Trained as an actress, Barbara Nadel used to work as a public relations officer for the National Schizophrenia Fellowship's Good Companions Project. Her previous job was as a mental health advocate in a psychiatric hospital. She has also worked with sexually abused teenagers and taught psychology in both schools and colleges. Born in the East End of London, she now writes full time, lives in Essex and has been a regular visitor to Turkey for over twenty years. She received the Crime Writers' Association Silver Dagger for her novel *Deadly Web*. She is also the author of the highly acclaimed Francis Hancock crime series set in World War Two.

Praise for Barbara Nadel:

'Nadel moves into the elite ranks of Michael Dibden, Donna Leon and Magdalen Nabb when it comes to blending foreign exoticism and impeccable mystery plotting. Exotic and atmospheric, this is superior police procedural sleuthing in which the locale is etched with precision and the city of Istanbul becomes an indispensable character and adjunct to the action'   *Guardian*

'Really refreshing to encounter something as idiosyncratic and evocative among debut novels as Barbara Nadel's Istanbul-set thriller'   *The Times*

'The delight of the Nadel book is the sense of being taken beneath the surface of an ancient city which most visitors see for a few days at most. We look into the alleyways and curious dark quarters of Istanbul, full of complex characters and louche atmosphere'

Independent

'Part of its appeal is the exotic setting and characters, especially the colour   memory'

Sunday Telegraph

DANCE WITH DEATH

BARBARA NADEL

headline

First published in Great Britain in 2006
by HEADLINE BOOK PUBLISHING

First published in paperback in 2006
by HEADLINE BOOK PUBLISHING

A HEADLINE paperback

10 9 8 7 6 5 4 3 2 1

ISBN 0 7553 3235 0 (B Format)
ISBN 0 7553 2131 6 (A Format)

Typeset in Times by Palimpsest Book Production Limited,
Polmont, Stirlingshire

Printed and bound in Great Britain by Clays Ltd, St Ives plc

Headline's policy is to use papers that are natural, renewable and recyclable
products and made from wood grown in sustainable forests. The logging and
manufacturing processes are expected to conform to the environmental regulations
of the country of origin.

HEADLINE BOOK PUBLISHING
A division of Hodder Headline
338 Euston Road
London NW1 3BH

www.headline.co.uk
www.hodderheadline.com

This book is dedicated to everyone who so generously shared their *iftar* meals with me during Ramazan 2003.

This book would never have been written without the help and inspiration provided by the people of Cappadocia. Both locals and incomers were endlessly generous and kind to me and for that I remain most grateful.

I am particularly indebted to Ruth, Faruk, Jeyda, and Hüseyin from Tribal Collections for their wealth of local knowledge and wonderful company. Thanks also to Ruth for taking the time to proof-read *Dance with Death* for me. Other heroic figures include Dawn and family at the Köse Pansiyan and Ali from the Kelebek, my neighbours during my stay in the land of the fairy chimneys.

Very big thanks also go to Pat who, like Ruth, proof-read *Dance with Death* and always made helpful suggestions. Big gratitude goes in addition to Pat for letting me stay in her beautiful house with Baris, Zeytin, Aslan, the 'one I called Arthur' and, at times, the mysterious Kismet too.

I had great fun with the lovely Caroline, experienced the grace and charm of Faruk's wonderful family on several enjoyable occasions and had a marvellous balloon flight courtesy of Kapadokya Balloons. Thanks to Lars and Kaili for making that flight so special for me, and by extension, for Çetin İkmen too.

List of Characters

Çetin İkmen – middle-aged İstanbul police inspector
Mehmet Süleyman – İstanbul police inspector, İkmen's protégé
Commissioner Ardiç – İkmen and Süleyman's boss
Sergeant Ayşe Farsakoğlu – İkmen's deputy
Sergeant İzzet Melik – Süleyman's deputy
Dr Arto Sarkissian – İstanbul police pathologist

İstanbul

Fatma İkmen – Çetin's wife
Hulya İkmen Cohen – Çetin and Fatma's daughter
Berekiah Cohen – Hulya's husband
Balthazar and Estelle Cohen – Berekiah's parents
Zelfa Halman Süleyman – Mehmet Süleyman's wife
Abdullah Aydın – injured victim of the criminal known as the 'peeper'
Mürsel Bey – louche habitué of the Saray Hamam

Cappadocia

Mensure Tokatlı – Çetin İkmen's cousin, hotelier
Captain Altay Salman – police riding school instructor
Ferhat Salman – Altay's nephew, a jandarma
Inspector Erten – police officer from Nevşehir
Haldun Alkaya – victim Aysu Alkaya's father
Kemalettin Senar – Aysu Alkaya's old sweetheart
Turgut Senar – a guide, Kemalettin's brother

Nalan Senar – Kemalettin and Turgut's mother

Nazlı Kahraman – daughter of the businessman Ziya Kahraman who had been married to Aysu Alkaya

Baha Ermis – Nazlı Kahraman's foreman

Dolores Lavell – American tourist

Tom Chambers – young English tourist

Rachelle Jones – Australian resident of Muratpaşa

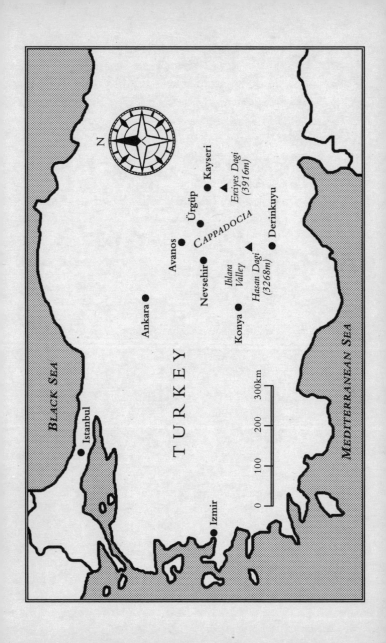

'I'm not sure that I should be here with him,' the prettier of the two girls whispered nervously.

Her friend, accustomed to these – to her – fussy little strictures, said, 'It's only Ferhat.'

They both turned to look at a young man in uniform shining a pencil torch up at the ceiling.

'Mum wouldn't have let me come out here without him,' the second girl said. 'Anyone could be lurking out in a place like this.'

'Yes, but Hande, he's also a jandarma. My mum would go mad . . .'

'Ferhat is my cousin, Türkân,' Hande said firmly. 'He wouldn't do anything to either of us. He is an honourable boy.'

Türkân hung her brightly headscarved head just a little and murmured, 'I'm sorry.'

'It's OK,' her uncovered friend replied, kindly. 'I'm not trying to make you do anything against Islam, Türkân, honestly. But if we want to come out here, we do have to be safe, don't we?'

'Yes.'

'Hey, come over and look at this,' Ferhat said as he shone his torch down into what looked like a deep, black hole.

The two girls walked across the uneven surface of the floor and joined him.

'What is it?' Hande asked, placing, just lightly, one hand on her cousin's arm.

'I think it might be a fresco,' Ferhat said. 'Even now people are still discovering new ones in these things.'

'How busy those old Christians must have been!' Hande said.

Ferhat laughed, 'Busy Christians!' he said. 'Just like Mr Dimitri. Do you remember him, Hande? The old Greek who ran the flower shop at the end of my road? Working day and night, all hours.'

'Oh, yes,' Hande said, her eyes lighting with excitement as she did so. 'He always had the most beautiful blooms, didn't he?'

'Yes.'

'Always such pretty flowers in İstanbul.'

And then for a moment they both became quiet, seemingly lost in their thoughts and memories. Hande and her family had moved from İstanbul to the small Cappadocian village of Muratpaşa just over a year before. Her father, who was an equestrian trainer for the police, had been sent to the area to take charge of a new facility just outside the regional capital of Nevşehir. He was very happy with all his new horses, his eager, if raw, recruits, and his man's world of flying gallops, football talk and rakı. Hande and her mother were, however, another matter. Unaccustomed to the restrictions of village life they both missed the glittering shops of İstanbul, the music in the streets and the easy access the city affords to entertainment. Until Ferhat had, quite coincidentally, been posted to the

2

local gendarmerie, both Hande and her mother had felt more at home with the tourists who came to the area to see the weird, lunar landscape that Cappadocia is famous for than they did with the 'locals'. Türkân was a good friend and the only girl Hande could really relate to at High School, but she was very, very different to herself, as this current trip out was demonstrating. Türkân, though interested in the frescos that Ferhat was pointing out, was neither comfortable with him nor with the ancient Christian paintings he was looking at.

'I think I'll go outside and see if it's raining,' Türkân said.

'If you want to,' Hande replied. 'But do be careful, won't you? You don't want to fall over and hurt yourself all the way out here.'

Türkân smiled. How nervous Hande was of the country-side! 'It's OK,' she said. 'I know the chimneys and they know me.'

And then she walked out through the rough-hewn doorway and made her way outside. This left Hande and Ferhat alone in a natural geological structure known locally as a Fairy Chimney. Made of a volcanic substance called tufa, the chimneys were conical structures that over the thousands of years of their existence had provided shelter and places of work and worship for the local inhabitants. There were, as Hande and Ferhat had discovered since they had moved into the area, tens of thousands of these things, many of which were decorated with frescos and carvings.

After they'd stared at the fresco, which featured indistinct figures weathered by time, Ferhat and Hande decided to go a little deeper into this cluster of chimneys through a small tunnel off to the left.

'Don't you think we should tell Türkân what we're doing?' Hande said as she nevertheless allowed her cousin to pull her along after him.

'We'll only be a minute,' Ferhat said. 'She can wait that long, can't she?'

He wasn't really taken with any of the locals, male or female. A lot of them were religious, which Ferhat wasn't, and those that weren't seemed to him to be interested in little beyond making quick money. Some of them were decidedly odd, too, something his friend and fellow jandarma, Abdulhamid, said was due to 'inbreeding'. 'You get that in villages,' Abdulhamid, who was from İzmir, had said. 'Family relationships that are far too close, if you know what I mean. And here with all of these penises around . . .' All of the young jandarma had laughed at that. The locals may well call them 'Fairy Chimneys', but everyone knew what they REALLY looked like, including young high school girls like Hande and Türkân.

Once through the tunnel, what Ferhat and Hande found themselves in wasn't actually another chimney, but a cave in the side of the escarpment behind the cluster of chimneys. It was very dark and smelt rather more earthy than the volcanic tufa had done. Ferhat switched on his torch once again and quickly flashed its beam around what appeared to be a considerable space.

'I expect these caves go on for kilometres,' he said. 'You know, back into the escarpment.'

'It doesn't smell very nice in here,' Hande said as she wrinkled up her nose at the rich smell of damp and rot. 'I think that we should go back for Türkân now.'

'I thought we were meant to be exploring,' Ferhat said. 'Just because she thinks I'm going to touch her or something . . .'

'Ferhat!'

'Well,' he said as he hunkered down and then shone the torch into yet another, even smaller, tunnel into the ground, 'I'm sorry, Hande, but this place does make me tired. Everyone looks at us as if we're some kind of threat. Even the tourists give us a wide berth! The gendarmerie is here for their benefit as much as anyone else's.' And then, almost folding himself in half, Ferhat slipped into the tunnel and disappeared.

'Ferhat!'

'It's all right,' she heard him say through the almost total darkness. 'I'll just be one minute.'

'But it's dark!' Hande cried. 'Don't leave me!'

'I'll be just one minute!' she heard his disgruntled and muffled voice pour through the rock. 'It won't kill you just to wait for a minute.'

Hande thought about trying to find somewhere to sit down but then thought better of it. This cave stank and who knew what 'things' or creatures it might have within its walls? Local people and even some of the jandarma told stories about bats and wolves living in the far-flung valleys of chimneys, like this one. Then, of course, there were supernatural stories, too – about malignant peris and djinn waiting in dark places to rob men and women of their souls. It was all rubbish of course, but as 'a minute' turned into several minutes, Hande began to feel an irrational panic settling on to her chest.

'Ferhat?' she said, quietly at first, and then, when he didn't answer, with more force, 'Ferhat!'

But neither sound nor light came from the small tunnel that

Hande could no longer actually see. What was going on? She hadn't heard any noise from where Ferhat had gone and so she couldn't imagine that he had fallen over or anything like that. Had he, perhaps, gone off somewhere else? He'd said that he wouldn't do that, but maybe if he'd found something, another tunnel, maybe that really interested him . . .

'Ferhat!' She was getting a little angry now and it showed in her voice. 'Ferhat, I'm all alone here, in the dark!'

But when that didn't appear to elicit any response, Hande wondered whether she should try to find the way they'd come into this cave and go outside to join Türkân. But she could no more find that tunnel than the one that Ferhat had slithered down and so, more out of frustration than anything else, Hande began to cry. She was, after all, only thirteen years old, little more than a child, really – even though the city-bred Hande would rather have died than admit it. If Ferhat did ever turn up again and he told anyone about it, she would just deny that she'd cried at all. İstanbul girls did not, after all, do such things.

'Hande!'

The torch caught the tears on her cheeks before she could even think of wiping them away. Not that it mattered much because Ferhat was back now and, suddenly, that was all that she cared about.

'Hande,' he said breathlessly, 'we have to get back to the gendarmerie.'

There was something different about her cousin that went beyond the sudden paleness of his skin.

'Ferhat?'

He grabbed her wrist and pulled her after him with what seemed to Hande to be tremendous urgency.

6

'Ferhat, what is it? What . . .'

But he didn't speak again except, when they got outside, to tell Türkân to come with them. It was raining a little bit now and so it would have seemed more sensible, to the girls at least, to shelter amongst the chimneys until the weather cleared up. But Ferhat wanted them all to go back to the jeep and quickly.

'Come on! Come on!' he said to the girls as they struggled to keep up with him. Rocky, uneven ground like the terrain around the chimneys isn't kind to ordinary, non-military shoes and so Hande and Türkân were at a distinct disadvantage when it came to following Ferhat.

'What's the matter with him?' Türkân asked as she and Hande watched Ferhat race down a slope towards his waiting jeep.

'I don't know,' Hande said. 'It's almost as if something in that cave frightened him.'

By the time the girls reached the jeep, Ferhat was already on the radio.

'Captain Göktaş?' he was saying and then he followed this with, 'Yes, sir . . . I've found a dead body, sir . . .'

Türkân and Hande looked at each other with big, frightened eyes.

'In a cave at the northern end of the Valley of the Saints,' Ferhat continued.

'Ferhat . . .'

He held up a hand to silence his cousin and then spoke again into the radio. 'Well, neither, really, sir . . . No, it's old but it isn't a skeleton. I think it's a, well it's sort of a mummy, I suppose, sir.'

7

A mummy? In that cave Ferhat had slipped into, the one next door to the cave where she had stood alone in darkness for all that time? Hande first put one fist up to her mouth and then buried her head in the folds of Türkân's headscarf. Türkân looked at Ferhat, at the fear she could now see in his eyes, and then gently stroked her friend's hair.

Something unpleasant had come to pass in the land of the Fairy Chimneys and for once Hande, the city girl, was a lot more frightened than Türkân. After all, as any Cappadocian will tell you, out amongst the chimneys anything is possible.

Chapter 1

It was one of those rare autumn days in İstanbul when the sun is hot enough to allow people to sit comfortably outside. Provided one goes to one of the old imperial parks or has a balcony or garden to sit in, days like this can be extremely pleasant. Indeed, one such private garden attached to a rather down-at-heel Ottoman house in the Bosphorus village of Arnavautköy rang to the sound of the companionable chatter of men, if not at peace with the world, at least getting along with it. Watched by a much older, elegant man sitting at a table, two attractive men in their forties were slouching in garden loungers, talking. The taller and more striking of the two was wearing swimming trunks and smoking a cigarette.

'Well, look, if you want to go out to a club, then you go,' he said to the other man who was slightly older and much more amused.

'Mehmet, you haven't been out for, how long?'

'I don't know, I don't think about such things,' Mehmet replied a trifle tetchily.

'Murad is only thinking of your happiness, Mehmet,' the elderly man at the table put in. 'It isn't right that you should be so lonely at your age.'

'Father, I am not lonely,' Mehmet said as he shot an arrogant glance across at Murad. 'But if my brother wants to go to clubs and probably make an idiot of himself with women half his age then that is his affair.' He stubbed his cigarette out in his ashtray and then immediately lit another.

Muhammed Süleyman looked upon all of this with gently amused eyes. Both of his boys were currently without a wife and, he felt, quite unhappy too. But Murad, his eldest, was at least admitting it. A widower since the terrible earthquake of 1999, Murad had sole custody of his daughter Edibe and was very happy with that. But he recognised that now, four years on from that event, he needed something more than work and fatherhood in his life. Mehmet, on the other hand, had thrown himself into his work as a senior police officer as never before. Separated from his wife for a year, he still loved her and the small son he was forced to spend most of his time away from. Mehmet was, his father felt, a deeply unhappy man, now quite incapable, for most of the time, of enjoying himself. That both of his boys had come home to live wasn't ideal either, mainly because their mother, who was mercifully out shopping now, nagged them about everything from remarrying to their choice of bread. Poor boys, Muhammed Süleyman thought sadly, it shouldn't have been this way for you.

'So how are you getting on with this new sergeant of yours?' Murad said brightly. It was always better to change the subject when Mehmet was being moody and his work was generally a pretty safe topic of conversation.

'İzzet Melik is an insufferable peasant!' Mehmet snapped.

'Ah, now come along, child,' his father put in, 'there is no class in modern Turkey. I know that we, our family, are of the old order . . .'

'I was speaking psychologically, Father,' Mehmet said. 'İzzet's people are probably far better off than ourselves. They're middle-class İzmir folk. But the man is coarse, devoid of taste, and I don't like the way he treats our female officers. It's crude and offensive. My dislike of him has nothing to do with what we are, or were.'

Until what was left of the Ottoman Empire became the Turkish Republic in 1923, the Süleyman family had been extremely wealthy. Related by marriage to several Sultans, the family had once owned property on the Bosphorus, which had only, finally, been sold when Mehmet was a child. Muhammed's father had actually been a prince and there were still some, generally elderly, people, who insisted upon referring to the older Süleyman by the princely title of 'Effendi'.

'It's a pity that İsak left,' the old man said. 'He was a nice lad, you seemed settled with him.'

'Yes . . .'

It had now been almost a year since Sergeant İsak Çöktin had resigned from the İstanbul police force. A follower of the native Kurdish religion of the Yezidi, İsak had felt unable to continue with his duties when his private and professional lives had come into almost disastrous conflict the previous year. Since then Inspector Mehmet Süleyman had suffered first one young woman who couldn't get on with what his department did and now İzzet. But then working in homicide was not, as Mehmet would have been the first to admit, for everyone. As the man who had been his own boss many years before, Inspector Çetin İkmen, was fond of saying, murder can be performed in any sick and foul way one cares to imagine and many that one cannot. Bringing those who engage in it to justice is not a task lightly done.

'But then maybe what we're doing at the moment isn't stretching İzzet to his full potential,' Mehmet said. 'Who knows what he's really like under pressure?'

What they were currently engaged in was not actually a homicide investigation. Someone, as yet unknown, had been first peeping in to rooms occupied by young, unmarried men and then, later, this had escalated to sexual assault. Nobody had been killed yet, but as Mehmet Süleyman knew from experience, these situations did tend to progress and the assailant, a large man by all accounts, was apparently armed. In addition, the victim of a male rape was currently so traumatised that his psychiatrist had put him on suicide watch. It was, as his wife would have said in her native English language, 'all going to come on top' very soon.

Muhammed Süleyman fitted a cigarette into his silver holder and waited for one of his sons to provide him with a light. It was one of the few vestiges that remained from the old man's servant-crowded past and so his sons generally indulged this small peccadillo without complaint. Murad got up and lit it for him just as they heard the front door bell ring.

'I'll get it,' he said as he looked at his elegantly unmoving father and barely clad brother.

'If it's your Uncle Beyazıt, come and warn us, won't you?' Muhammed said to Murad. 'You know how he is and if he sees us smoking in the hours of daylight . . .'

'He's still very strict about Ramazan?'

12

'My brother is still very strict about everything,' Muhammed said gloomily. 'But then I can remember when you were a good Muslim too, Mehmet. Not too many years ago.'

'When grandfather was still alive, yes,' Mehmet replied with a sigh.

When Murad had gone, the old man turned to his younger son and said, 'You know you should go out with your brother once in a while, Mehmet, if only to indulge him.'

'I know.' Mehmet first sighed and then leaned back into his lounger.

'And anyway you wouldn't make fools of yourselves, if that's what you think,' said Muhammed, smiling now, and adjusting his tie around his thin old neck until it felt just perfect. 'You are both stunning men. You are handsome, cultured and kind. You are my sons.'

Mehmet, amused, took off his sunglasses and looked at the old man with a twinkle in his eye. 'Yes, Father, of course.'

'Good.'

The sound of more than one set of footsteps emanating from the house caused Mehmet to look around for something to cover himself up with. However, before he could find anything, he found himself suddenly with his arms around what appeared to be a small human rocket.

'Daddy!'

'Yusuf!'

He was only two and a half but already he could run like a wild animal. Mehmet folded his arms around the child and covered him in kisses. Only when Murad cleared his throat did Mehmet look up to see his wife staring down at him.

'We were passing,' she said. 'I thought it would be nice.'

'Well, yes, thank you.'

His wife then walked over to his father and, taking one of his hands in hers, kissed it and said, 'Muhammed Bey.'

'Zelfa, dear, how nice it is to see you,' the old man said. 'I trust your charming father is well?'

'Yes, he is, thank you.' And then she walked back over towards her son.

Mehmet straightened up a little and after planting a few more kisses on his son's face, he looked at his wife who, he suddenly realised, had lost a considerable amount of weight. Somewhat older than him anyway, it made her look a little haggard. He automatically frowned with concern.

'What is it?' she asked as she too frowned at him.

'Oh, nothing,' he smiled. 'How are you?'

'Would you like some tea, Zelfa?' Murad asked before she could even begin to reply to Mehmet's question. Turkish hospitality must, after all, be performed before anything else. 'Assuming you're not keeping Ramazan, that is . . . ?'

'No, no I'm not. And yes, thank you, Murad, tea would be nice.'

'Father?'

'Oh, yes, Murad, tea would be . . .'

'No, I mean would you like to come indoors and help me?' Murad said as he attempted to indicate with his eyes that his brother and his family should be left in peace.

'Oh, yes, right . . .'

After they had gone, Mehmet put his son down on to the grass. The youngster had a passion for the family cat Aslan who would let Yusuf do just about anything he wanted with

14

him. He then offered Zelfa Murad's lounger and then leaned back and looked up at the sun.

Zelfa, whose mother had been Irish, came straight to the point. Speaking in English, she said, 'I think we should get a divorce. I think we should discuss it.'

Mehmet turned to look at her, suddenly both hurt and humiliated. It came out as anger. 'Is there someone else?' he said. 'Is that what the weight loss is about?'

'No!' she said, her face red with anger. 'Christ, Mehmet, can you be any more chauvinistic or what!'

'Well . . .'

'I've lost weight because I've been under pressure at work and because I've been smoking like a trooper,' she said and then, as if to prove her point, she dug into her handbag for a cigarette. 'Dad's going to be out of town this week and so I thought that, if it's convenient for you, you could come over and we could talk about it one evening.'

'What about him?' Mehmet said as he tipped his head towards the child throwing a ball for the cat in the flower beds.

'I thought that maybe you'd like to put him to bed and then we'd talk.'

Mehmet shrugged. 'If that's what you want.'

He could be such an arrogant bastard! And yet it had been Mehmet who had provoked this situation, Mehmet who'd gone off and screwed with a whore, been unfaithful to her! And yet, in spite of it all, Zelfa, who was after all a psychiatrist by profession, knew that she didn't really want to divorce him at all. What she really wanted, right at that moment, was to lick every centimetre of his body.

'I can't go back, in my mind,' Zelfa said. 'I can't trust you. And if I can't do that, what's the point?'

He first sighed, lit a cigarette, and then said, 'Is Wednesday convenient for you?'

'Wednesday's fine.'

'OK.'

And then he turned away to watch his son play with his cat and nothing more was said.

Later, when Zelfa and Yusuf had left, Mehmet told his brother that he thought the idea of going out to a club was an excellent one.

Menşure Tokatlı was not a woman to be trifled with. A soberly dressed old republican-style spinster, she was also the daughter of the late Faruk Tokatlı who had been something 'big' in the early tourist industry. Faruk, it was said, had been responsible for pushing tourism out into some of the more remote valleys as well as constructing several pansiyons and one hotel from existing fairy chimneys in Muratpaşa. Now Menşure, fifty-something and very determined, was in charge of the lot. Captain Salman of the Nevşehir police riding centre was openly afraid of her.

'It's about your daughter, Hande,' she said without preamble as she accosted the captain outside the Fairy Chimneys Carpet Emporium.

Captain Salman dropped what was left of his cigarette to the ground and very quickly brought one hand up to his cap in salute. 'Menşure Hanım.'

'She was with the boy, wasn't she, her cousin, when he discovered the body out in the Valley of the Saints?'

'Yes, Hanım, unfortunately . . .'

'Well, what I want to know is whether she saw it at all. They're not telling us whether it's male or female and I really . . .'

'Hanım, I think that you probably need to talk to the jandarma . . .'

'I've tried that,' the woman replied tetchily, 'but they're as obtuse as they can be. No, Captain, I need to get my information elsewhere, which is why I thought of Hande, or indeed yourself, because presumably as her father you will know what she knows.'

'Yes.' Captain Salman rocked backwards and forwards on the heels of his very shiny riding boots. 'Hanım, why, may I ask, is this of interest to you?'

'It isn't,' Menşure responded simply. 'But a member of my family may have an interest and if he does, it is important that he gets here and away as quickly as possible. I can't afford to have him around for too long during Ramazan.'

'Why is that?' Captain Salman asked. 'Is he foreign or . . .'

'No, he's from İstanbul where he smokes openly, as I see you do, in the day during Ramazan. But that is all right there, as you know. Here things are different and I really do not want him outraging my neighbours. You'd take note of that yourself if you have any sense. Now, Captain, can you help me or can't you?'

'Hanım, if I knew why your relative needs to know this . . .'

'I can't tell you that, Captain,' Menşure said shortly. 'That's his business. But if I tell you his name then, as an İstanbul police officer yourself, maybe that will change things?'

Captain Salman frowned. She was, it seemed, trying to dazzle him with 'big' names. Who was it to be? The Commissioner? The Director himself, maybe? Captain Salman's mind went, temporarily, wild with possibilities.

'Well, Hanım,' he said, 'you can try.'

And so she told him the name; Captain Salman smiled very broadly and then immediately told her what she wanted to know.

'Oh, he's such a big boy! He's such a hero!'

Strangely, when his pretty young mother considered how high in the air he was, little baby Timur was nowhere near to tears. But then he was in the hands of his grandfather who, whenever the baby was near to him, assumed the consistency of jelly and an IQ of 20.

'Dad, you'll make him dizzy,' Hulya said as she watched her father, Çetin İkmen, dance around the room with her infant.

'No, no, he's fine, aren't you, my little pigeon?' Çetin İkmen said, more to the baby than to his daughter. Little Timur just gurgled.

An older, plumper woman with her hair pulled behind her ears by a headscarf came into the room and tutted, albeit good-naturedly, at what she saw.

'I don't know who is the more childlike, the baby or your father,' Fatma İkmen said to her daughter.

'I think it's Dad,' Hulya said with a smile.

'I think you're right.'

Both of the women laughed, mainly because seeing the middle-aged Çetin İkmen so besotted was very amusing. He and Fatma had raised nine children of their own, but Timur was the first grandchild, named for Çetin's own father, and therefore very special indeed.

'Berekiah's father isn't quite as silly as Dad, but he has revealed a softer side in the weeks since we've had Timur,' Hulya said referring to the father of her husband with whom the couple and their baby currently resided. 'But then he isn't well, is he?'

'Mmm, Allah tests us all,' Fatma said. She didn't find it easy feeling sorry for her daughter's father-in-law, Balthazar Cohen. Although he had never risen through the ranks of the police as Çetin had done, Balthazar had been far more successful with women. In fact, for years he had made his wife's, Fatma's friend Estelle, life a misery. But all of that had stopped in the wake of the great earthquake of 1999 when Balthazar, trapped under the apartment building of his latest mistress, had lost both his legs. And now his son Berekiah had married outside the Jewish faith and Balthazar's grandson was to be a Muslim. Allah was, Fatma thought again, really testing Balthazar Cohen. But then the phone rang in the hall and Fatma left the room to answer it.

Once she had gone, Hulya said, 'So, Dad, are you busy?'

Inspector Çetin İkmen hugged the small baby to his thin chest and said, 'Not really. I suppose I should be glad, no one's killing anyone. I'm helping Mehmet Süleyman out with something, but . . . He's got another new deputy who may or may not work out.' And then he changed the subject. 'How is your house coming on?'

'Oh, slowly.' Hulya sighed. One of Berekiah's uncles had bought them a house up in the old Greek quarter of Fener on the Golden Horn. Almost derelict, the place needed a lot of work, which was what Hulya's husband was spending so much time doing.

'Too slowly, eh?' İkmen asked, knowing what the answer would be.

'Yes.'

Balthazar Cohen, as well as being very ill, was also very difficult to live with. He didn't like the fact that his grandson was to be brought up a Muslim and he didn't like the fact that his own sexual adventures were at an end. İkmen himself wasn't crazy about any of his relatives having any sort of contact with religion – he couldn't understand why his wife insisted on keeping the fast during Ramazan – but, like the rational secularist he was, he just lived with it.

'Çetin, it's your cousin Menşure,' Fatma said as she came back into the room and took the baby from her husband's arms.

'For me?'

'Well, of course for you,' Fatma said.

İkmen picked up his ever-present packet of Maltepe cigarettes and a lighter from the coffee table and went out to the hall.

'Is cousin Menşure the one who owns all of those fairy chimneys in Göreme?' Hulya asked, once her father had left the room.

'She owns fairy chimneys, but not in Göreme, in Muratpaşa, which is much smaller,' her mother corrected. 'Her father, Uncle Faruk, married your grandfather Timur's sister, Şerefe. They were both very business-minded, made a lot of money. Menşure owns pansiyons and tour companies and lots of things.

She never married. I wonder what she wants with your father?'

They both sat in silence until İkmen, puffing hard on a Maltepe, came back into the living room.

'Fatma,' he said as he braced himself against the side of a very old and threadbare settee, 'how would you feel about my spending some time in Muratpaşa?'

'Why? Has Menşure asked you to go for a little working holiday?' Fatma said with more than a touch of acid in her voice. Apart from Çetin's brother Halil, his wider family rarely made contact. When they did, however, it was usually because they wanted something from him – generally time or information. Fatma rarely saw her hard-pressed husband herself and was, as a consequence, unamused by his seeming desire to go off into the wilds of Cappadocia.

'No,' İkmen replied evenly, 'not exactly. Menşure has a few problems . . .'

'So why don't you and Mum go for a holiday together,' Hulya said excitedly. 'Berekiah and I could come and look after Gül and Kemal. You'd have a great time!'

'Well . . .'

'I think that your father would prefer to go to Cappadocia alone,' Fatma said. 'I expect this is business, or rather . . .'

'No, well, it . . .'

'Well? What?'

İkmen swallowed hard and then puffed furiously on his cigarette before saying, 'It's . . . well, yes, it is also a professional matter, Fatma. They've found a body . . .'

'Oh, so the local jandarma call you in, of course, Çetin,' she said with a huge ladle of irony in her voice. 'They can't possibly manage without you!'

21

'Fatma, it's an old body,' he said. 'It could be someone that I knew.'

'From your many holidays with Auntie Şerefe. How many times was it, two? Or did your brother go twice and . . .'

'If I can take a week's leave then I'm going!' İkmen said as he raised one silencing hand up in the air. 'It's just something that I have to do!'

And then he walked out on to the balcony, pausing only to coo at little Timur for a few seconds as he went.

Once he had gone, Hulya reached out to her mother and said, 'Don't worry, Mum, Dad won't do anything bad, he isn't like that. I'm sure it's all right.'

'Oh, so am I,' her mother said as she briefly dabbed her eyes with one corner of her headscarf. She was crying with frustration and anger as opposed to actual upset. 'Cousin Menşure has all the appeal of a bundle of twigs. No, I just worry about your father getting into trouble. You know what he's like when he becomes involved in something. Shooting his mouth off and upsetting people, putting himself in danger . . .'

'Well, he's always been like that . . .'

'Yes, but not hundreds of kilometres away,' Fatma said. 'Not in a place where I can't be with him when he wants me to be. People are very religious out in the villages, Allah alone knows how many ways your father will find to offend them! Drinking alcohol! Smoking in the street . . .'

Fatma shook her head with annoyance. Hulya did think that her father, once he had heard her mother's raised voice, might come in to offer some words of reassurance. But he didn't. He just stood out on the balcony looking across at the hazy sunset that was now falling across the great Sultan Ahmet mosque. Soon the faithful would be called to prayer and night, thankfully, for Çetin İkmen, would swallow what had, until only a few minutes before, been a very good day.

Chapter 2

Abdullah didn't like the new 'bedroom' his father had constructed for him. It was on the sixth floor and after a hard day at college the last thing he wanted to do was drag his big bag of books up six flights of stairs.

'But you can't expect the tourists to climb to such heights,' his father, Selcuk Bey, had said when Abdullah had suggested that perhaps some of the Emperor Justinian Pansiyon's guests might like to take advantage of the wonderful city and waterway views he now enjoyed.

'Dad, they all sit out on the terrace above my room every evening!' Abdullah replied.

'Ah, but they choose to do that, don't they?' his father said triumphantly. 'They don't have to worry about carrying bags up there.'

'But the staff carry them for them . . .'

'I have a pansiyon two storeys higher than that bastard next door, so my guests have the best views!' his father raged. 'You stay in that room and tell me the minute Ali damn Serpil starts building some awful shack on what he calls his terrace! I will be down to the Belediye before you can even cough!'

If only it had ONLY been the pansiyon next door with which Selcuk Aydın took issue. But as well as the Çinli Pansiyon next

24

door there was also the Aya Sofya Guest House across the road and its attendant hotel, not to mention the great Four Seasons five star hotel at the top of the street. All of them, according to Selcuk Bey, were 'far too tall and top-heavy for their foundations'. The fact that the Four Seasons was a sturdily built Ottoman building with a finely constructed terrace seemed to elude him. 'My place is the only place that can take great height,' he would say if challenged on the point. But other hotels and pansiyons in the historic Sultanahmet district of İstanbul begged to differ, and behind the Sultan Ahmet mosque particularly a war to 'capture' the best views for one's tourists had been hotting up for some time. Abdullah with his heavy bag of books was only one of its victims.

But this particular day was a Sunday and so Abdullah had not been to college but had been helping his father and brothers out with the pansiyon and its guests. Consequently, and because he, like most of the observant during Ramazan, wanted to eat as much as he could before going to bed, Abdullah didn't get up to his room until well gone midnight. So he was more than a little bit full when he did finally get into the shower and wash, but he went to bed quickly after that and fell asleep almost immediately.

What woke him wasn't a sound, but a feeling. Something cold and hard was pressing against his ear. As the fog in his brain began to lift, he could see that it was still pitch dark outside. He could also feel that the cold thing signified more than just a draught from a rashly opened window. The man, it had to be a man after all, the papers had said it was a man, was on the bed with him, his knife pressed against the side of Abdullah's ear.

'Turn over,' a strangely smooth voice ordered.

Abdullah knew instinctively what came next, and felt himself begin to sweat profusely.

'No . . .'

Quite where he found the strength to say it, Abdullah didn't know.

'Are you rejecting me, you filthy little homo!'

'Yes . . .' His heart was pounding like a hammer now. Why had he said that, why? Far away on the New City side of İstanbul the lights of Tophane and Cihangir twinkled seductively in the blackness.

With what seemed to be a complete absence of effort, the man flicked Abdullah over on to his stomach and then made as if to position himself above him. There was no face on account of his wearing a ski mask, but that didn't stop Abdullah from wanting to know who was about to rape him. Even through his fear he knew that he needed to know that at the very least. Using every last gram of his strength, Abdullah flung himself round on to his back and then pulled off the mask covering his assailant's face.

The knife that had been in the attacker's hand now found a new home in Abdullah Aydın's chest.

'So if I were to grant your application for leave, when would you want it to commence?' the very stout man with the unlit cigar in his hand said to the cadaverous individual smoking a cigarette in front of him.

'Tomorrow, sir,' Çetin İkmen said and then added, 'please.'

'So on a Monday morning you come to me, with no preamble at all, and tell me that you wish to go off to Cappadocia . . .'

'On personal, family business,' İkmen cut in.

The large man, Commissioner Ardıç, İkmen's superior, viewed him with reddened and unamused eyes.

'I do have leave owing,' İkmen continued, 'I . . .'

'You know that our peeper has now moved on from rape to attempted murder,' Ardıç said gravely. 'Süleyman and Melik are at the hospital with the victim now, for when he wakes up, if he wakes up. I'm surprised you didn't know, İkmen. You've been giving Süleyman some assistance with this one, have you not?'

'Yes, sir.'

Ardıç gestured expansively with his large, puffy hands. 'So?'

'So, what?'

'So don't you think that to just go off . . .'

'Sir, this is urgent family business!' İkmen pleaded. 'If it wasn't I wouldn't dream of asking at such . . .'

'Tell me something, İkmen,' Ardıç said as he tapped his lifeless cigar fruitlessly against the side of his ashtray, 'how are you going to get out to this village of Fairy Chimneys?'

'Well, sir, there's a bus that leaves at eight p.m., direct, getting in to Muratpaşa at around seven tomorrow morning.'

'From which I may infer, I suppose, that you are already packed and the ticket has been purchased.'

İkmen lowered his head as if he were a naughty schoolboy. 'Yes, sir.'

With a grunt reminiscent of that often heard on tennis courts, Ardıç pulled himself up by his desk and then moved rather painfully towards his open office window. Pigeons were feeding out on the small flat roof over the front office.

Ardıç, with his ever-ready supply of bread and seeds, made sure that they always came to his window. 'You know, İkmen,' he said as he threw yet more scraps out on to the pitted and damp-stained flat roof, 'a lot of people consider these birds to be vermin. My wife, for one. But I like them. They're greedy, aggravating and totally ubiquitous. Such a drive towards survival can give one a glimmer of hope in this world of suicide bombings and idiotic wars.'

'Yes, sir.'

First the World Trade Centre tragedy in New York and then the War that was supposed to be over, but wasn't, in Iraq had changed Ardıç considerably. He could still, on occasion, explode with anger in just the same way he had done before these events, but in general, wild tantrums were now a thing of the past. Of course such events were kismet and had to be accepted as such, but Ardıç, good Muslim that he always tried to be, struggled sometimes now. Ramazan was hard this time around, hence the unlit cigar he clung to so fiercely.

'How many children do you have, İkmen?' He was still feeding the birds, his head out the window, talking to the blue, autumn sky.

'Nine, sir. And one grandson.'

'Don't be offended, İkmen, but I have for some time seen you in very much the same light as these birds.' He slowly moved his head back into his office and then sat down. 'Survival. You just keep on producing, you are both admirable and ubiquitous. You don't look too nice, but . . . Oh, go wherever it is you need to go. Family is important, family is a gift from Allah.'

'Thank you, sir.'

He hadn't doubted for a second that Ardıç would allow him to go. He had thought that he might have to argue it, but apparently, that wasn't going to be necessary.

'So I'll just finish up . . .'

'You'll go and see Süleyman,' Ardıç interrupted as he looked back, smiling, at the feeding birds once again. 'He's over at the Taksim Hospital, waiting. The boy, the peeper's latest victim, is in a coma, I believe.'

İkmen, who had been slowly backing out of his boss's office for some time, edged his way closer to the door. 'Yes, sir.'

'Oh and İkmen . . .' Ardıç looked around suddenly and assumed a very serious expression.

'Yes, sir?'

'You know that the Fairy Chimneys don't really look like fairy chimneys, don't you?'

'Um . . .'

İkmen couldn't be at all certain what his boss was going to say now, but from the look on his large face it had to be something really quite serious.

'They look like male members,' Ardıç said with an utterly straight and unmoving face. 'But you try to get a Cappadocian to admit to that! Pah!'

He waved one dismissive hand and then turned back towards the pigeons again. It took a lot of effort, but İkmen did manage to hold his laughter in until he got back to his own office – just.

It wasn't really İzzet's fault, Süleyman thought as he sat and watched the older man suck his own teeth in lieu of having a drink. That everything about İzzet irritated him, including his personal habits, was unfortunate but nobody was actually to blame. The way he spoke, moved, ate, and even smoked, grated on him. However, it was the one thing that Süleyman could, to some extent, control that really rankled more profoundly than anything else. His sergeant's opinions and even some of his beliefs were, to Süleyman at least, beyond the pale.

'They've got to be queer, this man's victims,' İzzet said as he sat with his superior outside Abdullah Aydın's hospital room. 'That kid in there, he has to be queer.'

Heroically squashing down an urge just to tell him to shut up, Süleyman said, 'Why do you think that, Sergeant?'

'Well, if some man tried to have sex with me, I'd fight to the death,' İzzet responded passionately. As he spoke his eyes shone with an almost fanatical intensity.

'Well, maybe Abdullah Aydın did just that,' Süleyman said. 'After all, he is fighting for his life in there.'

'Maybe the peeper did him up the arse before he stabbed him . . .'

'It's unlikely,' Süleyman said as evenly as he could in the face of such bald language. 'If there had been any sort of penetration Mr Lewis would have heard something, wouldn't he? After all he was alone up on the roof terrace and it was very late.'

'Mmm.'

But İzzet was not, he knew, convinced. Even the peeper's early victims, those he had just stared at and masturbated in front of, İzzet had treated with barely disguised contempt. George Lewis, the elderly New Zealander who had responded to young Aydın's screams when he was stabbed, and who had probably saved Abdullah's life, İzzet had dubbed an 'old homo' on account of his unmarried state. Not even the fact that Lewis was a widower could sway the sergeant from this seemingly intractable opinion.

'You do know, İzzet, that this is not necessarily about sex, don't you?' Süleyman said.

İzzet wrinkled his already craggy brow. 'How do you mean?'

How do you mean, SIR would have been nice, Süleyman felt, but decided to let it go. After all it was an idea he wanted this Neanderthal to consider now – accepted procedure would have to wait. 'When one man forces himself on another man in a sexual act, he is exerting power over that individual,' Süleyman said. 'In exactly the same way as a man who rapes women is exerting his power over them, male on male rapists are making a statement about their feelings with regard to other men. Such men generally suffer feelings of inadequacy, of powerlessness within their own milieu, whatever that may be.'

'Oh, bravo!' a heavily smoke-stained voice said. 'Psychology at its finest.'

Süleyman looked up to see the thin face of Çetin İkmen smiling down at him. He stood up and embraced the smaller man immediately.

'This is a bad business, Inspector,' İkmen said, mindful of the presence of İzzet Melik at his friend's side.

'Yes . . .'

'But can't this peeper,' İzzet, obviously confused, put in, 'can't he just want to fuck them?'

'Well, that too is possible,' İkmen said with a smile. 'But

we have to look at every possibility and theory available to us, don't we? But look, Sergeant, I need to speak to Inspector Süleyman alone for a moment, so if you could just go outside and have a smoke for a few minutes . . .'

'Sir, it's Ramazan, I . . .'

'Oh, of course, of course. Well, look,' İkmen said, 'if you could just go and, I don't know, look around at nurses or something . . .'

As soon as he saw İzzet's sartorially inelegant form disappear down the corridor, İkmen came straight to the point.

'I've got to go to Cappadocia,' he said. 'It's possible the local jandarma have found Alison.'

'Çetin . . .'

'Look, I know that this peeper thing is very serious and that you're not having the best of times with Sergeant Reactionary, but Mehmet, it's Alison, you know. My and Max's Alison.'

Süleyman looked into eyes that were close to tears, sighed, and then smiled. For his mentor to go away now was inconvenient to say the least, but if it was about Alison then Süleyman knew that he could hardly argue. Back in the 1970s İkmen had met and fallen in love with a young British backpacker called Alison. A married man with children even then, he'd never done anything about this infatuation, which never progressed beyond a kiss and yet his friend Max, an English teacher who had also been in love with Alison, had been very jealous. The girl had, apparently, preferred İkmen over her own countryman and it had wounded the Englishman badly. In fact, so badly that Max, who was a man fascinated by and gifted in the occult arts, had brooded on what he saw as İkmen's betrayal for over twenty years. And when he finally arrived at

32

a punishment he deemed suitable for the Turk, Max had pursued his chosen course with fanatical intensity. He had kidnapped İkmen's daughter Çiçek whom he incorporated into a bizarre ritual designed, so Max maintained, to protect İstanbul against 'dark forces'. Ultimately he had been unsuccessful in this aim and had subsequently died in what İkmen still felt were mysterious circumstances. The point was, and had always been for İkmen, that just after Alison left İstanbul to continue with her trek along the hippy trail, she had disappeared. The last sighting of her had been in August 1978 in Nevşehir, the regional capital of Cappadocia. Alison was and remained for him unfinished business. Although no longer in love with her, he still cared about what might have been her fate. Süleyman, who had also been instrumental in preventing Max Esterhazy from completing his twisted ritual, was one of the few people who knew about the Alison connection.

'My cousin Menşure called to tell me that the local jandarma have found what they call a female "mummy" in one of the Fairy Chimneys,' İkmen continued. 'I don't know any more about it than that. But just the possibility it might be her . . .'

'Of course you have to go,' Süleyman said firmly. 'Has Ardıç given permission?'

'Yes.' İkmen looked down as if embarrassed. 'I go tonight.'

'I see. Does Fatma . . .'

'No,' İkmen frowned. He wasn't accustomed to keeping things from his beloved Fatma, but in view of the subject matter he felt that it was for the best. 'As far as she's concerned there's a body out there I might have some knowledge about – no names or anything. I also told her I'm going to help Menşure with some business problems too. Fatma either doesn't remember or chooses not to think about the fact that Menşure is the very last person who would need help with anything. Her mother, Auntie Şerefe, was exactly the same, as strong and determined as a lion. But then I told Ardıç basically nothing, only you, my dear friend, know the whole truth.'

Süleyman placed a hand on his mentor's shoulder. 'I'm, as ever, honoured that you should trust me with this, Çetin.'

The older man shrugged. 'You are my friend,' he said simply. 'I like working with you. I'm so sorry that I have to go. But I do have to.'

'I understand.'

And then they embraced again before İkmen left. Alone, briefly, with just the sound of the monitors bleeping rhythmically from Abdullah Aydın's room, Süleyman wondered whether the Cappadocian body was really this Alison or not. In addition he wondered what İkmen would do if it were not her and also what he would do if it were. Old infatuations and loves were very powerful things as he well knew. His trip out to a club with his brother had ended in his returning home almost as soon as he'd arrived. Somehow he just hadn't been able to get his ex-wife's face out of his mind.

Chapter 3

The literal meaning of the word 'Cappadocia', which is of
Persian origin, is 'Land of Beautiful Horses'. Quite why the
Persians had, apparently, overlooked its other delights, which
even in ancient times had been around for about thirty million
years, is puzzling. But then maybe the Persians were just simply knocked out by the bloodstock they came across in the
area, either that or they didn't feel confident enough to allude
to what can be extremely rude-looking rock formations. For
every cone-shaped column of tufa topped by a precarious-
looking lump of volcanic rock there are, in some parts of the
region at least, three that are exactly the image of an erect
penis. In some cases there are entire valleys populated by
'Fairy Chimneys' of this shape.

Lunar in character and deeply weird in more than a few
places, the landscape of Cappadocia was formed by the colli-
sion of two tectonic plates and by the eruption of the now
extinct volcanoes of Mounts Erciyes and Hasan. These erup-
tions caused the whole region to be blanketed in ash that eventually solidified into tufa, which in turn eroded into the odd
shapes that the region is famous for. Spooky and barren, even
from the earliest times, Cappadocia has a reputation for being
haunted not only by ghosts from its Hittite and Byzantine past,

but also by the peris or fairies for whom, some would say, a higher power had especially created the chimneys.

Not that much of this was on Çetin İkmen's mind as his bus pulled in to the bus station of the regional capital, Nevşehir. It was now eleven hours since he'd left Esenler bus station in İstanbul; he was exhausted and still irritated by the sight of the enormous bag of food Fatma had given him for the journey. It was so excessive. Even if he hadn't been travelling overnight, he wouldn't have wanted to stuff himself with the piles of börek, bread and tubs of cacık and patlıcan salatası that his wife had given him. He had wanted to smoke, but now that smoking was forbidden on buses, that had only been possible during the regulation stops at roadside service areas. So he hadn't slept at all and was therefore in no mood for what happened next.

'All right, this is it, end of the journey, everyone off!' the bus driver yelled down the bus waving his arms as if physically ushering his passengers into Nevşehir.

The young English student who had spent much of the night talking to İkmen about his plans to be an ancient historian, as well as eating a lot of Fatma's food, turned to the policeman and said, 'What's this?'

İkmen put his hand on the young man's shoulder and said, in English, 'Don't worry, it's nothing.'

Then, pushing past several ranks of barely roused passengers, both foreign and domestic, he made his way up to the front of the bus. The driver who, to İkmen's way of thinking, was smoking on board just to annoy HIM, leaned lazily across his steering wheel and only looked at the policeman when he tapped him on the shoulder.

'What do you mean, "everyone off"? Some of us have tickets through to Muratpaşa.'

'You have to change here for Muratpaşa,' the driver said with a shrug. 'There are minibuses.'

'Yes, but I and some of your other passengers bought tickets through to Muratpaşa.'

An attractive, Asian-looking woman who, İkmen reckoned from her accent, was probably American, made as if to get off the bus with her luggage.

'Do you have a ticket through to Muratpaşa, Miss?' İkmen asked, again in the English that was second nature to him.

'Oh, yes,' the woman said, 'but if the bus is stopping here . . .'

'You go and sit down,' İkmen said, 'I'll make sure we all get to Muratpaşa.'

'Oh, right. Thanks.'

As the woman made her way back to her seat the bus driver said, 'What do you think you're doing?'

'I've heard about this ticket scam before,' İkmen said angrily.

'What scam?'

'The one about paying through to Muratpaşa and getting dropped in Nevşehir,' İkmen continued. 'What is it? Being paid by the minibus company, are you?'

'No.'

'So, then, take . . .'

'No!' the bus driver waved his cigarette in İkmen's general direction and said, 'Fuck off! Get off my bus! Who do you think you are, anyway?'

İkmen put his hand into his jacket pocket and took something out which completely changed the driver's perspective.

When he went back to his seat, the young English student looked at him with admiration. 'How did you do that?' he said. 'That was so cool.'

And then İkmen showed him his police ID, which made the young man laugh rather nervously.

On the basis that she, as a hotel and tour company owner, was doing them a favour by providing them with accommodation, Menşure Tokatlı was not in the habit of meeting her guests at Muratpaşa bus station. It was the sort of thing that everyone in this village of but two thousand souls knew well and so any deviation from this norm was cause for comment.

'I wonder who she's waiting for?' the tall, blonde woman said in Australian English to her smaller, older companion.

'Who knows?' the other replied, also in English. 'Maybe we should ask her.'

'Are you serious?' the blonde said. 'Christ, Marion, if I got too close to her, she'd turn me to stone!'

'She's just a woman, Rachelle,' Marion said in what was very obviously a British accent and then she sat down on one of the bus station benches, one hand in the small of her back. 'Working in that bloody café will be the death of me.'

'Menşure Tokatlı is a scary woman,' Rachelle cut in as she sat down next to her friend and lit a cigarette. 'You know that when I was married to Kenan she was forever looking over the wall to see what we were doing. I swear to God she was around when Ali was conceived.'

Marion laughed. 'Oh, Rachelle, Kenan had the pansiyon next door to her place. Listen, you've been in Turkey a long time now, you should know that for Turks it is important what the neighbours are doing, especially in a village. You should also know that smoking in public in Ramazan is not really very respectful.'

'Yeah, I know. I'm a bad, bad person,' her friend replied, but without extinguishing the offending cigarette. Then, suddenly animated by something across the station forecourt, she said, 'God! I think she's coming over!'

Marion looked in the same direction as Rachelle where the slim and sensibly shod figure of Menşure Tokatlı was marching towards them at what appeared to be an alarming pace.

'God!' Rachelle reiterated. 'What the fuck can she want?'

Although what she uttered was in English, Menşure Tokatlı had understood completely what the Australian had said and so she waded straight in. 'I want nothing, Rachelle Jones, except to put an end to your and Marion Hanım's endless speculation.'

'Yes, but . . .'

'I'm awaiting the arrival of my cousin, Çetin, from İstanbul,' Menşure said. 'I called him in light of this ghastly body which I thought he might have some interest in. But now that we know it's all about that Alkaya business I should just feed him and then send him back to İstanbul. He's very busy. Should have telephoned him to tell him yesterday really, but . . .'

'Hanım?'

Menşure wasn't making much sense. The 'Alkaya business' to which she referred, however, was easy enough to decipher. The body Captain Salman's daughter and her cousin had discovered out in the Valley of the Saints had, the village had discovered the previous afternoon, turned out to

39

be that of a local girl called Aysu Alkaya. She'd gone missing from the village just over twenty years before and had finally been identified by her ageing father. What all of that had to do with Menşure Tokatlı's cousin from İstanbul and his 'interest' was a mystery. But then again, from what Menşure had just said, perhaps his concern was actually with something else.

'I want him to stay. He's honest and impartial,' the older woman said as if to herself. And then, turning back to the two women on the bench, she continued, 'Çetin is a senior İstanbul police inspector. Maybe he'll find the Alkaya situation diverting. Yes.'

And then, as if completely ignorant of the other women's presence, she made her way smartly back towards the bus company offices which formed a solid wall of commerce at the back of the forecourt.

Rachelle pulled her thick jumper tightly about her body and said, 'Bloody hell, more police! That's all we need!'

Marion smiled. 'I don't hear you complaining about the new training school for the police horsemen.'

'Ah, but that's different,' Rachelle said with a flick of her cigarette-toting hand. 'I can forgive a man in tight jodhpurs and with rock-hard buns almost anything – including being in the police.'

'Oh, Rachelle,' Marion shook her head and laughed. 'You are so naughty!'

'I am so bloody bored is what I am,' Rachelle replied. 'Ali's a great kid, don't get me wrong, and I like running the Tasmanian Devil, but I could do with some company, if you know what I mean.'

'You know that in Ramazan people are encouraged to think cleanly,' Marion said seriously.

Rachelle put her cigarette out and then lit another.

'Yes, I do. But that's got nothing to do with me or you. We're foreigners, we don't get involved. Anyway, what do you want to do, Marion, give me the glooms?'

Rachelle Jones had lived in Muratpaşa for over twenty years. She'd come to Turkey as a bog-standard Australian backpacker but, unlike most girls from Sydney, she'd met a local man and not only had sex with him but married him, too. Now that marriage was at an end she worked with her nineteen-year-old son, Ali, in her own pansiyon, which was called the Tasmanian Devil. However, twenty years or no twenty years, some things were still hard at times. Finding a suitable male companion was one, and Ramazan, when she had to think where she was every time she lit up, was another. Marion, too, had been in Turkey for many years and was married to a local man called Adem. Together they ran a café called the Cappudocia Coffee Bean. Marion was very happy to be out of Britain and loved living in Muratpaşa. She could, however, very easily understand some of Rachelle's frustrations.

A blue and white intercity bus swept into the forecourt, just briefly rousing a group of overcoat-clad local men outside the Tourist Information Office from their tea and tavla session. If there were any tourists on board, there wouldn't be many and, as all the men would know only too well, with Menşure Tokatlı meeting the bus, odd as that was, their businesses, whatever they were, didn't stand a chance. Rachelle squinted to see who was getting off and said, 'I suppose if the cousin is from İstanbul he can't be that bad. I mean at least he won't smell of goat, will he?'

Marion laughed. 'Oh, there are some fantastic people in this village, Rachelle, and you know it,' she said.

'Yeah, I do. I know how lovely the place is too, but . . .' She shrugged. She didn't need to go any further, Marion knew exactly what she meant.

The two women watched as first a couple of obviously European girls, an Asian woman and a headscarfed lady with multiple bundles, alighted on to the forecourt. Then there was a pause. Menşure Tokalı peered anxiously into the bus and for a moment Rachelle, at least, wondered whether this cousin had in fact arrived. But then a small, dark man who was accompanied by a much taller, pale boy got off and Menşure took the man by the hand with a smile. Fifty-something, the man was thin and a little shabby with his cheap shoes and cigarette hanging from one corner of his mouth.

'Well, if that's the best that İstanbul can do,' Rachelle said as she surveyed Çetin İkmen with some amusement. 'God!'

'Not as good as the men at the riding school,' Marion said with a twinkle in her eye.

'Are you kidding?' Rachelle laughed. 'They are hot! And that Captain Salman . . . Well, he can ride my pony any time he likes!'

'Rachelle!'

But the Australian was already on her feet and on her way back to her pansiyon. Menşure Tokatlı had come down from her vast complex of Fairy Chimneys to meet a coach, a new cop from İstanbul was in town as well as a sprinkling of tourists – it was just about as much excitement as Muratpaşa could take during autumn. Marion stayed and watched for a while as Menşure Tokatlı dragooned her cousin and all of

42

the tourists into her Land Rover and took off at some speed up into the hills. She drove like a lunatic but then, with this little traffic, why shouldn't she? Marion pushed herself up off the bench and made her way back to the Cappudocia Coffee Bean and more table moving. Adem was constantly changing the café's image in an attempt to attract more custom. Quite why, Marion didn't know. The Coffee Bean almost alone amongst local businesses was holding its own out of season. But then every foreigner in town knew it was a safe bet for food and drink any time of the day, Ramazan or no Ramazan.

Although he hated to admit it, Süleyman had to accept that İzzet could have a point about the boys who had been either observed or attacked by the peeper so far. Although he personally would have stopped at dubbing all of these boys homosexual, they were none of them particularly macho. A case in point, the object of some of the peeper's earliest attentions, was twenty-year-old Duruşan Efe. Like the most recent victim, Abdullah Aydın, Duruşan lived in the district of Cankurtaran just behind the Sultan Ahmet mosque. Also like Abdullah, Duruşan lived with his parents although not in a pansiyon but above his father's carpet shop.

Although Süleyman and İzzet Melik had originally interviewed Duruşan together, Süleyman now chose to be on his own with the youngster away from both the police station and the carpet shop. Although it wasn't in any way a warm day, it was bright and so the policeman and the young man drank tea in the çay bahçe opposite the Hippodrome and that dreadful gothic fountain that Kaiser Wilhelm II had given to Sultan

Abdul Hamid just prior to entering into the alliance that would lead the Ottoman Empire into the First World War.

Süleyman offered Duruşan a cigarette which the young man took, he thought, a trifle sulkily.

'I don't understand why you want to talk to me again,' the young man said. 'I've told you everything I know.'

'Yes, I know,' Süleyman replied. 'But ... look, you've heard, I know, about the latest victim. He's very badly hurt and could still die. We do need to catch this man, Duruşan.'

'Yes, I know. But what do you want me to do about it?'

Duruşan Efe wasn't exactly good-looking, his nose was far too large for him to be classically attractive. But he was tall and slim and, as Süleyman and almost everyone else with a brain knew, just that little bit too well groomed to be truly heterosexual.

'Duruşan,' Süleyman leaned in towards the young man as he spoke, 'I know that this isn't easy. But I must ask you to trust me ...'

'What do you mean?' Almost all of the colour had suddenly drained from his face now. 'What are you talking about?'

'I, or rather we, the police, we think that this individual might be targeting young homosexual ...'

'I'm not queer, Inspector!' Duruşan flung one long arm out in the direction of his home. 'Ask my friends, ask my mother!'

'Duruşan, look ...'

'I am not queer!' he hissed. And then, moving in still closer towards Süleyman's face, he said, 'And anyway, even if I was, do you think I'd tell *you*? I've heard what you do to such people. I've heard you take delight in telling their families.'

Süleyman shrugged. 'Some officers may do that, but not me. I am only interested in catching this criminal. I want to get hold of him before he kills someone.' He sighed. 'But I need help, Duruşan. I don't know, but I think that this man targets his victims prior to doing what he does. Maybe he does just spot a boy on the street, follow him and then climb up to his window late at night. But he may also be observing men in places where homosexuals meet. Now . . .'

'I'm not telling you anything.' Duruşan put his glass of tea down on to the table and went to take his jacket off the back of his chair.

Süleyman leaned back in his chair and watched him. 'If you've nothing to hide then there's nothing to tell.'

'No. But, well . . .' Flustered and now flushed too, Duruşan realised he'd made a mistake.

'So what can you tell me then, Duruşan?'

'I've told you, I . . .'

Süleyman drew in closer to him again. 'I am not a fool, boy,' he said. 'I know what you are and I honestly do not care. But if you want other boys like you to be free of this monster then I would suggest that you consider helping me.'

Duruşan sank back into his seat once again and picked up his half-finished tea.

'I don't want my parents or anyone to know,' he said quietly.

'Agreed.'

'And I'd rather you didn't tell that sergeant who was with you, either. I didn't like him at all.'

Allah, but İzzet was becoming a liability! Like a great, tactless ox.

Süleyman lit up a cigarette before replying. 'I will treat any evidence that you give me as anonymous,' he said. 'In effect it will be between you and me alone.'

'Are you sure?' Duruşan frowned. So young and so afraid! And yet wasn't this the fate of so many of these young gay men outside the very wealthy and enlightened districts of the city? Süleyman wondered.

'All right,' the boy said after a pause. 'All right, no parents and . . . You won't raid anywhere I tell you about, will you?'

'Duruşan, all I want to know is where you meet other . . . boys and I want to check these places out. I mean, look, if several different victims tell us about several different places they go to that they have in common then maybe we can start looking at other people who patronise these establishments.' And then, with a purposefully steely tinge to his gaze, Süleyman said, 'I want to catch this man and put him where he can't hurt anyone ever again. But until I do, no boy or young man will be safe. Do you understand what I'm saying, Duruşan?'

Duruşan did, and so the two of them had the conversation that Süleyman had wanted. The boy was nervous, of course, and Süleyman knew that the others would be equally as wary when he spoke to them. But there wasn't anything else to do at the present time. Forensic evidence on the peeper so far was very sketchy with no DNA samples in common at any of the sites. With this line of inquiry there was a possibility that staking out places like this gay hamam Duruşan had mentioned might be of interest. Although if he did that one thing was for certain, İzzet Melik was not to be a part of any resultant investigation team.

Chapter 4

Menşure put İkmen in one of her larger cave rooms. 'On the ground floor,' she'd said when she'd first shown him inside. 'You smoke too much to go upstairs.' But even so, even at ground level, he still had a spectacular view of the Muratpaşa valley and its almost straight ranks of chimneys in white, pink and even green shades of tufa.

As soon as he'd hurled what few clothes he'd brought with him into the wardrobe, İkmen opened the door out to the small balcony in front of his room and stepped into the dust-sodden air of Muratpaşa. He'd first come to the village as a child, to visit his Aunt Şerefe and Uncle Faruk. Both the pansiyon, now a hotel, and his cousin Menşure had been a lot smaller in those days and there hadn't been anything beyond a bakkal and a couple of bakeries down in the village. There certainly hadn't been carpet shops or restaurants with names like Turkish Delight and The Bedrock Pub. Even when Alison had visited the district in the seventies it had still, basically, been the same as it had been in the fifties. If, of course, Alison had ever got to Muratpaşa. Menşure had told him the news about the body as soon as she'd seen him. It wasn't, couldn't be her. In a way it was disappointing and yet in another way it was a relief – the thought that maybe Alison could be alive somewhere.

İkmen sat down on one of the little rickety chairs on the balcony and closed his eyes. Menşure said that she was going to come with a tray of tea and some börek for them both. She was also going to tell him something about the girl whose body had been found. It was, she said, an interesting and perplexing story. If he wasn't too much mistaken, İkmen sensed that his cousin might even want him to get involved with this 'case' or whatever it was. Not that that was possible. He was outside his jurisdiction and besides, given this new and potentially fatal twist to the peeper scenario, he was really needed back in İstanbul and so he'd have to go. Altering his ticket and cancelling part of his leave wouldn't be problematic.

'I don't know that we should sit out here where we can be seen.'

İkmen opened his eyes. Menşure and her tray of goodies had come in to his room almost without a sound.

'Oh, Ramazan . . .'

'You forget country bumpkins like Muratpaşa folk really take it seriously,' Menşure said as she set the tea glasses and börek down on the small table inside İkmen's room. 'Come in and let's eat.'

'OK.'

At first they talked about their families – or rather, İkmen spoke about his and Menşure spoke about her late parents and the odd visit she would sometimes get from another cousin from Ankara. Not so much lonely as alone, Menşure Tokatlı was not an unhappy woman – except when she didn't get what she wanted.

'Now look, Çetin,' she said at length, 'about this Alkaya body. I think that you . . .'

'Menşure, I'm out of my jurisdiction,' İkmen said as he lit up a cigarette. 'And besides, I really do need to be in İstanbul. I only came because I thought if it was Alison . . .'

'Yes,' she responded somewhat harshly. 'You know that it has been such a long time now, Çetin. You must give this Alison business up. I have never been comfortable knowing about it while your wife remains ignorant.'

'I know,' he said. 'But in the early days I needed you to keep a look out for her. The local police were never that bothered enough for my liking. I know we've never been that close, but I have always trusted you, Menşure.'

'I am flattered, Çetin, truly, but . . .'

'Menşure, I have always and will always love Fatma. But my wife is, if you can understand, always attainable.'

'What do you mean?'

'I mean that Alison as a foreigner, especially back in those days, was unattainable. I've never been under any sort of illusion about my own physical appeal. I'm an ugly man and yet here was a beautiful foreigner who wanted me over and above her own and very handsome countryman. Even I have some vanity. It was intoxicating.'

'And rather juvenile now, don't you think?'

'Yes, but,' he sighed, 'I have to know what happened to her, Menşure. What happened to that impossible dream?'

'Yes, but as I've said, Çetin, you must move on. Now look, I know you say you should be back in İstanbul, but hear me out,' Menşure said as she held up an imperious, silencing hand. 'When Aysu Alkaya went missing just over twenty years ago, this village was riven by suspicion and rumour. To some extent it has remained so ever since. But now that Aysu's body has materialised, well, it's about to get a lot more intense yet again.'

'What do you mean?' İkmen said as he mentally bowed to the inevitability of Menşure's argument.

Menşure, who didn't normally smoke, but who would occasionally 'treat' herself, took a cigarette from İkmen's packet and lit up.

'Aysu Alkaya was a very beautiful young woman of nineteen and the delight of her father Haldun's eyes. He was very indulgent and, for a peasant – Haldun has a few grape vines, a couple of goats, you know the score – really quite liberal. So much so that when a boy he knew his only child had eyes for made it known that he was interested in her, Haldun made himself ready for a wedding.'

'So what went wrong?' İkmen asked.

'Poverty, basically,' Menşure said with a sigh. 'Aysu and her father were poor. The boy, Kemalettin Senar, came from a much wealthier family, but he was very young . . . Anyway, somehow Aysu then caught the eye of one of our local dignitaries, Ziya Kahraman. He was a widower, he was seventy years old, and he spent months bothering Haldun Alkaya for Aysu's hand in marriage.' Catching the slightly raised eyebrows of her cousin, she said, 'You know it happens, Çetin. Even in İstanbul it still sometimes happens. But anyway, Haldun resisted. Despite his poverty he wanted what was best for Aysu. There were arguments, raised voices in the street. But then, suddenly, for no reason that anyone has ever been able to really fathom, Haldun gave in and Aysu married Ziya Kahraman.'

İkmen put his cigarette out and then immediately lit another.

'A seventy-year-old man with a girl of nineteen. Ugh! That's like my Hulya marrying my father!'

Menşure put a hand up as if to push that thought away. 'So Aysu went to live with Ziya and his maiden daughter, Nazlı, who must have been about fifty at the time.'

'Allah!'

'And of course partly because Ziya Kahraman was old he was traditional too. Aysu was rarely allowed to leave the house where, it was said, she was basically Nazlı's servant. Things would change, of course, if and when Aysu became pregnant' – İkmen pulled a disgusted face – 'but as far as we know, she hadn't become pregnant by the time she disappeared.'

'So what about the disappearance?'

Menşure shrugged. 'One night she was in the Kahraman house, the next morning she was gone. There was a rumour that when he wasn't actually sleeping with her, if you know what I mean, Ziya made Aysu sleep in his cellar – locked her in. There were lots of rumours. But anyway, somehow the girl got out and she had never been seen again until this week. At the time the jandarma and the police in Nevşehir questioned everyone. They were most enthusiastic, shall we say, in their questioning of poor Kemalettin. Half the village, including Aysu's husband, were convinced that he had somehow abducted her. For years the Kahramans and their supporters regularly accused the boy and his family of this, that or the other crime against Ziya and his missing wife.'

'So now that a body has been found, what does this mean?' İkmen asked. 'I mean, do you know how the girl died, Menşure?'

'No.' She put her cigarette out in the ashtray and then sipped her tea. 'But I do know that the police in Nevşehir think that she was murdered.'

'How do you know that?'

'I know, or rather I am acquainted with a certain Captain Salman who is an instructor up at the new police riding school. He's from İstanbul . . .'

'Yes, I know,' İkmen said, 'I know him.'

'Yes.'

'And so . . .'

'And so Captain Salman told me to tell you that the Nevşehir police think that Aysu Alkaya was murdered. No one else in the village knows. They will very soon, but Captain Salman felt that, if you were going to try and help out, you needed to know the facts now.'

'I never said I was going to help out, Menşure. I came here – well, you know why I came here. But I can't actually do anything here and I've a very stressful job waiting for me back in İstanbul.'

'Yes, I appreciate that, but this village will fracture once the truth is known, Çetin,' Menşure said. 'Fingers will be pointed and unless someone makes sure that proper evidence is collected, DNA or whatever it is, then someone could end up getting hurt or worse. They do their best in Nevşehir, but they don't have your level of sophistication . . .'

'Or my budget,' İkmen said with a sigh. 'Menşure, I cannot tell the police in Nevşehir how to do their job! They will do their best with what they have available to them. They will make decisions they feel are appropriate.'

'Some of them make decisions in line with how much

money certain people are willing to pay them. The police are poor here, Çetin. Even you are wealthy in comparison.'

'Menşure, I can't get involved with this!' İkmen stood up and threw his arms wildly into the air. 'I have no power in Cappadocia! And anyway, I need to get back to my own life. Fatma is alone and, as you have so rightly said, I need to at least try to put Alison behind me now. I need to accept, maybe, that I will never know the truth about her. But I think I have to do that at home.'

'Well, then, we'll all have to live with the possibility that we'll never know who really killed Aysu Alkaya, won't we? Innocent people will have to deal with malicious whisperings, pointing fingers and knocks on their doors at midnight! I thought of you immediately that body was discovered. I thought about the English girl and how desperate you have been to learn the truth about her. I've kept your secret for many years despite my own misgivings. You could at least repay my thoughtfulness.'

İkmen lost his temper. How dare she try to effectively blackmail him like this! 'You could have told me the body wasn't Alison's before I even got on that bus! You knew and you didn't call me, Menşure!' he cried. 'That is very manipulative, you know!'

She stood up and walked towards him. She was almost a whole head taller and for a moment İkmen thought that she might just shout him down. But in fact, when she spoke, she used a very gentle tone: 'Just talk to Haldun Alkaya, Çetin,' she said. 'Please.'

İkmen sighed and then sat back down again with his chin in his hands. Well, what an unusual day this had turned out to be!

No sleep, no Alison and now Menşure was begging for something from another human being. He took his gaze away from her face and looked out at the fairy chimney across the road. A woman wearing a long coloured headscarf was pulling a goat up a flight of outside steps into what İkmen knew was, traditionally, the family room in houses like this. What on earth was she going to do with a goat up there? And then he realised that he couldn't possibly know the answer to that question. This was, after all, rural Turkey, out among the chimneys where peris laughed and djinn danced and where anything and everything was possible. For just a very small moment he felt a tingle of excitement.

Quickly, before he changed his mind, he looked up at his cousin and said, 'All right. I'll talk to this Alkaya man but I'm promising nothing beyond that. Understand that, Menşure? Nothing.'

'I understand,' she said with a smile.

'And if I am staying, I may as well make some inquiries about Alison,' İkmen continued. 'After all, if I am to move on, I do have to know that the past is really behind me. I mean, what if she's living in some tiny hamlet hereabouts?'

Menşure viewed her cousin narrowly. 'I think it's unlikely,' she said. 'But if you must then you must.'

It had been a long day and what Mehmet Süleyman really wanted to do was go home and go to bed. But curiosity had got the better of him. And so here he was now, in the lee of a tall, brooding building belching steam from a rough steel chimney pipe, surrounded by several furtive-looking men.

When he had finished with Duruşan Efe, he'd decided to go

54

on and visit the peeper's first victim who lived in Kumkapı above his uncle's restaurant overlooking the Sea of Marmara. Small and terrified of almost anything one could name, Şevket Tezer had appeared before Süleyman shaking almost as much as he had when he'd first seen the peeper. It had seemed almost cruel to ask this lad any more questions, but Süleyman had done it anyway. He'd also told the boy he knew he was gay. Şevket cried by way of reply. Yes, İzzet Melik had been right about at least these two boys plus Ali Ceylan, who had woken to find the peeper actually masturbating in his room. They were all, at the very least, 'interested' in men and they had all mentioned two places that they all had in common. This, the Saray Hamam, tucked away amid the vertiginous and seedy streets of Karaköy, was one of them.

As Süleyman looked up at the forbidding black bulk of the hamam he wondered at why he'd never noticed this place before. He had, after all, lived in Karaköy for a number of years with his old colleague Balthazar Cohen when his first marriage to his cousin Zuleika had come to an end. A voracious appreciator of women with no morals, Cohen had quickly shown Süleyman all of the local whore houses, pavyons and gazinos that the district had to offer, but he'd never shown him this. Perhaps Cohen didn't know that this place even existed. One could be forgiven for overlooking such an ugly structure and men, after all, had never been to Balthazar's taste in any shape or form. There had been a time when he had suspected his friend Mehmet Süleyman of such practices, when the latter had, indeed, been young and painfully repressed. But that was a long time ago and Süleyman was now both a father and an erstwhile lover of his wife and, at times, of other women too. So this was a whole new world . . .

As he leaned up against the shuttered doorway of the hardware store opposite, he watched as the men around the hamam conformed to what seemed to be a standard routine. This started with hanging around looking as if one didn't know or even care where one was, perhaps accompanied by the lighting of a cigarette, either from one's own or another's lighter. Moving closer to the building and sometimes to other men in the vicinity then ensued, followed by a final dash to the main entrance at the side of the great, brooding structure.

Süleyman, now with a lighted cigarette of his own, watched it all. The eye contact, the almost imperceptible pout of the lips, the bolder holding up of the OK sign made with the thumb and index finger which, in this society had another, more directly sexual meaning.

'Trying to decide what to do?'

Süleyman turned quickly to find himself looking at a very good-looking man of about his own age. Expensively dressed, he smoked, like Süleyman's father, his cigarettes through a long, metal holder.

Süleyman smiled and said, 'Yes.'

'Well, I think you'll find a very . . . diverting group of people inside,' the man said. 'I think many might really take to you.'

'Oh.'

The man had a very sensual mouth that smiled easily and eyes that, Süleyman noticed, gazed quickly up and down his body with practised intensity.

'But it's up to you,' the man said with a shrug. 'It's always ultimately up to the individual, isn't it?'

And then he made his way forward towards the building, his thick dark overcoat swishing about his tall, elegant form as he moved. What had he been, Süleyman wondered, the man who had come on so casually to the lone policeman? A lawyer? An advertising executive, or someone 'big' in PR? Whatever he was he had wanted to get into the hamam and he had wanted to take Süleyman with him. For just a moment, he smiled. He'd only ever briefly entertained thoughts that he might be homosexual and, although he was now sure that he wasn't, it was still flattering to have been 'hit on' by another attractive man.

He was just about to leave when he saw another figure in another doorway about fifty metres down from where he was standing. Silhouetted against a glittering backdrop that featured distant glimpses of the Galata Bridge and the Golden Horn, he was tall, quite still and he was looking intently at the entrance to the hamam. Although he didn't want to stare, Süleyman tried to keep this unmoving party in at least the periphery of his vision. He would, the policeman imagined, eventually make a move towards the hamam at some point. It was not, as had been very well demonstrated earlier, always easy for these men to visit such places. The desire was obviously evident, but so were the guilt, the shame and any number of other attitudes towards homosexuality that had been drummed into them at home, at school and at work. However, thus far, they all seemed to manage to conquer their fear and to eventually go in – except for this man, seemingly pinned to his doorway. He, like Süleyman himself, just watched.

Time passed. Half an hour, an hour . . . Although he wasn't actually propositioned, Süleyman had to light a considerable number of cigarettes for people – unlike the watcher in the doorway further down the hill. No one, it seemed, except Süleyman, noticed him. The man, in his turn, watched the policeman back.

'Mehmet?'

The voice was familiar and so Süleyman turned around quickly towards it. 'Berekiah!'

It was his friend Balthazar's son, Berekiah Cohen, Çetin İkmen's son-in-law.

'What are you doing here?' the young man asked.

Süleyman, in spite of the fact that he wasn't doing anything illegal or immoral, felt his face flush. 'I'm, er, I'm' – he lowered his voice so that only Berekiah could hear – 'I'm working, actually, Berekiah . . .'

'Oh, right.' Berekiah smiled. He was young and had a really lovely face – a fact not lost on at least one other man in the vicinity who first smiled and then raised his eyebrows at the young man. Obviously accustomed to this sort of reaction in what was his home district, Berekiah just simply pulled a face and shook his head by way of reply.

'I'd better let you get on then, Mehmet,' he said to his friend and then he made his way off in the direction of his father's apartment.

Süleyman, sweating a little bit now in spite of the cold, gave thanks to Allah that it had only been Berekiah who had observed what he was doing. If it had been the lad's father, that voracious gossip Balthazar, then a story about Mehmet Süleyman having sex with another man in the street would already have begun to circulate amongst the law enforcement community. Süleyman breathed a sigh of relief and then turned back to look for his mysterious doorway man once again. But there was nothing to be seen. Some time during the course of his short exchange with Berekiah, the man had completely disappeared. As he started to move away, however, the attractive man who had spoken to him earlier emerged from the hamam. Passing Süleyman on his way up to Beyoğlu he smiled, exhibiting many shining teeth as he did so.

Allah alone knew what Menşure had told this poor old man about him! Probably a load of nonsense about how famous and powerful her cousin from İstanbul was. But whatever she had said had made Haldun Alkaya, a man already in grief, almost prostrate with humility and respect.

Even as a child on holiday with his parents, İkmen had never really had much to do with the really poor villagers. His uncle and aunt were wealthy and his father, whose forebears had originated from Cappadocia, had friends in the region who were, again, well off and educated. Places like Haldun Alkaya's semi-derelict chimney house were extremely alien. Halfway up one of the steep hills that led out of the village towards the road to Nevşehir, Alkaya's place consisted of just one conical chimney surrounded by a courtyard, the walls of which were topped with bundles of twigs. Usually chimneys, although at the heart of an individual's property, made up only part of the Cappadocian's home. Nearby caves would sometimes be utilised and for centuries people had built attractive stone houses on to the front or backs of existing chimneys. But that presupposed the occupants had money. Haldun Alkaya with his spare, two-room chimney lit only by the light from candles and his wood fire, was not one of them.

'The only thing I had, the only thing I have ever had, was my daughter,' the old man said as he lit his hand-rolled cigarette with a piece of paper dipped into the fire. 'I accepted she was dead long ago, Çetin Bey. But still it is hard. Allah's plan for us is sometimes difficult to bear.'

'Yes.'

There were no chairs, only those saddle seats, the more ornate varieties of which were frequently sold to charmed tourists. Old 'real' ones like these were, however, far from charming to a middle-aged İstanbullu with a rather spare behind. The thing was hard and hideously uncomfortable.

'Menşure Hanım has told me something about your daughter and the circumstances surrounding her disappearance,' İkmen said, 'so can you tell me, Haldun Bey, why she married Ziya Kahraman? I understand she had feelings for a boy of her own age, that he had feelings for her and that you knew about this.'

'I did.' The old man smiled, sadly. His face, like so many of the old, really hardworking peasants, was deeply lined and, in spite of the autumn weather, as brown as the earth. 'Kemalettin Senar was a lovely young boy in those days,' he said. 'He had eyes for my Aysu and she had eyes for him. But I am a poor man, Çetin Bey, a widower since the day my little girl was born. Her little dowry was of no interest to Nalan Senar. When I spoke to her of it she made it very clear that she thought her son could do a lot better than Aysu. Her own people were very bad stock but she married money and so she thought she was something. As it has turned out, Kemalettin remains unmarried to this day, so maybe Allah has punished Nalan's arrogance and greed.'

İkmen smiled. The majority of the villagers were religious, which was not something he was unaccustomed to, but, nevertheless, it wasn't something that he was necessarily comfortable with.

'When Aysu found out that Kemalettin's mother was against their union, she was very upset,' the old man said. 'In fact, for a time, I feared that she and the boy might try to run away together. I kept her inside. But then that wasn't really in Aysu's nature. She loved me. She would never have left me. She was a good girl.'

Haldun Alkaya paused for a moment while he dried the tears that had flooded into his eyes on the cuffs of his fraying shirt.

'I have never told anyone this before but Aysu offered to marry Ziya Kahraman, Çetin Bey,' the old man said. 'She knew he had been asking me for her and so, once she knew that Kemalettin's family would not accept her, she said she would marry Ziya.'

'But he was a lot older than her, wasn't he?' İkmen said. 'Didn't that make you feel uneasy? You are a man, are you not, Haldun Bey, of fine sensibilities?'

'I like to think so, yes,' Haldun replied. 'But I am also a poor man and, in those days, Çetin Bey, I was a poor man with a poor daughter no one but the most destitute peasant would consider. Aysu was a clever girl. Ziya Kahraman had only ever managed to have one daughter, Nazlı, by his first wife. His second wife he had divorced because she had been barren and Ziya Kahraman needed a son to take over his lemon empire . . .'

'Lemon empire?'

'The caves round here make very good storage for lemons,'

Haldun said. 'Ziya's father had left him many such caves as well as the Kahraman family lemon groves which are down on the south coast, by Alanya. Nazlı Kahraman is now a very wealthy grower of lemons. But that is beside the point. Aysu saw a way for us to maybe leave this poverty you see around you behind and so she married Ziya Kahraman.'

'But didn't you try to stop her?' İkmen said, knowing that what he was saying probably didn't make sense in the context of Muratpaşa circa 1983. After all, not everyone, even now, allowed their daughters to marry young Jewish boys they fell in love with as he himself had done.

'No,' the old man said. 'May Allah forgive me, I admit that I experienced greed! She went to him, he and that evil daughter of his, and I only saw her twice before she disappeared. They made me speak to her through that great gate Ziya had made for his courtyard. She told me she wasn't yet with child and I heard Nazlı order her about as if she were a servant. My daughter was used by Ziya and, I think that when he discovered that she, like his second wife, was not taking his seed, he killed her.'

İkmen, who had just reached into his pocket to retrieve his cigarettes, stopped and frowned. 'But the police seemed, I understand, more interested in the possibility of Kemalettin being at fault.'

'With respect to yourself, Çetin Bey, they would be.' The old man sighed. 'Ziya Kahraman used to be able to buy people. Miserly with those who worked for him, very free with money to people he wanted or needed. His daughter is just the same. Seventy years old she may be, but last year Nazlı Kahraman married a boy of twenty-five she met somewhere on the south coast. Oh, no, Ziya Kahraman was barely touched by the police at the time!'

'But you think that he killed your daughter?' İkmen said as he finally took a cigarette out of his pocket and lit up.

'Yes. I have always believed she was murdered. Half the village still think that, somehow, Kemalettin Senar killed my daughter, but I do not agree. I know that the boy has since become rather strange, but I really do believe that is because he misses Aysu. He loved her so much! Now he just drifts, talking to himself and . . .'

'So what do you think I can do about this, Haldun Bey?' İkmen asked. 'I am a policeman just like those in Nevşehir . . .'

'Ah, yes, but you are from İstanbul, aren't you!' the old man said. 'And in İstanbul you have tests that can be done to see who killed who sometimes years and years before. I have read it in newspapers.' His face assumed a proud glow. 'I can both read and write.'

İkmen smiled. Coming from İstanbul it was sometimes easy to forget that the ability to read and write was still, for some citizens of the Republic, a considerable achievement and one to be trumpeted.

'In Nevşehir they will not do such tests on my daughter's body,' Haldun continued. 'All they will say is that they will find out how she died. I said, "What about these tests to see who killed her?", but that inspector over there, the same idiot who came here twenty years ago, he just ignored what I said and told me they would release Aysu to me as soon as they could. They would not even tell me whether they think she was murdered. I know that she was. I know that you must know that she was, too, or else why would you be here?'

63

İkmen smiled. A simple man he may be, but Haldun Alkaya was far from stupid. 'So what exactly do you think I can do, Haldun Bey?'

'Menşure Hanım tells me that you are an honest man, Çetin Bey,' the old man said. 'You are also a clever man. Not just me, but this whole village needs to know who killed Aysu. We will never be at peace until this matter is settled. As it is, those who believe the Kahramans to be wronged will not speak or do business with the Senars or with me either. It is very bad for business.'

'But if, as you believe, Haldun Bey, Ziya Kahraman killed your daughter, if he's now dead . . .'

'Ah, but the tests can be performed on his relatives, can they not?' Haldun said. 'My friend Rahmi has a satellite dish and we saw this programme on his television about a murder in Ankara. The police there took some water from the mouth of a man who was the brother of a murderer.'

'Yes,' İkmen said, 'DNA testing. And yes, we do do that in İstanbul, Haldun Bey. But if Nevşehir do not have the facilities . . .'

'Then you will have to bring this DNA to them,' the old man said. 'Menşure Hanım told me that you came to Muratpaşa for some reason other than this. But the fact that you are here at this time is kismet and so you must help. Allah has sent you to us, Çetin Bey, in His infinite mercy, to heal the soul of our poor village.'

Even though he could feel the panic rising in his chest as the old man spoke, İkmen just nodded politely by way of recognition. How on earth was he going to 'bring DNA' to Nevşehir? If any of the local men were like the few country officers he'd met over the years who had been transferred up to İstanbul, introducing anything even slightly contemporary to them was going to be like trying to drag a caveman into the jet-age. And besides, he wasn't a scientist who could 'do' DNA himself. He had no jurisdiction, no scientific knowledge, and he didn't even really know the hellish village that well. Bloody cousin Menşure, he could have killed her, talking him up as if he were some sort of genius!

But then if he was going to stay, he would have to keep busy. Asking elderly Cappadocians about the possible appearance of an English girl in their midst in the 1970s was hardly likely to account for all of his time. And Muratpaşa, weird and lovely as he knew it to be, was also not İstanbul and İkmen knew that if he didn't go home immediately he would get very bored. So why not hassle the local grunts and see whether he could help this lonely, poverty-stricken old man for a few days? Allah knew there were already quite enough poor people suffering injustice. Why should Haldun Alkaya be just another statistic?

İkmen looked deeply into the poor man's fire and said, 'All right, Haldun Bey, I'll do what I can.'

'I knew that you would,' the old man said with a smile. 'It was written.'

Chapter 5

Captain Altay Salman was pleased that his old colleague had not wanted to meet him at Menşure Tokatlı's hotel. Although he had a lot of respect for the woman she did, he had to admit, make him feel both guilty – for his non-observance of Ramazan – and inferior in equal measures. But then meeting at the Tasmanian Devil was not exactly without its problems either. Just because Rachelle Jones was happy to serve non-fasting Muslims during the hours of daylight and even help them smoke their cigarettes, didn't mean that she was necessarily comfortable to be around – at least not for Altay. As he sat in her discreet courtyard, sipping his coffee and making conversation, the good captain wished that the Australian would not display quite so much of her chest quite so close to his face. İkmen was late, and considering that he had made this appointment, effectively dragging Altay away from his wife and daughter, the captain was not a little annoyed.

At length the İstanbul man appeared, and Altay Salman forgave him immediately. İkmen, although not exactly a close friend, had always been an honest and helpful colleague as well as, periodically, great fun to be with in one or other of İstanbul's numerous meyhanes. The Australian moved aside to allow the two men to embrace and then went off to bring the captain more coffee and İkmen a glass of tea.

After thanking his friend for coming, İkmen said, 'I'm sorry I rang you so late last night, but I'd just come back from visiting Haldun Alkaya and I was a bit fired up. Menşure believes that you know all there is to know about this Alkaya business.'

'I know it's split the village,' Altay replied. 'Alkaya and the Kahramans and their people don't speak. Kemalettin Senar, who, if you are staying, you will have to make your own mind up about, drifts around even now under a cloud of suspicion. He doesn't talk to anyone and behaves, well, oddly at times. I have no idea what might be wrong with him. His mother and brother can be quite vocal about Nazlı Kahraman, or, rather, what they think of her late father.' He sighed. 'But now that the police in Nevşehir have Aysu Alkaya's body maybe this puzzle is about to be solved.'

'And what do you know about the body?' İkmen asked.

'My nephew, who found it, said it was partially preserved,' Altay said. 'Scientists have believed for years that many of the caves round here can have that effect upon the human body, just like they do on the lemons. But anyway, the girl's father could, apparently, tell it was her. In addition there were certain artefacts identified as having belonged to Aysu.' He leaned forward and lowered his voice. 'Cause of death was a gunshot wound to the back. The father will be told later on today, then it will be all over the village. Nearly everyone here believes she was murdered anyway.' He sighed. 'There will be a ballistics investigation, but facilities with regard to DNA testing and those qualified to do that are limited. That's why when Miss Tokatlı told me you were coming I was anxious to make contact. If anyone can get someone down from the Forensic Institute it has to be you.'

Rachelle Jones appeared with their drinks. She smiled as she placed them down on the small metal table, principally at Altay.

Çetin İkmen smiled back. 'She seems impressed,' he said as he watched the tall woman walk back towards her kitchen.

Altay raised his eyes towards the heavens. 'It's the uniform,' he said. 'This is a village that has been hijacked by tourism, Çetin. All the old and the traditionalists spend half their time being scandalised while many of the young men and the foreign residents just want to jump on anything that moves. It's been known that some tourists and some of my boys at the riding school have been followed by one or other sex-starved individual.'

'Not keen on country life?' İkmen asked.

'Oh, I love working at the school,' his companion replied. 'It's great to watch boys who are just adequate riders become highly skilled. And we've got some very impressive horses. But socially it's a little dull. I don't, I must admit, mind that too much, but my wife isn't very impressed. In fact, I wish that Sevgi and Miss Jones would get together. Whatever I may or may not feel about her, Rachelle Jones knows this village, its people, and has a tremendous appreciation for the countryside and its history. Also, I know my wife is keen not to lose her English language skills while she's here. It would be perfect.'

'What about your daughter?' İkmen asked.

He sighed. 'Hande's okay. She's got friends and now that her cousin Ferhat is stationed here I feel I can let her explore

68

the area in the safety of his company. This landscape is fascinating by anyone's standards.'

'Yes.' İkmen smiled again, mainly at the sight of probably the most phallic chimney in the village, which was situated just next door to the Tasmanian Devil's kitchen. 'I don't know if I can do anything with regard to getting forensic movement on this,' he said. 'I'm only here for a week, but I can make some calls and see what I can do. I didn't, after all, come here to get involved with this. I came for other reasons.' He looked away briefly. 'But I can see how contentious this is and so I'll do what I can. I don't want to upset the boys in Nevşehir.'

'No.'

'Talking of which,' İkmen continued, 'what are they like?'

Altay shrugged. 'Rural. They tend to be conservative and they are notoriously hard up. I actually have much more contact with the jandarma myself who, as you know, are principally city boys.'

'We stick to our own, don't we?'

'We try to,' Altay replied. 'But they're not bad in Nevşehir. I mean, they would probably be quite impressed, shall we say, to see you. I can't say pleased exactly . . . I still get a bit of that attitude of "you're a big shot from the big city who thinks he's something special" from some of them, but . . .'

'Because it would help if I could see the body myself,' İkmen said. 'Then I could at least describe it to colleagues back home.'

Altay Salman let out a long, tired breath. 'It may be possible,' he said. 'Let me speak to the local jandarma, they've far more experience with the police around here than I have.'

İkmen offered his packet of cigarettes to Altay, who took one, and then lit up himself. 'I'd be grateful,' he said. 'I can't do much, but if I can get a proper forensic analysis underway it may, at least, go somewhere towards satisfying Haldun Alkaya. He seems to regard DNA as some kind of magical solution.'

'Well he might,' his companion said as he peered at İkmen through a curtain of smoke. 'Just like so many of them. But you know, Çetin, that some think he may have been responsible for his daughter's disappearance?'

'How do they work that out?'

Altay shrugged.

'Some think it might have been an honour thing.'

Both men looked up at the source of the Australian-tinged English that had just strolled up to their table.

'Miss Jones?'

Rachelle Jones put her cigarettes and lighter down on the slightly rickety metal table and sat down. 'One of the many theories that have flown around this village at one time or another is that somehow poor little Aysu Alkaya managed to get away from old Ziya Kahraman and that her father, shamed by what she had done to the lemon king, killed her.'

'Mmm.' İkmen looked at the tall, handsome woman in front of him with a critical eye. Probably in her mid-forties, Rachelle Jones had both humour and, now he observed it closely, a sweet, almost juvenile yearning for the dashing captain in her eyes. İkmen instinctively felt that he was going to like her. However, she was a civilian and so he didn't want to divulge too much about what he had discovered himself. Unlikely as it sounded, her theory was a point of view and one that was not unknown to İkmen. Sometimes runaway girls did fall foul of fathers and brothers wanting them to consent to or stay within abusive marriages with richer, often considerably older men.

'There's a lot of coercion put on some of the girls hereabouts,' the Australian said. 'That's not a criticism. I know that's just how it is, as I'm sure you do.'

İkmen smiled. This woman was rather good at being realistic about the village while at the same time retaining her own opinions.

'And then, of course, there's the theory about poor little Kemalettin Senar,' Rachelle continued. 'But I'm sure you've heard about all that.'

'Some people suspect him of involvement in the girl's disappearance,' İkmen said in the English that was obviously, in spite of her Turkish language skills, more comfortable for Rachelle.

'Listen, I've worked out she was probably murdered all for myself,' Rachelle said with a smile. 'Look at Kemalettin and tell me whether you think he's capable of murder? Oh, speak of the devil . . .'

İkmen turned and saw a rather stooped figure standing at the entrance to the pansiyon's courtyard. Extremely dark and probably in early middle age, the man surveyed the two officers and the woman with a frown that was almost fierce in its intensity. He wore a long brown overcoat that he now, very slowly, began to pull to one side.

'Ah!' The Australian was up and out of her seat like a rocket. 'You can put that away as quick as you like!' she said as she ran up to him and pulled his coat back around his body. 'Shameful!'

she said in Turkish and then, reverting to English, she said, 'Go on, get out of here!'

İkmen gave Altay a quizzical look.

'He tends to, er, manipulate himself sometimes,' the captain said coyly.

'Doing that in public places!' Rachelle, again in English, said as she sat down and lit up a cigarette. 'Dirty little tyke! Most of the time we all ignore it but when people are eating and drinking . . .'

'Has he always done that, um . . .'

'For years and years,' the Australian replied. 'Used to be quite a looker, but . . .' And then, seeing that the man was still in her gateway, she said, 'What did I say, Kemalettin? Go away!'

Slowly, almost as if he were in a dream, the stooped, dark man shuffled off down the hill and towards the centre of the village. Once he had gone, the Australian woman smiled broadly, especially at Altay Salman.

'It wouldn't surprise me for a minute if Abdullah Aydın took it up the arse,' İzzet Melik said with some gusto.

Süleyman, who had been talking to both his inferior and his colleague, Inspector İskender, turned to Melik and said, 'I don't think that speculation of the idle variety is of much value at this time, Sergeant.'

Melik, stung, sniffed and then said, 'No, sir.' He was, after all, accustomed to, if not approving of, Mehmet Süleyman's 'sensibilities'.

'Now if you don't mind retrieving my black shoes from the menders on Yerebatan Caddesi . . .' Süleyman put his hand in his pocket and gave the heavily moustachioed man a small ticket and a handful of banknotes. 'It shouldn't be more than five million.'

'No, sir.' Melik scowled and, as slowly as he felt he could get away with, he left.

Metin İskender was a younger and smaller man than Mehmet Süleyman. Dapper and intelligent, he was also a man who had fought his way out of one of İstanbul's most notorious slum districts. He was therefore rather more accustomed to rough talk and even rougher attitudes than his more aristocratic friend.

'You shouldn't treat him like your valet,' he said to Süleyman once Melik had finally gone. 'He isn't a constable.'

'He never has anything of value to say,' Süleyman responded haughtily. 'His only input to any investigation in which he is involved is simply a list of his own prejudices. I think he sees people as types, sort of caricatures. The screaming homosexual, the nosy kapıcı.'

'Most kapıcıs are nosy, Mehmet,' İskender said with a smile, 'but I take your point.'

Süleyman lit a cigarette. 'These incidents involving the person we call the peeper are a case in point,' he said. 'Melik believes that because the offender obviously enjoys the sight of attractive young men, his victims must of necessity be homosexual themselves.'

'And aren't they?'

'Well, a significant number of them are, yes.'

'Oh, so Melik's ideas do have some merit, then?' İskender said with a smile as he, too, lit a cigarette.

'The boy who was actually penetrated says that he isn't homosexual . . .'

'But even if he isn't, it still means that Melik, in the main, is absolutely right,' İskender replied. 'Come on, Mehmet, you just don't like Melik. And I can see why. He's dull, boorish and he makes some terrible noises when he eats. But İzmir reckoned he was a good officer, which is why you've got him.'

'I'd rather have your sergeant.'

'You keep your hands off Alp Karataş,' İskender said sternly. 'Not only is he my sergeant, we also get along as brothers. It's bad that you've not found anyone you can really like since Çöktin left the service, but you have to try to make something work with Melik, even if you can't really take to him.'

Süleyman sighed. 'I know.'

'And besides, by the sound of it, this idea that the peeper may be targeting men who go to homosexual places might just yield something. It is somewhere to start at the very least.'

This was true and was, indeed, the reason why Süleyman and İskender were having their meeting now. By climbing on to the ever-growing roofs of the old city, the person known as the peeper was demonstrating intention to look at certain and, possibly, pre-selected men. Some of the victims Süleyman had spoken to did seem to have some venues catering specifically for homosexual men in common. He knew that İskender had a very reliable homosexual informant whom he was quite keen to access.

'So, this Elma . . .'

'Is a very sweet little fruit whom I haven't used for quite a while,' İskender interrupted.

'But he's very involved in the homosexual life.'

'Elma is that thing that Melik would relate to oh so well: the screaming drama queen.' İskender shrugged. 'He's also a very good informant.'

'Could you ask him whether there's any mythology about the peeper amongst homosexuals?'

'Yes, although I'll have to pay him.'

'Of course,' Süleyman said. 'Just tell me how much it is and I'll reimburse you.'

İskender fingered his empty tea glass which he had placed on Süleyman's desk. 'OK, I'll set it up.'

The midday call to prayer interrupted their conversation. Because he smoked heavily, Süleyman was inclined to have his window open for most of the time. But with the imperial mosques of Sultan Ahmet, Beyazıt and Süleymaniye, not to mention all the little local mescits so close at hand, hearing oneself think could be a problem at times. And so because neither he nor İskender were of a religious nature, Süleyman got up and closed the window.

'I suppose it's too soon to start putting undercover officers into known homosexual haunts?' İskender said as he watched his friend walk back to his desk.

'Yes.'

He'd thought about it, though. He'd thought about whom he could and could not ask to perform such a task with more than a little shudder down his spine. Between the macho moustachioed variety like Melik and the horrified youngsters who were either too religious or too afraid of what their colleagues might think to volunteer for such an assignment there really wasn't a great deal of choice. It was why he himself had 'dabbled' a little at the hamam in Karaköy. And yet Süleyman, as well as most other Turkish men, was aware of the ambiguity that exists about homosexuality. Although rather an outdated idea now, there was a time when many Turkish men believed that only the passive partner was truly homosexual. The 'active' person could therefore screw his chosen boy to his heart's content and then go home to his wife and see to her with an entirely clear and, more importantly, masculine conscience.

'I'll consider the undercover option once I've explored some other ideas,' Süleyman said.

'So, how is the boy who was attacked on Sunday night?' İskender asked.

'Abdullah Aydın is still in a coma.' Süleyman put his cigarette out and then lit another. 'And you know how it is with those.'

'Yes. May it pass quickly.' The previous year İskender had been shot in the line of duty after which he had, briefly, fallen into a coma. Now fully recovered, he still bore the scar the surgeons had made in order to remove his shattered spleen. Sometimes it still hurt, when he was particularly tired or stressed. Unconsciously he put one hand over the scar now.

'As yet, no one has seen the peeper's face,' Süleyman continued. 'We know he's tall, slim but well built, wears a ski mask and something like a body suit, but that is all we know. What might be locked away inside Abdullah Aydın's head . . .'

'If anything,' İskender interrupted sharply. 'You know that I still can't recall everything about that time.'

'Yes, I know. But İnşallah . . .'

'He will be able to remember something, yes,' İskender said. 'But in the meantime I will speak to Elma.' He sighed. 'He's not exactly easy, but you are my friend, Mehmet.'

Süleyman smiled. It hadn't been all that long ago when Metin, his friend, had been almost unapproachable. Elevated through the ranks at a young age he had been very aware of both the resentment this had caused in some quarters and of the fact that it was well known he had originated from the crime-torn district of Ümraniye. Wanting to impress his superiors as well as his middle-class wife, Metin had been very rule-bound, self-contained and, seemingly, arrogant. However, as the years had passed and he had worked with and grown to trust people like Süleyman and Çetin İkmen, he had mellowed into the much more approachable person he was now.

İskender rose to leave. 'So when is Çetin returning to us?' he asked as he pushed the chair he had been sitting on underneath Mehmet's desk.

'Next Monday,' Süleyman replied. 'He has some family business in Cappadocia.'

'Oh.' İskender smiled. 'Strange place, Cappadocia, isn't it? My wife's company publishes some authors who live out there. She always says that although they all write different things – fiction, travelogue, et cetera – the one thing they all have in common is that they are all universally strange – as people, I mean.'

'I think that maybe that very special landscape has much to do with how people are there,' Süleyman said.

'How you said that without either laughing or using the word "penis", I do not know,' İskender said and then left the office, chuckling.

Süleyman smiled, just for a while, until he remembered where young Abdullah Aydın was and what he was doing. Even if the boy survived, the peeper was going to kill someone soon.

His behaviour had escalated from peeping and masturbating to assault in less than three months. He was obviously a very disturbed and dangerous person.

'Inti! Inti! Inti!'

The young man who had said these strange words and all of his colleagues collapsed into fits of laughter.

Çetin İkmen, laughing now along with the young jandarma, said, 'But what does that mean?'

'Apparently it's the name of the sun god,' the young man, Private Ferhat Salman, said. 'She's from Peru in South America and that is, so she says, what they worship over there.'

'But then she had to say something given how we found her,' the shorter, more serious, Private Büker, put in. 'I mean, dancing naked in front of some frescos in a chimney that used to be a church is not normal.'

Ferhat looked at İkmen and, suddenly serious, said, 'Nothing is normal in this crazy place, Çetin Bey. I never expected to find a mummy in that cave. It was gruesome.'

'It must have been a terrible shock,' İkmen replied.

'Oh, *I* was fine with it,' the young man blustered. 'But I was with my cousin and her friend. Girls.'

'But of course you had to protect them from the look of it,' İkmen said with a smile.

'Yes. Girls can become hysterical.'

After he had left Altay Salman, İkmen had gone for a stroll through the village. As well as wanting to reacquaint himself with the place he also needed some time to think about the disturbing vision that had been Kemalettin Senar. If the lovely

78

Aysu Alkaya had once loved him he must have been a very different man. It was, İkmen felt, as if the man had had some kind of breakdown. However, now that he was in the small gendarmerie at the edge of the village he was learning even more about the oddities of Muratpaşa. The young jandarma, and especially Altay Salman's nephew Ferhat, had welcomed the policeman from İstanbul with open arms. They were, he very quickly discovered, only too willing to share the gossip that jandarma everywhere are famed for collecting – like the Peruvian expatriate and her naked dances to the sun god.

'You know that Ümit Özal the carpet dealer sleeps with his kilims?' Ferhat continued. 'The story is that he's so afraid that someone will rob him that he even takes his best examples to bed.'

'There's old Selim who pretends he has Parkinson's Disease so that women will feel sorry for him and, possibly, agree to marry him out of pity,' Abdulhamid Büker said.

'But the foreigners are the worst,' another young man with a very prominent scar on his face put in. 'What about that English woman, Ferhat, the one with that slimy little gigolo?'

Ferhat scowled and then said to İkmen, 'European women who come up here with men from resorts like Side and Bodrum are not uncommon. But this woman is particularly of note because she's actually married this character. She must be fifty and I know for a fact that he is only twenty-two.'

'You think he's after a British passport?' İkmen asked.

'Oh, yes of course. But not before he's got her to buy him a nice little pansiyon here in the village,' Ferhat replied. 'In his name, of course.'

İkmen raised his eyes up to heaven and sighed. But then

needy European women and their sometimes rapacious beaux were not his problem. He'd seen this sort of thing before, back home in İstanbul, and he knew that such seeming exploitation was neither all one way nor all that simple.

'So what can you boys tell me about those people connected, as it were, to this body Ferhat has just found?' İkmen asked as he lit a cigarette and then handed the packet around to the rest of the assembled company.

'I found it out in the Valley of the Saints,' Ferhat said. 'It was ghastly, desiccated . . .'

'Yes, I know,' İkmen said. 'But what I'm asking is what you boys know about people like Haldun Alkaya, Kemalettin Senar and old Ziya Kahraman's daughter.'

'Nazlı Hanım,' Abdulhamid Büker said. 'She's very old, rich, by country standards, and very mean.'

'She's married to a boy called Erkan,' Ferhat added. 'People say he married her for her money but if he did then someone else put him up to it.'

'Why?'

'Well, he's, you know, he's simple. He can't read or write, stands around a lot with his mouth open. She's a covered woman, Nazlı Hanım, which is OK, but she also has a beard.' Ferhat pulled a disgusted face. 'Nazlı Hanım had never been with a man until she met Erkan – or so it is said.'

'People say that her father wouldn't let her marry until he himself had a son,' Abdulhamid said.

İkmen frowned. 'But he never did have a son, did he?'

'No.'

But then if Nazlı had seen her father's marriage to Aysu Alkaya as his last chance to have a son, could she not have just 'made sure' that he and his young wife did not conceive? Death is, after all, a most effective contraceptive. And there were an awful lot of lemons at stake, many of which had been preserved in just the same way as poor Aysu. Although if one or other of the Kahramans had planned her fate to be so intimately connected with their business that did seem rather stupid. And, in İkmen's experience, reasonably successful people like the Kahramans were rarely lacking in brain power.

'She waited a long time after her father died before she got married,' Abdulhamid said.

'She took a long time to find someone who could tolerate her foul temper and the look of her,' Ferhat said. 'Like a starved old eagle!'

'I suppose Nazlı Hanım has always lived in the village,' İkmen said.

Ferhat rolled his eyes. 'They've all always lived in the village, Çetin Bey, at least the older ones have. To give you a feel for it, you know the old man who owns the bakery?'

'I know the bakery,' İkmen said, 'it's at the bottom of the New Mosque hill.'

'That's it,' Ferhat said. 'Well, you want to listen to his story about the day he went to Ankara back in about 1960. It's amazing. To hear him talk you'd think he'd gone to the moon! Nazlı Hanım is a bit better than that. She's been to İstanbul, Ankara, and, of course, the coast – Alanya, I assume, where the lemon groves are; I don't know exactly. But wherever it was, that was where she found poor Erkan.'

The baker and Nazlı Hanım had to have been around when Alison allegedly passed through the district. In fact, İkmen felt that Nazlı Hanım might be just the sort of person who might

81

well recall the few foreigners who had got this far in the seventies. If she couldn't, he could at least use this as a pretext to see what she was like. Until Altay Salman got back to him about whether or not he could view the body in Nevşehir he'd have to amuse himself somehow. After all, listening to more stories about the Peruvian woman schooling her Turkish husband in the vagaries of sun god worship had a limited appeal.

İftar couldn't come quick enough for Erkan Erduran. All day, just like the day before and the day before that, he'd been starving. He knew, because Nazlı Hanım had told him, that his faith should sustain him through the hunger pangs, the raging thirst and the endless need for a cigarette. But beyond knowing that Allah existed and that Muhammed was his prophet, Erkan didn't have a tremendous grasp of the finer points and virtues of Islam.

'I sometimes think you have infidel blood,' his wife said caustically as she viewed him through crepey, half-closed eyes. 'That you should be so tormented by Ramazan is not right.'

'No.'

Erkan turned his fresh young face to one side. Sometimes when she spoke like this, about 'blood' and 'infidels', he became fearful that perhaps she knew his secret.

The Erduran family had always lived in the Aegean coastal town of Ayvalık – where Erkan had met Nazlı Kahraman. Even when the then new Turkish Republic had traded families, like the Erdurans, with Turks from Greece in 1923, Erkan's family had chosen to remain. But then his grandfather, Spiros Kazan, had changed both his name and his religion some years before the declaration of the Republic and so, naturally, he chose to remain with his fellow Muslims. Erkan's own mother was actually Turkish too, which was good. But his father remained 'close' about his origins, especially now that his son was married to 'money'. 'Now listen, Erkan,' he had said to his son on the eve of the latter's wedding to Nazlı Kahraman, 'this lemon queen has a lot of money which you can have provided you keep her happy and never, ever mention the . . . you know, the Greek connection.' Erkan had said that he wouldn't and he hadn't. He'd not mentioned anything about Greece and he had done everything that Nazlı Hanım asked of him. He had even taken her virginity, which had proved to be nothing like the sex he'd had with the tourist ladies on the coast. Nazlı Hanım had only wanted him the once. Ever since then there had been nothing, which was probably for the best. Nazlı Hanım wasn't pretty.

But Nazlı Kahraman was unconcerned. Ever since her sixtieth birthday, when she finally reasoned that she had mourned for her beloved father enough, she had been having and doing exactly what she wanted. Outside of Ramazan she ate, smoked and drank whenever she felt like it and Erkan was a lovely boy who looked good at her side. She did care for him and had indeed made some small provision for him in her will. That the bulk of her inheritance would still go to her cousin Gazi upon her death was more to spite Erkan's rapacious and so obviously Greek father than to upset the boy. Sitting beside her marble fountain in her vast courtyard overlooking the village, Nazlı Kahraman soaked up what was going to be the last hour of daylight like a sponge. Soon the girl she employed to cook and clean would call out to say that the iftar meal was ready and then all that would remain would be to wait for the call that signalled sunset had arrived. Then both she and Erkan would light their cigarettes simultaneously and she at least, would smile with pleasure.

But before any of that could happen, someone rang the bell outside the gate and Erkan, still unused to letting the 'help' do things, answered it.

Chapter 6

Dr Zelfa Halman Süleyman didn't keep Ramazan. Brought up in Ireland, her mother's country, she considered herself, if anything, a lapsed Catholic. She knew that her husband, though once observant, also failed to keep Ramazan. So as she waited for him to arrive to see his son and talk about the divorce she'd said she wanted, Zelfa knew that food was not a problem. Unlike her own feelings which were.

She didn't really want a divorce. What she and her son Yusuf, who adored his father, really wanted was for Mehmet to come home and be the family man he had been before all the trouble. But how could she trust him? Adultery was one thing, but going with a prostitute and then announcing that he had to be tested for HIV ... Oh, he'd been negative for that, which was wonderful, but the memories of that time, of the prostitute he'd screwed, of Zelfa's own obsessive suspicions and frigidity at that juncture, remained.

Hearing a car pull up outside the slightly shabby wooden house she shared with her father, Zelfa went to the front window and looked into the street. Mehmet, his face drawn and serious, was sitting behind the wheel of his great white BMW talking earnestly into his mobile phone. She wondered who he was talking to so seriously and then instantly wondered whether it was a woman. When he finally came into the house and took his son into his arms with a smile on his face, she asked him.

'It was Metin İskender, if you must know,' he said a little touchily. 'He's been speaking to someone who had some information we might be able to use.'

'Oh.'

What he didn't go on to say was exactly what İskender's informant had said. The peeper's activities, it seemed, were beginning to bite into İstanbul's gay community. The general consensus of opinion seemed to be that the peeper, far from being a homosexual man himself, was actually someone who 'got off' frightening and abusing other men. The mythology was that he was probably a straight man with some sort of grudge. The exotic Elma, İskender's informant, had said that some thought that perhaps the peeper was one of those who had at some time experimented with homosexuality and then been disgusted by what he had done – or maybe by the pleasant way it had made him feel. People gathering in gay places were watchful, although there had not, as yet, been any reports, as far as Elma knew, of any odd or disturbing people on the scene. The only thing that was happening was that people were not going out in public as often as they had before. Casual encounters and those expert in that field were also not quite so common as they had been. This man, though slowly and, to most people, imperceptibly, was changing the life of the city. The old whore İstanbul, as Süleyman knew right through to his city-bred bones, didn't like it when anyone tried to tame her wild spirit. No attempt to tackle vice in the city by Byzantine, Ottoman or Republican administrations had been even partially successful. There was going to be a lot of trouble.

Zelfa cooked pizzas for their dinner and then they all watched a video, *Finding Nemo*, before Mehmet finally put Yusuf to bed at nine. When he came back downstairs, Zelfa was sitting at the kitchen table with a fan of official-looking papers spread out before her. As he entered the room she looked up into his eyes.

'You've been busy,' he said as he sat down and lit a cigarette.

'I think that if we are going to divorce we should do it in as clean and civilised a fashion as possible,' she said. 'Delaying will only cause more aggravation and pain.'

'If that is what you think.'

'Well, don't you?' She lit up a cigarette and then exhaled jerkily.

Mehmet shrugged. 'What can I say? I'm in a position of weakness and guilt.'

'You could try saying what you really think.'

That was not an easy request and Zelfa knew it. Even discounting Mehmet's natural pride, there was also his sense of appropriateness, not to mention his adherence to the rules of etiquette, to take into account.

'Well, if you ask my worthless opinion . . .'

'Oh, Christ!' Zelfa cried out in English. 'Not those bloody Ottoman niceties again!'

Polite conversation in Ottoman court circles involved a process of constant self-abasement. Obvious arrogance was considered a sin and so a system of exaggerated self-deprecation evolved as each party in a conversation attempted to create a mismatch between themselves and the person being spoken to. This human 'doormat' phenomenon could only be brought to a close by one or other of the communicants reminding the assembled company that they were all, whatever their status, equal under God.

'Zelfa . . .'

'Look, do you want a divorce or don't you?' she interrupted, this time in Turkish. 'Because if you don't and you intend to fight me on this, then I think I deserve to know.'

His face wore an expression that had nothing to do with any sort of compassion. 'No, I don't want to divorce you,' he said.

Zelfa, furious, slipped back into English once again. 'Fucking great!'

'I don't want to lose my son,' Mehmet said. 'I know I am not the best man or the best father in the world, but I do love Yusuf. Even a stopped clock shows the correct time twice a day.'

Zelfa leaned across the table and pointed with one long, red-tipped finger into Mehmet's face. 'If you try to take my son away from me I will rip your head off and spit down your neck!'

'I'm not trying to take him away from you!' Mehmet said. 'And besides, you were the one who took him off to Dublin when all of this business began.'

'You mean when you fucked that tart!'

'I only did it because you were so cold at that time!' He stood up and walked round the table to stand in front of her. 'It was you I really wanted, it was you I thought about as she . . .'

'Bollocks!' She rose to her feet too, literally in order to stand up to him. 'You wanted a shag and anything female would have done!'

He reached one hand out towards her.

'Don't you dare raise a hand to me!' she said.

'I'm not,' he said, then suddenly he pulled her towards him. For just a moment she stared, half angrily and half fearfully, into his eyes.

'I'm doing this,' he said, and then he leaned down and kissed her full on the lips.

'Even in the 1950s we had people visit the chimneys from abroad. Some of them – Americans, I think they were – were black. People stared, amazed,' the old woman said as she leaned forward in order to let İkmen light her cigarette. 'But then in the 1970s we had a lot of foreigners passing through.'

'Yes, I appreciate that now,' he said.

Shortly after he had arrived at the Kahraman house, İkmen had been invited to join Nazlı and her ludicrously young husband for iftar. It had only been macaroni with cheese and tomato sauce and so it hadn't been too difficult to eat even for one as disinclined towards food as Çetin İkmen. But now that iftar was over and everyone could smoke he was much more at his ease even if this very lined and rather forbidding woman was more than a little disconcerting. Nazlı Kahraman, with her thick, weighty headscarf, her impossibly high-heeled shoes, 'from İstanbul', and her pale eyes of stone was not someone İkmen liked to think of as the wife of a young boy. Every time she looked at Erkan, İkmen felt a distinct shudder pass along his spine. For someone who had been a virgin for seventy years, Nazlı Kahraman had taken her revenge upon life in a most brutal manner.

'But I don't remember any Alison,' Nazlı Kahraman

continued. 'Although there was a Susan, and an English girl called Maud is still in the village. She married that stupid Kerem who used to run the Fresco Motel. He's dead now, but she still runs the place with his sister, Arın.' She leaned in towards him, conspiratorially. 'They have three Eastern European women in there, you know. Three!'

'Oh.'

The subtext behind this being, of course, that English Maud and her sister-in-law ran an illegal brothel. This was the third one İkmen had heard of so far – the other two, at the far end of the village, employed Bulgarian and Lithuanian women respectively.

'I would have noticed a pretty blonde girl with pink boots, even then,' Nazlı Kahraman said.

'She was rather distinctive,' İkmen replied. Especially to him. Alison with her long blond hair, her almost always laughing face and her huge army boots – the ones she had dyed pink 'to be different'.

'There isn't a lot of personal beauty around here,' Nazlı said. 'Maybe it's because so much of the loveliness exists within the landscape.' Her eyes twinkled almost naughtily. 'But then as most people marry their cousins that might have something to do with it too.'

'Nazlı Hanım . . .'

'You have, I know, heard a few things about my family, Inspector,' she said. 'I know that this Alison must have been important to you at some time. But I also know that what has happened here recently with this body out in the Valley of the Saints exercises your mind too. Haldun Alkaya has told everyone that Aysu was murdered. Shot, I believe. But anyway, to return to my family . . . My father was an intelligent man who, unlike most of the human detritus here, understood the dangers of in-breeding. You know that one of the reasons why he married Aysu Alkaya was because he knew that our family were not in any way related to theirs. The girl was lovely, intelligent, and there was nothing nasty, as far as Father could tell, lurking back in her ancestry.' She smiled unpleasantly. 'You know the carpet dealer, Ümit Özal? His parents were cousins. They had four children' – she counted them off on her fingers – 'Ümit, who is mad and sleeps with his kilims; Yaşar, who has a hare-lip; Ali, who suffers from fits; and the daughter who, Allah have mercy upon her, divorced her husband in Germany and now lives with a Dutchman in Amsterdam.'

'Well . . .'

'Inbreeding and bad blood,' Nazlı declared, 'that's what it is! There are so few families that are untainted by it. You either marry out or you choose the family with great care – like my father.'

İkmen picked up the tea glass which the distressingly shabby servant girl had given him and took a sip of the hot, amber liquid. Although dark now, it wasn't cold in Nazlı Kahraman's courtyard. In fact, surrounded by the many olive oil tins now used as plant pots, and looking down at the twinkling lights from the village below, was not an unpleasant way to spend an evening – even if Nazlı Kahraman's opinions were arrogant and bigoted. Of course, some in-breeding was inevitable in a small and once-isolated village. But not on the scale Nazlı or the young jandarma seemed to think it was. At least İkmen hoped that was the case.

'So did your father know that Aysu was sweet on Kemalettin Senar?' İkmen asked. 'I mean before . . .'

'Oh, he knew,' Nazlı Hanım replied. 'But once he'd identified the girl as suitable, he also knew that Kemalettin Senar couldn't possibly be any sort of threat.'

'Why not?'

'Because he paid Kemalettin's mother to make a big fuss about the girl's dowry.'

'I thought that the Alkayas were poor?' İkmen said with a frown.

'Oh, they were, are,' Nazlı Hanım said. 'But if Nalan Senar were not such a greedy woman, it would have been enough. After all, the Senars have some money but they are no one. They say that their blood is pure and untainted by all the ills that afflict so many other families here, but that is nonsense. Nalan's father was a raving lunatic.' She tutted her tongue and sucked on her teeth. 'And look at Kemalettin . . .'

'I thought that he was mentally damaged, on account of Aysu,' İkmen said.

Nazlı shrugged. 'Who knows?' And then rapidly changing the subject she said, 'I suppose some people have told you that my father or I killed Aysu.'

'Well . . .'

'It's all right, Inspector,' she said, this time with a genuine smile. 'I know that some ignorant people believe that. They say that Father locked her in, that I made her into my servant. But she was free to come and go and we shared the chores, she and I. I washed her clothes with my own hands.' She held two ravaged claws aloft for İkmen to see. 'I also know', she continued gravely, 'that Father was, and I am, innocent. The night that Aysu disappeared my father slept alone; I saw him retire. The three of us went to our own rooms. I slept all night and when I woke in the morning she had gone.'

'I understand she took some belongings with her,' İkmen said.

'Some clothes and personal effects, yes. She also left the courtyard gate unlocked when she left.'

'Really?' According to Haldun Alkaya his daughter had been a virtual prisoner in the Kahraman house. 'Did she have a key or . . .'

'My father kept the key always by his bed,' Nazlı said, tight-lipped around this admission, or so it seemed. 'She must have crept in and taken it.'

İkmen was just thinking about how he might ask her what she thought might have happened and why, when she said, 'Of course, she left to be with Kemalettin Senar who probably also killed her.'

'Why do you think that, Nazlı Hanım?'

'Well, look at Kemalettin and tell me whether you think he is normal.'

'Yes, but . . .'

'He's always been a bit odd. He was good-looking back then, but strange. Not in the least bit like his brother. But then Nalan has always over-protected him. Maybe she saw the seeds of his grandfather's madness in him and wanted to save him and her family from embarrassment. But anyway, I don't think that any girl would ever have been good enough for Kemalettin in Nalan's eyes. With regard to their children, Nalan and my father had a lot in common. Nothing and no one was ever good enough.'

Which had to explain why Nazlı Hanım had been a spinster for so long. İkmen turned briefly to look at the handsome young man who had been sitting silently underneath the kitchen window while they had been talking. The age gap between them was ludicrous and yet Erkan Erduran seemed too simple to be a typical, money-grabbing gigolo. He was also, on the face of it, completely clueless. He had no conversation, probably no education, and, when he did speak, a rather monotone voice. Of course he had to be good at something but that, İkmen felt, was probably something he didn't want to think about – especially with the wrinkled face of Nazlı Hanım right in front of him.

'No, I think that he did it,' Nazlı said, her elderly eyes looking sleepily over both her considerable property and the village.

'Who?'

'Kemalettin Senar,' she replied. 'I think she ran away to be with him and that he killed her.'

'But why?' İkmen said. 'If he loved her . . .'

'Maybe it was an accident,' the old woman said. 'Or maybe she wouldn't let him touch her until they could be married but he took no notice of what she said. Maybe he violated her and then killed her. But then, maybe, Allah forgive her, she killed herself once she realised all the money she had given up when she left my father. I hope that for the sake of her soul, suicide was not the case, but . . .' She shrugged.

İkmen didn't tell Nazlı Kahraman that Aysu Alkaya had been shot in the back and could not, therefore, have possibly committed suicide. But maybe some of her other ideas were valid. That some sort of accident involving a gun, possibly purloined as insurance against the couple's escape, could have occurred was not outside the bounds of possibility. That Kemalettin had been 'odd', sexually deviant or whatever, prior to Aysu's disappearance wasn't to be discounted either. After all, however much in love most men were with their youthful sweethearts, very few would descend so far into grief-induced madness as Kemalettin Senar had done.

Later, as he wandered back to his cousin's hotel, İkmen wondered again about these issues and about the money Ziya Kahraman had paid to Kemalettin's mother. Had Haldun Alkaya known about that, and, the odd strange villager aside, what was the obsession with 'untainted blood' all about? He resolved to ask Menşure about it in the morning.

The policeman from İstanbul, the one that was Menşure Tokatlı's cousin, had spent a very long time in the house of the Lemon Queen, Nalan Senar felt. He'd gone in just before iftar and she'd watched the gate, the only way in or out of the property, ever since. It had been pitch dark by the time he took his leave just outside on Muradiye Sokak.

Nalan Senar hadn't followed him. She'd heard some of what had been said inside by pressing her ear against one of the cracks in the gate. Some of it had concerned her, but there hadn't been anything that wasn't true. Yes, she had taken money from the Lemon King to keep Kemalettin away from Aysu Alkaya. What of it? The old man had had plenty of money and she hadn't wanted Kemalettin to have anything to do with the Alkaya girl anyway. No, what exercised the sharp brain that pulsed beneath Nalan's brightly patterned headscarf was what they had been talking about at the beginning of their conversation. Something about an English girl and outsiders coming to the village many years ago. That made Nalan sweat. The subject of foreign visitors to Muratpaşa many years ago was not one she wanted anyone to discuss. If talk like that began, Allah alone knew where it would end. It was almost too terrible to think about. As soon as the policeman had gone she raced down the hill in the opposite direction towards her own house, a double-coned chimney that she shared with Kemalettin and their great yellow kangal dog, Zeytin.

Once inside the courtyard, she lay back breathlessly against the wooden gate and pulled one plump hand across her sweating brow. The dog had barked in greeting when she arrived, but because she was indoors, Zeytin had soon shut up. Her son on the other hand was outside, naked in front of the shed that housed the gas cylinders. He looked across at his mother with an entirely static and unfathomable expression on his face. Nalan, for all her years of dealing briskly with him, suddenly felt her heart soften and she burst into tears.

He woke up in the very early hours of the morning and was completely disorientated. He was not in his bedroom. It was one of his bedrooms, places he had lived at and slept in over the years, but it wasn't his room at home in Arnavautköy. He would not, he knew, be able to hear his father's snoring coming from the old man's room across the hall. No, he was at Zelfa's house in Ortaköy, the one he had gone back to with her after their wedding. He was also in Zelfa's, and what had also been his own, bed.

Although it was dark, there was enough light in the room for Mehmet Süleyman to see his wife as she slept beside him. From the expression on her face, which looked like a slight *Mona Lisa* smile, it would seem that she was at peace. If only he could feel likewise. Now that he had woken he knew he wasn't going to be able to get back to sleep and so he got out of bed and walked, naked, over to the small table and chairs that Zelfa kept in the area where the bay window protruded over the garden. There were no curtains or blinds on the windows, nor was there any need for them, the garden being entirely secluded behind ancient trees. Mehmet lit a cigarette and sat down at the little table to think.

As soon as he'd kissed her, Mehmet had known that Zelfa was going to let him make love to her. For all her protestations about divorce he'd been able to feel an immediate response in her body as soon as he'd touched her. And because neither of them had had sex for a while they had both been greedy for passion and reluctant for it to end. The bedroom had only been the endgame as it were to the sucking and caressing that had started in the kitchen and passed briefly into the bathroom. That Yusuf seemed to have slept through all the groans and screams coming from his parents was nothing short of a miracle. The whole experience had been, on so many levels, fantastic.

But now that he'd slept, Mehmet was beginning to wonder whether what had happened was more illusion than reality. Clearly both he and Zelfa had wanted sex, but had it meant anything more than that? He didn't want his marriage to end, but whether that had more to do with Yusuf than Zelfa he still wasn't sure. Just as she couldn't trust him, he wasn't certain that he could trust her either. After all, as a psychiatrist, Zelfa came up against some very twisted states of mind on a daily basis – different mindsets and behavioural patterns that could, perhaps, give her ideas about revenge . . . How cruel would it be to fulfil him sexually, which she had done, and then tell him that she still wanted a divorce, still intended to rip the very shirt from his back? All he could do was wait and see what happened in the morning.

He looked out of the window into the garden, which was lit only by a weak quarter moon. Had he come to the house in Ortaköy with the intention of seducing Zelfa? Truthfully he could only answer 'maybe', but even that felt guilty as he thought about it. He'd come to see Yusuf and to talk and . . . one of the coniferous bushes down by the ornamental pond shivered slightly in the dead, night-time air. Moved, possibly, by a cat or a street dog passing through the garden, but there was something about the movement of this plant that caught Mehmet's attention. And as a shiver became an actual parting of the bush fronds, he leaned down to get a closer look at what was causing this to happen. Just as quickly as it had begun, it stopped and, assuming it must have been an animal of some sort, Mehmet looked away in order to put his cigarette out in an ashtray. However, when he looked back into the garden – for just a fleeting second, no more – there was a figure standing on the lawn. It was definitely human and it moved with a speed that reminded Mehmet of several martial arts movies he had seen.

He knew that even if his gun had been to hand it would have been useless to employ it. The human figure, man or whatever it was, had gone now. How long it had been there –

while he and Zelfa made love, while they slept, while Yusuf slept – was impossible to know. Mehmet quickly went to check on his son and then stood panting with fear on the threshold of what had once been his bedroom.

Chapter 7

'You know it never ceases to amaze me how quickly the weather can charge around here,' Çetin İkmen said as he looked out of the jeep at the snow-covered landscape. 'Yesterday evening was very mild, I thought.'

'Yes, and that's the danger of it for people hiking in the valleys without the proper equipment,' Altay Salman replied. 'Snow or rain can arrive very quickly and quite violently sometimes. Every year we get the crazies out there communing with the peris and of course the foreigners who want to find "spiritual enlightenment" or something amongst the chimneys.'

İkmen smiled. Although the road they were on now, which led from the village in to Nevşehir, was far from picturesque, it had been rather magical waking up in a white and sparkling Muratpaşa. Menşure had brought him tea and, although she had begged him not to drink it out on his balcony where everyone could see, he'd disobeyed her. He had stood for almost half an hour drinking, smoking and watching as pigeons, alighting on the overhead power cables, shook powdery snow down onto the streets below. Sand-coloured minarets, though not as grand as those he was accustomed to in İstanbul, pierced the silver-grey sky like elegant fingers, their tips just very lightly dusted with glittering ice.

Shortly after an elderly neighbour of Menşure's had called out the word 'shameful!' at the heavily smoking İkmen, Altay Salman had turned up with news from Nevşehir. The local police would allow the man from İstanbul to view Aysu Alkaya's body provided he came that morning. Ever helpful, Altay had offered to drive İkmen in to the regional capital through what was not thick snow but was nevertheless something more easily tackled by a jeep than an ordinary saloon car.

Once the formalities were complete, which included İkmen telling a very prematurely aged man – loosely his counterpart in Nevşehir – about the 'glamour' involved in working in İstanbul, they entered the mortuary. Small, its floors wet and muddy from numerous snow-covered boots, the place smelt strongly of formaldehyde and other disinfectants. One of the walls was covered with the refrigerated cabinets designed to store bodies and as he looked at them, İkmen was suddenly in his mind transported back to İstanbul and the laboratory of the Armenian pathologist, Arto Sarkissian. Friends since childhood, Arto, Çetin and their families had once spent a summer holiday together at what was now Menşure's place in Muratpaşa. Arto and his brother Krikor had loved exploring the chimneys with Çetin and his brother Halıl as well as the frighteningly independent young Menşure. As poor, tired-looking Inspector Erten pulled open one of the drawers, İkmen wished that Arto could be with him now. After all, whatever what was left of Aysu Alkaya looked like, it wouldn't mean too much to him.

'She was shot in the back,' Inspector Erten said as he removed the covering from the corpse. 'The ballistic tests have identified the weapon as a Colt 45. Not the sort of thing a Muratpaşa grape grower would have.'

'No.'

As İkmen looked down at what was indeed a mummified body he thought about the gun. A Colt 45 was a serious weapon by anyone's standards and Erten was quite right to point out that it wasn't something the average Cappadocian would have had access to, especially not twenty years ago. A Colt was a military weapon, however, and if İkmen wasn't mistaken, it wasn't a current Turkish military weapon. But then the ballistics department would know that and would, he hoped, have put that in their report to Erten.

'I assume, this being the country, that quite a lot of those involved with the girl have or had guns?' İkmen asked.

'The Kahraman family possess a selection of shotguns,' Erten replied. 'They have papers for them. And of course the guide Turgut Senar has a Beretta.'

'Why "of course"?'

'I understand Mr Senar goes out into some of the more distant valleys,' Erten continued. 'I expect you have heard stories about wolves, Inspector?'

'They're all true,' Altay Salman confirmed to İkmen. 'A very real threat. I know about Turgut's Beretta; he's an excellent shot.'

İkmen turned his attention back to the corpse.

'You were right when you described the body as "mummified",' he said to Altay Salman. 'How on earth did her father identify her?'

'She has six toes on each foot,' Erten replied. 'It wasn't well known, she was apparently ashamed of what she

102

considered a deformity. Girls are so sensitive about these things because they fear it may prevent them from finding a husband. But the father knew and identified her from her feet and the clothes she was wearing, the things she was carrying. Oh, and I did also check with the doctor in the village – about the toes. He confirmed the father's story. This is Aysu Alkaya.'

Poor child, İkmen added in his mind. In love with Kemalettin Senar, all but sold to the elderly Ziya Kahraman – and with those weird, overly wide feet to contend with, too. What, he wondered, had Ziya Kahraman's reaction been to his new wife when he saw those feet for the first time? According to his daughter, the Lemon King had been very keen to avoid any hint of in-breeding when it came to his theoretical son. Surely deformity, whatever its cause might be, had to have been forbidden too?

'Our doctor says that there is evidence of bruising on the body,' Erten continued. 'But whether that is connected to the murder . . .' He shrugged. 'We don't have so many facilities here as you have in İstanbul. This is an unlawful killing, but given the time that has elapsed all I can do is re-interview those remaining from that time and look for whoever may have owned or had access to a Colt 45.'

İkmen, still looking down at the shrunken, expressionless face of Aysu Alkaya said, 'If I could arrange for some samples of body tissue and clothing to be tested at the Forensic Institute, do you think that might help you?'

'You mean DNA testing?' Erten's thin face broke into what was the closest he had probably ever come to a smile. 'I've often thought that she must have some fibres or evidence of some sort from whoever killed her – maybe under her finger nails. I've seen a video of this. Now we know, in this age of scientific wonder, that it is almost impossible to commit an offence and not leave something of oneself behind.'

'Yes, although a lot of time has passed since this offence was committed,' İkmen cautioned. 'There may be little or nothing of use here.'

'No.'

They all looked down at the dry, brittle body just barely enclosed in what was left of its şalvar trousers and tunic. It was truly a very sad sight.

'Oh, you should also know that she was pregnant when she died,' Erten continued. 'Only in the early stages, but we will tell her father, of course.'

'Yes.' This from what İkmen had heard before was unexpected. It was also most illuminating. 'Maybe we can test for the paternity of the foetus too,' he said as he watched Erten cover the body once again. 'I'll do what I can.'

'Thank you, Çetin Bey,' his counterpart in Nevşehir said with a bow. 'You know that I was the original investigating officer in this case. I was very young then. It has haunted me ever since. To solve this mystery would be the highest point of my career – my life, even.'

İkmen, a little embarrassed by such emotional words from a fellow professional, just smiled. If all of this did come to fruition, he hoped that Erten's superiors would have the good grace to reward him properly. The poor man's broken and flapping shoes made even İkmen's hideous plastic faux brogues look stylish.

* * *

Altay Salman dropped İkmen off in the village before driving himself back to the riding school. They hadn't spoken much about what they'd seen at the mortuary, mainly because İkmen had been trying to get through on his mobile to Arto Sarkissian. After all if anyone could 'push things' through the Forensic Institute with no questions asked it had to be a police pathologist. However, Arto's assistant said he was on leave, and so İkmen tried to call him on his mobile. But he wasn't answering it and so the inspector was forced to leave one of his stuttering, terribly inept answer phone messages.

As soon as he got inside Menşure's hotel, İkmen lit a cigarette and wandered up into the restaurant area. Even if they weren't eating themselves, Menşure's kitchen and waiting staff had to be on hand for the needs and desires of her non-Muslim guests and friends. When İkmen arrived, Rachelle Jones and another, very heavily made-up foreign woman were sitting drinking coffee and eating börek with Menşure.

As soon as she saw him, the Australian smiled and said, 'Inspector!'

İkmen bowed. 'Miss Jones.'

'God, doesn't he have just the best voice ever!' she said in English to her companion. The woman merely smiled by way of reply. Menşure lifted her eyes to heaven in exasperation. Rachelle Jones was a woman she could respect, mainly because she alone amongst the foreign residents of Muratpaşa had never succumbed to any of the greedy young gigolos, but liking her was rather more of a stretch.

'This is Miss Lavell,' Menşure said in English as İkmen sat down beside her. 'From New Orleans in the States.'

The woman smiled. 'Oh, you don't need to be formal,' she

said in what İkmen found a most attractive Southern drawl. 'My name is Dolores.'

İkmen rose to stretch across the table and offer her his hand. 'Çetin.'

Menşure watched him sit down and then said to the American, 'Çetin has nine children, you know, Dolores. In İstanbul. With his wife.'

'Oh, how lovely,' Dolores replied. 'You know, Miss Menşure, I am a Catholic and we just love big families. I always wanted a whole load of brothers and sisters myself.'

'Indeed.'

Although not religious, Menşure Tokatlı was an intensely moral woman with what, to İkmen, had always seemed a very strange attitude towards personal relationships. Like the English philosopher John Ruskin, Menşure had a really quite morbid horror of the human body and of the intimate 'things' it was sometimes required to do. And although she knew that Çetin loved Fatma with all his heart, she had been disappointed by his admission with regard to Alison. This Dolores woman was therefore going to be kept very much at arm's length.

'So when did you arrive in Muratpaşa, um, Dolores?' İkmen asked.

'Dolores has been coming to Cappadocia for years,' Rachelle Jones answered for her.

'Oh?'

'My dad was a soldier stationed in Germany in the late fifties and early sixties,' Dolores said. 'He and his buddies went all over – Britain, France, Turkey.'

'To Muratpaşa?' İkmen asked.

The American laughed. 'Yeah, but hey, what is this? Twenty questions?'

Menşure placed a reassuring hand on Dolores' arm. 'My cousin is a police officer. Asking questions is a habit he has.'

Dolores smiled. 'Oh, how interesting,' she said.

İkmen braced himself for the foreigner's stock questions about human rights and how he, such a gentle man, could work within such a pernicious system. But strangely, neither they, nor any mention of a certain Alan Parker film* from the 1970s, materialised.

'I know Dad came to Muratpaşa because he sent me a postcard,' Dolores continued. 'I was only a kid and all the shapes hereabouts fascinated me. I don't know whether or not Dad stayed in this actual village, though. He used to tell stories about hiking through the valleys. I know he stayed in Ürgüp, which is where I went on my first trip. But then when I came to Muratpaşa I just fell plain in love.'

'With the village,' Rachelle Jones put in in Turkish. 'Not some conscript half her age.'

İkmen smiled. 'Has your father ever been back?'

'Daddy died in 1977.' Dolores' eyes instantly filled with tears, as if her father's death had taken place just the previous week.

'I am sorry,' İkmen said. 'I did not mean to bring back painful memories for you, Miss Lavell.'

'It's OK.' But she'd lowered her head now, carefully

---

* *Midnight Express* – the story of an American convicted of drug offences and confined in a prison in Istanbul. It was highly sensationalist and covertly anti-Turkish.

avoiding eye contact with anyone. Some people, as İkmen knew only too well, close down when they grieve.

It was Rachelle Jones who eventually broke the ensuing silence when she asked İkmen, 'So, Inspector, what were you doing out with the dashing Captain Salman this crisp, snowy morning?'

İkmen couldn't help but laugh. Very little got past village people, both natives and incomers. Rachelle Jones expressed this trait in a very direct way he found refreshing and amusing. But before he could reply he caught yet another of Menşure's disapproving glances and so his response was not quite as illuminating as it could have been. 'We had some business together,' he said noncommittally.

'Oooh,' Rachelle mugged dramatically. 'Old crimes. The murder of Aysu Alkaya?' She smiled. 'We all know now, Inspector, so you can be straight with us.'

'Can I indeed? You seem to know a lot about this village, Miss Jones,' İkmen said. 'I may need a guide out to some of the more distant valleys if or when the snow clears. Can you recommend such a person?'

'Yeah.'

He waited for her to continue, but she just kept on looking at him, smiling.

'Er . . .'

'Turgut Senar is the most experienced guide in the village,' Menşure said in Turkish. 'And yes, before you ask, Çetin, he is the brother of the somewhat unfortunate Kemalettin Senar.'

İkmen raised an eyebrow. Of course both Erten and Altay Salman had mentioned that Kemalettin's brother was a guide. He had a gun. If Turgut Senar was so knowledgeable about the valleys – including, he imagined, the fantastic Valley of the Saints – was it possible that his brother also knew a thing or two about the more obscure caves and chimneys?

'So maybe if you go out hiking with Turgut, you might learn a thing or two,' Rachelle said. 'Or maybe not. Turgut can be a bit tight-lipped, especially about his family.'

İkmen was rather more alarmed by the word 'hiking' than by the prospect of spending time with a man of few words. Exercise had always been anathema to the policeman and the guide he had imagined had had a jeep like Altay Salman.

When the two women finally left, Menşure turned a very stern eye upon İkmen and said, 'Can't stop yourself being the charmer with women, can you? You should smile less and not take their compliments as easily as you do. It's indecent. If you don't behave yourself, I will let Kismet into your room one day when you're out.'

In spite of the fact that it just wasn't logical to get so worked up about a dumb animal, İkmen felt his face blanch. 'He's still alive?'

'Oh, yes,' Menşure said with what seemed to be a degree of smugness, 'And despite being so very, very old, he is still quite capable of frightening his peers, small children and middle-aged policemen. Careful breeding, you see, Çetin. Healthy blood. My father, you know, said that my grandfather mated Kismet's mother with a lion.' She raised a warning finger up to heaven. 'So be warned, Çetin, no more smoking in public and no flirting with anyone. And remember that I have eyes in every place in this village.'

A whole society made up of informants! It put İkmen in mind of the tens of thousands of spies who had been employed by the paranoid nineteenth-century Sultan Abdul Hamid II. Although the snow had started to melt now, it was still very cold outside – but that didn't prevent İkmen from opting to continue his researches away from Menşure's hotel. As he left, however, he checked to make sure that he didn't inadvertently step on Kismet. After all if he was still alive and active he – and his 'healthy' blood – could be just about anywhere.

Mehmet Süleyman didn't mention what he thought he might have seen in Zelfa's garden in the early hours of the morning. In fact he and his wife didn't really speak at all before he left for work. If not exactly embarrassed by what had happened between them, they didn't know quite what to say to each other.

As he walked into the station, he saw İzzet Melik leaning against his office door talking to İkmen's deputy, Sergeant Ayşe Farsakoğlu. She, to her credit, was ignoring his leering expressions with some dignity.

'Shouldn't you be at the hospital?' Süleyman asked as he broke up this somewhat disturbing tableau with just the sound of his voice. Looking İzzet straight in the eye, he continued, 'The Aydın boy. Someone needs to be there in case he wakes up.'

'Well, there's Constable . . .'

'I mean someone with some experience of asking questions of – note I do not use either the word "questioning" or "interrogating" – victims of crime.'

'Yes, sir.' For a moment İzzet just stood there, awkwardly shifting from foot to foot, still half smiling at Ayşe Farsakoğlu.

'Well, off you go, then,' Süleyman said as he pushed open the door to his office and walked inside.

'Yes, sir.'

Süleyman was just about to close the door behind him, when he noticed that Ayşe Farsakoğlu was still standing outside, obviously waiting to see him.

'Yes?' he asked nervously. 'Sergeant?'

As well as being very beautiful, with long dark hair and a perfectly curvaceous figure, Ayşe Farsakoğlu was also a young woman with whom Süleyman had enjoyed a brief affair just prior to his current marriage. And although that was all very firmly in the past now, he was still not entirely comfortable with her. She was, he knew, if not still exactly in love with him, still vulnerable to feelings that he did not share.

'Inspector İkmen said that I was to help you as much as I could during his absence, sir,' she said without preamble. 'Sergeant Melik was just telling me about that poor boy in hospital.'

'Possibly the peeper's latest victim, yes,' Süleyman said as he sat down behind his desk and lit a cigarette.

She'd been off sick for a couple of days and so, in a sense, it probably had been useful that Melik had brought her up to speed. After all, it saved him from having to do so himself and he did, he knew, want to use Ayşe where he could in this investigation. Apart from anything else she was going to be a lot more sympathetic with the peeper's young, mainly gay victims than Melik was.

'I've received intelligence,' he said, referring to his recent conversation with Metin İskender, 'that there is a belief within the homosexual fraternity that the peeper is an enemy of their kind.'

'But I thought that he' – she swallowed hard before using the word – 'masturbated in front of them. And wasn't one boy sexually assaulted?'

'In the same way that misogynists sometimes assault or even rape women, so there is a school of thought that says men who dislike homosexuals sometimes seek to humiliate them by asserting sexual supremacy over them.'

Ayşe sat down in front of him. 'Yes, sir.'

'What I want you to do, Ayşe, is to check our records for men who have been convicted of offences against homosexuals in the past. Now, as you may or may not know, Sergeant Melik has already run a check, but what I'd like you to do is look at the details surrounding the offences committed by these individuals. There is a possibility that the peeper is connected to, or habitually present at, homosexual meeting places – clubs, hamams. Find out which of our offenders is either known to frequent such places or was maybe apprehended in a homosexual meeting place.'

'Yes, sir.'

He took several sheets of paper out of his desk drawer and passed them across to her. 'Here is the list,' he said, and then added with a smile, 'I'm sure I don't have to tell you which clubs are which, do I?'

She smiled too. 'No, sir.'

'All right then.'

Taking this as her cue to leave, Ayşe made her way towards the office door. Just before she turned the handle he added, 'Oh and Sergeant, if Sergeant Melik . . .'

'Oh come on, sir,' she said with a smile, 'I can handle a maganda.'

And with a slight raising of her eyebrows she was off. Süleyman laughed. The concept of the maganda, a coarse, arrogant, sexually inept macho man, had been born out of the satirical İstanbul weeklies of the early 1990s. Read, in the main, by youthful intellectuals, these magazines had sometimes slipped into Süleyman's world via his young friend Berekiah Cohen who found them very amusing. The maganda, Berekiah was fond of saying, bore more than just a passing resemblance to his father, Balthazar.

However, memories of Berekiah also brought to mind images of the hamam in Karaköy which he had spent some hours watching two nights before. In view of what he'd seen in Zelfa's garden, was it possible that someone had seen him there, followed him to his car and then pursued the white BMW home the following night? Could it possibly be the peeper who maybe thought that *he* was homosexual? He'd spoken to a rather smart man who had appeared to be attracted to him – they had indeed watched each other leave the vicinity. There had also been that fellow lurking further away, down the hill in a shop doorway. It was all speculative and tenuous, of course, but then it was well known that middle-aged homosexual life in the city was itself furtive and opportunistic. Süleyman ground his cigarette out in his ashtray and then shook his head impatiently. But this was all utterly ridiculous – and paranoid. Why anyone should follow him home was stupid. He wasn't young, he wasn't gay – not really. What he was was somewhat guilty about his unofficial trip to the hamam as well as being aware of the effect that his undisputed good looks had had upon some of the men outside the bath. But to think that one of them would go so far as to follow him home had to be a deeply paranoid and arrogant notion on his part. He resolved to put it to the back of his mind. He did not, however, resolve not to observe the Saray Hamam ever again.

'Up there it is a completely different experience,' the German said with a smile. 'In a sense you can almost see those ancient tectonic catastrophes as they happen.'

He was so enthusiastic, it was difficult not to be carried away by it all. However, as he had told İkmen in some detail, balloon flights were not cheap.

'Because we have to be expert pilots and because of the maintenance we have to do on the equipment,' he'd said in English and had then gone on to quote İkmen a price in US dollars which translated into a truly horrific lire tariff.

'I was actually thinking of hiking through the valleys, maybe with Turgut Senar,' İkmen said as he downed the last dregs of his cappuccino before calling for another. The Cappudocia Coffee Bean, or rather its signature product, did its Anglo-Turkish management proud. As a meeting place for expatriates of various hues it was also quite interesting too. Maybe outside Ramazan they were not so conservative in their beverage tastes, but certainly in the Holy Month cappuccino in the hours of daylight seemed to be de rigueur. Ferdinand, the German hot air balloon pilot, obviously used the place a lot because it was directly across the road from his own business, Muratpaşa Balloon Flights.

'Well, now that you say this,' Ferdinand said with a smile, 'did you know that we do a combined short flight and then a hike with Turgut through the White Valley and up into the Valley of the Saints?'

İkmen's ears pricked up at the mention of the latter destination.

'We fly out to the head of the White Valley where we land and then customers go off with Turgut to walk to the Valley of the Saints – five kilometres.'

Appalled at the way this man so glibly uttered such a vast distance, İkmen nevertheless managed to quash the urge to laugh nervously and instead smiled at the English partner in the Cappudocia, the very lively Marion.

'Cappuccino with cinnamon sprinkles, Inspector,' she said as she placed a huge white cup and saucer down in front of him.

'Thank you.'

'And when Turgut has shown you the Saints, one of our support vehicles will come to bring you back to the village,' Ferdinand continued. He then mentioned a rather smaller dollar figure for this service and, once İkmen had told him that he was related to Menşure Tokatlı, that figure reduced still further. It was good to see that at least one of the many foreigners resident in the village had some understanding of its hierarchies.

However, it was still rather a large amount of money for a mere policeman to afford and İkmen knew that he should speak to Fatma about it first. But then he thought about how hard he had always worked and how much he deserved that one, paltry credit card that only he knew about, and so he signed up with Ferdinand right away.

'You won't regret it,' the German said as he handed over a handwritten ticket for the next day's flight. 'The snow will be almost gone by the morning and the air will be as clear as spring water. I know these conditions, trust me.'

It was only then that Ferdinand hit İkmen with the news that they would be setting off at 4 a.m. in order to catch the sunrise over the valleys. But by then it was far too late.

Once the German had gone, İkmen, alone with his cappuccino, began to wonder about the advisability as well as the utility of what he had just done. In order to see where Aysu Alkaya had been killed he needed to get out to the Valley of the Saints and, had he asked him, Inspector Erten from Nevşehir would probably have arranged it for him. But there was a lot about being guided there by Kemalettin Senar's brother that intrigued him. That someone who had, at one time, been suspected of killing the girl had a brother who knew the valleys so well had to be known to the police in Nevşehir. He wasn't therefore doing anything that he shouldn't. The balloon flight itself was, of course, a total extravagance that so ably demonstrated his own physical laziness. But even so, five kilometres . . .

Leaning back in his chair, İkmen lit a cigarette and then closed his eyes. The American woman, Dolores Lavell, had said something rather interesting. Her father who had, apparently, been in the US army in the fifties and sixties had visited Cappadocia with his 'buddies'. Had any of them, İkmen wondered, brought their side arms with them, the odd Colt 45, perhaps? Considering that Dolores' father was dead, there was no way of knowing now. But it was an interesting line of speculation, namely because it raised the issue of how such a weapon had come to be in Muratpaşa. Mr Lavell had, of course, visited long before Aysu Alkaya's death, but other visitors from the US had been coming ever since as Nazlı Kahraman had told him.

116

İkmen's mobile phone rang, and so he opened his eyes, took it out of his pocket, and answered it.

'Çetin, it's Arto,' a familiar voice began. 'Something about forensic samples or . . .'

İkmen moved out on to the café's balcony and briefly explained what he had had in mind to the pathologist.

'I thought that if we could get their doctor in Nevşehir to take samples from the woman and the foetus, I could arrange for them to be sent to you,' İkmen said.

'Or I could take the samples myself,' his friend replied.

'You can't come all the way from İstanbul! I wouldn't ask it of you!'

'But I'm not in İstanbul,' Arto replied with an obvious smile in his voice.

'So where are you?' İkmen asked.

'I'm in Ankara. Four hours from you if I put my foot down.'

'What are you doing in Ankara?'

'I'm showing a guest the sights,' he said. 'The Museum of Anatolian Civilisations, Anıt Kabir. It's my cousin Atom – you know, my Aunt Sylvie's son. He's a lot younger than Krikor and me. Atom was born and brought up in Munich.'

With Arto one usually got the entire story of almost everyone's lives.

'But if you are showing Atom the country . . .'

'Then I could take him home to İstanbul via Muratpaşa,' Arto said. 'We're leaving here on Saturday. I could drive us all back home once I've collected the samples, if you like.'

After silently offering up thanks to Allah for his good fortune, İkmen resorted to an old Ottoman expression of self-abasement in order to express his gratitude. 'You know, Arto,' he said, 'that I am not fit to pour water for you to wash your hands.'

'The bus journey was not entirely pleasant, was it?' Arto replied.

'No.'

'Then I will see you at Menşure Hanım's sometime on Saturday morning,' he said.

'She will be delighted to see you again,' İkmen responded.

'And I, her.'

After the doctor had hung up, İkmen called Inspector Erten in Nevşehir. He wasn't in his office, and so İkmen called the mobile number Erten had given him. Against a background of what sounded like a dog fight, Erten declared himself almost ecstatic at the prospect of DNA testing on Aysu Alkaya's body. İkmen then went back in to finish his coffee. As he got up to leave he noticed that Kemalettin Senar was standing in the doorway of Muratpaşa Balloon Flights, quite still and not even close to playing with himself. He was in fact staring straight at İkmen, which made the policeman wonder just how long he had been doing so. What, İkmen wondered, was really wrong with Kemalettin Senar? Was it, as Nazlı Kahraman had implied, bad blood inherited from his 'mad' grandfather? Or was it something else?

Chapter 8

Only three of the names that Ayşe Farsakoğlu had identified so far had been completely unknown to Mehmet Süleyman. The rest were well-known bullies and thugs, most of whom had convictions for assaults upon women and sometimes children as well as the homosexual target group. And although it was his belief that this peeper character was more subtle, with a far more complicated agenda than just plain violence, Süleyman had won approval to have all of these men brought in for questioning. The following morning was going to involve an extremely early start and he knew that what he should really be doing was going home to get some rest. But when most people were gathering together for iftar, Mehmet Süleyman was still wandering the narrow streets of Karaköy, particularly those that were closest to the hamam. The bad feeling he'd had about this place when he'd spotted the unknown figure in Zelfa's garden hadn't gone away.

Because almost everyone had stopped what they were doing in order to eat, there was very little movement around the baths and certainly no one lurking where he shouldn't. Süleyman made his way up towards the Galata Tower and the apartment of his old friend Balthazar Cohen.

As soon as he arrived, Balthazar's wife, who had been Süleyman's affectionate landlady when he had lodged with the family some years before, began to fuss around him.

'Oh, Mehmet,' she said, more annoyed at herself than at him, 'if only I had known you were coming for iftar.'

'İftar?'

Estelle Cohen placed a hand on Süleyman's arm. 'Sometimes Hulya goes to her mother for iftar and sometimes we have it here. She isn't actually fasting because of the baby, but . . .'

'But you're Jewish.'

'Yes, *we* are,' Estelle said as she led him by the arm into the main living area of the apartment, 'but my daughter-in-law and my grandson are Muslims and so' – she smiled – 'we all do what we can.'

Süleyman bent down low and kissed her on the cheek. In so many ways Estelle Cohen was a second mother to him. Unlike his own mother, however, she didn't nag, criticise or judge.

With the exception of its patriarch, the entire family was seated around an enormous selection of food containers laid out on a tablecloth on the floor. Around the tablecloth Berekiah, Hulya – holding little Timur – and Estelle reclined on large cushions in emulation of how Hulya's nomadic ancestors would have taken their food. Balthazar, confined to his battered chair over by the television, waved his friend over to him as soon as he arrived.

'Mehmet! Mehmet!'

Mehmet stopped briefly to embrace Berekiah and greet Hulya and the baby, and went over to sit next to the crippled man and his television, which was, as usual, tuned to one of the sports channels.

'I don't know why I'm watching *Trabzon Spor*,' Balthazar said through what remained of a cigarette.

'No.'

Balthazar had always supported Galatasaray to the extent that he would, until recently, rarely watch even other İstanbul sides. To be watching an out-of-town team meant that he had to be bored. But then, sitting in almost the same place since 1999 could not, Süleyman knew, be very much fun.

'Mehmet, aren't you joining us for iftar?' Berekiah asked after he ravenously gobbled up a large piece of bread.

'My son is keeping Ramazan now!' Balthazar shrugged and huffed. 'The Muslim father-in-law doesn't keep it, but the Jewish husband does!'

'Çetin Bey has never kept Ramazan,' Süleyman said with a smile. 'He says that if he did, it would make him a hypocrite and be an insult to True Believers.'

'Mum made fodla,' Berekiah said as he pointed at what looked like a group of very large bread rolls. 'Mehmet!'

The fodla, a very old Ottoman dish, consisted of a rich lamb casserole encased in freshly baked bread. Süleyman had always liked it, especially the way that Estelle cooked the dish. But he placed a hand on his chest to indicate that he wasn't hungry. He was far too wired up to think about food. 'I was just passing,' he said.

'Oh?' Berekiah stood up and came to join his friend and his father by the television. 'Where are you going, Mehmet?'

Berekiah had seen him outside the hamam on Monday night and although Süleyman had, he thought, managed to explain his presence to the young man, he hadn't been certain at the time that his friend had believed him. Now, given the slightly suspicious look on Berekiah's face, he was even less sure.

'Oh, I said that I would go up into Beyoğlu to collect some cakes for my mother,' he said, knowing how lame he sounded.

'Oh, I see,' the young man responded with a smile and then he returned to his cushion on the floor and his food.

A rather awkward hour, for Süleyman, then ensued. Balthazar had always been a terrible gossip and some of his theories about the actions and behaviour of people they both knew swung between the salacious and the fantastic. Almost everyone, according to Balthazar, was engaged in some sort of activity he shouldn't be doing. And when sex came into the equation, which it did for much of the conversation, Süleyman noticed that Berekiah sometimes looked at him questioningly. Did the young man think that perhaps he had gone to the gay hamam for reasons other than those connected to police work? The boy had known him for most of his life, surely he was aware that his friend Mehmet wasn't like that?

As he was showing him out, however, it became apparent that Berekiah did have some anxieties in that direction.

'Have you got anything to do with the investigation into this queer who attacks people?' Berekiah asked as he watched his friend put his shoes back on at the front door.

'I have an involvement,' Süleyman replied. 'Why?'

'Well, you were at that hamam' – he laughed nervously – 'I mean, you weren't there for yourself, were you?'

'Why?' Standing up now Süleyman was a good bit taller than Berekiah and, at this point in time, somewhat graver too. 'Does it bother you that some men . . .'

'This one who attacks young boys is evil,' Berekiah said with some heat in his voice. 'Evil!'

Although married, Berekiah Cohen was both young and attractive and, maybe, he had some anxieties about becoming a target himself. After all, Süleyman had not, with very good reason, issued any sort of statement with regard to the peeper's obvious preference for gay men. That section of the city was already panicking of its own accord without the police making their lives even harder by pointing them out to the general public.

'We don't know for sure that this assailant is homosexual,' Süleyman said as he opened the door of the apartment to let himself out.

'But if he's assaulting men . . .'

'Berekiah, there can be a lot of reasons why people do things they do not like. Sometimes to punish others and in some cases, themselves, too.'

As soon as he was outside the apartment, Süleyman lit up a cigarette and made his way down towards the hamam. As he descended he passed the rather smart man who had spoken to him outside the hamam on that first occasion walking up towards Beyoğlu. As their eyes met, the man gave Süleyman a knowing look which could mean that he was still 'interested'. There was something else in that look too, something the policeman couldn't fathom. But it made his blood momentarily run cold. Was it possible this man had been in Zelfa's garden, obsessively stalking him, perhaps? Such things did happen. But how? No, that was just paranoia. It had to be. It was impossible, wasn't it? Once he was certain the man had moved on ahead of him, Süleyman turned back to follow him.

Although most of the bars in the village were effectively dead due to the combined elements of Ramazan and the end of the tourist season, there was one that still made a show of doing business. The Red Dragon bar, which was situated in a squat, windowless cone just behind the bus station, offered both a blazing open fire and a very comprehensive selection of rakıs. These were things that made it most attractive to Çetin İkmen and his friend Altay Salman, as well as a ragbag of local youth and bored expatriates.

'I've always had, Allah forgive me, this feeling that Miss Nazlı Hanim must have had something to do with the death of Haldun Bey's daughter,' one of the youths said to the two policemen as he joined them, uninvited, in front of the fire.

'And why do you think that?' Altay Salman asked with, İkmen noted, some exasperation on his face. 'You weren't even born when it happened.'

The boy waved a hand dismissively and then downed what was left of his Pepsi-Cola. 'Look how much money she has now,' he said. 'If Haldun Bey's daughter had lived after Ziya Bey died, Nazlı Hanım would have had to share some of her fortune.'

'I think it was a foreigner,' another young boy who also just sat himself down with the men said. 'Just because their own women are immoral they think that ours are like that too. I expect some American raped Aysu Alkaya – and then he had to kill her in order to avoid detection.'

'And this "foreigner", I suppose, also helped her to escape from the Kahraman house, did he?' Altay said wearily. He turned to İkmen and added, 'This village is full of chattering fools!'

'I would agree with that.' The voice came from the open door of the bar. Its owner, a tall, gaunt man in his early fifties, stood framed against the darkness outside for a moment before he sat down, without getting a drink, at a table on his own. The two boys then left the police officers' table and went, their eyes all the time on the man who had just entered, to sit quietly by themselves.

'Who's that?' İkmen asked in the lowered tone this apparition seemed to command.

'That's Turgut Senar, Kemalettin's elder brother,' Altay replied.

This striding fair-haired man and the small, shrunken figure he had seen earlier didn't seem, to İkmen, to have too much in common – apart from blood, that was. But then if Turgut was out and about in the valleys all day, exploring the countryside and talking to people from all over the world, his mind and his body were going to develop very differently to those of someone who lived only inside some sort of delusion. Kemalettin Senar, whether or not it was because Aysu Alkaya's death had messed up his life, was obviously a very disturbed man.

Another man, who was probably about thirty, and who had been sitting alone at the table next to İkmen's, got up and went over to Turgut Senar, a grim expression on his face. But even as the man, who was dressed in dirty brown labouring clothes, towered above him, Senar remained seemingly oblivious to his presence. İkmen, hearing Altay Salman draw in a very sharp breath, whispered, 'What is this about?'

Leaning in as close as he could to the man from İstanbul, Altay Salman whispered, 'That's Baha Ermis, head man out at the Kahraman lemon caves. Doesn't come into town very often. His father was head man before him for many years. When Aysu Alkaya disappeared Baha was staying at the Kahraman house and swore that he saw the girl meet Kemalettin Senar out in the street in the early hours of the morning.'

'Did he tell this to the police?' İkmen asked.

'Yes, but Baha was only a child at the time and a child, I understand, with a reputation for lying. I think that, although they put Kemalettin through it, Baha's evidence was largely ignored. But he's still fired up about it even now, as you can see.'

'You may be able to ignore me, but you can't ignore the truth!' Baha Ermis said through broken teeth to the top of Turgut Senar's head. 'Aysu Kahraman's murdered body will condemn that retarded brother of yours for the killer he is!'

Turgut Senar continued to look down at the floor as if nothing was happening.

'They're taking her body to İstanbul, for tests,' Baha continued. 'Tests that will show that your brother killed her and the child of Ziya Bey she was carrying in her belly!'

İkmen, frowning at Altay Salman, said, 'He knows about the baby?'

Altay Salman shrugged. 'Erten has told Haldun Alkaya. And we know he's been telling the world of his woes. This is a village . . .'

'Senar! Are you listening?'

In one smooth movement, Turgut Senar rose to his feet and

punched Baha Ermis full in the face. Almost as quickly to his feet, Altay Salman ran over and pushed himself in between the two men. 'Now come along, brothers,' he said. 'Don't fight . . .'

'Don't tell us what to do, city boy,' Turgut Senar said calmly.

'Mr Senar, I am, may I remind you, a police . . .'

'He's from İstanbul!' Baha Ermis cried as he pointed to Altay with one hand and held his bleeding nose with the other. 'And him!' he added looking across at İkmen. 'He's the one who's going to take her to İstanbul for tests!'

'Well, then, may Allah guide his steps,' Turgut Senar said. 'May . . .'

'I think you should get out, now, Turgut,' the thick-set old man behind the bar said. 'I don't want any trouble in my place! Especially not with policemen involved.'

'Hakan . . .'

'And Baha, you should go too,' he continued.

Stepping back a little from the centre of the conflict, Altay Salman said, 'I think that Hakan Bey has made a very good point, friends. Now . . .'

But Turgut Senar was already walking out of the door and into the street. Baha Ermis opened his mouth in order to have the last word only to be silenced by Altay Salman.

'If you say anything or follow him I'll arrest both of you!' he hissed. And grabbing hold of Baha by the scruff of his neck, he threw him towards the entrance before going back to sit down with İkmen. 'That's the only trouble with the country,' he said. 'The people.'

'Altay, how did Baha know so much about the tests on the body?' İkmen asked. 'You said he doesn't come in to town that often.'

The dashing captain shrugged. 'Maybe Haldun Alkaya went and boasted to Nazlı Kahraman about the tests when Baha was in her house. Haldun's accused the old woman of being directly responsible for his daughter's death on many occasions. And now with the baby . . . Or maybe that idiot Erten told someone else, someone he shouldn't have, and word slipped out. Or perhaps some nosy constable overheard our conversation in the mortuary. Who knows?' He shrugged. 'Anything is possible out here. What do I know? This is vendetta land where all the inbreds with two heads and a hump make it their business to know everything – and keep the city folk at arm's length while they do so.' He lifted up his glass to the barman and indicated that he wanted another rakı. 'Will you join me?' he said to İkmen.

'Only if I can have a double,' İkmen replied.

As if to symbolise his split from his troubled past, Turgut Senar had chosen to live in a modern apartment on the edge of the village as opposed to one of the chimney properties up on the hill. It hadn't always been so. When his father was still alive he had been happy to live with his wife and daughter at home in his parents' chimney. But when his father died at the same time as all the trouble over Kemalettin and the Alkaya girl, Turgut decided to move his own family out to a new apartment at the bottom of the valley, to a less oppressive atmosphere. Of course his 'new' property was not as picturesque as his parents' place, but it was more convenient for the bus station and the tourist office and it also meant that his daughter Zara was protected from her strange uncle Kemalettin's offensive behaviour. Though of course the girl could still see him out and about in the village just like every-one else, as Turgut was doing now.

Lurking in the doorway of the now defunct Bellydance Bar, which was almost opposite the Red Dragon, Kemalettin Senar was smoking a cigarette with one shaking hand whilst stroking his penis with the other. Turgut, still angry at Baha Ermis as well as the world in general, walked over to him and ripped his hand from his member with some ferocity.

'Put yourself away, you disgusting animal!' he said as he roughly zipped his brother back into his trousers.

'But now that Aysu has gone I have to pleasure myself,' Kemalettin said as his eyes began to water with tears. 'I like sex . . .'

'Then why don't you go to one of the whores at the Anadolu Pansiyon?' Turgut replied, naming one of the very thinly disguised brothels at the western end of the village.

'They're Bulgarian,' Kemalettin began.

'So? If it's money you're worried about . . .'

'No. No, I just want Aysu,' he said. 'I want to feel myself inside her body.' Kemalettin began to cry.

Turgut leaned in closely to him. 'But Kemalettin, it's all in your head, isn't it?' he said. 'You never had sex with Aysu.'

'Yes, I did! We had sex in the cave with the mummy on the wall. You know that, Turgut. We always had sex there!'

'No you didn't!' his brother insisted. 'And even if you had, you never own up to it. Not to the police, not to the Alkayas, the Kahramans, not even to me.'

'I told Father.'

'Father is dead,' Turgut said. 'Just like Aysu. Dead! You must forget about her, brother!'

'I didn't kill her, Turgut!' Kemalettin, his nose dripping with snot, wept.

'Of course you didn't!' Briefly, Turgut looked around to see whether anyone was looking. Then fixing his eyes on his brother once again he said, 'We were together that night, weren't we? You and me, together.'

'But . . .'

'*All* night, just as we told the police then, just as we will tell them now.' Turgut leaned in closer to his brother's ear. 'Not part of that night, not most of it, *all* of it.'

'Turgut . . .'

'On the life of our mother!' Turgut stood back and held one of his hands out to Kemalettin as if in offering. 'Imagine my hand is Mother's life, Kemalettin.'

'Yes?' He didn't have any idea where this might be going but he followed, slack-jawed, what his brother was saying anyway.

'Swear on Mother's life, Kemalettin!'

'Swear what? What?'

'Swear to me,' Turgut whispered, 'your brother, that you will tell anyone who asks, *anyone*, that you and me, that all of our family, were together all night the night that Aysu disappeared.'

'But . . .'

'Swear!'

'I . . .'

Turgut thrust his hand under his brother's long, dripping nose and said, 'Swear, you retard!'

Kemalettin Senar took his brother's hand limply between his cold, damp fingers.

*　　*　　*

'So what do you do?' the man, whose name Süleyman now knew was Mürsel, said.

'I work for a hotel chain,' Süleyman said without a flicker.

He had followed Mürsel to the bar of the Büyük Londra Hotel on Meşrutiyet Caddesi. Vaguely shabby in that old Ottoman way that the smarter Pera Palas Hotel does rather more stylishly, the Büyük Londra attracted an eclectic clientele fond of caged songbirds, enormous chandeliers, 78 rpm records and gin slings. Surrounded by fey, generally middle-aged European women, several middle-aged, Turkish men of a certain type, including Mürsel, were in attendance. Flopped into comfortable, if somewhat threadbare armchairs, Mürsel and the others regarded each other and Süleyman with soft, but hungry, eyes.

'So is it Inter-Continental, Kempinski . . .'

'It's a large chain,' Süleyman said with a smile, imagining as he did so the lush gardens of the Çırağan Palace Hotel where his brother Murad worked.

Mürsel raised his elegant manicured hands into the air and said, 'Well, if you'd rather be elusive . . .'

Süleyman, still smiling, lit a cigarette. He quite enjoyed the company of this educated, attractive, obviously very smitten homosexual. It wasn't an entirely uncomfortable experience.

'Of course you are married with children,' Mürsel said as he first sipped and then gulped at his gin and tonic.

'Why do you think that?'

Mürsel smiled. 'Well, you're not exactly a child, are you?' he said. 'And looking like you do, your mother is bound to have married you off to the highest bidder. Some very pretty, fertile girl who has furnished you with two perfect children. That's what happened to me.'

131

He raised his glass up to the barman who, trapped behind his minuscule bar in the corner of the salon, set to making another gin and tonic with a will.

'Join me?' Mürsel said while he still had the barman's eye.

'No, thank you,' Süleyman replied, placing one hand over his heart as he did so.

'Got to get back to the wife and children?'

'Something like that.'

One of the other men rose from his seat and went to sit down beside a particularly nervous-looking European woman. She spoke to him, Süleyman noted, in French.

'Well, you'd better be careful out there at night on your own,' Mürsel said darkly. 'Men are at a considerable risk in this city these days.'

Süleyman settled back a little into his chair. 'You're talking about the recent attacks?'

'I understand this criminal's penchant is for rather attractive men not averse, as it were, to the intimate company of their fellows. Or so it is said in some circles.'

The elusive, somewhat archaic language was, he had heard, typical of homosexuals of a certain age. 'Yes, but I am married . . .'

'And so am I,' Mürsel said with a straight, rather humourless face. Then leaning forward he whispered, 'But when someone wants you badly enough, that doesn't really matter.'

'Yes, but . . .'

'Maybe he, this criminal, is just a man of great passion. Maybe he just refuses to allow conventional morality to stand in his way. Maybe he just takes what he lusts for, what we would all have if we could.'

'Maybe.'

Süleyman's blood was quite cold now. Whether it was because of what had actually been said or because of the seriousness inherent in Mürsel's words, he wasn't sure. Here, however, was a man who was going to be worth watching. Süleyman suddenly gave him a brilliant smile.

'So what do you do?' he asked as he replaced his packet of cigarettes in his pocket. 'You never did say.'

'Oh, I trade,' Mürsel replied.

'In?'

'Oh, many things,' he said, smiling too.

'What? Carpets? Textiles?'

'Many things,' Mürsel reiterated.

'You're very . . .'

'Guarded? Yes, I am,' Mürsel continued. 'Some men have to be as we both know.'

'Yes.'

Before he brought Mürsel his drink the barman wound up the ancient gramophone on a table over by the window and the beautifully tortured voice of Billie Holliday rippled across the salon. Mürsel, responding to its plaintiveness, smiled.

'Oh, well, I must be going,' Süleyman said as he rose to his feet with one nervous spring. He had gained some small insight into this man's thinking with regard to the peeper but that was very far from having any notion that he had been following the policeman since their first encounter on Monday evening. Mürsel obviously liked him and, although it was tempting to string him along in the hope that he knew – or let slip – something as yet unknown about the peeper or his victims, he was extremely guarded as well as being unnerving.

'Goodnight,' Mürsel said as he left.

Once out in the street, Süleyman stood in front of the ornate nineteenth-century hotel façade and sighed. Going off on his own, pursuing what were in reality only gut feelings, wasn't really on. He'd have to mount proper surveillance on the baths and other places the peeper's victims had mentioned. Following Mürsel had been a reflex, reckless and probably ultimately fruitless, too. He was just a rather predatory man who fancied him, that was all. But Süleyman shuddered all the same; he still had the feeling that he was somehow being watched. He took his mobile out of his pocket in order to call Zelfa. They hadn't spoken since they'd slept together the previous night.

'Oh, Sunel Bey . . .'

He'd called himself Sunel for no particular reason, it had just simply been the first name to come into his head.

Süleyman turned to find Mürsel right behind him. 'Yes?'

'You left your lighter behind,' Mürsel said as he placed it into Süleyman's hand. 'There.'

'Oh, thank you,' Süleyman said. 'That's . . .'

'You're very welcome.' In one lightning move, Mürsel pulled Süleyman's head towards his own and kissed him full on the lips. 'I've seen you naked,' Mürsel breathed once he had detached his lips from Süleyman's. 'You can do with me what you will!'

Chapter 9

Although vaguely aware of someone coming into his room through the darkness, İkmen thought that it could only be Fatma and turned over to get some more sleep. When the light went on, however, he knew that he had to be mistaken.

'What . . .'

'It's three o'clock,' Menşure said briskly. 'Ferdinand Mueller is coming to pick you up at four.'

'What?'

'For your balloon flight,' Menşure said tetchily as she banged a small tea glass down by the side of İkmen's bed. 'Have a drink and wake up.'

He saw her, dressed and immaculate even at that early hour of the morning, through a sort of damp, sick fog. Businesslike and bustling, she was neither sympathetic nor alone.

'Ah!' İkmen, now that he could fully appreciate who it was, jumped to the head of his bed in one panicky movement. 'Why have you brought *him*?'

'Kismet?' Menşure looked down at the enormous ginger and grey cat at her feet and smiled. 'I knew that if anyone could get you up it would be him.'

'Just don't let him near me!' İkmen said as he reached across to his jacket and took out his cigarettes.

Menşure smiled. 'Afraid of a little cat? Shame upon you, Çetin İkmen!'

'He isn't a cat, *I* have a cat, Marlboro; he sits on my lap at night and purrs. He, this you have here, is a demon crossed with a fighting machine!' İkmen said. 'You said yourself he's part lion! I don't care if he's thirty or whatever he is, his father or his grandfather or whatever took a lump out of my brother's leg.'

'Forty-five years ago.'

'Seems like only yesterday,' İkmen said as he surveyed the enormously scarred head of the growling animal at the foot of his bed.

But even when Menşure and the cat left a few minutes later, İkmen knew that the animal had achieved his mistress's purpose. He was awake, shaking, and ready to get out of the hotel as quickly as possible.

Zelfa Halman Süleyman was barely conscious when her husband woke her up to make love yet again in the early hours of the morning. But he was so passionate as well as being so gloriously masculine that she could hardly refuse him. Usually far too cynical to be impressed by such blatant masculinity, Zelfa felt as if, on this occasion, she had just simply been swept along in the wake of his unstoppable desire. Maybe, she thought, as he kissed her mouth, he really does want to make our relationship real once again. Maybe she could just throw all of her legal papers away and, as she had dreamed so many times before, lick every centimetre of his body.

Mehmet Süleyman, it was true, wanted his wife badly. He also needed her body to cover up what had happened earlier that evening with Mürsel. The kiss, that terrifyingly comfortable kiss followed by the admission that had almost caused the policeman to scream. 'I've seen you naked,' he'd said. Only after offering his body to Süleyman had he added that he'd seen him naked 'in my dreams'.

But was he telling the truth or was he lying? Whether or not he was the peeper, had this man followed Süleyman back to Zelfa's house in Ortaköy on Monday night, gripped by a burning desire to see a man he had spoken but a few sentences to in the street? Homosexual life in the city could be, Süleyman knew, furtive, opportunistic and desperate, even in the twenty-first century. Then again was he – had he – seemed that available to this man? And what of Mürsel's take upon the peeper? There had been almost admiration in his voice when he had spoken about this criminal. Hardly the fear that İskender's informant had said was spreading in the homosexual community.

He entered his wife's body with a sigh, whispering in her ears that he loved her as he did so.

'Mehmet,' she murmured as he began to move inside her.

Then his mobile phone began to ring.

For some reason he spoke in English as he withdrew from her, kissing her head as he did so, and picked up the ghastly instrument with his free hand.

'Sorry, sorry, Zelfa,' he said and then with less than good humour he flicked the mouthpiece of the telephone down. 'Süleyman.'

'Sir' – it was a female voice, a little nervous, probably due to the lateness of the hour – 'sir, it's Ayşe.'

'What?'

'Sir, I'm sorry, but ... Sir, I'm at Taksim Hospital. Abdullah Aydın came out of his coma about five minutes ago.'

Within fifteen minutes Mehmet Süleyman was washed, dressed and in his car en route to Ayşe Farsakoğlu and whatever was left of Abdullah Aydın.

Two of them, İkmen included, had been required to get into the balloon basket while it was still lying on its side on the ground. The balloon itself wasn't yet inflated and so they slotted themselves into their individual wicker segments while the noise and heat from the gas jets above roared into the enormous red and gold bag. İkmen, disgruntled beyond belief that they were not allowed to smoke on the flight, eased himself painfully into his section, cursing the arthritis which recently seemed to be afflicting his joints. But then his father had suffered from it, and so why not he?

'This is fun, isn't it, Inspector?' his companion said. He was Tom, the young Englishman he'd met on the bus.

'At this precise moment, no, it is not,' İkmen said. 'I just hope that once we are in the air it all becomes worth the effort.'

Once the basket was upright they were joined by the other passengers who included Dolores Lavell and Turgut Senar who, İkmen had thought, they would be meeting up in the valley. Four young Korean boys, the rather attractive Asian/American woman İkmen had also met on the bus, and the pilot, Ferdinand Mueller, completed the party.

Taking off into the silence of the dawn was an exhilarating experience. The weather was perfect for ballooning. It was cold but bright and as they rose above the flat plain to the east of the village, they saw tiny lights come on inside structures that looked like things elves and trolls should live in. İkmen, who had foolishly refused the offer of the thick woollen poncho Ferdinand had given to all of his other passengers, breathed heavily on to his rapidly purpling hands.

Someone nudged his arm. 'Here, put these on.'

Dolores Lavell held out a pair of thick, fake leopard-skin gloves.

'No, Miss, er . . .'

'I know they're not exactly masculine, but the colour of your hands is giving me the horrors,' the American said. 'Please . . .'

İkmen shrugged and then with a small bow he took the gloves from her and put them on. It was, even he had to admit, a considerable relief.

İkmen, in common with the other passengers, had imagined a balloon flight to consist of rising to a certain height and then sailing along admiring the valleys, villages and small monastic settlements from above. As dawn began to burn into full daylight, the sky was an intense and, in places, almost lilac-blue, and he felt the urge to get even further into this soothing infinity of colour. But instead of going up, the German took the balloon down into one of the most famous valleys of the fairy chimneys, Beehive Valley.

'The early Christians were well known for their cultivation of bees,' Ferdinand said as he pointed to a large escarpment dotted with what looked like sightless windows. 'This place here was a monastery,' he continued, 'but look, you can see that modern farmers have placed hives in front of it. It is a tradition here.'

What was also traditional was the collection of guano or, as Ferdinand put it, 'pigeon shit'. Dove and pigeon cotes dug out from tufa had been constructed and also decorated by the now nameless former inhabitants of Cappadocia. That guano was still collected from these elaborate bird houses and used to fertilise the vineyards was another example of how things continued and persisted in this ancient place. İkmen felt it was a privilege to be able to get so close to the upper reaches of these ancient escarpments and chimneys. Unless one climbed, which was laughable even to consider, then this was the only way that close-up views of the dovecotes and the amazing geometrical decoration that adorned them could be seen. That the basket scraped along the tops of a couple of the larger trees was somewhat disconcerting, but neither the German nor Turgut Senar looked at all concerned about this. The latter was, in fact, apparently far too lost in his thoughts to be concerned about much that was outside his head. İkmen, intrigued by this dour brother of the strange Kemalettin, attempted to engage him in conversation.

'It's good to meet you under rather more convivial circumstances, Mr Senar,' he said as the balloon began to gain height over the valley below.

'I don't like it when people question the integrity of my family,' Turgut Senar replied tightly. 'The night that Aysu Alkaya disappeared my brother Kemalettin was with me, all night.' He looked up, challengingly. 'You can check with the police in Nevşehir if you don't believe me.'

'Right.' He was very vehement about it, İkmen felt, but he smiled anyway and said, 'Well, soon, İnşallah, you will be able to gain some comfort from the forensic tests our doctor in

140

İstanbul is arranging. Maybe the results from those will allow Muratpaşa to finally arrive at peace with regard to this matter.'

'İnşallah,' Turgut Senar repeated, then turned towards the American Dolores Lavell who was pointing down to the plain now so rapidly and amazingly far away from the balloon and its basket.

'Look at that!' she said as she pointed downwards, her eyes sparkling with amazement. 'God, isn't that just wonderful!'

İkmen looked down and saw a large troop of horses and their riders galloping wildly across the plain. Even from what Ferdinand said was nearly three hundred metres he could see that it was Altay Salman and his cadets roaring across the ground like their wild nomadic ancestors. Fulfilling the Turks' destiny as unparalleled horsemen, they looked so free and made such a romantic sight that all around him İkmen heard the click of cameras as the Americans, the Englishman and the Koreans attempted to capture that which cannot be tamed.

After first looking at İkmen for a moment, Turgut Senar leaned over to speak to Dolores Lavell and to join in her almost childish delight.

'Young Mr Aydın is very fortunate,' the doctor said as she led Süleyman and Ayşe Farsakoğlu down the corridor towards the guarded room of Abdullah Aydın. 'He's young and fit and, apart from the scar on his chest, physically, he should recover.'

'So you mean that psychologically . . .'

'I have no expertise in that area, Inspector,' Dr Arkın said shortly. 'All I know is that Mr Aydın's first words upon emerging from his coma concerned his desire to speak to the police. And now that I have examined him, I am satisfied that he is capable of doing so without incurring any ill effects.'

It had been nearly three hours since Süleyman had taken the call from Ayşe Farsakoğlu concerning Abdullah Aydın. Three hours during which the young man's doctors had tested his responses and measured his vital signs and reactions for traces of remaining physical trauma. Now, just after dawn, it seemed that they were satisfied he could talk to Süleyman. The doctors told him the young man was most anxious to do so.

As they drew level with the door, the police guard who had been outside the room all that night moved aside.

'Now look,' Dr Arkın said as she placed her hand on the still-closed door. 'I think that only you should enter, Inspector. Apart from anything else, Mr Aydın's voice is still very weak and so no one beyond a person leaning over him will be able to hear anyway. Also I must insist that I be present. If I detect any agitation in his condition I will ask you to leave.'

'Agreed.'

And so Ayşe Farsakoğlu sat outside while her superior entered the strange world of drips, monitors and catheters that was Abdullah Aydın's temporary reality. Inside the room the light was subdued and as soon as he entered, the nurse who had been sitting at the side of the young man's bed moved soundlessly to one side. There was an aura of contemplative calm in this spare, white place, almost like that encountered in a mosque.

At Dr Arkın's behest, Süleyman sat down next to the small figure of the very pale man in the bed. There was some sort of tube, green in colour for some reason, attached to his nose while both arms were riddled with needles, cuffs and pads that both invaded and monitored his body. Under the bed there was a bag of something that looked very unpleasant and which Süleyman was careful to step over as he sat down. Zelfa would have been instantly at home in this environment, but to him hospitals were and probably always would be places of fear and horror.

As he leaned in towards the man on the bed, Abdullah Aydın opened his eyes. All around him monitors beeped and flashed in time to the inner workings of his body. He had great dark brown eyes, like a tired faun. He was very young. Süleyman took one of his hands in his. 'The doctor has told me you want to speak to the police,' he said. 'My name is Inspector Süleyman. I work in homicide.'

'He didn't kill me, Inspector,' a small, rasping voice said.

'No, because you're far too tough,' Süleyman replied. Looking across at the doctor, he said, 'His throat sounds so dry. Can't he have some water?'

'Mr Aydın has had all the water he is allowed for the moment,' the doctor said.

A vague scrabbling near his wrist indicated to Süleyman that the young man wanted to speak once again. He leaned in still further in order to hear him.

'It doesn't matter,' he said. 'Just listen.'

'Yes?'

Abdullah Aydın took a deep breath and then said, 'The man who stabbed me.'

'Yes?'

'I saw his face.'

'How?' The peeper, so far, had always covered his face.

'I pulled it off,' the boy said.

'The mask?'

'Yes.'

'Abdullah, do you think that you could describe this man for us?'

He coughed, loudly, his throat straining against dryness.

'I think that's enough for now,' Dr Arkın said as she inserted a hand between Süleyman and the boy.

'Yes, but . . .'

'Inspector, he's had enough,' she said sternly. 'Come back in a few hours and things will be very different.'

The boy coughed while Süleyman, unmoving, continued to stare at him.

'Inspector, I must insist.'

'Right. Yes.'

He got up and moved aside. The nurse, who had been waiting for him to get out of the way, held a bowl under Abdullah Aydın's chin. The boy, red in the face now, looked at Süleyman as if he were again trying to speak as the latter left the room.

Once outside Süleyman sat down next to Ayşe Farsakoğlu and said, 'He says he saw the peeper's face.'

'That's good.'

'I don't know whether he'll be able to give us a description. We didn't get that far. But I'd like you to contact Mrs Taşkiran just in case.'

Ayşe Farsakoğlu widened her eyes in surprise. 'Really?'

'Well, Inspector İkmen still uses her,' Süleyman said. 'Although whether he does so because she's a brilliant artist or because he just enjoys her eccentricities, I don't know.'

'No.'

'But contact her anyway, will you? Tell her I may have a job for her.'

'Yes, sir. You do remember we're bringing in those known offenders for interview this morning?'

'Mmm.' He had in truth quite forgotten but he bluffed his way through as was his custom. 'Yes, well, we'll go ahead with that, anyway. I mean who knows what it may yield?'

They both returned to the station, then, Süleyman's mind at least partly focused upon the subject of the police artist Dorotka Taşkiran. The daughter of Polish refugees, Dorotka Taşkiran had married into considerable Turkish Republican money, which had allowed her to indulge her passion and talent for art. Although an excellent portraitist – on which her attachment to the police department was founded – Dorotka was also a very experimental artist who had been known in the past to mummify small animals and take castes of gross human deformities. Now in her eighties she was still working on and off for Çetin İkmen, who had always maintained that she was the best police artist in the business. Süleyman, although not as tolerant of Dorotka's strange habit of talking to her dead 'sitters' and usually frightening live witnesses a little, nevertheless felt that she would be the perfect choice of artist to work with Abdullah Aydın. Young people often responded well and with interest to her oddness and besides, if the Aydın boy did conform to the peeper's type, he was almost certainly homosexual. Gay boys and old women. Guilty at his readiness to stereotype, Süleyman nevertheless felt that it was a match probably made in heaven.

The Asian/American lady's name was Emily, İkmen discovered. She came from Los Angeles but was half Japanese.

She and Dolores Lavell had been so thrilled by the sight of Altay Salman and his recruits that they had talked animatedly about them for some time. Turgut Senar had then told them about the traditions of horsemanship that were native to the district while both women marvelled at the vast antiquity of such practices.

'Seeing all of this fabulous scenery from above is such a privilege,' Dolores said as she turned round to take in the full sweep of the lilac-blue sky, glimpsing the snow-capped peak of Mount Erciyes floating like an airborne island in the azure distance. 'I wish my dad could've seen this.'

'But I thought you said he came here?' Emily replied.

'I mean from up here in a balloon,' Dolores said. 'They didn't have all this back in the fifties and sixties when Daddy came here. Leastways, I don't think that they did.'

Turgut Senar, who could possibly have answered this question, merely stared out into the vastness of the sky.

'Your dad didn't mention it at all?' Emily asked.

Dolores sighed. 'Daddy was none too well for some years before he died. He didn't talk too much, you know.'

Emily took her long black hair down from out of the comb that held it behind her head and then pinned it straight back up again. 'I'm sorry.'

'It's OK.' Dolores smiled. 'Daddy, God bless his soul, wasn't himself towards the end.' She spent a few moments riffling in her handbag before producing a small photograph, which she handed to Emily. 'That's Daddy in his prime. He was a sergeant in the military.'

'Oh, er . . . He was a good-looking guy,' the other woman said.

'Yes, he was.'

Turgut Senar, now back from his reverie, looked over the Californian's shoulder at the photograph and said, 'Who?'

'My father,' Dolores replied.

He frowned. 'Really?'

'Yes.'

'I see.'

'That was before his illness came on him, poor sweetheart.'

'Illness?' the guide asked. 'What . . .'

'It's called St Vitus's Disease, it's . . .' She looked up and smiled. 'It's not important now. Gone and forgotten.' She put the photograph away again in some haste.

İkmen, who hadn't been close enough to the group to see the photograph, nevertheless noted that both Emily and Turgut Senar appeared a little embarrassed, or at least uncomfortable, about it. It was, he thought, probably one of those instances where a person shows you a picture of a relative they, and only they, find attractive.

'In a few minutes we're going to be landing at the head of the White Valley,' Ferdinand said as he abruptly brought the women's conversation to a close. 'Then I will hand you over to Turgut for your hike. You have a very lovely day for it, I must say.'

İkmen didn't think that any day could be considered nice if that day involved a lot of walking. But at least down on the ground he would be able to smoke – even if his lungs gave out and his feet collapsed beneath him. The altitude of Cappadocia, over one thousand metres above sea level, isn't easy for those visiting the area who are fit – much less some- one like Çetin İkmen. That and the dust from the tufa in the air

147

made his chest wheeze. Stiff and tired before he had even begun the wretched walk, it took İkmen some time to get out of the basket once they had landed. When he finally emerged, he noticed that Turgut Senar had insinuated himself amongst the American women again and was looking at some photographs Emily was now showing and smiling very broadly. Amazing how such a dour character could change around women, he thought. But then there was currently some interest in foreign women in and around the village. Mainly young gigolos from the coast who found it easy to home in on these lonely, generally middle-aged foreigners, like Emily and Dolores. İkmen wouldn't have taken Turgut Senar, middle-aged himself, for one of them, but then nothing in life, as İkmen knew only too well, was as straightforward as most people would like to think. Maybe Turgut's wife was no longer interested in him? Or maybe he had just simply been smitten by Dolores and Emily? Anything was possible.

'So this is the White Valley,' Turgut said in English. 'It is called the White Valley because as you can see all of the fairy chimneys in this area are very white. We will walk through the valley now and will pass some rock churches on the way. The first one on the left will be the Church of Mary the Madonna . . .'

Allah protect me, İkmen thought as he watched the seemingly endless whiteness of the valley stretch before him. The Valley of the Saints, their final destination, wasn't even on the horizon, and Turgut Senar hadn't so much as mentioned its existence. He looked down at his cheap, plastic shoes and tried not to imagine the colour or condition of the frozen feet inside.

Chapter 10

'Inspector Süleyman!'

Commissioner Ardıç didn't usually come out of his office unless it was to formally brief his men or meet some sort of dignitary. He certainly didn't come and get people himself, in the corridor. He had a telephone and minions to do that sort of thing for him. But on this occasion he seemed to be making an exception. Süleyman turned and smiled at the large, ravenously hungry figure behind him.

'Sir?' He'd just spent a fruitless hour with a man who, as well as frequently assaulting his own children, was known to have beaten up several homosexual men. But he hadn't been anywhere near any of the peeper's victims at the relevant times – he'd been getting drunk in quite different parts of the city.

'I need to talk to you, now,' Ardıç said.

And so Süleyman followed him into his office, noting the usual signs that Ardıç was fasting – unlit cigar, empty cups – as he did so.

'One of your people has called Dorotka Taşkiran,' he said without preamble as he eased his large behind down into his chair.

'Yes, Sergeant Farsakoğlu.' Ardıç rarely could remember names below the rank of inspector. 'Why?'

'The boy Aydın's physician, Dr Arkın, feels that further questioning of the lad is not advisable at this time,' Ardıç replied.

Süleyman frowned. Dr Arkın had been of the opinion when he'd been at the hospital that Abdullah Aydın would be fit enough to answer more questions that very same day. And so he told his superior this.

'Perhaps the boy has deteriorated,' Ardıç said. 'But, anyway, I have cancelled the mad Polish woman.'

'Sir, I hadn't given Mrs Taşkiran a date,' Süleyman said. 'I was simply lining her up . . .'

'Well, for the immediate future, there will be no need.'

'Sir, with respect, Abdullah Aydın claims to have seen the peeper's face.'

'Yes, I know,' Ardıç replied. 'It is most frustrating, but if Dr Arkın has said that Aydın cannot be questioned safely then we cannot proceed.'

'But Abdullah was, or seemed, so much better . . .'

Ardıç shrugged.

Süleyman shook his head. True, the boy had been suffering from a terrible cough when he had left him, but having just come out of a coma that was to be expected. When the throat isn't used it becomes dry and sore. Something else must have happened since Süleyman and Farsakoğlu had left the hospital – something of some seriousness. After all, how often was it that people like the commissioner paid heed to doctors? Usually if information was required and needed from a suspect or a witness in hospital it made little difference what the attending doctor had to say on the matter.

'So did Dr Arkın say when I might have access to Abdullah Aydın?' Süleyman asked.

Ardıç looked down at his desk. 'No. But I will inform you as to when you may visit the hospital in the future.'

'She'll telephone you?'

'Yes.' Ardıç looked up sharply. 'Do you have a problem with that?'

'No, sir, except that I can't really understand why Dr Arkın didn't contact me herself. Why she went through you . . .'

'Well, there's no mystery to it, Süleyman! I am your superior. You take your orders from me and I am ordering you not to bother that boy with your questions for the time being.'

'Yes, but . . .'

'İnşallah, the boy will soon be well again and you will be able to question him,' Ardıç responded tightly. And then, smiling, he continued, 'But in the meantime you will not go anywhere near him. Do you understand?'

'Sir, I . . .'

'I'm sure that you have other lines of inquiry in this investigation, Süleyman.' Ardıç rose from his chair with some difficulty. 'I would suggest that in the meantime you pursue those.'

Süleyman, standing as his boss stood, bowed his head. 'Sir.'

'I am confident the boy will recover soon,' Ardıç said, and then with a wave of his hand he signalled for Süleyman to go.

'Sir.'

Once outside the disturbingly un-smoke-filled office of his superior, Süleyman stopped to think for a few moments. In situations like that of Abdullah Aydın, doctors usually liaised with the investigating officer himself. Rarely, if ever, did they approach Ardıç unless it was to complain about police treatment of one of their patients. Süleyman knew he had done nothing wrong and so there were no fears there. But for the doctor to approach Ardıç, as opposed to himself, with news of Aydın's deterioration wasn't usual. It wasn't even as if he'd been unavailable – he'd been in all the time! But there was only one way to find out and so Süleyman went back to his office and retrieved his car keys from his desk. It was lunchtime now and, even if Dr Arkın was keeping Ramazan, she would almost certainly be having a break at this time.

The wonderfully weird Valley of the Saints, famed for its impenetrable caves and hermitages, might just as well have been the dull mining district around the Black Sea city of Zonguldak for all İkmen cared when he got there. He was out of breath and footsore; there wasn't a bone in his body that seemed to be happy about this latest, crazy, physical adventure. While Turgut Senar pointed up at one of the triple-coned chimneys that the valley was famous for, İkmen found a piece of ground that wasn't covered with snow, sat down on it, and rubbed his ankles.

'The Valley of the Saints has for a long time been famous as a place of mystery,' Turgut Senar said as the rest of his group, apart from İkmen, looked round with awestruck expressions on their faces. 'People who could not fit in with ordinary life would come here. Some Christian monks who chose to live in the way of St Simeon of the Stylites came here. They lived in caves and prayed many metres up in the air at the top of the fairy chimneys.'

'So this was like a place to escape from the world, I suppose?' Dolores Lavell asked.

'Oh, yes, many people, many, many things, have been hidden in this Saints' valley.'

Because she knew both Menşure and Rachelle Jones, Dolores Lavell had to have known about what had so recently been found in the Valley of the Saints, what had been hidden away in its chimneys for so long. But she didn't comment upon anything pertaining to Aysu Alkaya; that came from the Englishman, Tom.

'Wasn't a body discovered here recently?' he asked.

'Yes,' Turgut Senar replied. 'But it was not a monk. They have been gone many years.' And he laughed.

'But where was the body discovered?' İkmen asked in English. 'Do you know?'

'In a cave,' the guide said noncommittally.

'Which one?'

Turgut Senar frowned before replying in Turkish. 'How would I know? You're a policeman, ask the cops in Nevşehir.'

'Don't speak so that no one else can understand, Mr Senar, it's very rude,' İkmen said before reverting to English again. 'Well, maybe we'll come across it during our exploration.'

'Maybe.'

İkmen could see that the guide was displeased about his interest in this subject and so he pushed it that little bit further. 'There may even be an officer or two still at the scene.' And then looking up at the Englishman he said, 'Perhaps Tom and I will see what we can find.'

'That'd be cool,' the young man said as he reached down in order to help İkmen to his feet.

'You are supposed to stick with the group,' Turgut Senar said sternly. 'I am taking everyone to the St Simeon Stylites chimney in a moment. It is on three levels of caves.'

'OK,' İkmen said with a smile. 'I will just wait outside and have a look round. I don't suppose you would like me to smoke in the St Simeon chimney, anyway, would you, Turgut?'

'No.'

'Well, that's settled, then.'

And so the party made off towards one of the largest triple-coned chimneys with İkmen and Tom very obviously bringing up the rear.

'He's a bit of a control freak,' the Englishman said to İkmen as he watched Turgut periodically turn round in order to see what everyone was doing.

'He doesn't want to lose any of us,' İkmen replied as he winced against the pain from his feet.

'He's coming on to those American women though, isn't he?' Tom said.

İkmen smiled. 'I'm afraid it is a reality of our lives that some of our men will do this,' he said. 'Westerners have, in comparison to us, so much more money.'

The two men watched as the rest of the party, led by Turgut Senar, entered the large sand-coloured chimney that was the St Simeon Stylites chapel.

'Don't you think that Western women and Turkish men can really have relationships then, Inspector?' the Englishman asked.

İkmen lit up a cigarette and sighed. 'Oh, I think it can be genuine,' he said. 'Indeed, one of my own friends is married to a Western woman and loves her very much.' He didn't go on to talk about Süleyman's difficulties with Zelfa, but then they were largely irrelevant to this conversation. 'But they are matched in both class and intellect. It's important. The problem occurs I think, when older women come here looking for some fantasy dark, handsome young lover. Usually they find poor waiters, boys who rarely got beyond primary school. These boys take the women's money and they break their hearts with other Western women they are also involved with. Not that I am entirely sorry for these women. They are educated, they should know better than to fall for such a transparent fantasy. Why do you ask?'

Tom shrugged. 'I'm just interested. So what about this body, Inspector? Are we going to see what we can find?'

'We will take what you British call a little stroll,' İkmen said with a smile. And so the two of them set off down beside the chapel of St Simeon Stylites and very soon they disappeared from view. The valleys are like that. One can disappear and be rendered silent within them in a heartbeat.

Dr Hazine Arkın was not taking a break. In fact, as Mehmet Süleyman could see, she was actually running from patient to patient.

'We're very short-staffed today,' she said when he asked if he could just have a moment of her time. 'What is it?'

He explained to her what Commissioner Ardıç had told him about Abdullah Aydın.

The doctor shrugged. 'Then you'll know I'll tell your boss when it's all right for you to interview him,' she said.

'I thought that was going to be later on today, Doctor,' Süleyman said. 'You said . . .'

'Things can change, as I'm sure you are aware, Inspector,'

she said and then turned aside to speak to one of her nurses for a moment.

When she had finished, Süleyman asked, 'Has Abdullah Aydın's condition deteriorated?'

'Things have changed,' she said. 'As I told Commissioner Ardıç, I will let you know when . . .'

'Yes, but Doctor, is his life in danger? If it is and he dies without my at least attempting to engage with him about his attacker, I am in dereliction of my duty. If that boy dies then this investigation becomes a murder investigation.'

For just a moment she stopped, raked her hands through the tangle of her thick blond hair, and said, 'I know that! Allah! What do you want me to do, eh?'

'Let me see him.'

'You can't.' On the move once again she looked down at the watch that was pinned to her white coat and said, 'Look, Inspector, I have to be at a meeting in five minutes.'

Almost at a run in his pursuit of her now, Süleyman said, 'Doctor, if you can just tell me what the problem is . . .'

'The boy is too sick to see you!' she said as she rounded a corner and then opened a door into a room that appeared to be bulging with doctors. 'Be told!'

And then she slammed the door in his face and Süleyman was left alone. Whatever was wrong with Abdullah Aydın had to be serious to account for this total lack of co-operation from the medics. Usually they made exceptions for policemen. But not in this case. Whatever it was, this was serious. Not that Dr Arkın had been either willing or able to tell Süleyman in what way. In fact, she had been almost studious in not being specific about his condition.

Süleyman walked back down the corridor, wrinkling his nose at the hated smell of disinfectant as he did so. There was still an officer outside Abdullah Aydın's room when he finally drew level with it. But it wasn't the same man as before. This was someone Süleyman didn't know at all. The constable, however, knew him.

'I can't let you in, sir,' he said even before Süleyman had opened his mouth.

'I'm not asking to come in, Constable.'

'I think perhaps it might be better if you return to the station, sir.'

Allah, but that was arrogant for a mere constable! 'Do you indeed?' Süleyman responded sharply. 'What's your name, Constable?'

'Orders from Commissioner Ardıç,' the young man said. 'If you come here, sir, I'm to turn you away, and ask you politely to go back to the station. There's a very sick boy in this room, sir, very sick.'

'Yes, possibly with information . . .'

'The boy's quite unconscious at the moment, sir. Seen him myself.'

'Have you.'

The door to the room swung open just then and a small, harassed-looking nurse emerged. For just the briefest moment he was able to look into the room and could see that Abdullah Aydın was, as the rather unsettling constable had said, seemingly unconscious on his bed. But all the monitors, drips and drains had been removed, leaving Abdullah apparently free from any artificial biological assistance. Either his condition had to be improving or he had now actually died.

As she sped down the corridor, Süleyman chased after the nurse who had just come out of the room and said, 'Mr Aydın, is he . . . ?'

'He's very ill,' the nurse said sharply.

'But he's not on any machines . . .'

'He's very ill,' she reiterated and then, lengthening her stride, she pushed herself to outstrip him.

It wasn't right. Whatever was happening wasn't normal and he was, so Süleyman felt, being deliberately kept in the dark with regard to why this might be. And yet for doctors and other policemen to, seemingly, prevent him from getting a description of a criminal who was terrorising the city didn't make sense. Ardıç himself had prioritised catching the peeper right from the start. İkmen had been involved, the department had even consulted a criminal psychologist. Even the slightest chance of getting a description had to be taken – surely. As he left the hospital and went back into the street he wondered what İkmen would make of it all and even considered giving the older man a call. But İkmen was busy with his own concerns out in Cappadocia and the last thing he would need would be worrying developments emanating from İstanbul.

Just down the hill from the Taksim Hospital on the left-hand side of Siraselviler Caddesi was a shop called La Cave. It was Turkey's largest wine shop and was, Mehmet Süleyman knew, a favourite haunt of his aristocratic father, Muhammed. The old man, although virtually penniless these days, still fancied himself as something of a *bon viveur*, and he could quite often be seen in La Cave sampling some new and exciting shiraz. In part at least as a way of distracting himself from his current concerns, Mehmet Süleyman decided that it would be rather nice to buy the old man a bottle and to share it with him that evening. And so he made his way down, if distractedly, towards the emporium. He had just entered the cigar- and wine-scented shop and was about to be approached by one of the ever-smiling assistants when another, far more alarming presence, made itself known to him.

'Sunel Bey?'

The toffee-coloured voice, not to mention the immaculate appearance of Mürsel, made Süleyman jump.

'Mürsel Bey. What a surprise.'

Out of the corner of his eye, Süleyman spotted the look of confusion on the assistant's face. This, after all, was one of those places where Muhammed Süleyman Effendi and his family were very well known.

'I trust it is a pleasant one?' Mürsel said with a smile.

'Yes . . .' Afraid that the assistant could come over and blow his cover at any moment, Süleyman said, 'Actually, I've just realised that I don't really have time to look for wine properly now. I must go back to my er, my office . . .'

'Oh, then I will walk with you,' Mürsel said. 'I, too, must return to business. I've just purchased what I hope is a very nice Beaune.'

'Ah . . . Good.'

Süleyman almost ran towards the door, much to the confusion of the assistant who had to move very quickly in order to open the door for Mehmet Bey and that man who had spent so much money on that old bottle.

Once outside, Mürsel, who obviously thought Süleyman had another reason for wanting to get out of a shop he was in so quickly, smiled. 'So what, apart from La Cave, brings you over to Cihangir, Sunel Bey?'

In spite of being flustered, Süleyman didn't miss a beat. 'I have a sick relative in the Taksim,' he said. 'I came to visit her.'

'Oh. May it pass quickly,' Mürsel said, repeating the age-old formula of sympathy for the sick.

'Thank you.'

Mursel's perfume was strong when he was some way off, and close to, as he was now, it was almost overpowering. 'I'm going to the hamam tonight,' he said.

'Are you?' Süleyman looked him straight in the eye.

'If you'd like to join me . . .'

'I have to go home,' Süleyman said.

'To your wife and your little boy.'

'Yes.' Süleyman felt himself blanch. Had he told Mürsel about Zelfa and Yusuf? He couldn't imagine that he had, in fact he knew that he hadn't. A lucky guess, perhaps, on the man's part?

Mürsel moved in even closer. 'I think you'd have more fun at the hamam,' he said. 'I think you'd be so much more appreciated there, especially by me.'

Knowing that if he wanted or needed to find out more about this man, he couldn't just be blunt with him or rude to him, Süleyman found himself genuinely nonplussed. And so he started to walk away, back up the hill towards the hospital and his car.

'Sunel Bey!'

'I'm sorry, I really do have to go now, Mürsel Bey,' he said without looking back to where the man was standing outside the wine shop. 'Maybe another time.'

'Oh, you can count on that, Sunel Bey,' the other said with what sounded like a smile in his voice. 'I shall hold you to it.'

Süleyman shuddered. Whether he was the peeper, knew the offender or whatever, Mürsel seemed to have an uncanny knack of being where Süleyman himself was. Again, he wondered whether the man was following him and, if so, why. Sure he fancied or claimed that he fancied Süleyman, but İstanbul was full of attractive men, many of them considerably younger than he. Surely someone as attractive, wealthy and cultured as Mürsel could have his pick. No, there had to be something else – something that, only if he were lucky, would have nothing to do with his real profession. Ardıç had suggested that he pursue other lines of inquiry with regard to the peeper investigation. Having Mürsel followed could, possibly, be one of them.

There wasn't much to see beyond a few scraps of crime-scene tape and a rather sleepy jandarma on duty outside the chimney. Young and bored, he wasn't one of the lads İkmen was familiar with from the village. But he was suitably impressed by the older man's badge and quite cheerfully let the inspector and his English friend look at where Aysu Alkaya had breathed her last. Squeezing through into tunnels and dropping down through evil-smelling holes in the rough, flaky tufa wasn't the most fun İkmen and Tom had ever had, but it was an experience if nothing else.

'Not a lot to see,' the young man said as he swung his torch around a narrow, tall chamber in the very back of the chimney complex. 'Just another old monastery thing.'

'Hermitages,' İkmen said as he looked down at the rough-hewn floor beneath his feet.

'What?'

'Not monasteries, hermitages,' İkmen reiterated. 'The Christian mystics who came here did so to be alone, not in order to form a community. They were emulating the extraordinarily weird and solitary life of St Simeon Stylites.'

'There's a small fresco by the looks of it over here,' Tom said in English. 'Looks much better than those rough old things in the chambers up above.'

İkmen looked across at the foreigner who was pointing down with the spare torch the jandarma had given him into what almost appeared to be a well in the corner of the chamber. Although his feet were now throbbing as never before, İkmen went over and looked at a portion of wall just below the floor.

'What is it?' he said as he squinted down at what he was surprised to see wasn't like the usual 'new' frescos that were periodically discovered in one or other of the valleys. It wasn't a vague scribble but a colourful and detailed representation of two figures. Probably of Byzantine origin, the picture showed one haloed man leading another male, covered in bandages and carrying a stick, out into a garden. 'What does it mean?'

The Englishman sighed. 'Well it's a long time since I went to Sunday school, Inspector,' he said. 'But I think that the figure with the halo is Christ and the other man, well, the bandages would seem to denote that he is dead . . . Then again, the stick seems to point towards some sort of disability. It's either Christ raising Lazarus from the dead or Christ healing the leper.' He looked up into İkmen's face. 'You'd need to ask an expert. But it's a great fresco and if it *is* Lazarus, it's quite appropriate, too.'

'What do you mean, Tom?'

'Well,' he laughed a little to himself, 'you might think this is silly, Inspector, but there is a story in the New Testament about Jesus raising this bloke called Lazarus from the dead. This girl whose body was found here, well, in a way she has been sort of resurrected too, hasn't she? I mean, now whoever killed her can be pursued.'

'I like that.' İkmen smiled. 'Yes. Now Aysu may reach out and claim a new life of justice for herself.'

'Yes, and with your help she might just get it. Does this jandarma know anything about the fresco, do you think?'

İkmen asked the lad, and he told him that once the police had finished their investigations 'some art man' was going to come down from Ankara to look at 'that picture thing, whatever it is'.

'Does anyone else outside the gendarmerie, the police and the "art man" known about this fresco?' İkmen further enquired.

'What, the picture thing?'

'Yes.'

'Don't think so,' the jandarma replied. 'Once Inspector Erten and the men from Nevşehir have finished we'll guard this place because of the picture for a while. Don't know how long. I suppose it has to be worth something, does it, the picture?'

'I'd say so, yes,' İkmen said and then he made his way back over towards the Englishman who had just taken a small camera out of his pocket. 'It would seem that this fresco isn't common knowledge round here.'

'Oh?'

'The local police are expecting an expert from Ankara,' İkmen said. 'So maybe, Tom, you and I should keep its existence to ourselves.'

The young man shrugged. 'OK.'

'So no photographs,' İkmen said as he gently took the neat Olympus camera from out of the Englishman's hands.

'That's a shame.'

'Someone was murdered here, Tom,' the policeman said softly. 'People apart from our own photographers should not be taking pictures.'

'No.'

İkmen and the Englishman got back to the St Simeon chimney just as Turgut Senar and the rest of the party were emerging from inside.

'So did you find the place where the girl's body was found?' the guide said as he looked down, without warmth, at İkmen's cold, nipped face.

'Oh, yes,' the policeman replied with a smile. 'We did.'

'And?'

'And what?' İkmen said.

'And did you go in? Did you see . . .'

'I spoke to the jandarma on guard at the site.'

After placing one hand on İkmen's arm, Turgut Senar told the rest of the group that the transport to take them back to Muratpaşa would be arriving soon. He then turned back to the policeman with a grave face. 'Tell me something,' he said, 'this DNA test the people in İstanbul will put the body through, what does it do?'

'I'm not a scientist,' İkmen responded. 'I don't know exactly. Why?'

'Why do you think!'

İkmen shrugged.

'My brother didn't kill Aysu Alkaya,' Turgut said harshly. 'I want this thing finished!'

'Well, if nothing else, DNA analysis should do that, sir,' İkmen said. 'Any samples not belonging to the deceased will be analysed and checked against samples from all of those involved. If your brother wasn't in that chimney then nothing of him will be present.'

The guide frowned. 'What do you mean?'

'I mean,' İkmen said, 'that if we're lucky, if DNA samples have survived from that time, we will be able to find DNA in hair, skin fragments, on clothes, that will give us the identity of the person or persons who were with Aysu when she died. Your brother, as well as others connected to the investigation, will be asked to supply samples for comparison.'

'What?'

İkmen took careful note of the whiteness of Turgut Senar's face. 'We take a swab from inside the mouth,' İkmen said. 'It's quite painless. The material on the swab, which is unique to each person, gives our scientists everything they need to make a comparison. I doubt whether you will be required to give a sample yourself.'

'Why not?'

'Well, because although each sample is unique, yours will be, as a full brother to Kemalettin, very similar. The same will be true for your mother. Quite distant familial links can, I am told, be traced in this way. So only one sample from your family, I imagine from Kemalettin, will be required in the first instance. Although that is of course up to my colleagues in Nevşehir; they may want everyone tested at the very beginning.'

'Of course. I see.' He looked down at the ground. 'Well . . .'

'I hope, Mr Senar, that it will establish once and for all just who was with the poor girl on the night that she died. It should also determine the paternity of her child. İnşallah, what we discover will be satisfactory to all concerned.'

And then İkmen walked off to join his young English friend, Tom. There was not, he felt, any further virtue in discussing DNA testing with Turgut Senar. The guide had obviously understood what the policeman had said to him, but his fear was, İkmen felt, considerable. It could of course just simply be down to the fact that Senar was a country boy unaccustomed to the scientific process, but there could be more to it as well. And being of a naturally suspicious nature, İkmen decided to find out, if he could, some more about Turgut Senar and his family.

'I don't always have people over for iftar,' Menşure said as she watched over her cook and his daughter laying out the food on her huge kitchen table. 'But seeing as you seem to have made so many friends . . .'

'Mmm.' İkmen idly stretched out and took a date from a little silver platter.

He was just about to put the fruit into his mouth when he felt Menşure's hand on his wrist.

'It isn't time yet!' she said as she smiled at the shocked expression on her cook's face.

'Oh.'

İkmen put the date back down on the tray and worked at looking a little sheepish.

'Do try to at least pretend to keep Ramazan,' Menşure said. 'My cook has been preparing food for me for years, I don't want him upset.'

'No, Menşure.'

As well as her own guests at the Fairy Chimneys Hotel, Menşure had also invited Altay Salman and his family and Rachelle Jones, 'that Australian you like so much'.

'I see the good captain has brought his wife and kid,' she said in English to İkmen.

Now that the sun had officially set, İkmen was indulging his occasional yearning for pestil, a dried fruit toffee of quite alarming glutinousness. 'Mmm,' he said through a tooth-rotting mouthful. 'Lovely people. You know I think the captain would be very happy if you would befriend his wife. She's very lonely.'

'Oh, why not,' the Australian said with a wry smile. 'I'm sure she's a very sweet woman. Do you know why I always seem to go for married men, Inspector?'

İkmen swallowed what was in his mouth and then lit up a cigarette. 'No, Miss Jones, I don't,' he said. 'But the captain is a very charming and good-looking man and so he will always tend to attract attention.'

And indeed there was a demonstration of that phenomenon happening before their very eyes. Not only Dolores Lavell's friend, Emily, but also several other female guests were, or so it seemed, hanging on Altay Salman's every word. His wife, Sevgi, who was, as İkmen could see, used to this sort of thing, just looked on with mild amusement as her husband held court for almost every other woman in the place. But not all. Dolores Lavell had brought a man of her own.

'Turgut has invited me over to his mother's place,' she said when she briefly left Turgut Senar's side to speak to İkmen and Rachelle Jones. 'Tomorrow. Isn't that great?'

'Nalan Senar has quite a nice place. Some good frescos in one of her out-houses,' Rachelle said. 'Mind you, she's a miserable old bird herself, and if you don't like kangals, well . . .'

'I'm just fascinated to go into such an old and extensive chimney home. I mean I've only just glimpsed inside an authentic, inhabited chimney home before.'

'Well, if Turgut manages to persuade his brother to go out you should be all right,' Rachelle said with a shrug.

Dolores frowned. 'What have you got against his brother, Rachelle?'

'Nothing, but you've been coming here for long enough to know that all Kemalettin wants to do is wank, Dolores.'

'He's a sick man,' the American said sadly. 'I can relate to his pain. I've tended my own sick people.'

And then she went back over to Turgut Senar who greeted her with what was, for him, an unaccustomed smile.

Rachelle Jones, in emulation of the American, mouthed 'I can relate to his pain' at İkmen before saying, 'Christ! I know she's American, but . . .' Then looking across at Dolores and Turgut who were in close conversation she frowned. 'You know Dolores has been coming here for a number of years now and this is the first time I've seen her with a bloke. And Turgut Senar.' She shook her head. 'Blimey, he's got diplomas in being quiet and reserved!'

İkmen laughed. 'They started talking on our balloon flight this morning,' he said. 'Mr Senar is married, I take it?'

'Oh yeah,' the Australian replied. 'Like the lovely captain,

Turgut never strays. Or rather, he didn't stray until now. His wife's a mousy little headscarf. But he likes her – or he did.' She looked over again at Turgut Senar and Dolores Lavell and clicked her tongue in what seemed like irritation. 'Funny. He must've seen Dolores about over the years.'

'Maybe he has only just realised how much he likes her,' İkmen said.

Rachelle Jones looked at him through jaundiced eyes. 'You mean maybe he needs a few million lire for something or other.'

İkmen, smiling, shrugged.

'I don't trust him,' Rachelle said, as she continued to look at the strange sight of Turgut Senar, the lonely valley guide, flirting with the usually very restrained American. 'Look at the way he's making her behave. She doesn't come on to guys like that. Dolores is too sassy for that.'

And so she had seemed to İkmen, when he'd first met her. But then perhaps both he and Rachelle had been wrong. That or maybe something about Turgut, rather than Dolores, had changed. İkmen looked over at Altay Salman and raised his glass of sherbet in salute. Even back in İstanbul where people were accustomed to men like him, Altay had been 'bothered' by women. Maybe it was the connection with horses? After all, every man had his 'thing', his gimmick. With Altay it was his horses, with Mehmet Süleyman it was his aristocratic past, with İkmen himself, well, he supposed it had to be his voice. What it was with Turgut Senar was difficult to see.

When eventually Menşure Tokatlı had had enough of her guests she very skilfully got rid of them by announcing that the time had now come for her to feed her cat. Even those who didn't know about Kismet and his penchant for violence were soon put in the picture by all who did and so everyone left very quickly after that.

Later, alone in his room, İkmen smoked and thought about the fabulous fresco he and Tom had found in the chimney where Aysu Alkaya's body had been found. The fact that the body had been found in such a significant, if unknown, place couldn't be an accident. Maybe the fresco had even been 'their' secret, something known only to Aysu and whoever she had gone to meet in the Valley of the Saints. If she'd gone to meet anyone, that was, as opposed to being taken. Quietly, and probably willingly, she had left her old husband the night she had disappeared. But whether she'd gone to meet Kemalettin Senar or any other admirer she may have had for that matter was still unknown. It was hard to believe that Kemalettin had once been a desirable young man. Now obviously out of his mind in some capacity, at least Dolores Lavell could 'relate to his pain' in some way that, maybe, was at the root of Turgut Senar's sudden liking for her. Perhaps they'd talked of Kemalettin and Dolores' sympathy for the poor creature had touched the gruff countryman's heart. After all, from the little that İkmen had seen of him, Turgut Senar was very protective of his brother.

Chapter 11

It was dark, quite cold, silent and time to up the stakes. There had been rather more taunting and suggestion than had originally been envisaged, but all that was about to change now. This was pure skill. It could have been employed at any time over the past few months and weeks but holding back had been half the fun, if one were to be honest. Not that any of this was really about fun.

The boy, a waiter and part-time whore, so it was said, came out of the Saray hamam, Karaköy without looking to either left or right. The knife that severed his carotid artery came out of nowhere. Clean, quick, totally without sound. The kid probably didn't even know he was dead. Perfect.

Although he was not someone who breakfasted regularly, İkmen decided to join Menşure's non-Muslim guests for a cup of coffee and several cigarettes the next morning as it was to be his last day in the village. Her restaurant, which was at the top of the hotel complex, afforded views of the valleys almost as spectacular as those İkmen had seen from the hot air balloon. Although the American, Emily, waved to him as he entered, İkmen opted to sit with Tom, mainly because the Englishman was already puffing away at a cigarette, after the Turkish policeman's own heart. As he sat down, ordering a coffee from the cook's waitress daughter as he did so, İkmen noticed that Menşure was giving him a murderous look. If she had been one to keep Ramazan to the letter herself he would have shrugged his shoulders and tolerated her disdain. But he knew she cheated and so he dealt with her displeasure simply by ignoring it. After all, with Arto Sarkissian coming to pick him up later on that day, Menşure's threats of Kismet-based retaliation could be, at best, limited.

After passing the normal pleasantries people exchange at the beginning of a day, Tom said to İkmen, 'You know that fresco that we saw yesterday?'

'Sssh!' İkmen leaned across the table in order to encourage Tom to lower his voice. 'We don't know if we can talk about that, remember? What of it?'

'Well,' Tom whispered, 'I've been thinking. I know that cave we went into is quite remote, but the Valley of the Saints is on the tourist trail. How come no one has discovered such a treasure, or the body, for that matter, until now?'

İkmen lit a cigarette and then leaned back into his chair. 'I don't know,' he said. 'But I have puzzled upon that myself. I have wondered whether the body was moved to that cave, which is a possibility. However, that does not solve the mystery of the fresco.'

'Do you think that maybe someone has been making sure that no one enters that cave?'

But before İkmen could answer, Menşure came over and said, 'One of the boys has just told me that a policeman is downstairs for you, Çetin.'

'What policeman?' İkmen asked. 'You don't mean a jandarma?'

'No, not some gossipy boy! That incompetent from Nevşehir,' she said. 'Looks like a homeless person. Got something urgent to tell you, apparently.'

Erten. Although quite what he was doing in Muratpaşa İkmen couldn't think. As far as he was concerned he was going to see Erten at the mortuary with Arto Sarkissian.

'Better show him up,' İkmen said as his mobile phone began to ring. 'İkmen.'

Menşure left but with an expression of deep disdain on her face. She wasn't accustomed to being treated like the 'help' in her own place or any other place, come to that.

'Çetin, it's Arto,' a tired voice at the other end of the line said.

'I've a deep feeling of foreboding,' İkmen said as he first smiled at Tom and then turned away to speak into the phone more privately.

'And with good cause,' his friend replied. 'My gear box has blown, I'm having it fixed now, but I won't be able to be with you until tomorrow.'

'But you've only just bought that car!' İkmen said, appalled.

'I've had it five years, Çetin.'

'As I said, it's new,' İkmen said which, compared to his own sorry vehicle, was the case.

The Armenian ignored this last comment and said, 'Look, what you need to do is make arrangements with the mortuary in Nevşehir for me to take my samples tomorrow. Do you think that will be a problem?'

'If you give me a moment, I'll find out,' İkmen said as he beckoned the shambling figure of Inspector Erten over to his table. 'My opposite number in Nevşehir has just arrived.'

Erten, grey-faced, stumbled forwards. 'Inspector İkmen, I must . . .'

'My colleague the pathologist won't be able to get here until tomorrow,' İkmen interrupted. 'Some problem with his car. Can we still get in to the mortuary and take samples tomorrow?'

Erten, still nervous in his manner but smiling now, said there was no problem and so Arto Sarkissian made arrangements to pick İkmen up first before going on to Nevşehir the following morning. Once all of this had been organised, İkmen turned back to the young Englishman and said, 'So it would seem I have an extra night here, Tom.'

'That's great,' the boy replied. He had really taken to İkmen – a feeling the Turk experienced as mutual. 'Maybe dinner tonight, or . . .'

'I'd love to,' İkmen said.

Tom stood up and, nodding towards Erten, said to İkmen, 'About eight? Here in the restaurant? I'm off to the underground city at Derinkuyu today and I can see you're busy.'

'Fine. That's OK,' İkmen said, smiling as he watched the young man walk out of the large, bright restaurant. He then turned his attention fully on to Erten. 'So, you need to speak to me?'

'I came over here this morning, Inspector,' he said, 'because, as I understand it, we will need to take some samples from those involved in the Aysu Alkaya case for comparison with what may be discovered in İstanbul.'

174

İkmen, frowning, lit up another cigarette.

Erten, mildly shocked by this behaviour, muttered, 'Oh, I say.'

'Yes? And?'

'Oh, er, well, I was . . . Do we have to do that now, so that all the samples from everyone can be sent off to the laboratory together as it were?'

'That would be ideal,' İkmen said, 'although unless you actually have a suspect in custody, you will either have to ask permission from those you wish to test or get a warrant to do so.'

'Ah, yes . . .' İkmen noticed that he was looking hungrily at the cigarette he was so casually smoking.

'And you need swabs,' İkmen continued. 'Didn't you speak to your doctor about all this?'

'Yes. Yes.' Erten smiled his vague little smile and said, 'But he said he'd never done such a thing. DNA, you know. He's near to retirement, you see, and . . .'

'Look, Dr Sarkissian can't now get here until tomorrow, so let's just let him take his samples, have the tests done and see what happens,' İkmen said. 'It may well be that we don't get any samples to form comparisons with. And if that is the case, going through this process that I know some of these villagers fear will have all been for nothing.'

'You've spoken to some of the villagers about DNA testing?' Erten asked nervously.

'I've spoken to Turgut Senar,' he replied. 'A rather worried man, I felt.'

'Really?'

'Yes.'

'Mmm.' Erten placed one thin hand up to his lips and then said, 'You know I have to re-interview the Senars, the Kahramans and Haldun Alkaya. I have to do that anyway.'

'Yes, I know.' İkmen smiled. 'I've actually met most of them myself. I expect you know that I knew an English girl who went missing here some years ago.'

'I heard something about that, yes.'

'And so I've spoken to some people . . .' It was not, İkmen felt, a very good idea, even to one as mild-mannered as Erten, to let on just how much information he had gleaned about Aysu Alkaya from these individuals. However, there was one person he had not yet seen or spoken to, and in spite of his reservations he couldn't resist letting this slip to the man from Nevşehir. 'Not Kemalettin Senar's mother, though, Nalan, is it? I haven't yet seen her . . .'

'Oh, right,' Erten said, and as he watched İkmen first extinguish one cigarette and then immediately light another, he said it again, 'Oh, right.'

Menşure Tokatlı, who had been listening to some of this conversation from her position over by the breakfast buffet, sighed with impatience. All these niceties, hints and suggestions these grown men used, were such a waste of time! Çetin was much more intelligent and important than that little bundle of rags from Nevşehir. Why he didn't just tell the man he was going to see Nalan Senar and question the woman, Menşure couldn't imagine. Irritated, she went off to get more coffee for her guests.

It was impossible to know exactly what Zelfa was thinking about the situation just from idle conversation. Mehmet

176

Süleyman had telephoned his wife the previous evening in order, he hoped, to try to discuss their relationship – if indeed such a thing existed. But she had been too distracted to talk and so that was why he had arranged this small shopping trip to İstiklal Caddesi. Saturday was, after all, supposed to be his day off and so although his mind was still troubled by the peeper, by the disturbing Mürsel Bey and other worries, he decided that a trip to the music shops and bookshops along İstiklal Caddesi would make both himself and Zelfa feel better. And with his mother and father looking after Yusuf for the morning it would not only be like the 'old days' for the couple, but would also give them a chance to talk.

Usually when he went up into the Beyoğlu area, Süleyman parked his car outside the Cohens' apartment in Karaköy on Büyük Hendek Sokak. But Saturdays were a bad time for parking in that area. The Cohens' apartment was almost opposite the Neve Şalom Synagogue, and as there was a ban on parking directly outside it, combined with the many cars of those attending Saturday prayers in the vicinity, parking was virtually impossible. So, after an early and really quite promising start (Zelfa had kissed him passionately just after they left his parents' house in Arnavautköy), he parked up on Tomtom Kaptan Sokak, up by the rear of the Catholic church of St Mary Draperis. From Tomtom Kaptan it was a short walk up to İstiklal Caddesi and the Robinson Crusoe bookshop where Zelfa could indulge her interest in English language literature. One credit-card transaction for books including Peter Ackroyd's *Hawksmoor* and Mark Twain's *The Innocents Abroad* later, they left and were about to seek out coffee and maybe cakes when a familiar figure pushing a buggy came towards them.

'Hulya!'

The young woman looked up into the faces of friends she thought were no longer talking to each other. The fact that they were together and holding hands made her smile.

'Hello, Mehmet, hello, Zelfa,' she said, then looked around for the couple's child. She frowned. 'No Yusuf?'

'My parents are looking after him for the morning,' Mehmet said as he looked down and smiled at the sleeping infant in Hulya İkmen Cohen's buggy. 'You know how grand-parents like to spoil the grandchildren.'

Hulya rolled her eyes. 'Oh yes. Timur already has every toy that money can buy for babies his age, and older, and clothes . . .'

'Your parents?'

'And Berekiah's mother,' Hulya replied. 'Honestly, it's like a sultan has just been born!'

'How is Berekiah?' Zelfa asked as she looked into the buggy and clucked just a little. 'He's at work today, isn't he?'

'No,' Hulya said. 'Old Mr Lazar is religious and so Berekiah always gets Saturdays off to go to synagogue. Not that he ever does go.' She laughed. 'He's still asleep.'

Mehmet looked at his watch and saw that it was almost ten. He raised his eyebrows, but then he smiled again. 'Ah, but the gold merchants open early and shut late for the rest of the week . . .'

'When your husband works in the Kapalı Çarşı you don't get to see too much of him,' Hulya said to Zelfa.

'I know something of how that feels,' the older woman

178

said as she looked up at her tall, handsome husband. 'Yes, I do.'

Mehmet Süleyman was about to add something to the conversation which he felt was amusing, when the whole of İstiklal Caddesi seemed to take a leap sideways. People stopped talking, faces assumed a greying pallor and, as soon as some sort of grasp was gained about what may or may not have happened, men and women looked up to see a thick pall of smoke scar the morning sky. It hung, like a threat, over the Karaköy area.

For a second, Hulya just stared and then she said quietly, 'Berekiah.'

People were screaming now and first one, then what seemed like hundreds of sirens, rent the air with their ominous wailing.

Mehmet looked at his wife and said, 'Take Hulya and Timur to the car and drive home.'

He took his car keys out of his pocket and dropped them into her hands.

'Berekiah!' The girl turned as if to make her way back down İstiklal, the buggy under her hands, her eyes full of tears.

Mehmet Süleyman moved quickly to block her path. 'No, go with Zelfa now, Hulya.'

'Berekiah!' She looked up at the ever-rising pall of smoke and screamed.

'We don't know what's happened,' Süleyman said as he took hold of her shoulders and held her tightly in front of him. 'I will go and find out. I promise. But you and the baby must go with Zelfa. You must make sure that Timur is safe.'

Zelfa moved forward to get a hold on the young woman and thereby allow her husband to leave. For just a brief moment the two of them shared a terrified glance and then Zelfa said, 'Be careful, Mehmet. Please.'

He leaned in to kiss her quickly, and then he was gone, running down towards the Tünel funicular railway station, towards the raffish old district of Karaköy. Every step he took brought him closer to the smoke and to the ghastly and awfully familiar smell that accompanied it. The human body first cooks before incinerating when it comes into contact with fire. This was a gas explosion or, worse, a bomb. As his chest began to heave with the lack of oxygen, Süleyman couldn't help but think of other explosions in other parts of the world and of those who had perpetrated them. He thought also of those they had been perpetrated against. By the time he reached Ilk Belediye he knew. Everything was leading him towards Büyük Hendek Sokak and the Neve Şalom Synagogue. As he drew level with the intersection between Ilk Belediye and Büyük Hendek, he even closed his eyes for a moment, in order to give himself the illusion of denial for a few seconds longer. But when he opened them it was like the aftermath of the 1999 earthquake all over again – craters in the ground, bodies – some still living – pinned beneath glass and stone and wood, and the screaming . . .

'Sir!'

Although he was out of uniform, Constable Hikmet Yıldız was instantly recognisable and in this inferno was a slight comfort to him.

'Yıldız!'

The two men briefly, if fiercely, embraced.

'They've taken out the front of the synagogue,' the young man said and then, suddenly gripped by the full horror of what he had just seen, he screamed, 'There's a girl with no head! Allah, save us!'

'Who's taken out the synagogue?' Süleyman asked. 'What?'

'I don't know!' Yıldız replied. 'I don't know! I was just going up to buy a CD and then . . .'

He began to cry. Süleyman put an arm round his shoulders and moved him towards a group of uniformed officers who had arrived to keep the public back from the terrible scene and the work of the medics who were fighting to save what lives they could. As he approached the officers, he took out his ID card and showed it to them. They saluted.

'What's happening here?' he asked.

One of the men broke ranks and pulled Süleyman and Yıldız to one side. Crowds, many of them wounded and crying, were beginning to form and the officer was keen to keep this senior policeman out of their way.

'We think it was a car bomb, sir,' he said. 'Suicide. Driven into the front of the synagogue, right at the people at prayer.'

'Allah.'

'Men, women, children.' He shook his head in disbelief. 'They didn't stand a chance!'

And then once he'd torn his gaze away from the front of the shattered synagogue, Süleyman made himself look at what, for him, was an even more painful sight – the apartment buildings, or rather what remained of them, opposite the place of worship. Shattered windows were just the least of it. In some places whole chunks of the façades, people's living rooms, were hanging down into the street. On the first floor, the level upon which the Cohen family lived, a large iron bedstead hung from what had once been a window. There was no sign of life from that quarter. Amid the screams of the dying and the tears of the living there wasn't a sound from the apartment building or anyone in it. Berekiah Cohen had, Süleyman knew, been in his bed . . .

Chapter 12

Nalan Senar was a woman who, İkmen felt, liked to make an impression. On the one hand she was a pious, covered village woman, the very image of respectability, but on the other? Nalan Senar wore far too much jewellery on and around her heavy clothing to be the 'poor peasant' she purported to be. In addition, her house, as well as being home to a very large dog, was also the site of a huge amount of very sophisticated electronic equipment. Not that any of it was actually working when İkmen and Erten went to visit the woman that grey Saturday morning.

'Kemalettin knows how to do this stuff,' she said as she held a handful of remote controls up for the policemen to see. 'He is the watcher of television.'

'Where is Kemalettin, Mrs Senar?' Erten asked as he first took off his shoes and then sat down in the seat the woman directed him to.

'I don't know,' she replied with some resentment in her voice. 'Why? Did you want to see him?'

'No,' the Nevşehir man said with a smile. 'It is you we've come to see. I expect you've heard about Inspector İkmen from İstanbul and what he has arranged for Aysu Alkaya's remains.'

'Yes.' She eyed İkmen narrowly before offering him a seat alongside that of his rural colleague. 'Some tests,' she said as she, too, sat down, pulling her headscarf tightly down round what looked like a lot of blond hair as she did so. 'Turgut has told me a little about it. He says they show what a man really is.'

'In a way, yes. They're called DNA tests,' İkmen expanded. 'If tissue – skin, hair or nails – from whoever was with Aysu on the night that she died has survived from that time then our scientists will be able to match that to people known to have been involved with the girl.'

'Ziya Kahraman killed her and he is dead,' Nalan Senar snapped back unpleasantly.

'How do you know that?' İkmen asked. 'You don't, do you?'

'I know how badly he treated her.'

'And yet you prevented your son, Kemalettin, from marrying the girl in the knowledge that Ziya Kahraman would court her himself. Ziya in fact paid you to do just that.'

Nalan Senar shot İkmen a furious look. 'Yes, and why not? Haldun Alkaya has nothing. I wanted better for my son.'

'Who is now alone,' İkmen said. 'Your sons were together on the night that Aysu Alkaya disappeared, weren't they, Mrs Senar?'

She looked across at Erten and said, 'I told the police in Nevşehir where my sons and everyone else were twenty years ago.'

'Yes, but . . .'

'Kemalettin and Turgut were here with me and their father. My husband was dying then. He had cancer.' She looked

184

briefly across at a portrait of a fair-haired man that hung over the fireplace. Her husband. 'The boys were always with me then, they are good sons.' She turned back to look at İkmen again. 'Ziya Kahraman killed her. But he is dead and so we will never know.'

'On the contrary,' İkmen replied.

Nalan Senar frowned.

'Provided Nazlı Hanım is prepared to let us take a swab from inside her mouth we will be able to make a comparison,' İkmen said. 'We can identify family connections through these samples, Mrs Senar.'

'Which is why we don't need to bother everyone connected to Aysu Alkaya for samples at the moment,' Erten put in. 'Once we have the results from İstanbul I will ask our doctor to take samples only from one person in each family.'

'But what if that person is not connected to that murder? What if he or she is just related to the evil one?'

'Then at least we will know we are looking in the right direction,' İkmen said. 'Only at that point will other members of that family be asked to provide samples of their own.'

'So my boys . . .'

'One or other of your boys may volunteer,' İkmen said. 'Or you may yourself.'

'And Kahraman . . .'

'Nazlı Hanım will be asked,' İkmen said. 'Although as I'm sure your son Turgut has told you, Aysu Alkaya was with child when she died . . .'

'Baha Ermis spreads that poison! Pah!' Nalan Senar spat. 'That lying fool!'

185

'Our doctor thinks the girl was in the early stages of pregnancy,' Erten said.

'Which would seem to rule out Ziya Kahraman who so wanted a son, or so I am told,' İkmen said.

'But Nazlı . . .'

'Oh, Nazlı Hanım could have done it, yes,' İkmen said. 'She would have had a motive. Unless, of course, the child wasn't Ziya's. But we can determine the parentage of the foetus, or rather our scientists in İstanbul can and will do that.'

'Will they.' It was far more of a statement than a question.

'Yes.'

Their conversation was interrupted by angry voices from outside in the courtyard. Zeytin the kangal, temporarily locked into the Senars' kitchen, began to bark and howl. In fact the noise that she made was so terrific İkmen wondered whether the beast was in fact alone.

'What . . .' Nalan Senar got up and made her way over to the front door. She was closely followed by Çetin İkmen who peered round her shoulder as she opened the door.

Outside were Nalan's two sons, Turgut and Kemalettin, and the American woman, Dolores Lavell. Turgut, holding the American's hand as he did so, was shouting into his brother's face.

'You disgusting animal!' he screamed above the dog's wild howling. 'Apologise to Miss Lavell immediately!'

'But I . . .'

'It's really OK, Turgut,' the American said as gently as the furiousness of the situation would allow. 'I've seen your brother do it before . . .'

'Don't wank in front of her!' Turgut growled in Turkish. And then he hit his brother, already cowering on the ground in front of him, with a hard, closed fist. 'Not her!'

'Turgut!'

He looked across in response to his mother's voice.

'What are you doing?'

'This is the lady I told you about, Mother,' he said. 'Kemalettin was masturbating when we opened the outside door. Imagine! In front of her! Can you think of anything . . .' And then he saw İkmen with his mother and he stopped talking immediately.

'I'm sorry,' Kemalettin murmured as he nursed the blow he had taken on his head from his brother. 'I'm so, so sorry!'

'Shut up.' Turgut took another swipe at his brother.

'Stop it!' the American squeaked. 'This is just brutal! I can't be here for this!'

And with that she walked out of the courtyard and back into the street. Just as he was about to comment on this, İkmen's mobile phone began to ring.

A team of firefighters, together with some nurses and doctors from the nearby Italian and Cihangir Hospitals, were making their way gingerly but swiftly into the Cohens' apartment building. When Mehmet Süleyman asked if he could join in with their efforts he was told that he'd be welcome provided he allowed all of those present to do their jobs.

'I'm not interested in why this happened,' a young doctor from the Cihangir told him. 'My only priority is to make sure that anyone who is still living, stays that way.'

'The people on the first floor, the Cohens, are like my

second family,' Süleyman replied. 'I don't know what I'll do if anything has happened to them.'

The young doctor just smiled by way of reply. After all, what could he say? He didn't know whether all or any of the Cohens were alive any more than Süleyman did.

Because the Cohens' building was old, of nineteenth-century vintage, it was also strong, especially at its core. So in spite of the fact that the façade had crumbled to almost nothing, the stairwell and, the firefighters said, the back of the building was probably intact. So progress up to the first floor was swift for those not engaged in attending those very few survivors at ground level. Getting through the Cohens' stout old front door proved rather more time-consuming. As the firefighters attempted to smash it down with their axes, Süleyman found himself becoming both impatient with their efforts and afraid for what might be behind that door in equal measures.

'Come on! Come on!' he muttered as the door finally gave way under a ferocious assault by fire-axes and fell backwards into the Cohens' hallway.

Without a thought in his head save the fate of his friends, Süleyman rushed forwards only to be held back by the large, meaty arm of a senior firefighter.

'You can only be here if you're prepared to do what we tell you,' the man said roughly. 'There could be ruptured gas bottles or anything in there. This is our territory, Inspector. Keep back.'

Chastened, the policeman stood to one side as the senior fire officer and two of his men stepped over the shattered door and walked into the Cohens' apartment. A fourth officer stood at the entrance, holding the medics and the policeman at bay until his colleagues gave him the all clear.

After what seemed like an eternity, one of the men inside the apartment called out, 'Nazir!'

'Sir,' the man at the entrance replied.

'Clear in here. Three live ones. Send the medics through.'

Three live ones. Three! As the doctors and nurses pushed past him in order to get to the family, Süleyman just took a moment to revel in the fact that the Cohens were alive. He didn't know what kind of condition they were in but they were alive, and so as soon as the doctors had passed him, he followed them through into the apartment.

He had to climb over a lot of familiar but shattered furniture in order to get to the main living room. Once there, however, everything was unfamiliar – the paucity of flooring, the lack of anything even resembling furniture, the doctors and nurses leaning over tiny, hunched figures, the huge blood spatters on the wallpaper. And when one of the figures suddenly and piercingly screamed, Mehmet Süleyman felt his mind melt with the horror of it.

Although İkmen knew from what Fatma had told him that Hulya and the baby were all right, he felt his legs go weak and he had to sit down. What were believed to be terrorist attacks on two İstanbul synagogues, the Neve Şalom in Karaköy and the Beth Israel in Şişli, had resulted in heavy casualties. Mehmet Süleyman was, apparently, at the scene in Karaköy and had taken it upon himself to let Hulya know about her husband and in-laws as soon as he could. The Cohens lived opposite the Neve Şalom. İkmen could see their building or rather what remained of it, on Dr Ali's small black and white television set.

'Well, it's good that your daughter and grandson are safe, isn't it?' Inspector Erten said nervously as he watched the elderly doctor pass İkmen a glass of water.

'Yes.'

'And if her in-laws . . .'

'Balthazar Cohen is someone I've known all my life,' İkmen interrupted. 'As well as a grandchild, we share memories, you know . . .'

Erten looked away, although whether this was because he was embarrassed by İkmen's anxiety or alarmed at Cohen's Jewish name, the İstanbul policeman neither knew nor cared.

'Drink your water, Inspector,' Dr Ali said through what seemed to be a set of very ill-fitting false teeth. 'It will make you feel better.'

'Can I smoke?' İkmen asked as he dug a hand into one of his jacket pockets.

'This is Turkey,' the doctor shrugged as he, too, retrieved cigarettes and a lighter from his jacket pocket and lit up. 'I know as a doctor I shouldn't be saying this, but I've resolved only to give up once we're in the European Union. They'll have banned it by then, anyway – look at Ireland.'

İkmen, who had now lit up himself and who continued to stare open-mouthed at the television screen, didn't answer. In view of what was happening in İstanbul everything else that was going on seemed very trivial – even his own state of health. In the wake of Fatma's telephone call, İkmen had felt very sick and so Erten had immediately brought him across to the local doctor, Ali. When they had arrived, the elderly doctor was already glued to his television, watching the events Fatma had told İkmen about on the telephone unfolding bloodily across the screen. He duly took İkmen's blood pressure, which was surprisingly normal, and then gave him a glass of water. It was only when TRT switched their reportage from Karaköy to Şişli that İkmen began to think about the other possibilities inherent in his current situation. After all, if Dr Ali was the only local physician in the village, it was very possible he knew just what afflicted Kemalettin Senar. He had certainly, according to Erten, attended the late Aysu Alkaya. Not that Dr Ali, in the absence of an official order, was obliged to say anything about his patients to anyone, police or otherwise, as İkmen well knew. But Dr Ali was not, it seemed, averse to such a conversation.

'It is said, Inspector İkmen, that Nalan Senar's father, "deli" Yurt, as he was known in the village, was an idiot,' the doctor said.

With half an eye still on the television screen and half on the doctor, İkmen said, 'What do you mean?'

'I mean that Yurt drooled, talked nonsense and, on occasion, was known to expose himself.'

'Like Kemalettin.'

'Yes. In fact Kemalettin even looks a bit like old Yurt who was also dark, if not as dark as his grandson. But that is by the way. In spite of the nature of Kemalettin's distracted condition one cannot, necessarily, attribute it to his grandfather. That would be most unscientific. After all' – the doctor smiled – 'diagnostic techniques were very primitive when Yurt was alive.'

Although not entirely willing to tear his gaze away from

the television screen, İkmen did, however, do so and, intrigued, looked the old man hard in the eyes. 'Doctor,' he said, 'I know that you can't actually tell me what Kemalettin Senar is suffering from, but do I take it that some sort of genetic, er . . .'

'Some genetic diseases are now far more simple to track than they were in the past,' Dr Ali said. 'For instance, let us take, say, Huntington's disease.'

'What's that?'

'It is a form of early onset dementia. In Europe they called it something or other's dance, because of the trembling the disease produces, like some saint's movements, I don't know. Anyway, initial signs first manifest at around about thirty or forty years of age. If it hasn't started to show itself at fifty, one is probably OK. It is incurable and terminal but in recent years we have been able to test people both for the disease itself and for carriers of it.'

İkmen raised his eyebrows. 'And it's genetic, you say.'

'Yes. If a person has one parent who either develops the disease or is a carrier, he or she has a fifty per cent chance of developing the condition. If both parents are affected, it is one hundred per cent certain that any offspring will be affected. Of course with grandparents . . .'

'So this Yurt had this condition?'

'I don't know,' the doctor shrugged as he knocked his cigarette against the side of his ashtray. 'He was never tested, they couldn't do it in those days. Huntington's is only one possibility for Yurt's condition.'

'But then surely,' Inspector Erten, who had been listening intently to this conversation, now joined in, 'Nalan Senar, assuming that Kemalettin has this disease, has to carry it in her DNA, doesn't she?'

'Nalan Senar has never had a medical test in her life,' the doctor replied with a smile.

TRT's coverage of the tragedies in İstanbul switched back to the devastated scenes on the streets of Karaköy, forcing İkmen's eyes to fully attend to them once again. Not that he could make out anyone he knew from the small, grainy picture on the screen. Only what was left of the Neve Şalom synagogue and the façade of the Cohens' apartment building could be seen with any clarity. If only he had taken Hulya up on her offer for her and Berekiah to come and look after the children while İkmen took Fatma with him to Cappadocia. But that would have meant that he would have had to tell his wife about Alison, and that would never have done! It would, however, have been preferable to what had happened . . .

'But Kemalettin Senar has had tests?' Erten, less concerned with İstanbul than İkmen was, asked.

'Yes.'

'Which proved positive for this Huntington's disease?'

'That I cannot tell you,' Dr Ali responded.

'I understand.'

İkmen, who had been listening in spite of the television set, once again turned his eyes away from the horrors of İstanbul and said, 'OK, Doctor, let's look at it another way, then, shall we? If you tested Nalan Senar to see whether or not she was a carrier of Huntington's and you discovered that she was, would you be surprised? Or rather, would you be surprised if she wasn't?'

'I'd be very surprised if she wasn't,' Dr Ali said as he

193

ground his cigarette out in his ashtray and then leaned back into his chair. 'Nalan's husband and his family were always very normal. When something like a murder happens, outsiders can view villages like Muratpaşa as hotbeds of aberration. But most people are normal here, really. The Senars, as they were, were very nice people. Tatar Senar married Nalan because she was beautiful and, more importantly, blond. Shallow, I know, but men will be men as we know . . . The Senars were always more prosperous and therefore more educated than Yurt's family. Nalan was lucky that she managed to excite Tatar's lust to the extent that she did. Mind you, once they were married he lost interest in her and the children very quickly. Even when he was dying he was still harsh with poor Turgut, impatient with Kemalettin.'

'I see.'

'Poor Kemalettin. But then the village, in general, is very accepting of his peccadilloes,' the doctor continued. 'None of us enjoys seeing a grown man abusing himself in the street but as you have probably observed yourself, Inspector, we generally let it go without comment. There is not, after all, any point in telling the poor man not to do it. I know that some try, but his mother and his brother barely notice any more.'

Unless, İkmen thought, one is a certain American tourist that Turgut Senar seems to be taking a great interest in. He'd been furious when Kemalettin had manipulated himself in front of Dolores Lavell. And yet the American, as a previous visitor to the area, had witnessed this 'phenomenon' before. Turgut Senar also had seen the American probably many times in the past. This begged a question about why he was so enamoured with her now and not before? He was married, with a child, and so he had a lot to lose. Had the Lavell woman perhaps bought herself a face-lift since her last visit? He knew rich Americans did such things. But then maybe there was another reason for Dolores' popularity with Turgut, which had nothing to do with her looks. But İkmen couldn't think round that problem for the time being, and so after a few more seconds' thought he said, 'People in this village seem to be obsessed with blood, inheritance and what have you.'

The doctor frowned. 'Yes. There was considerable inbreeding in the past. Not now. It's caused trouble over the years.'

İkmen tore his eyes away from the television again, suddenly galvanised. 'Did you know that Aysu Alkaya was pregnant before her disappearance, Dr Ali?'

'No.' He looked down at his desk. 'I was as surprised, probably more so than many others, when I learned of it.'

'Why is that?' İkmen asked.

Dr Ali sighed and then looked up. 'Because of the deformity to her feet,' he said. 'I was convinced that Ziya Kahraman would reject her. I actually advised her not to marry him. Ziya was very anxious to produce an "untainted" son. I thought that once he saw her feet he would assume that they were the result of inbreeding and throw her out.'

'But that didn't happen.'

'No.'

'Doctor, is the phenomenon of extra digits always connected to in-breeding?' İkmen asked.

'Not always. But in a primitive place such as Muratpaşa was back in the nineteen eighties, that, as well as attributions of evil and ownership by Şeytan, were usually the assumptions that attend these cases.'

'I see.' İkmen turned his gaze back fully to the television once again. Someone was being brought out of the Cohens' apartment building on a stretcher. He or she wasn't moving.

Mehmet Süleyman had wanted to stay with his friend, but at the same time he fully understood why that just wasn't possible. He'd seen some terrible things – many of them worse than this – in the course of his career as a police officer, but he'd never felt so affected before; he'd never known a person's screams so tear his heart in all of his life. Even out in the street where he now sat with Berekiah Cohen's traumatised parents he could still hear the young man's screams of pain as the doctor and nurse attending him attempted to free his shoulder from the enormous shard of glass that held him impaled to the wall behind what was left of his bed.

'I don't understand why he's in so much pain!' Balthazar said as he wept into the folds of the blanket a nurse had draped in his lap to cover the stumps of his legs. 'Don't these people have morphine or something?'

'Morphine can only do so much,' his wife said as she held on limply to Mehmet Süleyman's hand, her eyes glassed over with shock. 'Berekiah is fixed to the wall. There is blood just . . . it's everywhere, it's down the walls, it's . . .'

And then she screamed. Mehmet Süleyman threw his arms round her and held on so tightly his hands went first white and then blue. 'They're doing everything they can for him, Estelle. He's young and strong . . .'

'I knew that no good would come of it,' Balthazar said as he shook his head violently from side to side. 'I told Çetin Bey.'

196

A man with a thick moustache and impenetrable, hooded eyes staggered across the piles of rubble in the street towards the ambulance beside which the Cohens and Süleyman were crouching.

'I told the woman, too,' Balthazar continued as he completely failed to register the face or form of the newcomer in their midst. 'A Jew and a Muslim cannot be together, it's like a dog and a cat . . .'

'This, this . . . whatever this is has nothing to do with Hulya and Berekiah,' Süleyman said. 'Nothing!'

'They've bombed our synagogue, Mehmet!' the crippled man yelled. 'And the Beth Israel over in Şişli!'

'I . . .'

'Inspector Süleyman . . .'

In response to this entirely different voice, Süleyman raised his head from Estelle Cohen's shoulder and looked up. 'Melik?'

'I've been trying to call your mobile phone,' İzzet Melik replied gruffly.

'Yes, I . . .' He'd been aware it had gone off once. But he hadn't been able to answer it. He'd been lost in the dizzying swirls of blood behind Berekiah Cohen's screaming face.

'Then I heard about all this and I came up,' Melik continued. 'It's terrible.'

Another scream from inside the apartment building caused Estelle Cohen to grasp on to Mehmet Süleyman still tighter. 'My poor child! My soul!'

'Sssh! Sssh!' Süleyman soothed. 'He's going to be all right, Estelle. He's young and he's fit. He has a wife and a son . . .'

Melik, who didn't know the Cohens or understand

197

Süleyman's relationship to them, cleared his throat. So harsh was the sound that it caused Süleyman to look up at him again. 'What?'

'Traffic officer on his way home found a body round the side of the Saray Hamam two hours ago. Little homo with his throat slit. I was just wondering what we know about this peeper when the Neve Şalom went up.' Just very slightly he smiled. 'What a day, eh?'

Chapter 13

The news that her father's young wife had been pregnant when she died hadn't come as a shock to Nazlı Kahraman, though she'd had to feign surprise for the benefit of that policeman from İstanbul. To not do so would have looked bad. Had he discovered that she had known that Aysu Alkaya hadn't had a period for at least two months prior to her death he might have come to a very damning conclusion. But then in the accepted sense, officially, for want of a better word, Nazlı hadn't known about Aysu's condition any more than her late father. Aysu hadn't told her husband, that man so desperate for a son, that man who would have treated his wife so much more kindly had he known. Ziya's daughter had failed to inform her father, too . . .

Nazlı Kahraman looked out of her kitchen window and into the courtyard where her young husband was chopping logs for the stove. He had his shirt off and his well-sculpted chest gleamed with sweat. But the sight of him didn't arouse any sort of interest or desire within her. That sort of thing was disgusting and besides, she was worried. Now that it was halfway through the afternoon she was very tired and hungry too. For all her protestations to her slack 'Greek' husband, she wasn't finding Ramazan any easier as the years progressed. Nazlı walked out of her kitchen and, ducking her head under the rough tufa doorway into the hall, she grabbed the telephone from off the wall and dialled a number. While she waited for someone to answer she chewed her bottom lip with the top plate of her false teeth.

When a man's voice eventually came on the line she said, 'Baha, it's Nazlı Hanım; we need to talk.'

Baha Ermis took a sharp intake of breath. 'What for, Hanım?'

'That policeman from İstanbul, he knows what I have always known about my "stepmother" and her delicate condition.'

'Haldun Alkaya has told everyone.'

'The İstanbul policeman İkmen wants me to have this DNA test at some point.'

'So?' Baha Ermis coughed suddenly and then, just as rapidly, he stopped. 'You have nothing to hide, Nazlı Hanım.'

'No, but maybe my father did.'

'What do you mean?' Ermis said. 'Ziya Bey didn't kill Aysu Alkaya. That madman Kemalettin did it. He got to her, got her pregnant . . .'

'Baha, I need to trust you with this . . .'

'Hanım?'

She knew that she could trust him. Baha Ermis, like his father before him, was devoted to the Kahramans. It was indeed one of the reasons why Nazlı could never quite believe Baha's story about how he'd seen Kemalettin Senar with Aysu Alkaya outside the Kahraman house on the night that the girl disappeared. Of course it was, had to be possible. But Baha was and always had been obsequious to her as well as being, in general, a gossip and a liar.

Nazlı Kahraman took a deep breath. 'I didn't see my father go to bed the night Aysu disappeared,' she said. 'And in the morning he looked dishevelled. He had not changed his clothes.'

'Ziya Bey was old, Hanım. Maybe he couldn't sleep. Sometimes he would sit up at night going over the accounts, you remember?' He didn't add that Ziya Kahraman frequently did this in order to find areas in which he might make still more savings.

'Only in his office,' Nazlı replied. 'And he wasn't in his office. He was ... elsewhere. Baha, did you really see Kemalettin Senar and Aysu outside our house that night?'

'Well, yes, I ...'

'The police, you know, can use this DNA to tell who killed her. There can be no mistake. They will be taking my sample to look at both me and my father. Look, Baha, I know you have always been loyal and faithful to this family and I am very grateful, but ...' She swallowed hard. 'Baha, on the life of your mother you must tell me the truth. Was Kemalettin Senar really outside the house with Aysu that night? Was it him or was it my father? I have to ...'

'I don't know who it was, Hanım!' the voice on the other end cried. 'It was a figure, slim and a little hunched. It could have been Kemalettin, most likely it was him! With respect to Ziya Bey, Hanım, it must have been Senar who made Aysu with child. Ziya Bey was old ...'

'He took her the night of their marriage. There was blood on the wedding sheet, I saw it. But, well, if the child was Kemalettin's then the police will be able to see that too with this DNA,' she sighed. 'What if my father knew he had been dishonoured, Baha? He would never have tolerated such a thing!'

'Ziya Bey was an honourable man. The girl was a whore, what choice did he have?'

'But we don't know that he killed her. We must never speak of it! Not to anyone!'

'No!'

'And yet . . .' She leaned heavily against the wall as if deflated. 'If the child was Kemalettin Senar's, why would he, even a madman like him, kill both it and Aysu? I can see how he could run off with the girl, but . . .'

'Kemalettin Senar is, as you have said, a madman. Who knows what he might do, Hanım?' And then through gritted teeth he continued, 'It was a bad day when the policeman from İstanbul came to this village. With his tests and DNA. Just because he is the cousin of Menşure Hanım, he thinks he can interfere . . .'

'He is an agent of the law,' Nazlı breathed fatalistically. 'What can we do?'

'There must be something,' Baha Ermis replied. 'Let me think about it.'

Suddenly angered by his arrogant and obsequious posturing, Nazlı Hanım said, 'Oh, for the love of Allah, you can do nothing! Stop fooling yourself, Baha! You are nothing! I'll give you nothing! Why make yourself so small and humble for no reason? A closed mouth is all that I want from you!'

And then she put the telephone back on the wall and closed her eyes. There was of course another dark and, Nazlı hoped, secret reason why her father could have killed Aysu Alkaya too. Those feet. Even if she had been pregnant with his child,

202

her father could never have tolerated those ghastly deformities. As soon as he'd seen them, as soon as Aysu had tearfully allowed him to see them the morning after their wedding, Ziya Kahraman, so he had said, had decided that the girl was to be little more than his servant. Nazlı had been so pleased – then.

The policeman from İstanbul was going to blow the village apart with his strange and frightening medical tests and there was absolutely nothing she could do about it now.

'But of course Ziya Bey was the father of this child you say my Aysu was having!' Haldun Alkaya cried as tears gathered at the corners of his eyes. 'She was a good girl, untouched when she married! There was blood on her marriage sheet . . .'

'Haldun Bey, I do not mean to cause offence,' İkmen said. 'But I must explore every possibility, it is my job.'

'It was I who suggested this DNA testing, if you remember, Çetin Bey,' the old man said. 'To find the true killer of my daughter. Why would I bother for a whore? Maybe I would even have killed her myself?'

İkmen did not respond to what had been one of the theories that had crossed several minds about Aysu Alkaya's death over the years. Some men did, after all, consider it their right to kill any female relative who even remotely threatened the honour of their family. Sexual indiscretion was the most common cause of this type of scenario.

'Apparently neither Nazlı Hanım nor her father knew of Aysu's condition . . .'

'Well, she would have been afraid to tell that monster Nazlı,' Haldun Alkaya replied bitterly. 'I would not have put it past her to abort my poor daughter had she known, to protect her fortune and her interests. And anyway, you only have her word that she didn't know of my daughter's pregnancy. She could have killed Aysu.'

'But Haldun Bey,' İkmen said, 'with your daughter's deformity . . .'

'Ah, you know . . .'

'You identified her body in part by her feet, sir,' İkmen said. 'You must have known how Ziya Kahraman felt about such "defects" . . .'

'Yes. Yes.' The old man put his head briefly into his hands and then said, 'I suppose you could say that we set out to trick the Lemon King, in a way, Aysu and I. We thought that once she was pregnant with his child none of that would matter. Ziya Bey was so captivated by my daughter.'

'It didn't occur to you that Ziya Kahraman might become angry or feel cheated or . . .'

'He never spoke a word of it to me,' the old man said.

İkmen silently wondered whether the Lemon King had felt too humiliated by this deception to speak. After all, it had been perpetrated by someone who must have been, to Ziya Kahraman, a very inferior person.

'Haldun Bey,' Inspector Erten said. 'You never mentioned anything of this to us at the time, twenty years ago. We didn't know . . .'

'You've never known anything, stupid police in Nevşehir!' Haldun Alkaya said as he waved his arms agitatedly in the air. 'Twenty years and you do nothing! Nothing! Why should I parade my poor daughter's defects in front of you, eh? Why don't you have DNA as they do in İstanbul? Nevşehir is a city, İstanbul is a city . . .'

İkmen smiled. 'I think, Haldun Bey, that İstanbul and Nevşehir are rather different cities.'

'So I'm a peasant who has never been to İstanbul, what do I know?' the old man said.

They all sat in silence for a few moments. Almost without thinking, İkmen had started to take the lead on this ancient case of Aysu Alkaya. Erten was not very forthright which, İkmen knew, one could get away with in the countryside. In İstanbul he would have been eaten for breakfast and his bones sucked dry many years ago. But then one was paid to be like that back in the city. And yet İkmen knew that he, too, was hardly on top form now. He wanted to be back in İstanbul. Fatma had said she'd heard from Hulya again and that the Cohens were all right, but Berekiah had been taken to hospital. No one as yet could comment upon his condition, but İkmen was anxious about it. Berekiah was, after all, not just the son of a friend. He was his little girl's husband, the father of İkmen's own precious grandson, Timur. But then to go now was not going to do İkmen any good. He only had to wait until the following morning for Arto Sarkissian to give him a comfortable and rapid ride back to the city.

'If we find useful samples on Aysu's body, we'll need to take a DNA swab from you, Haldun Bey,' İkmen said gravely.

The old man shrugged. 'I don't have a problem with that. Why should I?'

'Inspector Erten will keep you informed,' İkmen said.

'You are going, Çetin Bey?'

İkmen looked round the shabby sparseness of the lonely old man's chimney house and shook his head sadly. In a way it was a shame to leave now just as he felt he might be getting somewhere, working his way through this village's psychological wounds. But what choice did he have? His life and problems were back in İstanbul.

'Yes, I'm going,' İkmen said. 'But my colleagues at the Forensic Institute and Inspector Erten will keep me informed about this case I am sure.'

Erten smiled weakly, which gave İkmen very little confidence in what he had just said but he acknowledged his temporary colleague anyway. After leaving Haldun Alkaya, Erten and İkmen discussed how matters might proceed when Arto Sarkissian arrived the following day and then, once their business was concluded, the local policeman went back to his car for the journey home to Nevşehir. It had just started to get dark when İkmen met Dolores Lavell coming out of the Cappudocia Coffee Bean. She still looked upset and so he went over to her and said, 'I'm sorry, Miss Lavell, I should have come after you when you left the Senars' house today. I could see that you were upset. But I had some news from İstanbul . . .'

'The bomb explosion.' She shook her head in disbelief. 'I heard about that. I hope your family are OK, Inspector.'

İkmen shrugged. 'My son-in-law has been taken to hospital. That is all I know. İnşallah he will recover.'

'Yes.' She looked down at the ground, her brow furrowed with what looked like anxiety.

'Miss Lavell, Dolores,' İkmen began, 'may I ask if it is not too intrusive, what your connection to Turgut Senar and his family might be? I believe you have been here before . . .'

'Turgut and I just knew each other by sight until we took that balloon flight together,' the American replied.

'Apparently he'd tried to speak to me before but never had the courage to do so.' She smiled. 'I mean, at my age I should be flattered. He's not young but he's a fit, attractive man and all. I know he's married . . .'

'It didn't strike you as strange that he, a married man, should wish to take you to meet his mother?'

'I went to see a real traditional chimney house, Inspector,' Dolores replied spiritedly. 'Not hang out with Turgut's mom.'

'I beg your pardon,' İkmen replied.

'I'll freely admit that me and Turgut had a thing together last night. I'm an American, I don't have to live by these strict sexual rules you have over here. And I'm a grown-up. I can, so I do, and it isn't as if I'm going to tell the guy's wife. It's casual . . .'

'I'm not so sure whether that applies in Turgut's case,' İkmen said as he watched her nervously attempt to smooth the foundation cream that so liberally covered her face. 'Turkish men are generally – serious.'

'Well, I can assure you, Inspector, I've given that man no cause to believe he's my one and only true love,' Dolores said forcefully. 'The sex was just sex, I can assure you. We did it then shook hands and went our separate ways like a couple of regular guys. The most intimate thing I've done with that man is show him an old photograph of my dear old dad. But then maybe for someone like him, someone who had such a minimal relationship with his father, my love for Dad is just endearing. Who knows?'

And then with a toss of her head she left him to go, she said, to visit a small and apparently heavily frescoed rock chapel just behind the launderette on the Nevşehir road. İkmen, alone now, pulled his jacket closely in around his thin shoulders against the increasing cold and then phoned Fatma. Surely by now there had to be some more news about Berekiah.

Zelfa wrapped the largest towel she possessed around her husband's dripping body and then led him from the bathroom into their bedroom. When he had eventually managed to get home he had been covered in dust and blood, which was why she had taken him straight to the bathroom. He had been horrified by the blood. He'd said he didn't know whose it was. He feared it had belonged to Berekiah Cohen. But now it was gone, washed away, unlike the images that would keep on replaying hideous sequences of terror on and on in Mehmet Süleyman's head.

As he sat down on the bed, he said, 'Shouldn't somebody be with Hulya at the hospital?'

'Her brother Sınan is with her,' Zelfa responded gently as she sat down next to him. 'Fatma has taken Timur.'

'Balthazar and Estelle are not capable,' Süleyman said. 'When Berekiah comes out of surgery they will go mad, I know they will! I must get back to them . . .'

'No!'

'Yes!' He stood quickly and then raced, naked, over to where his wife had dropped his bloodied clothes earlier.

'Mehmet, you can't go back to the hospital. You've done enough today! You . . .'

'I don't know who bombed those synagogues,' he said as he pulled his clothes on to his body with some violence. 'But we should have known!'

'What? The police?' Zelfa switched rapidly into her own

native language, English. 'God Almighty, Mehmet, it was a terrorist attack! The whole point is that the security services don't know it's about to happen!'

'It's a failure,' he said, 'it's part of a catalogue of failure! The peeper struck again last night! I know it was him. At the hamam, where the gay boys go. I know it! This time he killed. A young boy is dead because I don't get it! I don't understand what pattern this offender conforms to! Up on rooftops, down on the ground . . .'

'Well, maybe there isn't a pattern! Or maybe if there is, it's something you can't understand,' Zelfa replied. 'If he's mentally ill there could be some sort of logic at play that you can't get. I mean, I know we haven't been together for a bit, but you've surely been married to me for long enough to understand the basic irrationality behind most disordered events.'

'Yes, of course, but . . .' He put his heavily stained jacket back on and then fumbled in its pockets for cigarettes.

Zelfa moved forward and handed her packet to him. 'Here, have these,' she said. 'I threw yours away. They were covered in . . .'

'Berekiah's blood.'

They both stood looking into each other's eyes for a few seconds as the import of his words really took hold. He then leaned forward and gathered Zelfa into his arms, squeezing her body tight against his ribcage.

'If that boy dies . . .'

'Sssh, sssh,' she soothed, rubbing the back of his head with her hand as one would comfort a baby. 'Come on, there is nothing you can do for the moment.'

'I can go to the hospital. I can wait.'

She pushed herself a little away from him and said, 'Like that? Mehmet, you'll frighten everyone, covered in blood. Please, please get some rest.'

'But . . .'

'I'll stay awake. I'll let you know as soon as the telephone rings.'

'As soon as it rings?'

'The very second,' Zelfa said as she led him back to the bed and, almost without his noticing, removed his jacket. 'Lie down.'

Oddly for him, he did as he was told and for a few minutes Zelfa, who had lain down beside him, was convinced that he was drifting off into some kind of, albeit fitful, sleep. But then it would hardly have been a restful sleep for Mehmet. With the exception of a brief detour to view what could be the body of the peeper's latest victim, he had spent the entire day either at the hospital or amongst the ruins of the Neve Şalom Synagogue and its environs. He had as a consequence seen things that, hardened officer as he was, no one can see and not be affected by. Loss of life had been heavy.

But Mehmet Süleyman was still destined not to sleep for a while. A shrill beeping from the table beside the bed indicated that he had a text message on his mobile telephone. One still tense arm shot out and he grabbed the instrument.

'What's this?' he murmured.

'Whoever it is, tell them to fuck off,' Zelfa grumbled in English. 'You need to sleep.'

'Yes.'

But as he read the message, Mehmet Süleyman knew that he couldn't ignore it. İzzet Melik was not a man given to either high drama or unnecessary contact with his boss. So if İzzet wanted to see him, immediately, at the Saray Hamam in Karaköy, there had to be a very good reason.

Whilst waiting for İkmen to appear in the restaurant, young Tom the Englishman had got into conversation with the only other American woman, apart from Dolores Lavell, currently resident in the village. Emily Bronstein, though by no means a prudish woman, was nevertheless not entirely approving of her countrywoman's behaviour.

'To just go off with that guide,' she said as she twirled her napkin in her fingers, 'well, it's a little cheap, I think. I'm not judging her, you understand, but . . .'

'Oh, the Med is a place where Western women do go mad,' Tom replied with a smile. 'Years ago an aunt of mine . . .'

'Tom!' A small, thin hand landed on the Englishman's shoulder, causing him to look up.

'Inspector.'

'I am so sorry that I am late,' İkmen said as he pulled the chair next to the Englishman out and sat down.

'That's OK,' Tom said cheerily. 'Emily here has been keeping me well entertained.'

İkmen looked across at the attractive, smiling woman and bowed his head just very slightly.

'But now maybe I should go,' Emily said. 'Tom . . .'

'Oh, no, please do stay, Miss, er . . .' İkmen stuttered.

'It's Mrs Bronstein,' the American said as she came to his rescue. 'Emily. Remember?'

'Yes, of course, but . . .'

'Em and I were gossiping, actually, Inspector,' Tom said

211

and then, lowering his voice, he continued, 'about Em's fellow countrywoman.'

'Miss Lavell?'

Tom raised his eyebrows. 'Seems it's all on between her and that Turgut chap,' he said. 'Moved in for the kill on that balloon flight we took.'

Menşure Tokatlı herself came to take their dinner order. Unnervingly she had Kismet the cat at her feet. As disinclined towards food as ever, İkmen just ordered a plate of mantı while Tom and Emily went for İskender kebab and chicken şiş kebab respectively. As Menşure and the cat moved away from the table, İkmen said in Turkish, 'Is Kismet after scraps or does he have his eyes on perhaps a still-warm limb?'

Menşure turned and said, 'He, unlike you, Çetin, is a creature of high breeding. People willingly tend to his every need.'

Once she had gone, İkmen turned back to his fellow diners and the English language that they used.

'So at the risk of being a gossip myself, what do you think about Dolores Lavell and Turgut the guide?' he said. 'Do you have any theory about why he is suddenly interested in her? She has been coming here for some time, it would seem.'

'Dunno,' Tom said. 'He just seemed to latch on to her in that balloon.'

Emily picked up her knife and fork from the table and fiddled with them for a moment before first grimacing and then frowning. 'That whole thing with that old photo of her dad was creepy,' she said.

Dolores Lavell's 'dear old dad' as İkmen recalled her saying herself. Not that he'd seen the photograph with his own eyes.

'Creepy? In what way?'

Emily shrugged. 'Maybe I just feel like I do because I know she comes from the south.'

'What do you mean?' İkmen asked.

'Well, you know that until the sixties we had segregation in the south. Whites and blacks couldn't mix.'

'Yes.'

'That's all over now, at least according to the law,' Emily said. 'So it's weird to come across someone who's obviously so freaked about it still.'

İkmen frowned.

'Well, look, you must have noticed how shocked that guide and I were when we saw her photo,' Emily said. 'It was a shock.'

'Why?'

'Because the guy, her dad, was black. I don't know about the guide, but it suddenly hit me what she'd been doing. Creeped me out.'

Tom poured out water for everyone from a large bottle on the table and said, 'What was that, then?'

'All that make-up all over her face, it's to cover up her colour,' Emily said. 'With her hair dead straight like that and all that stuff on her skin . . . she's trying to be white and it's just creepy. And people don't need to do that these days. My mom was Japanese, you can see that and I'm proud of it. I don't know, maybe it's to do with her being from the south.'

'I've never been there myself, but I've heard that places like Alabama are still quite primitive and prejudiced,' Tom said gravely. 'Maybe poor Dolores has suffered discrimination. Maybe it's a sort of a protection – the make-up and what

213

have you. I mean, her mother must have been white, I should imagine.'

'It's a bit Michael Jackson,' Emily replied. 'It . . .'

'It's my business is what it is,' a southern drawl interrupted. Dolores Lavell was right behind Tom's left shoulder.

'Er . . .'

'And for your information, Miss Bronstein, my hair is naturally straight and I wear make-up because I have acne scars.' Then, turning to Tom, she said, 'But you were right about my mom. She was white. My parents never married; you couldn't in those days because of segregation.' Her eyes blazed. 'It isn't me who's prejudiced! I leave that to trendy-in-denial Californians like Miss Bronstein. If I was prejudiced, why would I show folks that picture of my dad? He always took an interest in me even when, years ago, we could hardly see one another. I'm proud of him. Turgut understands that.'

'I don't think so!' Emily said.

'It's a pity he does not seem at times to understand his brother with such sympathy,' İkmen said gravely. 'If indeed he has exhibited that emotion.'

'He just gets tired of poor Kemalettin's ways sometimes,' Dolores replied. 'I can understand that.'

'Can you? You seemed quite upset this morning.'

'I don't have to give any sort of account of myself to you! I understand about Kemalettin and how it all is!'

'I'm not certain that you do, Miss Lavell,' İkmen replied.

'Well, screw you!' And then with a toss of her head she walked out of the restaurant. Menşure, who had been watching the 'action' from the bar, shook her head at İkmen as Dolores Lavell left the building. The American had said that

214

she would be taking her dinner in the restaurant – something that had been, apparently, ruined by Menşure's cousin and his friends. She made a mental note to add one extra meal to his bill.

After a few moments' embarrassed silence, Tom said, 'Well, that was us told.'

'What?'

'About inheritance, Inspector,' Tom continued. 'Em and, I expect, you and I, once we knew, assumed that because Dolores' father was black she could not have straight hair. But that is perfectly possible. I went to school with a chap whose mother was Sri Lankan and he was whiter than me! No one can predict how inheritance will play out in reality. Genetics is such a lottery.'

'Yes, I'm learning rather a lot about that subject this week,' İkmen said as his cousin approached the table with a basket of bread. 'Menşure . . .'

'You upset Miss Lavell . . .'

'She's having it off with Turgut Senar!' İkmen said in Turkish. 'So sorry for her now, are you?'

'He shouldn't go with anyone outside of his marriage, especially not a foreigner,' she retorted.

'Why? Scared the experience will cause him to grow horns on his head?' İkmen turned back to his fellow diners and reverted to English. 'This village makes me tired,' he said. 'It's very picturesque, but the people . . . I want to go home.'

Chapter 14

The two constables on duty at the crime scene were not surprised to see him. İzzet Melik had warned them of his coming.

'Sir,' they both said, saluting as Süleyman passed them and walked down beside the now dark and silent hamam.

It was easy to see where İzzet Melik was. An inveterate smoker, just like his superior, the glowing end of his cigarette guided Süleyman to his side. What was surprising about this scenario was that Melik wasn't alone. Dr Mardin, Arto Sarkissian's assistant, was with him. She looked particularly anxious.

'So, Sergeant,' Süleyman said as he drew level with the pair, 'what is all this about?'

'Someone has tampered with the crime scene,' İzzet Melik said baldly.

'How do you know?'

'When the body was removed, after it had been measured and photographed, a forensic team moved in.'

Süleyman shrugged. 'Quite right.'

'If they'd been from the Forensic Institute, yes, Inspector,' Melik said sharply. 'But they weren't.'

'How do you know?'

'Because when the corpse failed to turn up at Dr

Sarkissian's laboratory, Dr Mardin called me and I called the Institute, thinking it might have gone there with the other data by mistake.'

'And had it?'

'No,' the young female pathologist cut in anxiously. 'I don't know where it went. It was missing for a good two hours.'

'So you do have the corpse of, what was the young man's name?'

'Nizam Tapan. Yes,' Dr Mardin said, 'but only since he's been cleaned.'

Süleyman frowned.

'Whoever took him, not boys from my laboratory, cleaned him up,' she continued angrily rather than fearfully now. 'There's not a scrap of evidence on him! I was all set to send my boys out to get him when I received a call from your boss, Commissioner Ardıç, to say that the police had taken care of transport and the boy was on his way. I counted on it taking an hour at most for them to get to me – it took three!'

'I see.' Süleyman took his cigarettes and lighter out of his pocket and lit up. Fortunately, the darkness of the night hid the many blood stains that still marked his jacket and trousers. Zelfa had nearly gone mad when he'd left the house in such a state. 'So you telephoned Sergeant Melik?'

'Yes. He'd called me originally from here.'

'I checked to see whether the body had turned up at the Institute by mistake,' Melik continued. 'It hadn't and neither had the samples from the site – the blood-soaked dust, the rubbish around the body.'

'Have the samples turned up since?'

'Apparently, yes.' Melik frowned. 'At a laboratory out of

217

town, or so the Institute told me a couple of hours ago. They will get the results from this unknown place and, I am told, pass them on to you, Inspector.'

'But you don't like it, do you, İzzet? Dr Mardin?'

'No, Inspector.'

'No.'

He looked at them both and then sighed. He didn't like it either. First he was, seemingly, prevented from talking to a live peeper victim, Abdullah Aydın, and now his people were having dead bodies and vital evidence on the case disappear from view. Furthermore, the commissioner seemed to be involved in both instances. It was something he knew he'd have to take further on both his own and Dr Mardin's account.

'These teams who came to pick up the body and the samples,' Süleyman said to Melik, 'did you recognise anyone?'

'No, but then I've not been in the city for very long, have I, Inspector? I mean, if this had been İzmir . . .'

'Yes, it's all right, İzzet,' Süleyman said, 'I'm not blaming you for anything. I take it these constables are unaware of these matters.'

'Yes. They think you've just come out to see the site again.'

'Good.' He coughed. 'Leave it with me and keep what has passed here just between ourselves.'

'Why do you think I sent you a text?' İzzet Melik snapped. 'Why do you think we're out here in the dark? I'm not James Bond and neither are you, Inspector Süleyman.'

His manner was, to Süleyman's way of thinking, unnecessarily brusque. But he let it pass – for the moment. After all, Melik's attitude was hardly top of his list of things to deal with if one compared it to speaking to Ardıç about misplaced evidence. If indeed 'misplaced' was the right word. Süleyman and Melik escorted Dr Mardin back to her car and then stood in the street, in front of the Kamondo Steps on Voyvoda Caddesi. Constructed at the behest of a once-powerful Karaköy banking family, the strange art decoesque staircase had always fascinated Süleyman. When he had lived in the district with the Cohens, when the Cohens had still had an apartment to call their own, he had often come to the steps to sit and enjoy their stylish strangeness – and of course to get a little peace away from Balthazar's endless complaining. Suddenly he experienced terrible guilt about these old feelings he was having and so he turned back to Melik and the problem in hand.

'You were right to come to me with this, İzzet,' he said. 'I don't know why these things are happening, but it is better that I try to get to the bottom of it rather than you.'

'I agree,' Melik said as he put one cigarette out and lit another, trying to get as many in as possible before sunrise. 'I don't get paid an inspector's wage.'

'Nor do you always address me as "sir", which you should,' Süleyman responded sharply. 'You've done well to bring this malpractice to my attention, İzzet, but I am having problems with your attitude as I am sure you know.'

'Inspector . . .'

'Let me finish!' Süleyman then lowered his voice, unwilling to share his observations with small groups of people leaving iftar meals with very stuffed bellies. 'Your prejudices are, on occasion, stomach-turning, and your attitude towards women is offensive.'

'I'm a traditional man . . .'

'Who is going to have to shape up when all of this new legislation designed to bring us into line with the European Union really starts to bite.' Süleyman lit a cigarette of his own and then breathed out shakily. The events of earlier that day were still reverberating through his body. 'You are not my sort of person, İzzet, I could not call you my friend.'

'Nor I you, sir.' İzzet Melik scowled. 'But you're wrong if you think that I don't respect you. I know you're honest and I'm proud to be able to work for you. I'm old-fashioned and I'm not going to change, but I won't betray you, Inspector. I won't tell anyone about this evidence tampering and if you want my support with your superiors then you can have it. I always do my job to the best of my ability, up to the limits of my responsibilities as a sergeant.'

Süleyman looked down at the stocky figure of İzzet Melik, so clearly the very image of the coarse maganda of the 1990s' youth magazines. But instead of causing him to feel disgust, now he felt a sort of, if not affection, gratitude towards this man who had been nothing but honest with him. Melik didn't like him any more than Süleyman liked Melik. But that was all right because, for all his faults, Melik didn't let that colour his attitude towards his work. He knew what was right and what was wrong and what to do if the latter situation applied.

'Thank you, Sergeant,' Süleyman said eventually. 'I appreciate your candour.' The two men would then have gone their separate ways. But, seeing as he was now in the area, Süleyman had decided to go to the Italian hospital on Defterdar Yokuşu Sokak, which was where Berekiah Cohen was currently being treated. Melik, rather oddly, expressed a desire to accompany him.

'I speak Italian,' the sergeant offered as the two of them made their way up into Cihangir.

Süleyman, a little taken aback by this information, frowned. Italian and Melik did not somehow seem to go together very easily.

'And anyway,' the sergeant continued, 'you look a mess, sir, if you don't mind my saying . . .'

'Yes, well, it's been quite a day.'

'Not so bad for us as those poor people in that synagogue, though, eh?' Melik said. 'We've a Jewish population in İzmir as I expect you know. One of them was my Italian teacher. I've got friends in that community. I hope the young Cohen boy is all right.'

They threaded their way through the now heightened security measures in the district in, now companionable, silence.

İkmen had decided upon a walk before bedtime. Alone, by choice, he had declined the offer of company from Tom. It had just started to snow lightly once again and he wanted to get one last magical view of the chimneys before he headed on back to İstanbul. As the days had progressed he'd become increasingly jaded in his attitude towards Cappadocia, something he knew was not really right. After all, not everyone in the district was obsessed by blood purity and revenge. Most Cappadocians just wanted to get on with their lives, just like he did. İkmen took his mobile phone out of his pocket, looked at it and then replaced it once again. If Fatma or Hulya had any news about Berekiah they would let him know. Mehmet Süleyman who had, apparently, been at the scene when Berekiah was rescued from his family's apartment might have called. But he had not and so İkmen had to assume that his son-in-law's condition was unchanged.

'Penny for 'em.'

İkmen looked up into the smiling face of Rachelle Jones. She was muffled against the weather in a very long, thick fur coat.

'Penny for what?' İkmen replied in English.

'Your thoughts,' the Australian said. 'It's a saying. You say "Penny for your thoughts" when you want to know what someone is thinking.'

'And do you want to know what I am thinking, Miss Jones?'

'I'd like to know what you're doing rolling around the village in the snow with no coat on,' she replied as she boldly took one of his arms in hers. 'You must be perished!'

'I'm not warm, it's true,' İkmen said with a smile. 'But it's not cold like this in İstanbul yet. I brought the wrong clothes. As you see, I am not a man of fashion. One of my colleagues, Inspector Süleyman, now he knows how to dress. He is a very elegant man, younger too, you would like him, Miss Jones.'

'I might fancy him, but I'm sure I'd have a better time with you,' Rachelle said as she kicked into a small drift of snow underneath a street lamp. Powdery, the snowflakes flew into the air like tiny swan's feathers. 'You've shaken things up a bit since you've been here.'

'I've done little beyond putting some more advanced technology at the service of the police here,' İkmen replied. 'Oh, and I've upset some people by smoking in the street.'

'You and me both! And that's another reason why I like you,' Rachelle said. 'But you're married and . . .'

'Oh I am very married, Miss Jones. But then you know that from my cousin.'

They both laughed and then when they drew level with one of the roads leading up to her Tasmanian Devil pansiyon, Rachelle Jones stopped and took her arm away from the policeman's.

'I think I'm done with handsome blokes,' the Australian said as she turned her face upwards into the freezing cold snowflakes. 'I'd like a guy like you, someone who's unconventional, makes me laugh.'

'Not the good Captain Salman? He is an excellent fellow.'

'Yeah, maybe.' She looked very, very sad as she sighed. 'So you're off back to İstanbul tomorrow.'

'Yes.'

'Well, I hope you have a good journey and I hope your . . . son-is-law, is it?'

'Yes.'

'I hope he's going to be OK.'

'Thank you.'

She then leaned forward and kissed him very quickly on the lips. Her mouth felt cold and wet but not in any way unpleasant for all that.

'Miss Jones . . .'

'See ya, İkmen,' she said as she turned and waved him goodbye. 'Christ, this hill is shit!' she added as she began puffing her way up towards her property.

İkmen watched the Australian, with a smile on his face, until he could see her no more. Rachelle Jones was, he felt, a fine and excellent woman who deserved to be with a man who would treat her with the respect a knowledgeable expatriate like her was due. Just not him – or Altay Salman, for that matter. As he walked to the very edge of the village he saw the captain riding slowly towards him through the ever-thickening snow.

'Çetin?' He leaned forward in his saddle and squinted.

'I'm just going for a last look around,' İkmen said. 'I'm off tomorrow.'

'But it's snowing and you have no coat.'

'Rachelle Jones just made me aware of that fact, too.'

Altay Salman's whole body tensed. 'Rachelle Jones? Is she here?'

'No, no.' İkmen laughed. 'You're quite safe. She's gone . . .'

'Because she is a very predatory woman . . .'

'Who, if you were not married, would probably make you a very happy man,' İkmen said. 'I like her. She makes me smile.'

'Yes, well . . .' The top of the captain's cap was entirely covered with snow now, as were his long, thick eyelashes. They reminded İkmen of Süleyman's. He wanted to be home very much now.

'So where on earth are you going, Çetin?' the horseman continued. 'It's snowing.'

İkmen pulled the jacket of his suit tightly around his chest and said, 'I'm only going to the chimneys at the edge of the village. I'd like to be able to look back at Muratpaşa and see it looking snowy, quiet and romantic.'

'Minus the people, then?'

'Something like that.'

Altay Salman's horse stamped against the cold and he patted his flanks to soothe him. 'There, Süleyman, good beast.'

224

İkmen laughed. 'You called the horse Süleyman! You know my ex-sergeant . . .'

'I remember Mehmet Süleyman,' the captain said with a smile. 'But this horse isn't named for him. This beast was born and bred in Cappadocia and came with his name when the riding school purchased him. You know, Çetin, if something does result from this DNA testing you have organised, you will be quite a local hero.'

'Except with the perpetrator.'

'Of course,' Altay Salman said. 'But one way or another the rifts that cross this village do need to be resolved.'

'I know.' İkmen looked up at the man on the horse, his eyes now squinting against what had become driving snow. 'I hope Dr Sarkissian will be able to get here tomorrow.'

'İnşallah,' the horseman responded. 'I'll come by Menşure Hanım's place in the morning to take my leave of you, Çetin.'

'I would appreciate that.'

'Don't be out too long,' the captain said as he spurred Süleyman the horse to trot onwards. 'You don't want to go back to İstanbul with a cold.'

İkmen put his head down and pushed on towards the edge of the village. When he reached the last outpost of Muratpaşa, a collection of dark and derelict fairy chimneys, he turned to look at the village as he had said that he would. Altay and his horse had long since disappeared and so all İkmen could see through the swirls of snow and ice were higgledy-piggledy cones and chimneys and what looked like sugar-coated fingers – ice-bound minarets – pointing up into a sky of almost total blackness. Street lighting in the village, unlike back home in İstanbul, was of a minimal nature and so all of the rocks and caves appeared unadorned and natural underneath snow that looked as if it were materialising, as opposed to falling through the night sky. And although there were no peris or indeed spirits of any sort that İkmen could detect present in what he was viewing it was a very magical moment for the policeman. But it was also very cold and so as soon as he had savoured the moment sufficiently, Çetin İkmen made ready to go back to Menşure Tokatlı's hotel. If he hadn't heard a noise coming from one of the derelict chimneys behind him he would most certainly have left that place in quite a hurry.

There was no light anywhere in the chimney that he could see and so İkmen flicked his cigarette lighter and held it out in front of him. He already had a cigarette between his teeth on the basis that if he wasn't going straight back to the hotel he might as well have a smoke in this chimney before he set off for his room. After all, out in the billowing snow once again smoking was going to be a tough call even for someone as practised as Çetin İkmen.

This chimney, just like the other one he had explored before it, obviously hadn't been lived in for a very long time. As well as possessing that dank, musty smell that chimneys get when areas of their interiors are exposed to the elements, there was also evidence, in the form of empty rakı bottles, that the place was sometimes used by Muratpaşa's small cabal of drinkers. İkmen looked up and, through a hole in what had once passed for a ceiling, he felt a little snow and saw a little sky.

It had probably, he thought as he lit his cigarette and surveyed the scene around him, been an animal of some sort that had made the noise that had caught his attention. A cat or a dog. Just conceivably it could have been a wolf, not that they came down out of the mountains and into the villages on a regular basis. But it was very cold now and wolves, like all other sensible creatures, would be seeking shelter wherever they could find it. İkmen felt himself go colder than he already was. Perhaps he should telephone the jandarma just in case . . . But as well as feeling stupid, weak and cowardly for even thinking about calling for help, İkmen was also suddenly intrigued by something that had caught his eyes over by what used to be the old dwelling's fireplace. Something large was wrapped in what looked like a blanket but turned out to be a considerably large wall tapestry. Of course 'it' could, İkmen knew, very well be a bundled-up alcoholic, and so he approached whatever or whoever it was with care. Holding his lighter out in front of him, he made a sweep down from the top of the bundle to the bottom. At the bottom he saw two very unpleasantly coloured feet. Inwardly he groaned. The last thing he needed on the eve of his return to İstanbul was some lengthy process involving getting medical attention for a dead or dying alcoholic. Then, however, for some reason he found himself counting the number of toes on each ghastly foot. There were six.

The blow, when it came, arrived hard and fast from behind İkmen's head. By the time he hit the floor he was already unconscious.

Luckily the baby, Timur, had taken the formula milk Fatma had given him without either complaint or obvious distress. Of course he had to be missing his mother's – Hulya's – milk as well as the comfort of her breast, but the girl had other things besides her baby to think about now. Her husband, as far as

Fatma knew, was still in intensive care over at the Italian hospital.

'Hulya and her in-laws will have to come and stay here,' Fatma said to her daughter Çiçek and son Orhan who had come to be with their mother in the wake of the Neve Şalom tragedy.

'Isn't the house Berekiah's uncle gave them ready?' Orhan asked. He was a pleasant-looking man in his thirties and one of two İkmen boys who had qualified as a doctor.

'No, and with Berekiah sick for Allah alone knows how long, it could be standing empty for some time to come,' Fatma said.

Çiçek, İkmen's eldest daughter, looked out of the window at her side and through the darkness at the old imperial buildings across Divanyolu. The Sultanahmet Mosque with its six minarets could be seen as a smudged grey shape against the deep velvet of the midnight sky.

'There were police all over the airport this morning,' she said. 'Looking for something, someone. I thought of Dad.'

The flight that Çiçek had been due to work on that morning – she was a Turkish Airlines hostess – had been cancelled. At first she hadn't, like a lot of people, really known why. But when the airport TV screens began to fill with images of dead and dying people in Karaköy she had asked to be allowed to go home to her family. As she left she heard some of her colleagues ask each other, in hushed tones, whether Çiçek was indeed Jewish or whether that was just a rumour. She hadn't bothered to stop to put them right on that point. Only her sister Hulya and the safety of her family had mattered then, as it did now.

'Your father will be home tomorrow, İnşallah,' Fatma said with a sigh, 'to this madness.'

'Berekiah is alive, Mum,' Orhan said as he took his cigarettes out of his pocket and lit up. 'He may not be as we would wish him to be . . .'

'That Italian doctor told Sınan that Berekiah may lose the use of his right arm,' Fatma said. Sınan, her eldest, was also a doctor, and was currently at the hospital with his sister Hulya. 'He is a jeweller. He is right-handed. How will he work?'

'If he does indeed lose some function he may get that back in time,' Orhan said as he passed a cigarette across to his sister.

'And if he doesn't?'

'Lazar Bey won't get rid of Berekiah,' Çiçek said as she lit up and then exhaled shakily from tiredness.

'Lazar is fortunate to be alive himself,' Fatma responded with a shudder. 'Only a bad cold and the mercy of Allah kept him away from his prayers this morning. Lazar's is only a small shop, Çiçek; he must make a profit and he has his own son and grandson to think of. If Berekiah can't work properly, can't make the pieces that Lazar needs made, then he will have to let him go. Making a living is hard.'

They all sat in silence for a few moments while the truth of Fatma's words sank in.

'But to have Berekiah's father here . . .' Orhan began.

'Oh, I can, if necessary, manage Balthazar Cohen,' his mother said with some conviction. 'And anyway, Estelle would be here too. I've only got Gül and Kemal left at home now.'

'And Dad,' Çiçek put in.

'Yes, and . . .'

'Dad won't be able to support the Cohens as well as this family, you know,' Orhan said. 'The rest of us will have to contribute.'

'Of course,' Çiçek said simply, before she returned her gaze to the window once again.

Their mother looked at them, from one to the other, and smiled inside. Of course it was to be expected that well-raised children should help support their parents in times of trouble. There was a time when only female children ever left the parental home, anyway. Mothers were the empresses of their sons and daughters-in-law. But in İstanbul at least, that way of life had changed for a lot of families, including the İkmens. Çetin had, after all, worked hard all of his life in order to give his children, both sons and daughters, choices in their lives. That the older children, without question or complaint, always assisted with the cost of their younger siblings' upkeep and education was a great help. That they should now volunteer for more of the same on behalf of just one young sister was nothing short of heroic. Fatma was in fact so proud that in that moment she broke down and wept.

Chapter 15

'Menşure Hanım!'

One plump hand slipped out from inside the sleeve of a heavy Astrakhan coat and brought Menşure Tokatlı's knuckles up to a pair of fleshy lips.

'Arto Sarkissian,' Menşure responded dryly as she watched the Armenian bend down and kiss her fingers. 'It must be forty years since I've seen you. You haven't changed.'

'And neither have you,' Arto said with a smile. 'Still . . .'

'I'm still wealthy, more suspicious than ever, but I'm no longer young,' Menşure said tightly. 'So don't try to flatter me, Arto Sarkissian.' And then she turned to the rather younger and slimmer man standing beside her cousin's old friend and said, 'And who is this?'

'Atom Boghosian. He's my cousin. From Munich.' He then translated what he had just said into English, for Atom's benefit.

Menşure, irritated that Arto Sarkissian had either forgotten or didn't know that she could speak English, said, in that language, 'So your journey from Ankara, was it difficult?'

'Only when we got into Cappadocia,' Arto responded as he and Atom followed Menşure into her restaurant. 'It was not snowing in Ankara.'

Menşure motioned the two men towards a table and called to her cook's daughter to bring them coffee and breakfast. 'I won't join you myself . . .'

'Ramazan,' Arto smiled.

'Of course. Please sit,' she said sternly. 'I will go to find Çetin. He is generally up at this time.' She then swept out of the restaurant with what looked like some sort of small fox in tow.

It was only 10 a.m., which, as far as Atom Boghosian was concerned, was still very early. In fact, he was a little bit resentful that his cousin's friend wasn't around to greet them. They had, after all, left Ankara very early in order to do this business in Muratpaşa and then Nevşehir.

In response to what he perceived as his cousin's grave expression, Arto said, 'Don't worry about Nevşehir, Atom. You don't have to come into the mortuary. And I'm not taking a whole corpse back to İstanbul, only samples.'

'Mmm.'

'Çetin is excellent company and speaks very good English,' Arto continued as the cook's daughter laid plates of bread, cheese, honey and olives in front of both of them. 'We will not go on in Turkish, I promise. In fact, maybe you and Çetin can speak German together and confuse me. I don't know how fluent he is, but I know that his father insisted he learn to some level. His father taught European languages.'

Atom didn't comment. He had enjoyed Arto's guided tour of Turkey so far and had been amazed when he had first seen the Fairy Chimneys, but he was starting to reach his limit. Whatever his mother said, he was German – he spoke German, thought in German – and he wanted to be home in Munich.

None of this exotica had very much meaning, of any sort, for him.

They'd started their breakfasts by the time Menşure Tokatlı and what Atom Boghosian could now see was an enormous cat returned to their table.

'Çetin isn't in his room,' Menşure said with a frown.

'Maybe he's gone out for a walk,' Arto replied.

The woman fixed the Armenian with a very cynical eye.

'I didn't mean he was having a walk for pleasure,' Arto corrected. 'I mean that maybe he's out getting cigarettes, or . . .'

'Have you ever known Çetin to be without cigarettes?' Menşure interrupted tartly. 'Arto, please. You know Çetin.'

'Yes.' Arto sighed. It was unlikely. But then if İkmen were out and about, knowing that Arto and Atom were due to arrive, it had to be because of some sort of emergency. Maybe he'd received more bad news from İstanbul.

'I've got his mobile number,' Arto said as he slipped his hand into the pocket of his jacket. 'I'll give him a call. He's always got it with him.'

But the phone just rang and rang.

'Maybe he's out of range, in an area with bad reception.'

'Try again in another few minutes,' Atom suggested.

He did but still to no avail. By this time someone that Arto knew, though vaguely, Captain Salman, had arrived. He had, he said, last seen Çetin at the edge of the village the previous evening in the snow. As usual, he had been poorly clad for the dire weather conditions, but then that was Çetin all over. Arto said that he would try to ring Çetin's mobile again in another few minutes. In the meantime, however, he asked Altay Salman to join Atom and himself for coffee and some background on just what had been happening in Muratpaşa since Çetin İkmen's arrival.

He knew that he'd come to at some point during the course of the night, but just when that was, Çetin İkmen couldn't even begin to know. He'd been in a vehicle of some sort, his face pressed hard up against the tapestry that had covered poor Aysu Alkaya's body, but he hadn't been conscious for long. Another, even harder, blow to the head had taken care of that. Who had hit him, he didn't know. He'd seen and heard nothing of any consequence beyond the gruesome presence of Aysu Alkaya's mummified corpse – or rather nothing that he could as yet recall.

İkmen sat up, his head thumping with pain. There was sky above him, grey and heavy with yet more of the snow that lay underneath his hands as he pushed himself into a sitting position. Out in the open, somewhere amid what looked like a very densely packed group of chimneys, he was strangely rather warmer than a man wearing only a thin summer suit should be. Not that it took İkmen long to find the source of the heat that seemed to be ensuring his survival. There was a smouldering bonfire in front of him, and for about two metres all around it the snow had melted into the cool rivulets that had eventually woken him. At first he had thought that maybe he had wet himself, but it had, to his relief, been only this melted snow.

That whoever had attacked him was now warming him with this bonfire did seem strange. But İkmen moved towards it, clutching his bruised and in places bloodsticky head as he did so, simply in order to dry out his trousers and jacket. On closer inspection, however, İkmen discovered that the bonfire was a far-from-benign presence. Scooping up what he could of the melted snow around the pile he threw it wildly on to what was still unconsumed. Seeing that one brittle, six-toed foot was sticking out of the smouldering pyre, pointing towards him, İkmen made a grab for it. If he could just salvage something of her! But it came off in his hands leaving him holding just a dry pile of something that made him whimper into the harsh morning air.

Someone had tried to destroy Aysu Alkaya's corpse. Someone had also tried to destroy him, too, and, given the total alienness and isolation of his surroundings, they were really quite likely to succeed. But then he remembered his mobile phone and his cigarettes. He put his hand into his jacket pocket to retrieve his smokes. They did not appear to be where they should. That did not, İkmen felt, bode well for his telephone.

Mehmet Süleyman had reached what, for him, was a momentous decision. Inclined by nature to be rather impulsive, he had opted, in this case, to take what İkmen called the 'do nothing' approach. Commissioner Ardıç was in, and he could have gone straight to his office screaming about compromised crime scenes and the seriousness inherent within the situation. But he didn't. After he had called the Italian hospital to check on Berekiah Cohen, he just simply reviewed what he had so far on the Saray Hamam murder victim. Even when Melik arrived, neither he nor Süleyman spoke of what had passed between them the previous night. Only when Ardıç eventually called the inspector into his office did the two policemen exchange tense and worried looks.

'Seems that young Nizan Tapan is not any more use dead

than alive,' the commissioner said as Süleyman entered his office and sat down.

'Sir?'

'Trading his arse around the Saray Hamam and other disreputable places,' Ardıç continued. 'Parasite!'

'Maybe. But sir, he was murdered. His throat was slit . . .'

'Indeed. But by who, eh, Süleyman?'

'Sir?'

The older, larger and very hungry man turned a piece of paper over in his hands. 'Dr Sarkissian's assistant, Dr Mardin, tells me that Tapan's body is clean. There are no signs of sexual activity and beyond asserting that the killer wielded the murder weapon with his left hand she can tell us very little. Preliminary forensics have yielded nothing also. Whoever killed Tapan was very careful.'

'Yes, sir.'

Süleyman saw the commissioner raise an eyebrow which caused him to turn slightly to one side. The older man was, he felt, searching his face for signs of recognition or suspicion. Either that or Süleyman himself was becoming ever more paranoid.

'So, Süleyman,' the commissioner continued, 'do you have any thoughts?'

Süleyman cleared his throat. 'Well, sir, Tapan's death is obviously unconnected with what we now know were terrorist attacks on the Neve Şalom and Beth Israel synagogues. Tapan was not Jewish and I believe that his death in the Karaköy area was in all probability purely coincidental.'

The older man moved his head just slightly in order to signal his assent.

'In addition,' Süleyman continued, 'an immediate connection between Tapan's death and the current peeper investigation should not necessarily be taken as a given. Tapan was, like some of the peeper's victims, a practising homosexual. In common with several boys the peeper has abused, he frequented the Saray Hamam. However, all of the other victims were attacked and subjected to sexual activity in their own homes.'

'Yes. This may not be attributable to the peeper.'

'But we have to keep an open mind, don't we, sir? You say that the killer was left-handed?'

Ardıç frowned. 'Yes?'

'Well, that could be something, sir,' he said. 'Left-handers are a minority group, after all.'

'I am left-handed, Süleyman.'

'Yes, but . . .' He leaned forwards on to Ardıç's desk. 'Sir, the handedness of the peeper has never been subject to discussion before. It could be important. I think I might re-interview some of the previous victims with that in mind. Of course, if I could speak to Abdullah Aydın who was actually stabbed and survived and who saw . . .'

'That boy is still far too sick,' Ardıç cut in, reaching as he did so for one of his unlit cigars. 'He's still on life support. I told you I'd let you know when you can have access to him, and I will.'

'Oh, sir, I wouldn't dream of . . .'

'You've already turned up there once,' Ardıç said with a scowl. 'Dr Arkın called me.'

'But sir . . .'

'However, in view of this business at the synagogue which

237

was admirable on your part, I mention it now only to warn you for the future. Do not attempt to contact Abdullah Aydın until you get the say-so from me.' He cleared his throat. 'Now, how is Cohen's son? Is there anything we can do?'

And for the rest of their time together, the two men spoke only of Berekiah Cohen and about how good it was that he was now out of danger. That he may possibly never work in the jewellery trade again was not discussed. It was far too early, so Süleyman felt, to be indulging in speculation about something as uncertain as the recovery of a damaged limb. When he did finally leave the commissioner's office, Süleyman tried to call İkmen on his mobile in order to talk to him about what had happened in Karaköy. Fatma İkmen, he knew, had been in contact, but he had not spoken to Çetin himself and he suddenly felt the need to do so. However, the older man wasn't answering for some reason and so Süleyman went back to his office where he sat and thought for a while about Nizan Tapan and Abdullah Aydın, who, last time he'd seen him, had most certainly not been on life support. By the time he had come to any sort of conclusion as to how he might proceed, İzzet Melik had gone off on his mid-morning break.

Midday came and went with no word at all from İkmen. News of his apparent disappearance had travelled fast and Menşure Tokatlı's restaurant was now full of those concerned or just curious about the İstanbullu's current location. Altay Salman who, it appeared, had been the last person in the village to see İkmen the previous evening, took a group of his recruits out to the collection of half-ruined chimneys towards which the inspector had been headed. But beyond a few empty rakı bottles scattered on the dirty tufa floors there was nothing to be seen in any of those structures. On his way back to the hotel, Captain Salman called in at the gendarmerie to canvass support for a possible search party. The young jandarma were keen to help and so several of them accompanied the horsemen back to Menşure Tokatlı's place.

'Do you think there's any possibility that Çetin just kept on walking once he'd reached those chimneys at the edge of the village?' Altay Salman asked Arto Sarkissian once he had shaken the snow from his clothes. It was still coming down hard.

The Armenian laughed. 'Çetin? No, Captain, not Çetin. He doesn't "do" country walks; he doesn't really like the country.' As he sighed, his face fell. 'No, if he's still out there in the snow, I fear that he must have either had an accident or become unwell. He only suffers, to my knowledge, from stomach ulcers, but he was, as you've told us, poorly dressed, and then there is the matter of this body he wanted me to take samples from.'

'Meaning?'

'Meaning,' Arto said, 'that knowing Çetin as I do, I don't suppose his offer of DNA testing was entirely to everyone's taste. Some people object to it on religious grounds, while others . . .' He lowered his voice so that only Captain Salman could hear him. 'From what you and Çetin have told me I gather that the death of this "mummy" you have in Nevşehir is contentious. I understand that many and various people could have been involved.'

'That is true.'

'So maybe Çetin's disappearance is . . .'

'Captain Salman, will you stop chattering on to Arto Sarkissian and organise a search?'

Both men looked around to where Menşure Tokatlı was standing with her hands on her hips in the middle of her restaurant. She looked impatient, angry, and she had Kismet the cat with her to emphasise her point.

'That scruffy creature from Nevşehir, that Erten, has just telephoned to ask why my cousin and Dr Sarkissian are not at the mortuary,' she said. 'I told him Çetin has gone missing and he's driving over now. But we'll need to tell him what we're doing when he gets here. He hasn't got the wit to do anything himself.'

'All right,' Captain Salman said with a sigh. 'I understand your anxiety, Menşure Hanım. Look, why don't the jandarma get out on to the Nevşehir Road while my boys start riding into the valleys at that end of town.'

'Is there anything I can do?' a voice in English cut in suddenly.

They all turned to look at a young, slim man wearing a very heavily padded parka.

'My name's Tom Chambers,' the young man said. 'I've got to know the Inspector quite well over the past few days. I'd like to help, if I can.'

Altay Salman, who had seen Tom with İkmen several times, frowned. 'That is very good, Mr Chambers. But I am worried about civilians getting involved. The weather is very bad . . .'

'I could take him with me,' another voice, this time in Turkish, interrupted. 'I know these valleys better than anyone.'

'Ah, Mr Senar.'

Although he had been in the room for some time, this was the first anyone had heard from Turgut Senar. But as the local, expert guide to the area he did have a point.

'My jeep is gassed up and ready,' Senar continued. 'I could take the Englishman and anyone else who wants to help.'

'That's me.' Rachelle Jones raised a fur-clad arm into the air. 'I like Inspector İkmen. I want to help him if I can.'

'Well, as the local guide . . .'

'I could go with him,' Arto Sarkissian said to the captain. 'After all, if this goes on for some time, Çetin could very well need a doctor.'

The horseman nodded slowly. 'I agree. Although, given that my boys, simply by virtue of being on horseback and therefore having more comprehensive access to the valleys, stand more of a chance of finding Çetin than anyone else, I was hoping that you, Doctor, could come with us.'

'What? On horseback?' The Armenian's face instantly drained of all colour.

'Well, we're not going out for a gallop, Doctor. I do have several quiet, older horses.'

'Yes, but I'm a big man, Captain!'

'Yes, I can see that, Doctor, but . . .'

'Well, you can all argue about who is doing what until the end of the world, if you like,' Menşure Tokatlı's imperious voice boomed above everyone else, 'but I'm going to see what I can find.' And with that she picked up Kismet the cat and made her way towards the stairs.

'Menşure Hanım!' Captain Salman shouted after her.

'Kismet and I will go into the little valley behind Ferdinand Mueller's place,' Menşure said as she and her cat began to

241

descend. 'We'll go no further than that, I give you my word. And besides, the German should know what is happening. Maybe he can take one of his balloons up . . .'

'I think that the weather conditions might preclude balloon flights, Menşure Hanım.'

'Well, why don't I ask him, anyway?' she said as her head disappeared from view.

Altay Salman looked at Arto Sarkissian and shrugged. 'She takes the cat . . .'

'Kismet.' The Armenian nodded. 'The latest, I believe, in a line of similarly named psychotic cats. One of its forebears bit Çetin's brother. Kismet and Menşure have a relationship . . .'

'Is there anything I can do?' Atom Boghosian said to his cousin in English. 'I know I don't speak Turkish . . .'

'Atom . . .'

'We have to get organised, Doctor,' Altay Salman said to Arto Sarkissian. He then rapped on the table in front of him with his fist in order to get everyone's attention. 'My recruits and I are going to wait here until Inspector Erten arrives from Nevşehir, so that we organise our search along with him,' he said. 'If the jandarma can get out on the Nevşehir road and perhaps up in to Çavuşin, then that is a start. Menşure Hanım has taken it upon herself to cover the eastern side of the village.' He looked across at Turgut Senar. 'If you could take the Englishman, Mr Senar . . .'

'Yes.'

'And me.' Rachelle Jones yet again raised a fur-clad arm.

'Miss Jones, I . . .'

'If you're going to give me any nonsense about being a woman . . .'

'No, no,' Captain Salman said wearily. 'No, I . . . Look, Mr Senar, how many people can you take in your jeep?'

'I'll take the Englishman, Miss Jones and the doctor.'

'OK. But I think that the doctor is coming with me. His cousin wants to help; you can take him.'

'All right.'

'I'm quite happy to go with Mr Senar,' Arto Sarkissian said. But Captain Salman fixed him with a hard eye that reduced the Armenian to silence.

'So, then, let us get about our business,' the captain said as he turned back to the assembled company once again. 'Apart from Menşure Hanım, we have three search parties. Take mobile phones and radios and let us all keep in contact. No one wanders off alone or moves out of contact, and everyone dresses for the weather. With the help of Allah we will find Inspector İkmen.'

Those of a more religious bent mumbled their assent.

Chapter 16

Only one of the boys who had either seen or been attacked by the peeper so far could recall which hand the offender appeared to favour. But then he changed his mind three times before he, either by accident or design, finally settled on the left. Süleyman then listened to what Ayşe Farsakoğlu had discovered about and from those convicted of violent offences against homosexuals and whether their records showed them to be left-handed or not.

'There are three,' she said as she looked up from her computer screen at Süleyman and Melik. 'We've had one, Battal Oz, in already – with the group we interviewed the other day. He was at work, he's the night manager at a pansiyon in Laleli, when Abdullah Aydın was attacked. He has the same alibi for the dates and times of the other offences. I think he's clean, sir.'

'And the others?' Süleyman asked through an ever-thickening pall of cigarette smoke.

'Karagöz Tarih,' Ayşe said with a sigh.

'Allah!' Süleyman murmured in reply.

'I don't see him crawling around on rooftops with only one leg,' Ayşe elucidated.

'And the other?' her superior asked.

'One Aslan Yılmaz.'

'Aslan Yılmaz, small time enforcer for the Edip family?'

'Yes, sir,' she replied. 'He roughed up a transsexual known as Hazelnut Hanım February before last. Hazelnut, otherwise known as Onur Bavur, claimed that the Edip family godfather, Yaban, had made advances to him which he had rebuffed. His punishment, so Hazelnut claimed, was to be roughed up by Yılmaz.' Then still looking at the screen, she frowned. 'Interesting.'

'What's that, sergeant?'

'Well, it says here,' Ayşe said as she peered intently at the computer, 'that Yılmaz, so Hazelnut asserted at the time, masturbated over him after he had beaten him up.' She looked up. 'Excited by his pain, maybe?'

Süleyman frowned. 'Asserting his dominance over a lesser creature.'

'Maybe he was just in the mood at the time,' Melik put in, his voice tinged with that strangled desperation only lack of food and cigarettes can bring.

'There's nothing else on Yılmaz, in relation to homosexuals, here, sir,' Ayşe said as she pointedly ignored İzzet Melik. 'He's married with four children. Officially he's a car mechanic but, as we know, he fetches and carries from time to time for Yaban Edip's crime family up in Edirnekapı.'

Süleyman leaned back in his chair and blew smoke at the ceiling. The Edips had once been a particularly powerful crime family, although since the coming of gangs from Eastern Europe and central Asia, people like Yaban Edip had kept a somewhat lower profile than before. As far as Süleyman knew, they confined themselves pretty much to dope with regard to drugs now, augmenting their income mainly by people trafficking into the European Union. Aslan Yılmaz was, he recalled, probably in his mid-thirties. The last time Süleyman had seen him, he had been a fine physical specimen. Aslan Yılmaz liked to box; he was good at it. He was, however, less successful in controlling what a judge had once described as his 'psychopathic temper'. The fact that the transsexual had reported him and he had been questioned for that assault must have made Aslan very angry indeed. 'İzzet and I will pay Aslan a visit, I think,' Süleyman said at length. 'Whatever the outcome, it doesn't do to overlook scum even of the small-time variety.'

'No, sir.'

Ayşe Farsakoğlu stayed for just a short time after that. It was easy for her to see that, for some reason, Süleyman wanted to be alone with that oaf İzzet Melik. As she left she saw the sergeant sit down in front of Süleyman's desk and bend his head in close to that of his superior.

Ever since the panic-stricken and grisly task that Çetin İkmen had set himself had mercifully come to an end he'd been entirely at a loss as to what to do. Shortly after he had come round from whatever beatings he'd been given by whoever had performed them the previous night, he'd seen Aysu Alkaya's burning body and acted. A person or people unknown had wanted the mummified corpse destroyed and, with the exception of her head, plus a few other ghastly 'lumps', they had succeeded. Obviously, someone amongst the living had a problem with the prospect of DNA testing.

Serious for them, but not nearly as earth-shattering as İkmen's own immediate problems.

The fact that he was in a place that he did not in any way recognise was bad. It was frightening that no towns, villages or, for that matter, lone dwellings could be seen even from the top of the chimney he had been dumped in front of. That someone obviously thought he was already dead or at least wanted him to be so was terrifying. On top of this, whoever had brought him to this place had either stolen or destroyed his mobile phone. All these things were bad, but whether they were as bad or worse than the fact that İkmen's assailant had taken his cigarettes was open to question.

'Fuck! Fuck! Fuck! Fuck! Fuck!' he roared as he emerged from the chimney into which he had placed what he'd managed to salvage of Aysu Alkaya.

Staying where one was in an unknown landscape was, İkmen knew, the only sensible way to proceed. He didn't know where he was and, if he wandered about too far from this chimney and Aysu Alkaya, he knew there was a possibility he would never find either of them ever again. And that would never do. Whoever had tried to burn her body, whoever had stolen his cigarettes, could well have left some forensic evidence on either himself, the corpse, or both. It was evidence that could, İkmen knew, make the evil bastard pay for his or her crimes. 'Not least of which involves this nicotine-free torture!' he shouted, giving vent to his frustrations as well as, hopefully, alerting someone to his predicament. Mad Peruvians dancing for their Sun God, perhaps . . .

İkmen put both hands up to his endlessly throbbing head and wondered how, amid so much freezing whiteness, he was going to stay both alive and sane. It was beyond just ordinary cold and with only his paper-thin jacket and trousers between himself and the elements, İkmen realised that his chances of emerging unscathed from this particular 'adventure' were slim. He walked round the now-dead funeral pyre and surveyed his surroundings. He was outside a white chimney in what looked like the middle of a very long valley of white chimneys. That this and all of the other chimneys in this area had once been inhabited was evident from the fact that they possessed many roughly hewn windows and upper 'storeys', one of which he had briefly climbed up into in order to look at still more chimneys: they seemed to go on and on into infinity, like a hellish succession of oddly hewn Emmental cheeses. Allah alone knew for how far the wretched things continued.

For one brief, shining moment, İkmen thought that because his chimney had been inhabited at one time, then perhaps he wasn't too far away from the rest of humanity. But then he remembered just what type of people had come to Cappadocia to live in these structures and he felt his heart sink. Hermits. Bloody, fucking lunatics with no friends.

'I have no idea who could have done such a thing, Doctor,' the shivering, scruffy little man told the Armenian. 'To steal a body . . .'

'Don't you have security at the mortuary?' Arto Sarkissian asked Inspector Erten.

'Well, yes of course. We have guards,' the policeman replied. 'But if people are determined, even the most efficient systems will be of no use. Quite how I am going to tell Haldun Alkaya I really don't know.'

'When did the body go missing?'

'I saw it with my own eyes yesterday, so it must have been taken last night,' Erten said as he nervously chewed on his bottom lip.

'We think that Inspector İkmen has been missing since last night, too,' Arto said. 'The two events may not be unconnected as I am sure you are aware.'

Erten frowned.

The Armenian moved in closer to the man from Nevşehir and lowered his voice. 'If İkmen were on to something or someone who didn't want me to take samples from that body . . .'

'Oh, I see.'

The sharp clack of riding boots against the hard, marble floor of the restaurant signalled to Arto Sarkissian that Captain Salman had returned. Though smiling at one who was a very nice man, inwardly Arto cringed.

'I've sorted out a nice quiet mount for you, Doctor,' the captain said rather too cheerily, Arto felt. 'He's a noble old retiree called Yıldırım.'

'Oh, how thoughtful,' the Armenian said through clenched teeth. How he was going to mount Yıldırım, much less ride him, was going to be interesting.

'Come on, then!' Captain Salman said, and looking across at Erten, continued, 'So you'll stay here, will you, Inspector?'

'I think I should,' Erten replied. 'Someone needs to be a central point of contact and also I am going to have to explain what has happened to Haldun Alkaya.'

Captain Salman looked briefly around the room – at Ümit Özal the carpet dealer who liked to sleep with his kilims, at

Marion from the Cappudocia Coffee Bean Café, at the Kahramans' old friend, Baha Ermis, plus several other less prominent villagers. All had been listening intently for much of the time and all were well equipped with mobile telephones. When he looked back at Erten he said, 'I imagine, Inspector, that unless Haldun Alkaya has himself expired, he already knows what has happened to Aysu's body.'

Turgut Senar had offered to search in the valleys just to the north of those Altay Salman and his cadets had opted to explore. On the basis that İkmen, had he had an accident or become unwell, was unlikely to be too far from the derelict chimneys he had been exploring the previous night, the horsemen were more likely to be successful than any of the other search teams. But Senar as a professional wasn't taking any chances and before he, Rachelle Jones, Tom Chambers and Atom Boghosian hit the road, he loaded his jeep up with blankets, waterproof clothing, food and drink.

Rachelle was just folding herself into the back of the vehicle when their small group was joined by Dolores Lavell. Her face was full of concern.

'I've just heard,' she said as she placed a hand on Turgut Senar's arm, 'about Inspector İkmen.'

'Yes,' the guide responded, 'we are now going to look for him.'

'Oh, can I . . .'

'I am sorry, there is no room in the jeep,' Turgut said coldly.

'She can always crush in between me and Atom,' Rachelle said from her cramped position behind Tom Chambers.

'I do not think so,' Turgut said as he swung himself into the vehicle and fired up the engine.

'But . . .'

'Why don't you go to see my mother?' the guide said as he squeezed his foot down on the accelerator. 'Kemalettin will behave himself this time.'

And then he was off, leaving Dolores behind, looking small and doe-like in the thick-falling snow.

'That was really nasty, you know, Turgut,' Rachelle said once they had gained the main Nevşehir Road.

'She has no business . . .'

'So you've just used her and now you don't want to know any more,' the Australian said in Turkish.

Tom, who hadn't been able to understand the previous comment said, 'Last time Dolores spoke to the inspector she was really quite angry with him – and me – and that nice Emily. We were gossiping about her, and she . . . she's sensitive about her family, it turns out.' And then twisting around to look at Rachelle he said, 'Did you know that Dolores' father was black?'

'No.' Rachelle frowned. 'I . . . Well, is it a big deal?'

'She comes from the south and so I suppose it could be,' Tom said.

'Mmm.' And then slipping back into Turkish in the full knowledge that Turgut Senar knew exactly what had passed between herself and the Englishman, Rachelle said, 'A black woman, eh? Well, Turgut . . .'

'If you want to get out and walk, Miss Jones,' the guide said menacingly.

'No.'

'Then do not question or even mention my motives,' he replied.

And then they all fell into silence, which continued until Turgut took the jeep off the main Nevşehir Road and began to drive up into a valley both he and Rachelle Jones knew as the Valley of the Goat. Tom Chambers, who had not known its name, was intrigued as to its origin.

'At the end of the valley there is a church with a fresco showing the father of Jesus, Yusuf, milking a goat,' Turgut said as he steered his vehicle over a large flat expanse of tufa and into a narrow valley of mainly pink-tinged chimneys.

'But not all the valleys are named for the frescos that have been discovered in them, are they?'

'No. We have the White Valley, named for its brilliant colour, and the Valley of the Dervishes. It is only occasionally that a fairy chimney is given a name because of the frescos it has inside.'

'Usually they call those the church of something or other,' Rachelle Jones put in. 'Like the Church of the Snake down in the İlhara Valley. There's a painting of a snake in there; I saw it a long time ago.'

'Well then, the chimney where that girl's body was discovered will probably end up being called the Church of the Leper,' Tom said, thinking only after he had spoken that he had in fact said something that he shouldn't have. İkmen had, after all, told him not to mention the startling fresco of Christ and the strange bandaged figure to anyone. But it was too late.

'Why is that, Mr Chambers?' Turgut Senar enquired.

* * *

Nazlı Kahraman pulled Baha Ermis into her courtyard and then pushed him back against her father's old great wooden door.

'Did you take that body from the mortuary?' she said in a low voice, keeping one eye as she did so on her oblivious young husband humming away to himself in their kitchen.

'No! I swear! Why would I?'

'You had better be telling me the truth!' she hissed.

'I am,' Baha Ermis replied. 'Believe me, Hanım . . .'

'Because when I said that we needed to find a solution to the problem of who killed Aysu, I didn't mean that I wanted you to kidnap her body!'

'But I haven't!' the man protested. 'Someone else has done that, Hanım. Someone also worried and concerned about what this DNA business might reveal.'

'And who might that be?'

'Well, Kemalettin Senar, of course!' Baha said with a shrug. 'Or rather his family. I doubt he could do such a thing himself. But that brother of his will do anything to protect him. They've taken the body and destroyed it, no doubt.'

'And this policeman from İstanbul? What is this I hear about him?'

Baha Ermis made a face. 'He's missing, apparently. Maybe he got too close to what was going on with the Senars and the body and . . .'

'If I find you've been lying to me, Baha, about Aysu's body, if I find you have taken it . . .'

'But . . .'

'You've always been a liar!'

'But Hanım,' Baha pleaded, 'whatever has happened, your

late blessed father's good name is now no longer in any doubt. Now, with no body, the situation returns to what it was before the girl was discovered. I didn't take the body, on the life of my mother, but I am not unhappy that others may have done so. Anything to shield your father's sacred name.'

Nazlı Kahraman took in one deep breath which she then let out slowly.

'I have always worked only for the greater honour of the Kahraman family,' Baha Ermis continued as he looked down at her with obvious sympathy. 'I have never expected anything in return apart from the honour of . . .'

'Someone must go to the Senars',' she interrupted. 'Find out what they are doing. I don't want that body to just turn up again.'

'No, Hanım.'

'I can't go and you shouldn't . . .'

'Turgut Senar is out helping to look for the İstanbul policeman. Nalan may be alone.'

Nazlı Kahraman put her hands up to her head, seemingly rubbing away a headache. 'Nalan Senar would never kidnap a dead body!' she said, her voice tired and exasperated. 'She certainly wouldn't keep it in her house. Underneath all her fancy jewellery she's just a peasant. She believes in peris and ghosts, she wouldn't want an "unquiet" spirit in her home. No, if any of them has done this thing, it has to be Turgut. I must talk to him, away from here . . .'

'He is out looking for the policeman, Hanım. He is with the Jones woman, some German and a boy from Menşure Tokatlı's hotel – an Englishman.'

'Do you know where they've gone?'

254

'Out into the valleys, somewhere,' he shrugged. 'I don't know.'

Nazlı Kahraman sat down on one of the empty oil cans that was awaiting transformation into a plant pot. 'Then we will have to await his return,' she said. 'But after this, you must follow him. I want to know where that body is. I want to know that Nalan Senar will not try to use whatever it conceals against me.'

'But why would she? Your father . . .'

'The Senars have always maintained that my father killed my stepmother.'

'But that is a lie, Hanım!'

She turned on him like a fury. 'You don't know that, you lying little creep!' And then looking through the kitchen window at her husband yet again she said, 'Why do people always lie to me? Why can no one face the truth?'

Mehmet Süleyman lay down on what had recently reverted to being 'their' bed and stared at the ceiling. His friend, Berekiah Cohen, was making what looked like a good recovery up at the Italian hospital. It would have been excellent news had it not been tainted by that telephone call from a frantic Fatma İkmen. Çetin had gone missing somewhere in Cappadocia – in the snow. That Dr Sarkissian was in Muratpaşa, and apparently helping to look for İkmen, was a consolation. Mehmet, however, would have much rather been there himself. But he couldn't go anywhere now, something that İkmen, knowing Mehmet's situation, would have agreed with. Although he didn't know what to do about what looked to him, and to İzzet Melik, like evidence and witness manipulation

255

in the peeper case, he knew that he couldn't just stand by such things in good conscience. He didn't have a clue as to how he might, for instance, tackle Ardıç on these issues, however . . .

'Mehmet?'

He looked up to see his wife coming towards him carrying a cordless telephone.

'It's Arto Sarkissian,' she said as she handed the instrument to him.

Mehmet, standing now, took the telephone from his wife and walked over to the table and chairs Zelfa had placed in the bay window overlooking the now-darkening garden. 'Doctor?'

'Oh, Inspector, I wish I could say that I had some good news for you, but . . .'

'You haven't found him.'

Mehmet heard Zelfa leave the room with a frustrated sigh.

'No,' the doctor replied. 'And now it's too dark to carry on the search tonight.'

'You must be exhausted.'

'Not really, I'm too worried,' he said. 'Or rather, my brain is too worried. Another part of my anatomy is extremely tired, I must admit. It is many, many years since I rode a horse, Inspector. Both the beast and myself are at the end of our patience.'

In spite of himself, Mehmet smiled. The doctor was a heavy, very unfit man. Riding one of Altay Salman's horses had to have been pure torment.

'We're resuming the search tomorrow at first light,' Arto continued. 'A lot of the villagers have volunteered to help and so we must remain hopeful. How is young Berekiah?'

Mehmet told him.

'Well, at least we have that to be thankful for,' he said in response to the positive news from the Italian hospital. 'We will find Çetin, you know, Mehmet.'

He didn't often use Mehmet's first name, he only used it in times of tremendous strain.

'İnşallah,' the younger man said, and then repeated the formula again just for good measure.

Nothing much more beyond mutual assurances to keep in touch passed between them then. They were both relieved to end what had been an essentially miserable call and when Zelfa came back into the bedroom a few moments later she had to make an effort to gain her husband's attention.

'Come back to the bed and lie down for a bit,' she said as she pulled him gently to his feet and guided him across the bedroom. 'Father's back home tomorrow, so if you want some really noisy sex . . .'

Mehmet lay down, pulling Zelfa after him and smiled as she too sank towards the mattress.

'Can I know what it means yet?' he asked, watching her face intently as he spoke.

'What?'

'Your attitude towards me,' he explained. 'I mean, I know that you want me . . .'

As if to underline this point, Zelfa slipped a hand underneath his shirt and began massaging his chest.

'But . . .'

'I have to give our marriage one more chance,' Zelfa said with, he observed, something of regret in her tone. 'For Yusuf and . . . I don't know what it is about you . . .'

She leaned over and kissed him. Then when she had finished she said, 'You've let me down, you've fucked about. Why I can't be rid of you, I . . .'

'I won't let you down any more,' he said. His heart was now racing with the thrill of being back with his family once again. He pulled her body close in towards his own and said, 'I promise.'

Although during the course of their love-making he thought of nothing but her, as soon as Zelfa was satisfied and asleep his mind turned back to other things. To how he might discover who or what was blocking his progress on the peeper case, but mostly he thought about İkmen and how an underweight man in a thin summer suit could possibly survive outside in the wilds of Cappadocia. For, although winter had not yet, officially, arrived in the land of the Fairy Chimneys, temperatures of -10°C had been recorded already at night time. In full winter that could fall as low as -25°C. Mehmet, in an attempt to blot such thoughts out and to comfort himself, took one of his wife's breasts between his hands and then buried his face in its softness.

Chapter 17

Had his mouth not been frozen shut or his body wracked with uncontrollable shivering, Çetin İkmen would, he thought, have jumped up as soon as dawn arrived and cried, *Oh joy, it is morning! Another day without warmth or cigarettes!* But he was too cold even to get excited by his own cynicism. That he had actually survived the night was a miracle. He hadn't slept and had been obliged to drape himself in the half-burned remnants of Aysu Alkaya's tapestry winding sheet, but he'd made it. What was more, his brain had been busy all the time even if his body had not.

One of the things that had, seemingly, become lost in all the speculation about who killed Aysu Alkaya and why, was the story that had to surround the weapon that had killed her. As had been observed right at the beginning of the investigation, Cappadocian grape growers were not famous for carrying this particular weapon. Made in the US, the Colt 45 was, İkmen knew, an iconic American gun. That said, of course by virtue of the fact that American military bases had existed in Anatolia for many years, a US weapon in the hands of a local was not outside the bounds of reason. In addition, he knew that Americans had been coming to Cappadocia for some time. Nazlı Kahraman had mentioned it and the American Dolores

Lavell had said that her father and his fellow GIs had visited too. It was because she'd enjoyed her father's Cappadocian stories so much that Dolores had decided to follow in his footsteps.

But Americans walking around with Colt 45s was one thing – Turks having such weapons was quite another. How one of these revolvers had come into the possession of a local was a problem that İkmen found very interesting. Had an American perhaps given his gun to someone he met, and liked, in the village? Some people did after all, see guns as quite legitimate gift material. Not İkmen himself, he rarely carried the gun he was actually required to have in his possession, but if a serviceman made a present of a weapon to someone outside his own unit then surely his superiors would be angry to say the least? Maybe he was a deserter or perhaps the gun was not given at all but stolen by someone in the village? Maybe it hadn't come via anyone from the US, but had entered the village by another, less obvious route? Effectively trapped inside a chimney riddled with ice-encrusted holes with only various mummified body parts for company was not conducive to finding solutions to these many, many questions İkmen was asking himself. But thinking about them was better than thinking about the whereabouts of his mobile phone, if Berekiah was continuing to recover from his wounds or, worst of all, if he himself was going to live long enough to smoke another cigarette. He moved his still sore and bloodstained head just a little so that he could see the outside world. It was no more appealing than the last time he'd looked – all rocks and snow and a distinct lack of vegetation. He knew, however, that somehow he'd have to make himself move outside soon. If he didn't, anyone who might be searching for him wouldn't stand a chance of finding him. And people had to be searching for him now. In fact, knowing his friend Arto as he did, İkmen knew that he at least must have been looking for him for some time.

Captain Salman had decided to extend the search for İkmen into the valleys at the opposite end of the village up towards the troglodyte town of Ürgüp.

'If the inspector has been taken as opposed to his becoming unwell or having an accident, any of the valleys hereabouts are fair game,' he said to the assembled cadets, watching as he spoke, Dr Sarkissian allowing himself to be eased up on to a horse for the second day running. 'The police from Nevşehir are searching house to house here in Muratpaşa,' he continued with a nod towards a violently shivering Erten. 'The jandarma are touring the local towns and villages, almost every able man in Muratpaşa is searching and Turgut Senar is out with his jeep once again. We will ride out in the valleys that lead to Ürgüp and beyond – if necessary.'

Horses already slick with sweat from early morning gallops, stamped against the cold snow-covered ground as their riders mounted up for another day amongst the Fairy Chimneys. They had gathered in front of the bus station, which, though at the very heart of the village, was also very convenient for entrance to the tiny, narrow path that gave access to the Ürgüp valleys. As they began to move off, Altay Salman made sure that he was level with Arto Sarkissian who, he now saw, was wincing with every movement of his mount, the ancient Yıldırım.

'What's your cousin going to do while we're out?' the captain asked, knowing from the previous day that to ask the Armenian about riding, his horse or his level of comfort only aroused his fury.

'Atom got into conversation with that young Englishman, Mr Chambers, yesterday,' Arto said through just slightly gritted teeth. 'Got on well, apparently. He and Mr Chambers have gone out with that guide, Senar, again. That lovely Australian lady, however, Rachelle, has some business today.'

The Australian had, apparently, shared more than a few glasses of wine with the doctor the previous evening and, according to a somewhat disapproving Menşure Tokatlı, got along rather well with him. Her 'business' today probably included some sleeping off of the night before.

But then Turgut Senar's jeep would be quite heavily filled without Miss Jones. As well as Tom Chambers and Atom Boghosian, he was also taking someone who was, to all intents, his enemy – Baha Ermis. How that had come about he couldn't imagine.

Just before the riders turned into the pathway leading out of the village, Ferdinand Mueller came running across from his Land Rover and trailer which were parked outside his business. Menşure Tokatlı was standing next to the vehicle carrying the cat, Kismet, in her arms.

'Captain!' the German called out as he approached. 'Can I speak to you?'

Altay Salman held one hand aloft to bring his men to a halt and then looked down at the German with a questioning expression on his face. 'Mr Mueller?'

'Ingrid and I are going to take a balloon up,' he said, shrugging as he did so. 'I know the weather isn't ideal . . .'

'It's still snowing,' Altay said with a frown. 'Not so much now, but . . .'

'Menşure Hanım was knocking on our door at four this morning,' the German continued. 'She's frantic about her cousin. She's convinced that a balloon will prove a much better method of finding him and she is probably right. I said no, but my wife, on the other hand, was of a different mind.'

Ferdinand Mueller's Swedish wife, Ingrid, was both a very experienced balloon pilot and a very determined woman.

'So you're going up?'

'Yes. I'm launching from Ürgüp.'

'Not with Menşure Hanım or the cat, I trust,' Captain Salman said as he nodded his head towards the woman and her feline.

'No.'

'Well, Mr Mueller, I have to trust you know what you're doing.'

The German smiled. 'I do and I know it isn't strictly OK. But I'll do it anyway.'

'I've always found it hard to say no to Menşure Tokatlı,' Arto Sarkissian put in miserably. 'She's a formidable woman and as for that animal of hers . . .'

The captain and the balloon pilot made sure that they could contact each other with ease and then Ferdinand Mueller went back to his Land Rover. As the vehicle with the balloon basket in tow made off for the flatlands north of Ürgüp, the horsemen watched Menşure Tokatlı march, in a very satisfied fashion, back to her vehicle and then drive off to her hotel.

As the mounted party entered the narrow pathway out of the village, Altay Salman turned round in his saddle and spoke to Arto Sarkissian. 'With a balloon up, we stand much more of a chance today,' he said in as reassuring a way as he could. 'The Muellers are excellent pilots.'

And yet just the mere fact that he said what he did filled the doctor with dread. Balloons did not usually go up in the snow, not even in the kind of faint powdering they were experiencing now. The Cappadocian terrain, both at ground level and above, could be challenging at the best of times, but in the snow it was that much worse. Arto Sarkissian shifted his large behind uncomfortably in the saddle and allowed Yıldırım to follow Altay Salman's magnificent horse, Süleyman.

'I don't know why Abdullah can't come home now! Your lot, the police, they say no!'

Mehmet Süleyman watched in some admiration as Selcuk Aydın talked to him, gave out and received keys from his guests and berated what appeared to be one of Abdullah's older brothers.

'So the police say that Abdullah must go to this convalescent hospital in . . .'

'Kaş, Kalkan – I don't know! My wife knows.' And then turning to his son he said, 'Are you going to study or are you just going to sit there doing nothing?'

The young man, who was behind the reception counter with his father, ignored a key in the outstretched hand of a Canadian woman and said, 'It's physics. I don't like physics.'

'Please . . .' the woman said.

'Oh, thank you very much,' Selcuk Aydın replied in English

264

as he took the key from the woman. Then glaring at his son, he shouted in Turkish, 'I don't care whether or not you like physics . . .'

'Mr Aydın!'

Selcuk Aydın gave out one key and took in two while his son slowly moved out from behind the desk and walked towards the stairs. The lobby of the Emperor Justinian Pansiyon was typical of such establishments in the lee of the Blue Mosque and Aya Sofya. Dark and labyrinthine in layout, it served as a repository for keys and valuables, an office, and as a meeting place for those guests who liked to sit about, watch television and drink endless glasses of tea. It was not somewhere Süleyman had been since that very first day, the day when Abdullah Aydın was attacked. It wasn't somewhere he was supposed to be now. Other officers, however, had been to see Abdullah's family. Other officers had 'recommended' this convalescent hospital the boy was apparently going to be moved to the following day.

'So you would prefer to have your son at home, Mr Aydın?' Süleyman continued.

'He's made a good recovery,' Selcuk Aydın said. 'That doctor says so.'

'Dr Arkın?'

'Yes. A woman. Good though.' He cleared his throat noisily. 'He's moving around now, is Abdullah. Slowly, but . . . There would be nothing to stop him answering the telephone here if you ask me. But then your colleagues will disagree.'

'What was the name of the officer who spoke to you?' Süleyman asked. 'Who told you about the convalescent hospital?'

Selcuk Aydın thought for a few moments before he said, 'Doğan. Inspector Doğan.'

Süleyman had never heard of such a person, although for the moment he kept that to himself. 'Oh,' he said, 'I know him, about thirty, short . . .'

'More like forty-five!' Aydın retorted as he typed something into his computer system underneath the reception desk. 'Tall, like you.'

'Oh, yes,' Süleyman said as he watched the pansiyon owner type yet more information into his computer. 'That Doğan.'

'And his boss, of course, but that was earlier on when he came up here. Just after my son woke up in hospital.'

Süleyman moved closer to the desk which was now, mercifully, free of clamouring tourists. 'His boss?'

'Big fat man,' Selcuk Aydın said as he quickly looked up at Süleyman. 'Commissioner.'

'Commissioner Ardıç?'

'That's it,' Selcuk Aydın said with a smile. 'Commissioner Ardıç. It was him that told me you weren't going to be working on Abdullah's case any more. It was Ardıç who put me on to that Doğan fellow. He said he was going to be doing whatever needed to be done from now on.'

This was the first that Süleyman had heard of his demotion from the case and the first, too, that he had heard of this mythical Inspector Doğan. That all of this strange and, as yet, incomprehensible activity around Abdullah Aydın had come in the wake of the boy claiming to have seen the peeper's face gave the policeman the shivers. If Abdullah had seen the peeper, then why wasn't Süleyman himself allowed to have that information? He was being purposefully prevented from visiting the boy in the hospital. Could it be that this Inspector Doğan and Ardıç were dealing with this on their own for some reason? Why he should now be excluded from an investigation he had been pursuing since the first attack had happened, he couldn't imagine. All he knew was that in order to make any sense at all, Ardıç's actions had to be connected to what Abdullah Aydın, the peeper's only witness, as far as Süleyman knew, had seen on the night of his ordeal. The peeper's face was what had to be exercising the commissioner and his unknown colleague, Inspector Doğan. Did one or either of them know this face Abdullah possessed in the dark recesses of his mind? Or was it a face everyone would recognise? The face of someone famous or powerful? After all, if the peeper really was 'someone' then it was logical to assume that certain people would not want that fact to be connected with those crimes.

But Ardıç? Involved in corrupting evidence? Süleyman couldn't in all honesty see that, but as he walked away from the pansiyon towards the opulence of the Four Seasons Hotel he knew that he couldn't rule out that possibility either. There was, however, a somewhat dangerous way in which he could test his various theories.

For a moment he thought about putting his idea to İzzet Melik and perhaps enlisting his aid into the bargain. The İzmir man was currently interviewing that thug, Aslan Yılmaz, the one that Ayşe Farsakoğlu had identified as a possible peeper back at the station. It was just a bluff, of course. Yılmaz was far too stupid to be anything as clever as the peeper. But then Süleyman thought better of dragging Melik in any deeper than he already was and just continued on back to his office in silence.

*   *   *

The Englishman and the German Armenian didn't have a clue about what was happening between their fellows. Tom Chambers had gathered, mainly because Rachelle Jones had told him the previous evening, that their driver Turgut Senar and their new passenger Baha Ermis were long-time enemies. But, though quiet, they seemed to be managing to be together with some level of equanimity.

As they passed from the reasonably flat roads of the village and out into the countryside, Turgut Senar broke his silence and said in English, 'This valley is called the Valley of the Birds. It is because there are many bird houses up in the rock faces here.'

Both Tom and Atom looked up at the sheer white rock faces that rose up on either side of their vehicle. At intervals, brightly decorated dovecotes or pigeon houses had been roughly cut out of the tufa.

'Captain Salman and his horsemen are in the valley to our right,' Turgut continued. 'That is the Valley of the Trees, although not everyone knows that it has a name. It is not famous.'

Baha Ermis, who Tom reckoned was in his thirties and rather unkempt for one who had introduced himself as an estate manager, said something to the guide who replied with a shrug. Rather than satisfy the younger man, this soundless response just seemed to suddenly and spectacularly infuriate him. Shouting erupted in the front of the jeep with both men attempting to raise their voices as high as they could as well as waving their hands aggressively at each other.

'I don't like the way this is going,' Tom said to Atom as their vehicle swerved wildly to the left. He didn't trust Turgut

Senar as it was. The guide had, Tom thought, been rather more aggressive in his questioning of him about the 'new' fresco out at the Valley of the Saints than was comfortable.

'Put your hands on the wheel!' Atom shouted at Turgut Senar. Unfortunately in his panic he spoke in German, which was not a language anyone else in the jeep could understand.

'Mr Senar,' Tom began, 'would you . . .'

'Stop! Stop! Stop!' Baha Ermis said this in English, shaking Turgut Senar's shoulders as he did so.

The guide responded with a furious welter of Turkish, but he nevertheless did as Ermis had requested and stopped the jeep immediately.

After a few moments of what was, for everyone concerned, tense silence, Tom Chambers said, 'What on earth is wrong with you guys?'

Slowly, both the Turks turned round to face him. 'You want to know what is wrong, Mr Chambers?' Turgut Senar asked.

But before Tom could even think about replying, Baha Ermis was screaming again, this time with his face so close it was almost touching that of Turgut Senar.

'For God's sake!' the Englishman said as he looked, in despair, at his German-Armenian companion.

Then the jeep rocked as the two men in the front got out to continue their argument in the cold morning air. As their passengers looked on helplessly, Turgut Senar and Baha Ermis went from shouting at each other to pushing and making obscene gestures. Something that had been said, or perhaps left unsaid, had caused this sudden and now rather frightening escalation.

'Quickly goes off around here, doesn't it?' Tom said to Atom as they watched the two Turks square up for a fight.

Standing up, although far more conducive to staying awake than sitting down, hadn't been an option for İkmen for some time. Inside the chimney it was probably possible, but outside in the snow it was just beyond him. To have any chance of being rescued he had to be visible and yet with the snow coming down again, though lightly, he knew that it wouldn't be long before his rigid and battered body was indistinguishable from the rock he was sitting on. The possibility of death was, he realised, upon him. But just like every other time mortality had reared its head at İkmen in the past, he pointedly chose to ignore it. Although apart from his shivering he was completely unmoving now, his brain was working overtime on as many things as it could manage. Things which puzzled him about Muratpaşa and its inhabitants.

Why had Turgut Senar suddenly developed a passion for Dolores Lavell and why had he been so appalled when his brother masturbated in front of her? He'd been so upset he'd even pointed the dastardly action out to his mother. Why? Dolores Lavell was a foreigner who, so she claimed, had no connection to the Senar family or anyone else in the village for that matter. But her father had been to the area before, her father who had been in the US army, together with his fellow soldier 'buddies'. When Dolores had shown that photograph of her father to Turgut and Emily in the balloon, perhaps the former hadn't been as shocked by the colour of the American's father, so much as by his familiarity. Perhaps Turgut Senar, who must have been a child in the late fifties and early sixties, knew him. Perhaps the big, friendly black GI had taught the cute little Turkish kid to shoot – Turgut Senar was as Altay Salman had said, a very good shot. Did Dolores' father perhaps give the kid a keepsake, a Colt 45? GIs had, after all, done such crazy things in Vietnam; he'd read about it.

But why would Turgut Senar kill Aysu Alkaya, whether he had an old American weapon or not? He had no motive that İkmen could see. Both Nazlı Kahraman and her father had several motives, not least of which was the fact that the girl and her father had effectively duped the Lemon King into matrimony. And if Nazlı Hanım had in fact been lying about having any inkling of Aysu's pregnancy . . . It wouldn't, after all, have been difficult for a wealthy woman like Nazlı to get hold of a weapon, American or otherwise, that was impossible to trace back to her or her father's estate.

Kemalettin Senar might have had a motive no one knew about or maybe he had killed the girl by accident. He would have to have had access to the Colt 45 in order to do this, however, and İkmen couldn't see Turgut actually giving his strange and much younger brother what had probably been a prized possession. Perhaps Kemalettin had stolen the gun? He and Aysu planned to spring her and their unborn child from their 'prison' in the Kahramans' house. Kemalettin brought the gun along for their protection, but the boy was clumsy and there was an accident. That İkmen himself had had an accident of sorts was something he considered as he gazed fixedly at the ground straight beneath his face. Someone who probably had not counted on his being with the corpse of Aysu Alkaya had hit him. Later, that person or someone else, because he now remembered that there had been a lot of people around at some

time during that night, had hit him again – and then again . . .
His brain was working now, but slowly, oddly.

'Inspector İkmen!'

Oh, and now voices in the head for company too!
Concussion maybe. Fantastic. It sounded just like that idiot
who lived in the apartment next to the İkmens, Mr Gören.
Stupid idiot lived with his great dollop of a daughter who just
sat and ate lokum all day long. Why the voice couldn't be his
Fatma's sweet tones, he didn't know. 'Fuck off,' İkmen murmured. 'Fucking Mr Gören!'

'Inspector İkmen! Is that you?'

It took a while for the reality of what he'd just heard to fil-
ter through, but when it did, İkmen frowned. Mr Gören did
not, as far as he was aware, speak English, or any other foreign
language, come to that. Slowly, İkmen raised his face upwards
into the falling snow. Above him was a great big silver balloon
that made a roaring sound as flames shot hot air up into its
huge body. Someone whom he couldn't recognise because of
the snow was waving at him from the basket underneath the
balloon. The policeman hoped that it wasn't just an illusion.

'What are we going to do?' Tom Chambers said to Atom
Boghosian. 'We're supposed to be looking for the inspector!'

'There's nothing we can do,' Atom replied as he leaned
against the side of the jeep, watching, together with the
Englishman, the progress of the fight between Turgut Senar
and Baha Ermis.

'I wish I knew what it was all about,' Tom said. 'One
minute they were OK and the next minute – this.'

Atom shrugged. 'Without language we are helpless,' he

said. 'I would have felt better if my cousin had come with us.'

'Me too.'

And then the fight, which had up until that moment involved only the two men's fists, took a sinister turn. Baha Ermis reached into a pocket in his jeans and took out something which he then held in front of him. There was a small clicking sound and the innocuous-looking instrument revealed its deadly secret – it was a knife.

'Oh, my God!'

Atom turned to look at Tom and said, 'We are not too far into this valley. I think that maybe we should leave to go and get some help.'

'Well, why don't I phone someone?' the Englishman said as he took his mobile telephone out of one of the pockets in his parka. 'We can't leave them!'

The sound of a thick blade swishing through the air caused them both to look just as Baha took an unsuccessful swipe at Turgut.

'But what if they turn upon us?' Atom said. 'If the one with the knife kills the other one then he will not want any witnesses to his crime. No, he will . . .'

A strange puffing or sucking noise was coming from somewhere. It was nothing to do with either of the men fighting in front of the jeep. In fact it had a most alarming tone to it. Atom turned around in an attempt to locate its source. But then Tom Chambers prodded his shoulder with his finger and said, 'Look, up there!'

He looked up at the very same moment that the two combatants also looked at the sky above the valley.

'Kismet!' Turgut Senar said as he first looked up at Ferdinand Mueller's hot air balloon floating above the valley and then back down at Baha Ermis once again. 'Kismet.'

Baha, his face now white with cold and with fear, dropped his flick-knife on to the ground, and the instrument slipped down a crack in the snow-covered rock and disappeared.

Chapter 18

'I want a cigarette! Give me a cigarette!' İkmen demanded from inside the folds of the enormous blanket Altay Salman had draped round his body.

The horseman looked up at the puffing and overweight doctor, who had just finished looking into İkmen's eyes and taking İkmen's pulse, then shrugged.

'Oh, give him one, for God's sake!' the Armenian said as he shook his head from side to side in disbelief. Then bending down towards İkmen just as Altay Salman placed a cigarette into his mouth he said, 'Don't blame me if you throw up!'

'Fuck off, Arto,' İkmen replied as he breathed in heavily as soon as Altay Salman lit the end of the Marlboro cigarette.

The doctor held his arms aloft in a gesture of submission to the inevitable while İkmen, bent double over his own empty stomach, coughed on to the rock underneath him.

Altay Salman's radio began to crackle and so he turned aside in order to answer it.

'I telephoned Fatma as soon as the balloon pilot told us you were alive,' Arto said as he lowered himself down beside İkmen and then placed an arm round his shoulders.

'Fatma knew I was missing?'

'Everyone knew you were missing,' the Armenian replied. 'I told them.'

'But with Berekiah . . .'

'Fatma told me to tell you that Berekiah is doing very well,' Arto said and then, lowering his voice so that none of the young cadets could hear him, he asked, 'Do you have any idea who did this to you, Çetin? Who brought you here?'

'No. Not really.'

'Maybe it will come back to you,' the doctor said. 'You've had a shock and been through a terrible ordeal.'

'Yes.' İkmen let the smoke permeate every fibre of his being. It hadn't made him feel in the slightest bit nauseous – unlike the sight of the young cadets going into that chimney with its bits of Aysu Alkaya all over its uneven tufa floor. 'Someone wanted to destroy that body. They were afraid of what our tests might reveal.'

'Yes.'

'But the whole village knew about the tests and so . . .'

'Sssh, sssh!' Arto put his hand on Çetin's arm to help to calm his sudden agitation. 'The boys are going to stay with the remains until I get back out here with some proper receptacles for them. You did a really heroic thing when you took them out of that fire, Çetin.'

'I just reacted,' the policeman said as he ground the little that remained of his cigarette out in the snow by his feet. 'Can I have another cigarette now?'

'Yes, I expect so.'

Altay Salman, who had now finished speaking on his radio, said, 'That was one of the boys I sent into the Valley of the Birds. Your cousin and Mr Chambers are safe, Doctor.'

Arto Sarkissian sighed. 'Well, that's a relief.'

İkmen, for whom news about anyone in the Valley of the Birds was all new, said, 'What was Atom Boghosian doing out in some valley in the snow?'

'Looking for you.'

'Turgut Senar took Mr Boghosian, Mr Chambers and Baha Ermis out in his jeep to help with the search,' Altay Salman added. 'Just after Ferdinand and Mrs Mueller found you they also saw Senar, Ermis and their passengers. Although this valley is effectively sealed off from those around it, the Valley of the Birds where Senar and company were searching is only a few hundred metres away. Ferdinand radioed to say that Senar and Ermis were fighting which was why I sent a couple of my lads over there. Apparently one of them had a knife.'

'Why were Ermis and Senar even together?' İkmen asked. 'They're enemies.' And then looking up at the captain he said, 'Altay, can I have another cigarette?'

With a smile the captain leaned down and gave İkmen a whole packet of Marlboro plus his one and only lighter.

'Çetin, do you have any idea how you came to be out here?' Altay Salman asked once he had straightened up again.

'No.' He shook his head. 'I know a vehicle was involved at some point, with people. Lots of people . . .'

'Sir!' One of the captain's cadets came over and snapped his superior a salute.

'Yes?'

'Sir, the snow is thickening. I think that we should get the inspector out of here now.'

The captain nodded his assent. 'Yes, you're quite right,' he said, and leaning down towards İkmen he said, 'If the boys lift you on, are you all right to ride a horse?'

İkmen's eyes widened. 'On my own?'

'I had to, why shouldn't you?' the doctor put in without a great deal of humour.

Altay Salman smiled. 'No, you'll ride with me,' he said. 'You're only light and my Süleyman is a big, strong fellow.'

And so İkmen was lifted on to the horse and left with Altay Salman, the doctor and three of the cadets. The original plan was to get İkmen checked out by a proper medical doctor at the hospital in Nevşehir, but as the snowfall increased that possibility began to recede. When they finally got back to the village, the local doctor, Ali, was brought over to the Fairy Chimneys Hotel in order to check the policeman out. A lot of other people were at the hotel too, some of whom, once he had warmed up a little, İkmen was eager to see.

During the course of the doctor's examination he suddenly remembered one thing about his ordeal. Just one.

The tiny two-roomed apartment reeked of alcohol. As soon as Estelle Cohen opened the door to him, Mehmet Süleyman could see that she was embarrassed.

'Hello, Mehmet,' she said as she failed to immediately usher him inside as she usually did. 'It's very nice to see you.'

'And you, Estelle.'

He bent down in order to remove his shoes and saw her face descend into panic. 'Is it OK?'

'Er . . .'

Shortly after the Karaköy bombing, Balthazar Cohen's brother Leon had contacted the Italian Hospital and offered

278

to take in whichever of his relatives was fit enough not to require medical attention. It was a very generous offer. Leon, although a bachelor, didn't have a lot of space in his fifth-floor apartment in Yeşilköy, but he was prepared to share it with Balthazar and Estelle for the time being. Not that Leon Cohen was often bothered by his new guests. When not out in the city's rougher meyhanes with his group of like-minded male friends, he could generally be found passed out in a puddle of rakı either on his bed or across the floor of the tiny toilet and shower room just beside the front door. Like his father before him, Leon Cohen was a hopeless alcoholic. Unlike his late father, however, he did not, mercifully, have any children or even a wife or girlfriend to suffer his drunken incoherence – only, and latterly, his brother and his wife.

'Who's that at the door?' Mehmet heard a familiar voice call from inside the dingy apartment. 'Estelle?'

'It's Mehmet, Balthazar,' she said. 'Is Leon . . . ?'

'Snoring like a pig in his bed,' Balthazar replied. 'Mehmet knows all about Leon. Let him in, woman!'

The hall floor felt disturbingly sticky as Süleyman walked across it to the small, nicotine-stained living room.

'Come in,' Balthazar said from his place propped up in what looked like a settee in the midst of an explosion. Horsehair and rubber foam spilled from every numerous rent in the body of this terminally disfigured item of furniture.

'I'm sorry about this, Mehmet,' Estelle said as she ushered him over to one of only two dining chairs that stood in front of a slightly listing table.

'We live in reduced circumstances, but at least we are

alive,' her husband said. 'More importantly, Berekiah is alive and we must all thank the Almighty for that.'

'Yes.' Mehmet sat down. In spite of these dismal surroundings he was feeling better now that Fatma İkmen had phoned and told him that Çetin had been found alive. No one had felt the Cohens could take any more bad news at the time when the inspector had first disappeared. But now Süleyman did fill them in on what had been happening out in Cappadocia. It was part of the reason he had come to see them.

'Well, thanks to the Almighty yet again for Çetin Bey's safety,' Balthazar said just as the snores from the bedroom next door reached a crescendo.

'Balthazar . . .'

The small Jew leaned forward in his seat and said, 'You know it was good of Leon to take us in, but . . . My brother Jak called, from England. He's coming over. Jak will sort things out.'

Jak Cohen, Balthazar's older brother, was a very successful night-club owner. He had married and then divorced a British woman, and operated a series of gentleman's clubs across London. It was an occupation that had enabled him to put his son through Cambridge University and buy a lot of property including a picturesque, unrenovated house in Fener for Balthazar's son Berekiah and his family.

'Do you think that Jak will help Berekiah to finish renovating his house?' Mehmet asked as Estelle wordlessly passed him a glass of tea from the huge samovar that stood on the floor over by the window.

'I don't know,' Balthazar shrugged. 'Who can say? Jak is worried about us . . .'

'To be honest, we are all hoping that Jak will make the place habitable so that we can all live there for a while,' Estelle said as she sat down next to Mehmet with her tea.

Her husband lit a cigarette and then sighed. 'It's true,' he said. 'It's a big place and if we could all live there . . .'

'Not for ever,' Estelle interrupted, 'but until the apartment has been repaired.'

'If it is ever repaired . . .'

What they had all been through, coupled with the now nebulous nature of the Cohens' old apartment, temporarily silenced them all. Hulya and the baby were safely ensconced at the İkmen apartment which was where Berekiah would probably go when he was released from the hospital. At least that was were Mehmet hoped he would go. The broken furniture, the reek of alcohol and just the fact of being around an alcoholic as profoundly addicted as Leon, would certainly not help the young man's recovery. But after several minutes had passed Mehmet knew that he couldn't think about any of that any more. He'd come to visit the Cohens for his own reasons and time was moving forward. In the morning Abdullah Aydın would be transferred out of the city.

'Look,' he said, 'I need your help, both of you.'

Balthazar frowned. 'Then ask. Whatever it is, it will be given to you. You know that, Mehmet.'

He took a deep breath. 'I can't tell you why but I need a legitimate excuse to go to the Taksim Hospital tonight.'

'What?'

'I need to speak to someone in there, a patient,' he continued.

'So why don't you just . . .'

'I'm not supposed to speak to this person,' Mehmet said. 'Ardıç has forbidden me to do so.' He looked across at Estelle. 'But I must.'

'Is this for yourself? Or is it business?' Balthazar enquired.

'Oh, it's business,' the younger man replied. 'Life and death. If it was only for myself I would deal with it myself, as you know.'

A terrible jangle of bed springs from the other room signalled that Leon Cohen was either shifting his position or getting up. Estelle looked across at the door with an anxious expression on her face.

'All right, whatever it is, we'll help you, Mehmet,' Balthazar said. 'Because it's you.'

'Thank you.'

'Just, in return, encourage my wife to take the tranquillisers the doctor at the Italian hospital gave her yesterday. Her nerves need to rest, they're stretched like piano wire.'

But before Mehmet could answer, a terrible, rakı-scented presence entered the room wearing nothing but a stained pair of pyjama trousers.

'Who the hell is that?' Leon Cohen asked as he stared, red-eyed, down at Mehmet Süleyman.

'You know I've always wanted to do this,' İkmen said to Altay Salman as the two men walked up the stairs towards Menşure Tokatlı's restaurant. 'My father was very fond of Agatha Christie books. I'd read most of them before I was sixteen. In English, too. I think maybe I've been influenced at a very deep level. What do you think?'

'I don't think anything,' the captain responded darkly. 'All

I know is that if any of the civilians in that restaurant want to leave, I have no reason or means to stop them. You could end up playing Hercule Poirot to an audience of police officers, your cousin and that dreadful cat of hers.'

'Oh, Arto, Atom and Tom will be there,' İkmen said. 'I've told them something of what I believe.'

'I can't arrest the entire village,' Altay said, pausing just below the level of the restaurant for a moment.

'Oh, I'm sure that won't be necessary,' İkmen responded with a smile. 'By the way, did you manage to speak to someone at the mortuary?'

'Yes.'

'And was it as I suspected?' İkmen asked.

'It would appear so,' his companion said, but with some sadness in his voice.

'I see.'

The sun had not yet set over Muratpaşa and so not everyone present was taking advantage of the free tea and coffee that Menşure Tokatlı was providing. Everyone had, however, stayed around to see what was about to happen. After all, the policeman from İstanbul had been found, alive, and in company with, it was said, some very gruesome human remains. Even some of those who hadn't been involved in the search had turned up to see what was going on. One of these, İkmen noticed, was Nazlı Kahraman.

As he walked past the Lemon Queen, İkmen smiled and said, 'I'm surprised that Baha was out with Turgut Senar, looking for me. I'm flattered that he should be so concerned.'

'I sent Baha,' the elderly woman snapped. 'I wanted him to see what Turgut Senar was up to.' She looked briefly across at the object of her hatred and said, 'I don't trust Senar. I thought he might have hurt you, Inspector.'

Turgut Senar just curled his lip in response.

'But now I can see that he has not, I am content,' Nazlı Kahraman continued. 'But it is my fault that Baha got into that fight, Inspector. I put him in that position. You must not think badly of him.'

İkmen noted that Baha Ermis still continued to hang his head in what looked very much like shame, in spite of his employer's supportive words.

İkmen made his way over to a row of padded seats beside the table upon which bubbled both the samovar and the coffee percolator. After he had helped himself to tea, an unusually large amount of sugar and, of course, a cigarette, İkmen called for silence.

Everyone in the room immediately stopped whatever they were doing and looked at him.

Of course Balthazar Cohen had been very ready and willing to indulge in a little off-the-record police assistance, but the logistics of getting him away from Leon's and over to the hospital were not that simple. The apartment lift was broken and Leon was totally useless when it came to assisting with the lifting and carrying of his brother. Though not quite so willing, Estelle Cohen agreed to help Mehmet Süleyman in his mysterious quest at the Taksim hospital. She wasn't entirely certain that she could create a diversion for him, however.

'If you want to go away from the waiting area and into the hospital, why don't you just go?' she said as she sat beside him in the car.

'I'm not supposed to go into the Taksim,' he said, patiently reiterating what he had already gone over with her several times now. 'Somebody doesn't want me to talk to one of the patients in there. But that is exactly what I have to do. Hence my need for your help, Estelle and that of,' he looked up at the shabby wooden building that the car was parked in front of and sighed, 'İbrahim.'

Just at that moment a dark, lanky young man wearing way too much jewellery about his person came out of the shabby house and smiled at the occupants of the car. İbrahim İnçesu had been Berekiah Cohen's best friend ever since they had played together in the streets of Karaköy as little boys. Even when the İnçesu family moved away to Hasköy, Berekiah and İbrahim remained close. Not even İbrahim's more latterly developed tastes for drinking, fighting and generally breaking his poor mother's heart could do any more than occasionally shake their friendship. So when Berekiah's 'big brother' Mehmet Süleyman had called İbrahim to ask whether he would like to do him a favour, the twenty-six-year-old had responded immediately.

'Does it involve any danger?' had been his first question.

Süleyman replied that danger was possible and, what was more, shouting and general obnoxiousness was required in some quantity. İbrahim had agreed to do whatever the policeman wanted immediately. It was worrying: İbrahim was what many people would have called unhinged. Just his voice, when shouting, could chill the blood. But then what Süleyman needed – someone to create a diversion for him – did of necessity require a high level of noise and general bad behaviour. Balthazar, of course, could have created exactly the same effect just by sobbing at the top of his voice. The sight of a man with no legs weeping is difficult for even the most hard-hearted bystander to ignore. But Balthazar was not with them and İbrahim was.

As soon as the young man got into Süleyman's white BMW, they headed off towards the Taksim Hospital. The sky was beginning to darken now and in just over an hour it would be iftar. Süleyman, aware of just how erratic the driving of those anxious to get home to eat can become, drove rather more carefully than usual. After all, Abdullah Aydın wasn't due to be moved from the Taksim until the following morning and so theoretically Süleyman could have the entire night at his disposal. That was of course provided his 'Auntie' Estelle wasn't either seen by a doctor immediately or failed in her task of pretending to be in pain. The latter case was possible but that the former was almost laughable was underwritten power-fully as Süleyman, Estelle and İbrahim entered the hospital waiting area.

'What do you want?' a small, but staggeringly hard-faced nurse asked them as they approached the great mass of moaning and grimacing people waiting for some sort of medical attention.

'My aunt was injured in the Karaköy bombing,' Süleyman said as he looked affectionately at Estelle. 'She was taken to the Italian Hospital at the time . . .'

'They were very kind,' Estelle said by way of explanation.

'But now she is having pain again, in her arm,' Süleyman said.

'Well, what is she doing here?' the nurse enquired. 'Take her back to the Italian Hospital.'

'I can't,' Süleyman looked, he hoped, with dewy eyes at the nurse in front of him. Then moving in more closely to her he dropped his voice. 'My aunt is poor,' he said. 'My brother and I have brought her because we don't want her to suffer. But we cannot afford medical bills for our entire family. We have parents, wives . . .'

'Well, we'll need to have photocopies of her papers first,' the nurse said as she gestured limply towards an endless line of people. 'Over there.'

'I presume it's my job to get in line for Auntie,' İbrahim said as he helped Süleyman lead Estelle towards a group of five elderly ladies who immediately made room for her on the three small chairs that they shared.

'Yes, please, my dear brother. Auntie can't possibly stand in her condition.'

As she sat down Süleyman noticed that his 'aunt' winced with pain in a very convincing manner. Estelle Cohen was an amazing woman. After all the shocks and traumas she'd been through – both recently and in the past – she was still giving this latest little adventure her all.

'Dear Auntie,' he said as he took her documents from her then planted a kiss on her cheek and straightened up. He then went with İbrahim over to the disgruntled line of people waiting to photocopy their documents.

'So when do I start screaming?' the younger man asked with rather more relish in his voice than Süleyman would have liked.

'When I tell you.'

'Which . . .'

'I'm going to go and find the toilet now,' Süleyman said as

he looked around in order to get his bearings. 'You stay here in the line with Auntie's documents and no noises until I say so. OK?'

'If that's the deal, that's the deal,' İbrahim responded breezily.

'That's the deal, İbrahim.'

And stepping carefully over those patients who had probably lost hope long ago and were now lying asleep on the floor, Süleyman began to make his way to the front of the waiting area and the corridor which, he knew, eventually, led to the back of the premises and Abdullah Aydın's police-guarded room.

Chapter 19

İkmen first looked out of the window towards the darkening, snow-blizzarded Fairy Chimneys opposite before he spoke. Soon the muezzin would call the faithful to prayer and the Ramazan fast would be broken. But as he looked at the assembled company around him in Menşure's restaurant, he couldn't imagine any of them rushing home to eat on this particular occasion. With just one more glance towards an anxious-looking Altay Salman, he said, 'Before we start I should just tell you all that I know who kidnapped and attempted to kill me and who killed Aysu Alkaya twenty years ago.'

There wasn't so much as a sharp intake of breath. Only the sound of Arto Sarkissian's muted English translation of his words – for Tom's and Atom's benefit – made any impact upon the almost corporeal silence in that room. If he had dropped what remained of Aysu Alkaya, which the captain's recruits had now transported back to the village, on to one of the dining tables in front of them all he could not have stunned or shocked them more. Almost a minute had passed before the only person capable of speaking did so.

'Then give us the names, Inspector,' Dr Ali said in that elderly, almost casual tone of his.

İkmen smiled. 'I will,' he said. 'But not before we've all

gone on a journey – into both the distant and the recent past history of this lovely village of Muratpaşa.'

Menşure Tokatlı, upon whom the irony of İkmen's words were not lost, cleared her throat and then she busied her hands rearranging the cat Kismet on her lap. He started purring into the silence which was eventually only brought to an end by Çetin İkmen.

'All right,' he said as he surveyed both Nazlı Kahraman and the small figure of Haldun Alkaya who had come in with one of the jandarma at the back of the room. 'Let us get some things out in the open in this village of secrets, shall we? Ziya Kahraman paid Nalan Senar to object to a match between Kemalettin and Aysu Alkaya.' He looked round the room to see whether Nalan was present, but she wasn't. Turgut, however, sat gloomily beside his erstwhile adversary, Baha Ermis. 'He wanted the girl because he believed her to be without either genetic taint or deformity. But, sadly for Ziya Bey, he was duped by Haldun Alkaya because Aysu was deformed and he was not happy.'

A lot of people in the room turned to look at Haldun Alkaya who nevertheless remained silent.

'She had six toes on each foot,' İkmen continued. 'Ziya Bey must have had a very nasty shock on his wedding night.'

'He took her!' Nazlı Kahraman protested fiercely. 'The whole village saw her bloodied sheet!'

Various people murmured their agreement.

'I'm sure that a bloodied sheet was held aloft and I'm sure that the celebrations of Ziya Bey's marriage were most enthusiastic,' İkmen said. 'But whether Ziya Bey made Aysu Alkaya pregnant is another matter. If he did then it would seem unlikely he would have killed her – unless you subscribe to the view that the perfectionist Lemon King would have hated the possibility of having a deformed child.'

'My father would never . . .'

'Or that the child wasn't indeed Ziya's own,' İkmen interrupted. 'But we will leave aside who may or may not have been the father of Aysu Alkaya's child for the time being except to say that I know that you, Nazlı Hanım, knew that the girl was pregnant.'

The old woman looked at him with real hatred on her face.

'That first time I met you, you told me that you had washed Aysu's clothes with your own hands.'

'Not every day!'

'Maybe not,' İkmen said. 'But if you were washing clothes at all you would know who was bleeding or had bled and who was not. You are a woman, Nazlı Hanım, a much older woman than Aysu Alkaya, but I think you would have known whether or not the girl was pregnant.'

'I did not . . .'

'Having said that,' İkmen said as he raised a hand to silence her, 'I don't believe for a moment that you killed her, Nazlı Hanım. I don't think either that you genuinely do know who killed her.'

All eyes were now turned towards Nazlı Kahraman who said, 'In that, at least, you are correct, Inspector.'

'I think you worry that people think that your father killed his last wife . . .'

'But he didn't.'

İkmen didn't answer her. Some moments of what was almost silence, save for the English translation whispered by

Arto Sarkissian, passed before he spoke again, this time to Turgut Senar.

'What is so special about the American Dolores Lavell's father?'

The American was not in the room as far as İkmen could see, but he saw Turgut Senar look for her before he answered.

'Nothing.'

'I disagree,' İkmen responded.

Everybody looked at him.

'For years you've seen this woman come and go. You've taken no notice of her at all. Then she shows you a photograph of her father and you are suddenly the woman's best friend.'

Turgut Senar shrugged. 'Are you saying I killed somebody, or . . .'

'No, I'm saying that I think you remember Dolores' father from when he used to come here years ago, when he was in the American forces. I think that his presence here has some meaning for you.'

'What do you mean?'

İkmen panned his gaze around the entire room. 'Do you know what kind of weapon was used to kill Aysu Alkaya?'

'No . . .'

'A pistol called a Colt 45,' İkmen said. 'An American weapon, carried by soldiers like Dolores' father in the late 1950s and early 1960s.'

Turgut Senar turned his head away.

'It is not a weapon one comes across every day in Turkey.' İkmen put his cigarette out and then immediately lit another. 'At least not in a place like Muratpaşa. Of course, all that we have of the weapon is the bullet that was fired from it back in 1983. How old the gun actually is, I don't personally know, but I suspect it is of 1950s vintage.' He looked for and found the pale face of Inspector Erten and asked him, 'Have ballistics come back to you with any more information, yet, Inspector?'

'Er, no, not yet.'

İkmen smiled. 'Ah well,' he said, 'no matter.' And then he turned back to Turgut Senar once again. 'I'm not accusing you of killing anyone with a gun or otherwise, Turgut,' he said. 'I just want to know whether you knew Dolores Lavell's father and his friends back in the 1960s . . .'

'No.'

'What's he saying about me?' a voice with an American accent asked in English.

Dolores Lavell stood at the top of the stairs, panting from the climb.

İkmen switched to English and said, 'I just asked Mr Senar whether or not he knew your father, Miss Lavell. He said that he did not. Do you think that he is telling me the truth?'

She moved further into the room, shrugging as she did so. 'I don't know,' she said. 'Why don't you ask his brother?'

'Kemalettin?'

'Yeah.'

'Why should I ask Kemalettin, Miss Lavell?' İkmen asked.

Dolores Lavell sat down almost opposite a now wide-eyed Turgut Senar and said, 'Kemalettin told me to get away from Turgut while I could earlier today. He said that his brother was only interested in me because he used to know my daddy when he was a kid. I asked Kemalettin how that could be, how a little Turkish kid could have known a big black man like my daddy, but he said he couldn't tell me that.'

'Why not?'

'Because, Inspector, Kemalettin said that his brother and his mom had told him never to talk about it. Could all just be in Kemalettin's head, I don't know . . .'

İkmen moved to stand over Turgut Senar and said, 'Where is your brother Kemalettin now, Mr Senar?'

There was still a police guard outside Abdullah Aydın's hospital room. Again it was an officer Süleyman didn't recognise although, in spite of the fact that the man didn't speak to him as he passed – he appeared barely sentient – the inspector knew it would have been foolish to assume he had not been seen. Without looking at the officer again he pushed his way into the men's lavatory and then leaned back against the wall with a sigh.

It would have been more pleasant for Süleyman had he been alone in the toilet, but he wasn't. The hospital was packed and so it was logical that the toilets should come in for a lot of punishment as a consequence. Not all of the men in there with him were bleeding, but a significant minority were engaged in doing just that into the sinks and, in one case, on to the floor. Some groaning was going on, too, as well as a lot of coughing, which was not made any better by the fact that everyone was smoking. Süleyman, braced against the wall, closed his eyes. In order to force the police officer away from Abdullah's room, İbrahim was going to have to make a scene so terrible he would probably end up being imprisoned for years. Now that he'd walked the route Süleyman realised just how far it was. With great impatience he sighed. İbrahim making an exhibition of himself in the waiting area just wasn't going to be good enough.

'Kemalettin was standing outside the Cappudocia Coffee Bean last time I saw him,' Rachelle Jones said to İkmen. 'That was, I suppose, about half an hour ago. He was just letting the snow fall on his head. Looked like a snowman.'

'Go and see if you can find him,' İkmen said to the small group of jandarma that had gathered around him. 'Oh and bring his mother here, too, if you can, we need all the "actors" in this drama now.'

'Yes, Inspector.'

As the jandarma left, İkmen went back over to Turgut Senar, still uncomfortably seated beside Baha Ermis, and said, 'You know that it's my belief all of this – Aysu Alkaya's death, my abduction – is about money.'

'I thought you said you knew who killed Aysu Alkaya,' Turgut Senar replied. 'And who kidnapped you.'

'I don't know why, if you know, you don't just come out and tell us,' Nazlı Kahraman put in. 'It seems to me, Inspector, that you're getting some sort of pleasure out of our discomfort.'

'I've just been stuck out in a frozen valley with a half-burned corpse!' İkmen blustered. 'I've been beaten up. Of course I want to make you suffer, Nazlı Hanım.'

The room became very still. İkmen caught Altay Salman's nervous eye. Menşure Tokatlı cleared her throat in what could only be described as a threatening fashion.

'The people who abducted me tried to burn Aysu Alkaya's

body,' İkmen said rather more calmly now. 'I rescued what I could of it from the flames and what remains will accompany Dr Sarkissian and myself back to İstanbul for analysis.' He swept his gaze quickly around the room. 'In view of my abduction everyone in this village will be DNA tested and if anything matches what remains on Aysu's body or on my clothes, that person will have to give an account of his or herself . . .'

'But, I repeat, if you know who did it, Inspector,' Nazlı Kahraman said, 'why not just tell us? Surely you want to arrest this felon . . .'

'*Felons*,' İkmen corrected. 'Quite a few people kidnapped me, Nazlı Hanım. One was wearing very distinctive items of clothing.'

And then came the call to prayer, signifying the end of the fast for that day. Considering the fact that most of those present were fasting, the number of people moving over to the samovar for tea was surprisingly small even if a veritable host of individuals lit cigarettes once the call was at an end.

'God, this is exciting,' Tom Chambers whispered to his Armenian companions. 'The inspector is magnificent.'

'Çetin can at times overcome the impression that his small and shabby appearance can sometimes give,' Arto Sarkissian replied. 'I just hope that everyone is as awestruck as you, Mr Chambers.'

'Why's that?'

Arto Sarkissian leaned in more closely to the Englishman. 'Because while they are dazzled by him, they will not be asking themselves whether he is telling them the truth about what he says he knows.'

'Oh.'

'He is taking a sort of a gamble if you will,' Arto said.

İkmen watched closely the comings and goings from the samovar. The German, Ferdinand Mueller, gave him what İkmen interpreted as a knowing look.

'Yes, I know, I will get to that,' he said to the balloonist in English.

'It may be nothing . . .'

'It may be, but we will see,' İkmen said.

He may have said more had not the jandarma returned with a very white-faced Nalan Senar. Behind her, but holding her hand, was a snow-drenched Kemalettin. They moved straight away to sit next to Turgut. İkmen did not try to stop them.

Süleyman made İbrahim wait ten minutes before he allowed him to set off for the lavatory along the corridor. Following at a distance, the older man just hoped that his young protégé didn't go too far over the top with his unreasoning crazy person act.

In view of the distance involved, from the waiting area to Abdullah Aydın's room, Süleyman had decided that a rather more local diversion was what was needed. So, if İbrahim could pick a fight with one of the men in the lavatory across the corridor, the officer on guard was much more likely to become involved with it. After all, he was a young man and, important assignment or no important assignment, it was unlikely he'd be able to resist the opportunity of a good brawl. Süleyman followed his friend as far as the bend in the corridor just before the private room and the lavatories. He then leaned back against the sickly green paintwork, sweating. İbrahim was, he knew, a real force to be reckoned with once he got into a fight. But the officer was armed and, although he desperately wanted and needed to know what Abdullah Aydın might know about the peeper, Süleyman was also quite nervous about what might happen next. For some time there was only silence.

At first it wasn't İbrahim who broke the silence, but the sunset call to prayer. The police officer first sighed and then took a large simit roll out of his jacket pocket and bit into it. Only when he was halfway through his supper did things in the lavatory begin to kick off.

At first it was impossible to make out what was being shouted or by whom. A rumble of male voices tumbled out on to the corridor, eliciting only one fleeting glance from the police officer. He, like Süleyman, knew that things can get heated in hospitals and that more often than not disputes between patients or patients and staff blow over quickly. This, however, went on. Over a minute passed and then Süleyman distinctly heard İbrahim's furious voice.

'You did it on purpose, you filthy pig!' İbrahim screeched.

The other man or men involved said something to which the boy replied, 'You can get AIDS from blood! If you've given me AIDS . . .'

The police officer looked up from his simit.

'I haven't got AIDS!' A huge and furious voice boomed from inside the toilet. 'Only queers get AIDS!'

'Well, maybe you are queer!'

Allah, but when İbrahim did something he really did it thoroughly! Süleyman had no idea about the size or appearance of the man he had obviously accused of getting his blood

298

on him somehow. But if he sounded as big as his voice then İbrahim could be in trouble.

'Queer!'

'Bastard!'

Someone or something fell to the ground and the police officer got off his squat hospital chair and took his baton from out of its holster. For a moment he just stood outside the toilet listening to the noises of heads and elbows hitting the hard, concrete floor. Süleyman, wincing at what sounded like İbrahim's pain, held his breath as he waited for the officer to go inside the lavatory. Just go in, he thought as he watched the officer first look at the lavatory door and then back at Abdullah Aydın's room. He had obviously been told not to leave his post under any circumstances, but would he obey? Süleyman could almost see the arguments and counter-arguments pass across the poor man's brain until suddenly, at the moment when it seemed most likely he would return to his post, he opened the lavatory door and went inside.

'What is all this?' he yelled. 'Are you mad?'

Checking quickly that no one else was about to see him, Süleyman ran from his hiding place and, barely daring to breathe, he stood in front of Abdullah Aydın's door.

'If you hit me again . . .' he heard İbrahim scream as he let himself inside the dimly lit room and then took a moment to catch his breath.

The boy, Abdullah Aydın, appeared to be asleep on the bed. Lying on his side facing away from the door he breathed even-ly and without noise. None of the machines that Süleyman had seen inside that room on his first visit seemed to be either attached to anything or working. Abdullah did not, it seemed, need any help from outside sources any longer. The men in the toilet were still screaming and so Süleyman moved quietly towards the bed and the boy inside it.

'Abdullah,' he whispered.

The pain as his arm was pushed way beyond where it should go up his back was so intense that it momentarily rendered him speechless.

'Ah, Sunel Bey,' an eerily familiar voice said, 'we've been expecting you.'

Chapter 20

İkmen smiled. 'Well, now that most of those who I think should be here are here, let us continue.'

Both Turgut and Nalan Senar looked down at the floor while Kemalettin stared, as usual, into space. Everyone including the Senars expected İkmen to now question Nalan and her family, but he didn't.

'Inspector Erten.' İkmen looked at the Nevşehir man and beckoned him forwards.

'Yes?' He shuffled out of his seat and went towards İkmen with a smile.

'Would you like to tell us how Aysu Alkaya's body came to be missing from the mortuary in Nevşehir?'

'Well, I don't . . .'

'Please sit,' İkmen said as he made room for Erten beside him. 'When did it go missing, exactly?'

'On Saturday,' he began. 'I saw it on Saturday morning, just prior to coming out here . . .'

'But why did you come out here?' İkmen asked. 'Dr Sarkissian and myself had agreed to meet you with the body in Nevşehir.'

'Well, as I told you at the time, Inspector, I felt I should at least ask about the possibility of taking DNA samples from the villagers . . .'

'Yes, but you didn't have to do it then, did you?'

'I thought that Dr Sarkissian might have those swabs they use with him . . .'

'You went to the mortuary at six a.m. on Saturday morning,' İkmen said. 'We've checked.'

Erten looked up, confused. 'Checked? With whom?'

'With the authorities at the mortuary. One of the guards was coming to the end of his shift when you arrived. His replacement wasn't due to take over from him until six thirty a.m. You told the first man to go. You said that you would cover for him until his replacement arrived.'

'Which I did.'

'Yes, indeed.'

'It was the last time I saw Aysu Alkaya's body. I went to make sure that everything was in order.'

'No, I don't think that's entirely true,' İkmen said.

'But . . .'

'I think that you went to steal Aysu Alkaya's body, Inspector Erten,' İkmen said. 'I think you then drove it over here and deposited it with someone for future disposal.'

The country policeman's face, though white, did not appear to be ruffled. 'And why would I do that?'

'Because somebody gave you the two things I believe you most crave in this world, Inspector,' İkmen said.

'And what are they?'

'Knowledge of who committed the crime that has haunted you for most of your professional life, and money. I think that you were paid to make sure that Aysu Alkaya's body never reached İstanbul and I know, Inspector Erten, that you were instrumental in abducting me.'

Various people around and about turned to look at each other with confusion on their faces.

Erten, shaking now in his thin grey raincoat, said, 'How? How do you know or think that you do?'

İkmen looked down at Erten's feet and said, 'Your shoes really are an outrage, Inspector. They're even worse than mine. Even by deprived rural standards, they are appalling. You don't forget shoes like that in a hurry and I got to have quite a close-up view of them when someone was smacking me around the head in that vehicle. It took a while for my poor old brain to recall . . .'

'That proves nothing and you know it!'

'Do you want to take the risk of your DNA evidence turning up on either my clothes or what remains of that body?' İkmen said.

'But we have been round one another, Inspector . . .'

'But you haven't been round that body without gloves, have you?' İkmen said. 'Unless of course you carried it out to your car. Leaning over it with bits of your hair dropping down on to its face, fragments of your skin falling on to the clothes it was wearing. The head, Inspector, is intact, as are some limbs, some tapestry, some other human remains I pulled from the fire . . .'

'All right!' He put his head in his hands and for a moment appeared to be weeping. But when he lifted his head again his eyes were dry.

'Somebody,' İkmen said, 'had to get that body over to those abandoned caves from Nevşehir. You were, according to the log, the last person to enter that mortuary before Aysu's body was reported missing, by you, on Sunday morning. No one went in or came out. Do you know what I think?'

Erten stared at him dumbly.

'I think that Dr Sarkissian and I were meant to find that Aysu's body was missing on the Saturday morning when we accompanied you back to the mortuary. I think you had a nice little story ready about giving us all a lift into town. But when you realised that the doctor wasn't going to be able to make it until Sunday you had to change your plans which was why we went off on that fruitless quest to see the Senar family.' He coughed. 'Now I'm not saying you had anything to do with it but that terrorist attack in İstanbul certainly helped you, didn't it? I might have thought a bit more critically about what was happening if that hadn't happened. Now are you prepared to take the risk of forensic evidence further condemning you or are you going to tell me who paid you to take part in this little enterprise?'

Erten first looked at İkmen, then at the Senar family, then at Nazlı Kahraman.

'Well?'

There were three men in the room with him apart from Abdullah Aydın. But even before Süleyman was turned round to look into Mürsel Bey's hard and unamused eyes, the third man had taken the boy away into another room.

The elegant homosexual moved over to the now-vacant bed and sat down. 'Let his arms down just a little, will you, Haydar,' he said to the man who was holding Süleyman so hard it took his breath away. 'Bring him over here.'

Whilst pushing him from behind, the man holding

304

Süleyman slackened his grip upon his arm just a little.

'Now, Inspector Süleyman,' Mürsel said as he took the policeman surprisingly gently from his previous captor, 'I must ask you not to even think about trying to get away from us. I don't want to have to ask Haydar to kill you.'

There was every reason to suppose that he meant every word of it.

Süleyman looked up at him and said, 'Who are you?'

'Someone who is a lot better at concealing his identity than you,' the man replied. 'Now you will listen and I will talk and when I have done you will give me your word that nothing I have told you will go any further. If you can't do that I will kill you. If you break your word I will kill you and anyone you have shared this information with. Is that clear?'

'Who are you?' Süleyman reiterated.

The man he knew as Mürsel took a gun out of his jacket pocket and held it against Süleyman's head. 'Is that clear?'

'Yes . . .'

He smiled again. 'Good. If you go to the hamam, dear boy, you have to be ready to sweat as the saying goes.' He put the weapon away. 'Now, Mehmet,' he said, 'what you must understand is that I am a man who loves his country. I love it so much, I would deem it an honour to give my life for it. In fact almost my entire adult life so far has been dedicated to the protection and care of my country.'

'So . . .'

'I'm talking, Mehmet.' He put one large finger across the policeman's lips. 'You are listening. Now, like most people, I do not work in isolation. Haydar here, for instance, works and has worked with me for many years.'

Süleyman looked up at the tall, rather spare man who was now blocking his path towards the door. There was something familiar about him.

'There are many people like us both inside and outside the country.'

What he was saying was obvious. He worked for MIT. Süleyman shuddered. The CIA, Mossad, MIT, *those* sorts of people might have a different name in every country across the globe, but what they did was chillingly uniform.

'Now it is a well-known fact,' the man continued, 'that from time to time somebody like me finds what we do rather too much to cope with. Caring for the nation is a tremendous strain. Usually, Mehmet, such people are informed of their lack of fitness, shall we say, long before their condition may become problematic for the rest of us. However, sometimes when one has been working abroad, particularly in an area of, let us say, tension and for a considerable amount of time, certain early warning signs may be overlooked. Sadly, this has happened in what is becoming one spectacular case.'

Süleyman swallowed hard.

'You know what comes next, don't you, Mehmet? You know because suddenly your investigation into the person you call the peeper seems to have hit a brick wall. That is me, Mürsel, otherwise called that nice Inspector Doğan who has been so kind to the Aydın family.' He smiled. 'Poor Commissioner Ardıç tried his best to stop your meddling and I haven't lost sight of you for days but you would persist. I blame Çetin İkmen.'

'How do you know . . .'

'Don't talk!' He slapped him once, hard, around the face. It stung like hell. 'Now although we were not a hundred per cent certain that your peeper was one of ours, young Abdullah's description of his assailant would seem to confirm our fears. This is a very dangerous, as well as a very disordered individual. He has been taught to eliminate those who pose a threat by those who, let us say, know more about the ways in which a person may die than most. Make no mistake, you will not catch him. He will kill others and he will kill you. Haydar and myself together with our other colleague have been given the task of neutralising this individual, which we will do. We have, after all, been trained in the same school as this person. However, because of the nature of this person's activities and the fear that he has engendered in the public it is important that a police input is maintained. After all, people like Haydar and myself, like our friend who has lost his sense of proportion, do not usually interact professionally with the ordinary man or woman in the street. Mürsel Bey goes to work at his import-export business on a daily basis. He even has a wife, although no children; I lied to you about that.' And then suddenly he smiled again and said, 'Now you can speak.'

Nazlı Kahraman began to cry. 'I don't know why you're looking at me!' she said to Erten. 'I didn't steal any corpse! I asked that idiot Baha Ermiş if he did and he told me no.'

'I didn't kill Aysu.' Kemalettin Senar shook his head while his mother and brother looked at him, their eyes full of fear. 'I did meet her outside Ziya Bey's house and I did take her to the chimney with the picture of the mummy on the wall, but . . .'

'Kemalettin!'

'I told you that I saw him outside Ziya Bey's house that

night and you didn't believe me, did you?' Baha Ermis said as he pointed an accusatory finger at Inspector Erten.

Kemalettin Senar turned to his mother and said, 'But then she disappeared.'

İkmen, his attention now caught by the strange snow-covered individual in front of him, said, 'Kemalettin, I believe you. I don't think that you killed Aysu; you loved her, didn't you?'

'Yes.' He put his head down then and murmured, 'She was having a baby.'

'Was it your baby, Kemalettin?'

'You have no right to ask him that!' Nalan Senar said as she jumped to her feet. 'My poor son is an idiot, like my father. He doesn't know what he's saying!'

'Let me be the judge of that, Nalan Hanım,' İkmen replied and then turning back to her son he said, 'Well?'

'Aysu said that it was mine.'

Several people amongst those present gasped. Menşure Tokatlı shook her head sadly while one elderly matron said, 'Shame!'

'We were going to run away together,' Kemalettin continued. 'Aysu was so unhappy with Ziya Bey.'

'And so you went out the night that she disappeared and you took her to this cave with the mummy which was special to you.'

'Yes. It was a secret between Aysu and me. We went to the cave with the mummy. I left her there with food and drink.'

'And what happened then?' İkmen asked.

'I went home and went to bed,' Kemalettin said. 'Then in the morning when I went back to go with her – we were going to go to İstanbul – she was gone.'

Which meant that whoever had killed Aysu had moved her

body to another chimney, one without the picture of the mummy on the wall.

İkmen turned to Inspector Erten who was still sitting, shamed, at his side. 'I assume you know who killed Aysu Alkaya, Inspector. I don't think that Kemalettin has a clue. Would you care to enlighten him?'

The policeman passed his tired gaze around the room once again and then said, 'Inspector İkmen, you must understand . . .'

'Did Ziya Kahraman follow his wife and her lover out to the Valley of the Saints, or was someone else involved?'

'My father didn't leave our house all night!' Nazlı Kahraman yelled. 'How dare you make such an accusation against a dead man!'

İkmen looked across at Erten and said, 'Well? We're going to find out anyway, Inspector. You might as well do yourself a favour and tell us. The rift that crosses this village has to be healed some time. Who killed Aysu Alkaya?'

Inspector Erten sighed. But before he could actually speak another voice, that of a woman, interjected, 'It was me.'

'It was Kemalettin's mother,' Arto Sarkissian translated for Tom and Atom. 'Good God!'

'So what you're saying,' Süleyman began, 'is that MIT . . .'

'I didn't say that I was with MIT, did I?' the man cut in gravely and looking up at his colleague, he said, 'Haydar, did I ever say that we worked for MIT?'

'No, Mürsel Bey.'

'No.' He turned back to Süleyman. 'We are patriots who get paid for being patriotic, Inspector. Let us not name names we do not understand.'

Süleyman breathed deeply as he tried to get a hold on his shaking nerves. 'OK, if you will. Well . . . Look, if you know this man, then why is he doing this?'

'Killing queers? I don't actually know,' Mürsel replied with a shrug. 'I have a good idea, but that isn't something I'm prepared to share with you.'

'Yes, but if you accept that input from the police is still necessary . . .'

'We, as I have told you before, Inspector, will apprehend this person, not you.' He offered Süleyman a cigarette and then took one for himself. Mürsel had, Süleyman noted with some amazement, even brought an ashtray. 'You will, of course, continue to investigate these crimes. The public must not have any notion of any difference or oddness at play here. You will even be required to share information with us about whatever you may discover on your own account. But information will only be shared in one direction. I will ask you a question and you will answer it, you will not ask me anything.'

'So we will assist you?'

'If you want to look at it like that, yes,' Mürsel replied. 'But you will not apprehend this person. If by some miracle it looks as if that might be likely, you will contact us immediately. Let us be clear you are not to arrest this person, you are not to wound or kill him, you are not even to speak to him. After what Abdullah Aydın has told us, we are now certain that our suspicions have been confirmed. We've been following clues and hints of this person for some time. He belongs to us; he's lethal and we will take care of him.'

Süleyman smoked in silence for a few moments as he attempted to absorb what he had just been told.

'Our aim is to remove him from circulation. After that these crimes will stop. Unfortunately for the police these crimes will remain unsolved which will not look good for you, but there it is.'

'What will you do with this person?' Süleyman asked. 'When you . . .'

'That's none of your business,' Mürsel said shortly. 'But I'm not going to deliver a convenient body to you, if that is what you're asking. The peeper will just simply disappear. People do it all the time.'

Süleyman felt a cold shudder snake down his spine. Mürsel was so casual about it all. But then people like him were, or so it was said.

'Now I will give you a number to ring which you can use at any time,' Mürsel said. 'Give me your mobile and I'll put it in for you.'

Süleyman did as he was asked.

As Mürsel plugged the number into the telephone he said, 'I've put it under "Haydar" who will never be very far away from you.' He looked up and smiled. 'You may or may not know this, but it was Haydar who first spotted you outside the hamam. We both agreed you were very obviously a policeman.'

Süleyman put his head down a little and shrugged.

'Oh, don't be upset!' Mürsel laughed. 'You stared at Haydar for quite some time yourself! Lurking in that shop doorway he looked like a pervert!'

So that was where he'd seen this Haydar before, outside the hamam in Karaköy.

'Was it Haydar in the garden of my house?'

'No, but I know who it was,' Mürsel replied.

'And?'

'And I'm not going to tell you,' he said with a shrug. 'I don't have to.' He then handed the mobile back to Süleyman. 'Now I will inform Ardıç that we've had this conversation and I imagine he will want to see you. You will continue your investigations but I suggest that you now reassure your colleagues that everything is in order. Young Mr Aydın didn't have anything of value to say on the subject of his attacker and by tomorrow he will have left to convalesce at a nice resort on the south coast.'

'Which is just where he won't be, I assume?'

'We will keep Mr Aydın safe until all of this unpleasantness is at an end.'

Suddenly aware that he could no longer hear any noise from outside the door, Süleyman said, 'Er, I have a friend . . .'

'You have dear little Mrs Cohen still lining up to get her documents photocopied and some lunatic I believe you encouraged to fight in the toilet, yes.'

'Well?'

'Well, if you promise not to leave, I will ask Haydar to find out what our young guard might have done about that.'

Süleyman said he wouldn't leave. Mursel's gun if nothing else was inducement enough.

'I expect your lunatic is all right,' Mürsel said as Haydar left to go about his business. 'You'll tell him and Mrs Cohen that you spoke to the person you needed to see but that he had nothing of value to tell you.'

'Yes . . .'

Mürsel put his cigarette out in his ashtray and then leaned

in towards Süleyman. 'You know,' he said, 'I did enjoy our drink at the Büyük Londra Hotel. You may not be very good at hiding what you are, but you lie quite convincingly.' His eyes sparkled with mischief, 'And the kiss was delightful.'

'Oh, so you didn't lie about . . .'

'I enjoy beautiful things,' Mürsel responded. 'I avail myself of sexual pleasure whenever it presents itself. I have been married to this woman for some years – it suits me and what I purport to be. But if circumstances were to change I wouldn't give a thought to leaving her. She is transitory. I like women, but I like men too. I enjoyed our little frisson.'

'I am not gay, Mürsel Bey,' Süleyman said very properly.

'Neither am I, but I'm sure that we could both enjoy having sex in spite of that.' He placed one large hand on Süleyman's thigh.

'Mürsel Bey . . .'

'Oh, don't worry, I'm not going to force you,' Mürsel said, amused at the look of cringing horror on Süleyman's face. 'That wouldn't be any fun. But you will come round, I believe, my dear Sunel Bey of the Büyük Londra Hotel. It is just too fortuitous that you became more involved with this problem of mine than you should have. I sometimes think that maybe I organised it to be this way. Having seen you . . .'

'The lunatic has been delivered back to his aunt in the waiting area,' Haydar said as he re-entered the room. Mürsel let his hand linger for just a moment on Süleyman's thigh before removing it. It seemed he needed Haydar to see this for some reason.

'Thank you, Haydar,' he said and then looking back at Süleyman again he smiled. 'Now you have a lot of people to reassure, don't you, Inspector? Auntie Estelle, your lunatic, that oafish thing İzzet Melik, that pretty girl who works for Çetin İkmen . . .'

İkmen again. 'How do you know Çetin İkmen?'

Haydar laughed. 'Oh, everybody in the world knows Çetin İkmen,' he said. 'You might be beautiful, but he is a legend.'

Although her son Turgut attempted to silence her, Nalan Senar pushed him roughly away from her. 'Oh, it is over, Turgut!' she said with a weariness in her voice that powerfully and immediately struck İkmen as absolutely genuine. 'It is kismet. I have committed many sins and now I must pay.'

'Yes, but Mother . . .'

'And so must you, my son,' she said as she looked down at Turgut with what seemed to be pity in her eyes. And then she looked away towards İkmen. 'Not that my son Turgut killed Aysu Alkaya,' she said. 'I did that entirely on my own.'

'You killed Aysu?' Kemalettin Senar's lower lip trembled with both sorrow and fury. 'I loved her! Why . . .'

And then he was on her, punching and clawing and screaming his misery into her outraged ears. It took Altay Salman and two of his recruits to pull him off. When he was finally removed, Kemalettin Senar was trembling violently and his mother was bleeding from the mouth. Turgut Senar, who had briefly entered the fray on behalf of his mother, had to be held away from his brother by one of the recruits.

'You animal!' he screamed at Kemalettin as the young horseman held him. 'This is all your fault!'

'Shut up and control yourself!' İkmen yelled as he stood up in order to assert his authority over the proceedings. He then stepped forward to give Nalan Senar some tissues. Her mouth was not badly damaged but the bleeding needed to be staunched before they could proceed. When he eventually returned to his seat, İkmen glanced out of the window and saw to his horror that the snow was coming down even more intensely now that darkness had fallen. No going back to İstanbul for me, he thought gloomily. But then with so many criminals, or so it seemed, to deal with in Muratpaşa was that ever going to be possible anyway?

'Nalan Hanım?'

After looking first at one son and then the other, Nalan Senar stood up again. 'My son Turgut saw his brother Kemalettin with Aysu Alkaya in the Valley of the Saints once before the girl married Ziya Kahraman and once afterwards. They were having relations in that place Kemalettin calls the cave of the mummy.' She looked down at the floor, ashamed by her admission. 'After the second time, my son Turgut scolded his brother. Aysu belonged to Ziya Bey, it was not his place to take her. It was then that Kemalettin told Turgut that Aysu was having his child.'

'Mother, if you do this there will be no one left to look after that maniac!' Turgut Senar screamed as he pointed at his brother. 'We will lose everything!'

But his mother just simply ignored him. 'Turgut told me and, of course, I was horrified. My first thought was to punish Kemalettin until Turgut told me the rest of the story, which was that my younger son and Aysu were planning to run away together. I asked Turgut to try and find out when this might be taking place.'

'You promised me you hadn't told anyone!' Kemalettin

Senar said to Turgut. 'You told me to tell the policemen that we were all in the house with Father all night. But I heard you leave, Turgut, I heard you. You lied about everything!'

'Yes, Kemalettin,' Nalan continued, 'he lied. Turgut told me you had gone. He knew you would take Aysu to the Valley of the Saints, to the cave with the painting of the mummy on the wall. And so when you came back and went to bed, I went out. I went to the cave with the mummy and I saw Aysu. I wish I could say that I talked to her, that we argued and that the gun I had taken with me to protect myself against wolves had gone off accidentally. But it didn't happen that way. I took the gun, Turgut's, without his knowledge, and I went to your special cave to kill Aysu. I shot her in the cave with the mummy and then I started to panic. What if other people knew of that place and of your love for it? If Turgut knew, then why not others?' She sighed. 'And so I went home, got Turgut out of his bed and took him to the Valley of the Saints to see what I had done. He was so shocked. His father was dying at the time, I thought he might go mad like his grandfather . . .'

'But he didn't, did he, Hanım?'

'No. No, he helped me to move Aysu's body out of the cave with the mummy and we put it into a tiny deep cave just along the valley. When, later, the area was being searched, Turgut moved it about but we eventually put Aysu back into the cave with the mummy because we knew it was the one place that Kemalettin wouldn't look for it. He has always been too scared to go there ever since.'

'I did go back for Aysu in the morning,' Kemalettin said. His face looked calmer now, even a little dreamy. 'Aysu . . .'

Altay Salman just caught Kemalettin's hand as it began to snake down towards the front of his trousers. 'No.'

'Of course Kemalettin didn't say anything to me about Aysu's disappearance,' Nalan said. 'But he did tell his brother. Turgut said that she must have gone off somewhere but that Kemalettin wasn't to say anything because otherwise Ziya Bey would kill him.'

'And so you waited for the Kahramans to raise the alarm,' İkmen said.

'Yes.'

Nazlı Kahraman, who had been listening like the rest of the people in the room with a growing sense of horror, said, 'How did you know that the child was not my father's, Nalan Senar? I admit I knew Aysu was pregnant and I had some doubts as to whether or not the child was my father's, but there was blood on her wedding sheet . . .'

'Kemalettin told his brother that Aysu smeared blood from her arm on the sheet in order to save your father's reputation,' Nalan Senar replied. 'As soon as Ziya Bey saw those feet of hers he lost his ardour completely and never touched the girl ever again. The child had to be my son's.'

Nazlı Kahraman shook her head in disbelief. 'Then why didn't my father just divorce the girl! Why didn't he tell me?'

No one gave an answer to this question immediately. Only after a while did Haldun Alkaya say in his old, reedy voice, 'Because he was ashamed. He was old and had been tricked. I had tricked him.'

'My father was the most powerful man in this village!'

'Which was why he could not be laughed at,' İkmen said.

317

'Which was why, I assume, he would have allowed a reasonable amount of time to elapse before he divorced his young wife, probably on the grounds that she was infertile.'

'She had my baby inside her,' Kemalettin Senar said dreamily.

'Which meant that she had to run away,' İkmen said. 'Why did you stop her, Nalan Hanım? You didn't "officially" know that Aysu was carrying Ziya Bey's child. You could have let the two of them run away, you could have allowed your own grandchild, your own flesh and blood, to live.'

'Ziya Bey would have punished our family,' Nalan replied. 'As soon as it was known that Kemalettin was with her . . .'

'And yet even now – Ziya Bey has been dead for years – you still attempt to conceal what happened,' İkmen said. 'By trying to destroy Aysu's body, by trying to kill me . . .'

'I did not! How . . .'

'It was very unfortunate for you that I survived,' İkmen said as he moved in towards the now very frightened-looking woman in front of him. 'Why didn't you finish me off, eh, Nalan Hanım? It would have been very easy to just get hold of that old Colt of Turgut's and put it up to my head. I mean, I assume you do still have the weapon . . .'

Mehmet Süleyman went to the İkmens' apartment as opposed to just going straight home. He'd already lied – under the direction of Mürsel – to Estelle Cohen, İbrahim (who had a black eye and bleeding lip and was really very happy) and to İzzet Melik on the telephone. He wasn't yet ready to lie to his wife and so he went to visit Fatma and some of her brood, none of whom knew or could know what he was now involved with. After all, who could, outside of fiction, even dream about such a thing? A 'spy', if indeed that was the right word to use about this person, gone 'wrong' in some way. It was fantastic, troubling and, if Ardıç hadn't been involved at some level, Süleyman would have dismissed Mürsel's story as the fantasies of an obviously wealthy and probably bored libertine. But it was true, and the threat to himself if nothing else was very real.

As Fatma bustled around him making tea, shouting at her youngest son, Kemal, and cooing over Hulya's baby, Timur, Süleyman found himself thinking about the character he knew as the peeper. Mürsel had implied that this person had worked or rather served abroad at some time. He wondered where. Spies, of course, went everywhere, even to friendly countries where he imagined their presence was both known of and tolerated. But Mürsel had implied that the place the peeper had been sent to had been dangerous; a place of 'tension' was the way he had expressed it. Where had this man been? To one of the wilder former Soviet Republics? Or maybe to Afghanistan or even Iraq . . .

'Arto Sarkissian has told me the snow has got even worse out there now,' Fatma said as she set a glass of tea and an ashtray down beside her guest.

'Eh?'

'In Cappadocia.' She sat down opposite him with a tired sigh. 'That Çetin in that thin suit of his survived at all out in such a terrible landscape is a miracle for which we must thank Allah.'

Süleyman shrugged his agreement. 'Do you know when he'll be getting home?'

'No. Arto says it is like January or February out there. So bad.' She shook her head and then continued, 'And of course Çetin is meddling.'

Süleyman smiled.

'They tried to kill him, those country people!' Fatma said. 'Arto says it is very exciting, that Çetin is solving a mystery that is decades old. But I am still angry with him, Mehmet.'

He knew that she didn't have a clue about Alison and so it couldn't be that. 'Why?'

'For being manipulated by that Menşure Tokatlı. That woman has never needed help with anything related to business in her life and yet what do I get? Some rubbish about her not being able to cope. Why he didn't just come out and say that Menşure wanted him to try to solve some old mystery in the village, I don't know. What am I, a monster that he doesn't tell me these things?'

As Fatma turned away to shake her head in despair, Mehmet and Hulya shared a smile. No, Fatma wasn't a monster, but they both knew that she didn't like him leaving the city no matter what the reason.

'And as usual my husband has involved others in his schemes, too,' Fatma continued. 'I don't yet know how, but in some way Arto Sarkissian was in Muratpaşa and ended up searching for Çetin. Then there was his cousin Atom from Germany.' She looked over at Hulya who was now laughing. 'You may snigger but it isn't very funny for innocent people who get caught up in your father's investigations.'

'But it sounds as if Çetin is doing a good job out there in Cappadocia,' Süleyman said.

'Well . . .'

'The police in a place like that have few resources,' he continued. 'They need help from those of us in the cities sometimes.'

'Oh, but the people out in such places just feud and fight all the time!' Fatma said. 'I read the papers. If I were policing such places I'd give up, let them do what they want to each other! But Çetin . . .'

'As an outsider Çetin can make clear-headed, unbiased judgements . . .'

'Even when those barbarians try to kill him?' She was, as usual, hiding her concern and her affection for her husband very badly.

'Of course,' Süleyman responded. 'You know how he is. He cares.'

'I don't know why,' Fatma said. 'Country people. What are they to do with us, eh? The papers are saying that it is people from the country who blew up the synagogues, who nearly killed Berekiah.'

Süleyman looked across at Hulya again. The girl very quickly turned her face away.

'They say, these country people, that they are fighting for Islam when they do these things. But I am a Muslim, I love the Prophet, blessings and peace be upon Him, and I know He would condemn such slaughter . . .'

'Mum!'

Now that she had turned back again, Süleyman could see that Hulya's eyes were full of tears.

But rather than go to comfort her daughter, Fatma, her own eyes wet around the edges, said to Süleyman, 'Berekiah will recover, but he won't be able to do his own job again. His right hand is useless. The doctors haven't told his parents yet, but Hulya has been told, haven't you, Hulya?'

The girl just nodded her reply.

'Oh, I'm so sorry,' Süleyman said. The fact that he had, to some extent, helped to rescue Berekiah from his shattered apartment did not now, he felt, make up for the tiny amount of time he had spent with the young man since. If poor Berekiah wasn't to be a goldsmith any more, what was he going to do? Süleyman knew he had spent far too much time in pursuit of his own mystery, that which surrounded the peeper, to give what was a tragedy for the İkmen and Cohen families too much thought.

'Yes, well, I won't be happy until Çetin is home now as I think you will appreciate, Mehmet,' Fatma said. 'I want him back here where I can keep my eyes on him. What kind of a world exists outside this city, eh? What sort of a place is that?'

'I threw Sergeant Lavell's gun into the Kızılırmak River the day after I killed Aysu Alkaya,' Nalan Senar told İkmen. 'I made a special trip to Avanos to do just that.'

It was unfortunately only too easy to see how the local police and jandarma had missed a Colt 45 in the Kızılırmak all those years ago. Avanos was not Muratpaşa, the main focus of their search, and so they probably hadn't even bothered with it. The Colt 45, if it still existed at all, was probably now in the hands of some elderly shepherd who had come across it on one of his lonely journeys with his flock.

'So you recognised Miss Lavell's father from that picture,' İkmen said to Turgut Senar.

'It was a shock,' the man replied as he looked very quickly over at his mother. 'He was a nice man, Sergeant Lavell.'

İkmen beckoned Dolores Lavell over to him and said, 'Turgut has just told me he knew your father, Miss Lavell.'

'So Kemalettin was telling the truth.' She walked across to İkmen whilst looking at Turgut Senar.

'I was a child,' Turgut explained in English. 'My father was never home. Sergeant Lavell was very kind, he taught me to shoot.'

'And he left you a gun to practise with,' İkmen said, also in English.

'Yes.'

'That doesn't explain why you then suddenly wanted to get close to Sergeant Lavell's daughter . . .'

'No, no,' Turgut Senar put his head down and then said in Turkish, 'I just did, it just happened.'

And maybe it had. Maybe he had just wanted to get close to someone who was related to a man he had respected. Such hero worship could explain why Turgut had been so disgusted at Kemalettin when he had attempted to masturbate in front of Dolores. But from the way that Nalan was looking at her son, with almost a visible threat in her eyes, İkmen also knew that he could be wrong about that. There could be something else at play there, too, even though he didn't know or understand what that might be. But then a woman who would knowingly kill her own grandchild had to be, by her very twisted nature, entirely enigmatic.

İkmen settled Dolores Lavell next to him and then turned to Nalan Senar once again. 'So Kemalettin is completely inno-cent?'

'Yes.'

'Did he know anything about your plan to kill me?'

'I didn't plan to kill you, Inspector! Turgut didn't plan to kill you either!'

'Oh, so hitting me over the head several times and then leaving me to freeze to death doesn't constitute a threat to my life?' İkmen asked with a cynical smile on his face. 'Come on, Nalan Hanım!'

'He wanted you dead!' the woman said as she pointed one spiteful finger at Inspector Erten. 'And him,' she added as she swung round and nodded her head at Baha Ermis. 'But I said no, you can't kill someone during Ramazan!'

İkmen looked towards the back of the room at where Arto, Atom and Tom were sitting and said, in English, 'The country-side – the quiet, the serenity, the nature, the spite! Thank whatever God you favour for İstanbul.'

The two Armenians and the Englishman smiled. But just before İkmen spoke again he was distracted by a loud, snapping sound which turned out to be the flat of Nazlı Hanım's hand against Baha Ermis's face.

'So you did steal that corpse!' she screamed. 'Liar! And with the Senars!'

'I didn't know what I know now,' Ermis sobbed. 'I did it to once and for all put Ziya Bey's reputation beyond all harm.'

'Liar! You did it for the money!' Nalan Senar sneered at him and then, turning to her rival, Nazlı Kahraman, she said, 'If you didn't pay your people in goat dung they would be loyal!'

'I saw Turgut Senar drag you out of that chimney on the edge of the village, after he had hit you,' Baha Ermis said to

İkmen. 'You interrupted him as he was getting the corpse. Then I came along. It's true the Senars have money, I don't. He and I, we did a deal.'

'Which all fell apart when amazingly I survived,' İkmen said and then, looking across at Ferdinand Mueller, he added, 'What was it you said when you saw Mr Mueller's balloon, Mr Senar? Kismet. And you were not talking about my cousin's cat. You knew it was all over then, inevitable, your fate.'

'He was driving far too close to where we'd left you!' Ermis said as he looked with contempt at Turgut Senar. 'I told him and he tried to kill me – in front of the foreigners.'

'My mother and I are the only reason you are alive at all,' Turgut Senar said to İkmen. 'Ermis and your scruffy friend from Nevşehir wanted you dead!'

İkmen turned to Inspector Erten and said, 'Is this true?'

For a moment it seemed as if the Nevşehir man would attempt to dissemble but instead he just sighed and said, 'Yes.' And then rather than look away he gazed into İkmen's eyes and spoke again. 'Nalan Senar offered me money to take Aysu Alkaya's body and then help her and her son to destroy it. I went to see her just after you came to the mortuary. I was going to question her but she saw a great need in me. She offered me such a vast amount of money . . .'

'So that was the Senars' dog I heard barking in the background when I phoned to tell you about Dr Sarkissian,' İkmen said. 'But what about your job, man, your profession?'

'What about it? What's it done for me? I didn't want or plan to kill you, Inspector, but when you threatened to come between me and money I've never had, well . . . I knew we needed to kill you and destroy your body. You'd taught me that much about DNA testing. But the Senars wouldn't have it. Too religious, too superstitious, too rural. They stopped Ermis and myself doing what should have been done. I knew the cold would not necessarily kill you.' He cleared his throat. 'And it didn't and my poor man's shoes gave me away. As I know you have observed before, Inspector, I have very bad shoes. These are, however, only a pale reflection of my life. I have never married, I – you know I have a degree from Erciyes University – have never been able to afford to do so. My father was sick for most of his life, someone had to pay for his treatment. I am an educated man and yet I eat plain pilav most days, I smoke the cheapest brand of cigarettes. I have nothing! I am fifty years old and I live with my mother and my maiden sister in a three-roomed flat in Avanos . . .'

'You and fifty per cent of rural Anatolia, yes,' İkmen responded sharply. 'If police work in Nevşehir was not glamorous, or lucrative enough for you, why didn't you move to İstanbul or Ankara? Millions of people do that. They send money home.'

'My mother . . .'

'I looked after my father until he was so old he didn't even know what his name was!' İkmen cut in savagely and then bearing down upon his rural counterpart he said, 'I have nine children, Inspector Erten, a wife, a grandchild, a son-in-law who is currently unable to work, and a cat. I work both for and in spite of all that. The people in my life are what keep me going. İstanbul is a tough place.'

'Yes, but you get paid more money . . .'

'Because everything is much more expensive in İstanbul!' İkmen said. 'I'm sorry for you, Erten, in a way, but my life is no party either, you know. I can't afford a new car or new furniture, my wife has worn the same winter coat for the last five years and, as you can see, I am not exactly an advertisement for Armani myself.' And then suddenly and savagely, he grabbed Erten by the throat. 'But I don't throw a man into the snow to get my hands on some extra money! I don't burn a dead body and the evidence it might reveal!'

'All right, Çetin.' He looked up into the face of Altay Salman who already had one hand on İkmen's shoulder.

'Arrest him,' İkmen said as he pointed at the Nevşehir policeman.

'Yes.'

'And them,' he said as he tipped his head in the direction of Turgut and Nalan Senar and Baha Ermis.

'But my son didn't kill anyone,' Nalan Senar said as she watched one of Altay Senar's recruits walk over to her and put his hand upon her arm.

'You, Turgut, Baha and this creature here,' İkmen said as he looked with contempt at Inspector Erten, 'tried to kill me. You will all, as far as I'm concerned, face the full force of the law.'

And then İkmen sat down in his seat again, his face grey with strain, and wept. Dolores Lavell, who was closest to him, put one of her arms round his shoulder until Arto Sarkissian lumbered over to comfort his friend.

'All of this and I didn't even find Alison,' he sobbed in English to the Armenian.

'Alison?'

'I had an aunt Alison once,' Tom Chambers said as he came up behind the policeman and the doctor. 'She died before I was born. She came to Cappadocia, you know.'

327

Chapter 21

Menşure Tokatlı pulled the curtains across her living-room windows, shuddering at the sight of the thick snow outside as she did so. If it went on like this for much longer Çetin, Arto and Atom could be stranded in the village for weeks.

'God, this is amazing!' Tom Chambers said as he finished his tea and then placed the empty glass down on to the coffee table in front of the fire. 'Mum's always wanted to know who it was Auntie Alison fell in love with over here.'

'I didn't know she loved me myself until recently,' İkmen replied with a smile at the memory of his old British love on his lips.

'How did you find out?' the Englishman asked.

İkmen sighed. 'That's a long story, Tom,' he said. 'There was another man, an English friend of mine, who loved your aunt. He told me. But what happened to Alison? You say your mother knew her sister came to Cappadocia.'

'My grandparents got a postcard from Ürgüp, yes.'

'As I told you,' İkmen said, 'I traced Alison to this area myself. The police in Kayseri made inquiries, but then the trail suddenly went cold as you say.'

The young Englishman shook his head sadly. 'She met some blokes out here, white South Africans with lots of money and a car of some sort. Alison's aim had always been to get to India and these guys offered her a lift. Her body turned up in Peshawar in Pakistan about six months later.'

'But there is no record of her leaving Turkey,' İkmen said. 'I checked in those early days. The police in Kayseri kept looking for several years.'

'It's thought they must have got over the border into Iran illegally. My mum got a postcard from Tehran,' Tom said. 'The South Africans were drug dealers, Inspector. People in Pakistan remembered them. Two cheery white blokes and a pretty blonde girl with pink boots. They used Alison to deflect attention away from themselves while they did their deals.'

'But why did she die?'

'The Pakistani authorities believed that Alison didn't know what her chauffeurs were doing for a long time. Mum said she was a bit naïve. But then she found out and was appalled. Alison didn't do drugs, Inspector.'

'No, I know,' İkmen said.

Tom put his head down a little. 'Yes. But anyway, the Pakistani police told my grandparents that once Alison knew about the drugs she wouldn't play these blokes' game any more and so they killed her.'

'How?'

'Shot her up with a mega dose of heroin. I imagine the idea was that when she was found the police would think she was just another Western junkie. But my grandparents had been making inquiries in Pakistan for some weeks by that time. She'd written a short note to them from Islamabad. I don't know whether she knew about the drug dealing by then, but things had certainly turned sour for her by that time. Mum showed me this letter. It's a sad little thing. It's how we know about you, actually.'

İkmen frowned.

'My aunt said that she wanted to go back to Turkey. She said she'd met a man she liked very much in İstanbul. But he was a policeman and he was married with children . . .'

'You know nothing about any of this,' İkmen said in Turkish to Menşure and Arto. 'Fatma . . .'

'But if you were never unfaithful to Fatma,' Arto said, 'I think you can tell her the truth.'

İkmen looked his friend very hard in the eyes and said, 'Do you really think so? Tell me you believe in what you just said.'

A moment passed after which the Armenian sighed and then said, 'No, no, you're right, Çetin. Maybe some things are best left unsaid.'

'And I've spoken not a word about it to anyone except you for nearly thirty years, Çetin,' Menşure Tokatlı said as she sat down beside a slightly bemused Atom Boghosian. 'I'm not about to start now.'

İkmen first shook his head and then looked up at the Englishman again and smiled. 'So does Alison have a grave?' he asked.

'Yes, in a cemetery in Guildford, that's in Surrey where my grandparents used to live. My mum still visits sometimes, takes flowers . . .'

Quite suddenly İkmen began to cry. He'd felt fine until that moment but now, maybe because Tom was talking about Alison's grave, the place where her body was and now always would be, suddenly he could no longer control his emotions. Alison was dead and even though he had really known that she

330

had to have died all along the reality of it hit him hard. Poor Alison, she'd left to continue her journey to India in a state of some agitation. She'd had to rebuff the unwanted advances of İkmen's English friend Maximillian while at the same time she'd had to tear herself away from the man she did love: himself. If only they had both been single! But not only had İkmen been married, he had also had several children by that time, too. Only once had he kissed the lovely blonde girl with the big pink boots. It was just as she was leaving the city, at her pansiyon. It had been the most passionate moment he had ever shared with any other person apart from Fatma. He still on occasion dreamed about it.

No one went to İkmen as he cried. Not even Arto felt it was appropriate for him to share in his friend's misery. Whatever was going on in İkmen's tired and unhappy head was between himself and what he recalled of this girl he apparently had had such a profound effect upon. Quite how he was holding together at all after the ordeal he had been through out in the valleys, not to mention what he had put himself through up in Menşure's restaurant, was a mystery to everyone. Atom Boghosian for one could very easily have fallen asleep where he sat. And after a while he did indeed do this while the others just watched anxiously as İkmen cried himself slowly into silence.

'He is your brother's child!' Altay Salman hissed through the snow at the heavily bundled-up woman at the door. 'He is your blood!'

'He's a devil!' the elderly woman replied fearfully. 'Like the father of his murderess mother, he is mad. The woman my

331

brother married has been taken to prison with that eldest devil-child of hers . . .'

'Nalan and Turgut Senar are under arrest at the gendarmerie,' Altay explained as he watched Sebla Ek's tiny dark eyes dance nervously above her covered mouth and nose. 'We can't get out of the village until the snow clears a little. Then they will be taken to Nevşehir along with Baha Ermis and Inspector Erten.'

The old woman waved a dismissive hand at the policeman and his vacant-faced charge. 'I don't know anything about it, only what my son has told me. Kemalettin made that Alkaya girl pregnant, Nalan has killed and Turgut knew about it. They are all damned.' She leaned out of her door and forward into the snow a little and whispered, 'I will be contacting my lawyer, too, you know. I have never been comfortable that my brother died under the care of that woman.'

'Mrs Ek . . .'

'Take the madman away, for the love of Allah!' she said as she waved them away from her house and then closed the door behind her.

Altay Salman turned to look at Kemalettin Senar. 'I'll have to take you home,' he said with a sigh. 'I'm sorry.'

It was three o'clock in the morning and the captain wasn't happy about leaving Kemalettin, the only remnant of the immediate Senar family not in custody, alone. After what he had heard and with only his mother's dog for company it was anyone's guess what he might do either to himself or to the house for that matter. Sebla Ek had been Altay's last hope. He'd already spoken to every other member of Kemalettin's family in the village including Turgut's wife, but none of them wanted to know even though several of the uncles had admitted that they could see why Nalan had done what she had. One had even expressed his gratitude towards her. After all, for a very long time, Nalan had saved the name of Senar from dishonour.

'Come on,' Altay said as he placed a hand on Kemalettin's shoulder.

They walked in silence along the top of the escarpment, their boots crunching through snow that was now at least fifteen centimetres deep. This 'high' road was where the wealthier residents of Muratpaşa lived – the Eks, the original Senar family, Menşure Tokatlı's elderly uncle Fatih Tokatlı, and the Kahramans who had the biggest establishment of them all. Although there were street lamps, they were pale and insignificant even in this privileged part of the village and so Altay was quite grateful when they eventually made the lee of the Kahraman place with its large and bombastic outside light.

'Now we'll be able to see where we're putting our feet,' he said to Kemalettin Senar.

'Yes . . . Aysu was murdered, wasn't she?'

'Yes, Kemalettin. I'm sorry.'

'Mmm.'

The captain was as shocked as the strange man in his wake when the total silence of the night was broken by the sound of the Kahramans' great wooden door creaking open.

'Oh!'

Nazlı Kahraman looked drunk as she swayed in the doorway in front of them. She was loosely covered in a voluminous lace nightdress, her head swathed in a very vibrant pink scarf. For a moment she just smoked as she watched the two men look at the vision of her through the falling snow.

'Nazlı Hanım?'

'I heard you talking,' she said in a voice that now sounded more dreamy than drunk.

'Yes, Hanım,' the captain replied. 'I'm taking Kemalettin home.'

'To an empty house?'

'What else can I do?' Altay spread his arms out wide to indicate the scale of his helplessness. 'I've tried to get him taken in by his family but they don't want to know. I have to take him home.'

Nazlı Kahraman sighed.

'Good night to you, Hanım,' the captain said as he saluted the elderly woman and prepared to go on his way once again. It was so cold and he was so tired he just wanted to get home to his own bed for a few hours.

However, before he had a chance to move forward, Nazlı Kahraman spoke again. 'Kemalettin can stay here,' she said. 'He can't be alone at a time like this.'

The horseman frowned. 'But, Hanım, you were at Menşure Hanım's place, you heard . . .'

'He cuckolded my father, yes.' She took a drag from her cigarette and then ground it out in the snow with one pink fluffy slipper. 'But he and Aysu were young and my father was wrong to have married her. My father, you know, Captain, he was not a nice man. He didn't kill Aysu and like Kemalettin he was falsely accused, but he wasn't a good person.'

'Hanım . . .'

'I was never enough for him, you see,' she said as she put her hand out towards Kemalettin and beckoned him forwards.

334

'I adored him, but I was a girl and so I wasn't enough. My father wanted perfection, a perfect boy.'

'I'm not perfect,' Kemalettin said as he tramped through the heavy snow to join her. 'Mum always told me I was broken.'

'Which you are,' Nazlı Kahraman said. 'But that doesn't make you bad, Kemalettin.'

'Are you sure about this, Hanım?' the captain asked once the strange man had joined the old lady between the thick wooden posts of the courtyard gate.

'If you mean will I exact revenge against this poor, wild creature, then no,' she said. 'You have my word.'

The captain saluted once again.

'Someone has to make a start to heal this village,' Nazlı Kahraman said. 'And because of, or maybe in spite of, the fact that I have more money than anyone else, I think it is appropriate that person be myself. Maybe if I'd taken a bit more account of others, spoken to Aysu, paid Baha a living wage, some of what has happened would not have done so. Good night, Captain Salman.'

With one hand on Kemalettin Senar's shoulder she pulled the gate closed and walked back towards her house. The captain for his part first lit a well-earned cigarette and then began to make his way down towards his home and hopefully a few hours' sleep.

Chapter 22

Commissioner Ardıç spoke more to himself than to Mehmet Süleyman. 'We live in terrible times,' he said as he replaced his unlit cigar into his mouth. 'But then if it is the will of Allah that we suffer in this way . . .'

Süleyman, still standing to attention in front of his superior's desk, did not reply.

For a few moments Ardıç just looked up at him before he said, 'Well, sit down, sit down!'

Süleyman did as he was told and then waited for his boss to take the initiative in the coming conversation they both knew they had to have.

'You know of course that I tried to protect you from Mürsel Bey and whatever it is his kind do,' the older man said wearily.

'Yes, sir.'

'But' – he shrugged – 'you went your own way and now you as well as I have to actively work with Mürsel, and . . .'

'From what he said to me, sir, it would seem that we give them information but they do not reciprocate.'

'That is so,' Ardıç said. 'Yes.'

'And so MIT . . .'

'Let us not use names we do not understand, Süleyman,'

Ardıç said, in what Süleyman felt was a chilling echo of Mürsel's own words. 'You do not know who Mürsel works for and I, even if I did know, am not obliged to tell you. Do you understand?'

No, he didn't, but he said that he did just in order to keep the peace.

'You will continue to work on this peeper case for reasons I believe Mürsel has already discussed with you,' Ardıç said. 'But, in common with this latest peeper outrage, this murder, Mürsel and his people will have access to bodies and forensic material prior to our own specialists.'

'But, sir,' Süleyman began, 'how will we keep people like Dr Sarkissian away from scenes? Last time, with Dr Mardin . . .'

'Last time was a mistake, a mess, and I take full responsibility for that,' Ardıç said as he looked gravely down at the shiny surface of his desk. 'In future Mürsel's team alone will be employed. Sarkissian and the head of the Forensic Institute will be told as much as they need to know. Such an event as happened on Saturday will not happen again. A lot happened on Saturday . . .'

Süleyman did not answer. Yes, a lot had happened on Saturday. People had been killed both inside and outside of two of the most popular and sacred synagogues in the city.

'Berekiah Cohen . . .'

'Is making good progress, sir.'

Ardıç nodded. 'Good. İkmen will have been worried about him. I don't like it when my men are upset.'

'No, sir.'

Süleyman smiled a little to himself. Ardıç liked the world to believe that he was a hard and heartless being with no sense of either artistry or humour. And that was largely true. But at little moments like this he did show that he cared, if in a limited way, for those who were responsible to him. In fact İkmen always felt that Ardıç had more sympathy for his 'men' than he did for his own family about whom he spoke rarely and then mostly with intense exasperation.

'Out there in the wilds of Cappadocia' – Ardıç shook his head – 'I would have been furious with İkmen if he had died out there! Said he was going out there about family business, but he ends up getting involved with some ancient homicide. I don't suppose you . . .'

'I know nothing about it, sir,' Süleyman said. And in part that was true. He hadn't actually spoken to İkmen since he'd left to go off in search of English Alison. Even now he only had a very vague grasp upon what had happened to İkmen and no idea why. 'Do you know when Inspector İkmen is coming home, sir?'

Ardıç pulled a face and then sighed. 'You know what it's like in the country in the winter,' he said. 'Snow. Masses of the stuff. When it clears İkmen and Dr Sarkissian will return to us. But until then?' He shrugged. 'I understand he has had an inspector from Nevşehir arrested for attempted murder. The creatures from the caves will be wanting him to stay to "clean up" their locality next!' And then he laughed but without either warmth or mirth. 'Officers should stay in their home towns or cities, if you ask me. İstanbullus are İstanbullus; we are different. No one can understand us like ourselves.' He looked up sharply. 'How is İzzet Melik coming along?'

Süleyman considered the question carefully. In light of

what he and Melik had shared with Dr Mardin with regard to evidence tampering, the man from İzmir had proved himself honest and trustworthy. In general, however, he was his usual self – superficially boorish and unreconstructed. He would, Süleyman knew, irritate him enormously from time to time and the way he chewed sandwiches was particularly revolting. Melik, however, spoke Italian. Melik had sat by Berekiah Cohen's hospital bed with Süleyman and talked to the young Jew about the little synagogue he knew in İzmir and all the friends of his who went there.

'I think that he will work out – in the end,' Süleyman said finally in answer to his superior's question.

Ardıç nodded sagely and then smiled just a little. 'Good.'

The snow had finally stopped falling just before dawn. And so although most of the inhabitants of Muratpaşa awoke to the prospect of yet another day's fast, the idea that the snowfall may have finally come to an end was cheering – for most. Çetin İkmen, although well aware of how impossible the roads out of Cappadocia would be, was almost unreasonably anxious to get back to İstanbul. And although he had spoken to his wife, his son Orhan and daughter Hulya, he knew that wasn't enough and he needed to be with them.

However, before any of that could happen he also had to make his own statement with regard to his own ordeal and so, once he had finished his breakfast, he went down to the tiny gendarmerie at the edge of the village. The three young jandarma not with the prisoners at the back of the building greeted him warmly, as did Altay Salman when he eventually arrived at lunchtime. The roads, he said, were getting clearer now and

Nevşehir were anxious to have their four prisoners in the rather more secure environment of the police station. Transport, he told İkmen and the others, was apparently on its way. One of the young jandarma went to tell the prisoners this piece of information. When he returned, he came over to İkmen with a message from Nalan Senar. She apparently wanted to see the İstanbul man alone before she was transferred over to Nevşehir.

'You don't have to speak to her if you don't want to,' Ferhat the jandarma said. 'To be honest, it won't be easy if she wants to see you alone. We'll have to move all the men in here.'

But İkmen, true to his nature, was intrigued. He also still had unanswered questions of his own about the Aysu Alkaya affair, questions he had been unable to formulate in the immediate wake of his frozen ordeal. He said he'd see Nalan Senar. And so the men were taken out of the cells at the back of the building and İkmen went in to see the woman alone.

'Your eyes are very red, Nalan Hanım,' he said, as he eased his thin behind on to the one small chair in front of the heavily muffled woman.

'It's cold and I haven't slept.'

İkmen shrugged. 'This is a cell, Nalan Hanım. It is not a pansiyon.'

'I know that!' she snapped. 'I know . . .'

'What do you want, Nalan Hanım?' İkmen asked as he took out his cigarettes and then lit up. 'Do you want to apologise perhaps for trying to kill me?'

'I didn't try to kill you, Inspector,' she replied. 'It is Ramazan. I saved both you and the souls of those who did desire your death.'

340

'The cold would have killed me. It nearly did and you know it.'

'You were never meant to be involved.' She shrugged. 'It was unfortunate.'

'This carnage was all so that your family could retain their honour . . .'

'It wasn't only that,' she said. 'I was afraid of Ziya Bey and what he would do if he discovered what Kemalettin had done with Aysu but there was something else, too.' She raised her face to look into his eyes. 'Something I have never, with the exception of Turgut, told anyone.'

'Something you wish me to keep secret now?' İkmen asked.

She shuffled uncomfortably on the thin pallet she had been given to sleep upon. 'Yes . . .'

'I don't know if I can do that,' İkmen said. 'But then . . .'

'You know, Inspector, that there is more to this than just my family's honour, don't you?'

İkmen puffed hard on his cigarette and then said, 'I suspect it, yes.'

'What I may tell you will not change anything. I will still be punished for what I have done, I am resigned to my fate. It will make no difference to what will happen.'

'So why tell me?'

She sighed. 'Because you are not from this district, because I must tell someone. And maybe for you it will help. What you suffered out in the valleys had a reason that is not one I believe is trivial.'

He opened his arms and spread his hands wide. 'Then speak.'

'You will keep my secret? You . . .'

'I will listen to what you say, Hanım, and then make a judgement,' İkmen said.

For a few moments she sat in silence, thinking about what his words meant and then she said, 'All right.' She took a deep breath. 'My son Kemalettin is not Tatar's child. It wasn't only Turgut who was friendly with Sergeant Lavell from America. As soon as my looks began to fade, my husband rejected me most of the time. He called me the Madman's Daughter, went with whores in Kayseri and Nevşehir.'

'I see. But Turgut . . .'

'Oh, Turgut knows. He is the only one who does,' she said. 'When Kemalettin made Aysu pregnant I had to tell him.'

'Why?'

'Because of the colour!' She wrung her hands until they became red. 'When Kemalettin was born I was so relieved that he was white. For many years, in fact, I made myself believe that he was in reality my husband's. He could have been Tatar's, after all. But then as he grew I began to notice things – the colour and curl of his hair, different even from that of my dark father, a difference about the cast of his features . . . Then when he made Aysu pregnant . . . I had been to see Dr Ali about my husband. Tatar was dying by then and the doctor said he wanted to see me. He said that because I was soon to be alone he wanted me to consider having some tests for the disease he always believed had killed my father. It wasn't entirely a shock to me as I imagined he felt it would be.'

İkmen recalled his own conversation with Dr Ali. 'Huntington's Disease.'

'Yes.' She looked surprised. 'How . . . ?'

'Just carry on, please.' It was cold, and although he was

pleased in a way that his suspicions about there being something more at play here than just 'simple' honour, he was also sickened by both the effects of his recent ordeal and the Byzantine nature of some of these relationships.

'My father's brother died in the same way, you see, and . . .' She swallowed hard. 'I wouldn't have the test. But Dr Ali told me about how things are inherited, how some physical things and illnesses can suddenly come back in a family. Like a curse, like Allah exacting rightful punishment of the wicked. And so when Aysu became pregnant . . .'

'You feared she would give birth to a baby with black skin. You feared that your infidelity would finally be exposed.'

She looked down at the floor once again. 'Yes.'

'I'm amazed that your son Turgut helped you in this,' İkmen said. 'Were his actions not dishonourable to his father?'

'If Tatar and his family had ever found out they would have killed me and disinherited my boys. Even Turgut's place in the family would have been questioned. He would have been the son of an adulteress. Turgut is a practical man, he always has been. He doesn't love me, he moved his family out to get away from me and my bastard.' She looked up, her eyes now full of tears. 'Why do you think that he went with that American woman, Sergeant Lavell's daughter? To get back at me! We both recognised her name years ago, Turgut and myself but because she was white we didn't think she could be the sergeant's daughter. But when Turgut saw that photograph of Dolores' father, he knew. And so he took revenge to show me that he could have a foreigner, too, that he could in fact have his own brother's sister!'

'Half-sister.'

'Yes, I know, I know!'

And yet when Kemalettin, poor unaware Kemalettin, had attempted to masturbate in front of Dolores, it had been too much for Turgut and he had become furiously angry with him and with the strangely incestuous act he was unwittingly committing.

'When you killed Aysu, didn't you realise that Kemalettin might have wanted to possess or even marry another woman? How were you going to deal with that?'

She shrugged. 'I didn't know – then. After Aysu's death, Kemalettin was very depressed.' She looked up. 'And then he was strange, like my father.'

'And so you had him tested for Huntington's?'

'Yes.'

'And he was positive, wasn't he?'

'Yes. His sister, you know, the American woman, she doesn't have it.'

İkmen frowned. 'Well, she wouldn't, Hanım. That comes from your father.'

'And hers too,' the elderly woman said. 'Sergeant Lavell and I met through Turgut and his interest in him. But we talked about my father when we spoke together. The sergeant was interested in my father because he saw some similarities between my family and his. His father and his father's sister had something he called St Vitus's Dance . . .'

And then İkmen remembered what Dolores Lavell had told him about her father's disease, about the 'dance' Dr Ali had alluded to.

'Turgut doesn't have it, but poor Kemalettin, well, it was a certainty, wasn't it? First his depression and confusion over Aysu and then his bizarre behaviour meant that he would never want to wed or be asked for in marriage. My secret was safe until . . .'

'Aysu Alkaya came back to haunt you,' İkmen said. 'Why didn't you or Turgut burn her body, Hanım, years ago?'

'We, like you, are Muslims, Inspector. You know that we do not burn our dead. Although lots of tourists go to the Valley of the Saints, the cave with the mummy is not easy to get to and Turgut has always directed the more adventurous people away to other sites.'

'Then if you're such good Muslims why was her body burning when I finally came round out in that frozen valley!'

'Ah, that was Baha, he is a person entirely without religion . . .'

'You let him do it!' İkmen said and then pushing his face into hers he said, 'Allah, but you are a deluded woman, are you not, Nalan Hanım? I bet you couldn't believe it when Aysu turned up almost intact. Ziya Kahraman would of course have understood about the preservative qualities of some of the caves and wouldn't have made such an error. But you? The only way that body could be safe from forensic examination was if it were to be completely destroyed. You and Turgut knew that! I as much as told you and Erten, of course. All right, so I accept that Ermis may well have lit the match, but you didn't stop him, you even encouraged him!'

'His soul is not . . .'

'Oh, but of course, he is just a money-grabbing little heathen, isn't he, not an upright person like you!' İkmen stubbed his cigarette out on the floor and then lit up another. 'If you believe that Allah is all-seeing, don't you think that he is aware of your deception?'

'Aysu Alkaya was a harlot!'

'Aysu Alkaya, just like you, Hanım, was a young girl who was unloved by her husband and who fell in love with a nice young boy. Your families, yours and the Kahramans! Allah!' He threw his hands up in disbelief. 'All of you talking about inheritance – of money, of physical features. Laughing at others like that carpet dealer who sleeps with his kilims. You all laugh at him! You all talk about the fact that you believe his parents were cousins. Ziya Kahraman, the richest man in the village, he wanted a "perfect" wife. Was he mad? If he was so concerned about in-breeding, why didn't he go out of the village to find a woman? There were some tourists around even in those days. With all his money he could have had his pick of "perfect" women – both Turks and foreigners.'

'I don't know!' She put her head in her hands so that she at least didn't have to see his tirade, his infuriated, reddened face. 'Maybe because it is wrong to lie with those not your own kind. Look at me.'

'You were already married!' İkmen cried. 'And you were unfortunate. Dolores' father was, I understand, a very nice person . . .'

'He was very kind! He bought many things for Turgut.' She looked up into his eyes again. 'Then one day when Tatar was in Kayseri, Sergeant Lavell came to show Turgut how to shoot in the yard. Later when my son went off to play with some friends in the street, he came in to the house. I gave him water. We'd . . . noticed each other before. It happened almost without my knowing. I loved him! May Allah forgive me!'

And then she looked down at the floor once again. İkmen, rather more deflated now since his tirade, said, 'Yes, I believe that you did love him. You took an awful risk. I'm sorry.'

Nalan Senar looked up. 'It was a terrible, terrible . . .'

'Tell me, Hanım,' İkmen said, 'does Dolores Lavell know?'

'No! No!'

'I ask because I know that she is alone in the world and maybe if she knew that she had a brother . . .'

'Kemalettin?' She shook her head. 'Who would want him? My son is mad, Inspector, and he can only now get madder.'

'I do think that Miss Lavell should be given that choice,' İkmen said.

'But if you told the American you would have to tell Kemalettin too. No, no. No, he is never to know.' She fixed İkmen with a harsh stare. 'He loved his father Tatar. He loved me and his brother. Don't take us away from him, for his sake.'

She leaned forward in a pleading motion and İkmen shook his head sadly. 'I don't know. I don't know.'

'You are not to tell anyone about this,' Nalan Senar continued. 'Look, if it's money you want, to buy your silence, I still have . . .'

'I don't want your money!' İkmen instinctively cringed away from her.

'Then . . .'

Quickly and suddenly, İkmen stood up. 'I need to get out of here,' he said. 'I need to leave this place and get back to my reality.'

'Yes, but you mustn't . . .'

'You,' he pointed rudely into her face, 'will not know

whether I have told anyone or not about your secret for some little time. That,' he said spitefully, 'is my personal punishment to you.'

'For what?'

'For trying to kill me,' İkmen said as he banged his fist on the door to attract one of the jandarma in the office. 'But mainly for making my wife and my children so worried. My son-in-law had just been injured in an incident in İstanbul, they had enough to worry about. How dare you.'

'I was simply trying to retain my family honour . . .'

'And keep the Senar money.' The door opened and İkmen went through it. Just before it shut behind him again, he looked at the woman, so small and old sitting on her bedroll, and said, 'By the way, I have a secret too. I'll tell anyone. Even you.'

'What is it?'

'I didn't know who killed Aysu Alkaya when I stunned you all with my "genius" yesterday. I just hoped that someone would either reveal themselves to me or simply give themselves up. Hang themselves, as it were.'

The jandarma pushed the door shut and locked it up again.

Chapter 23

'Jak!'

Mehmet Süleyman took hold of the small, dark man in front of him in a firm and almost grateful embrace. Although a lot cleaner and much more mobile, Jak Cohen looked remarkably like his brother Balthazar.

'Mehmet,' Jak said in his rather strange English-tinged Turkish. 'Good to see you again, if in such sad circumstances.'

'Jak, I . . .'

'Oh, Jak, thank God!' Estelle, who had been beside Mehmet and Zelfa Süleyman at the arrivals barrier, threw herself into her brother-in-law's arms and began to weep hysterically.

'It was very good of Leon to let Estelle and Balthazar stay in his flat,' Mehmet began. 'But Jak, you know Leon . . .'

'I understand,' Jak said as he gently stroked Estelle's hair with his one free hand. 'Don't worry, Mehmet, I'll sort it out.'

Mehmet smiled and then, taking one of his wife's hands in his, he said, 'I've got my car. Shall we?'

'Yes.'

The Süleymans led the way. Behind them, Jak and Estelle talked in a language Mehmet recognised as Ladino, the ancient speech of the Sephardic Jews of İstanbul. It made him smile. People almost without thinking always did tend to revert to the language of their youth when in pain or in trouble. Even passion could bring it back. Whatever she might say when they were making love, Zelfa always said it in English. The memory of the last time she had done this, just the night before, caused him to squeeze her hand affectionately.

'What is it?' she said as she looked into his eyes with a frown on her face.

He smiled. 'Oh, just happy, that's all. Glad you and I are, well, what would you call it, together . . .'

'Married,' she said. 'I'd say we're married, wouldn't you?'

'Well, I hope . . .'

'Well, let's go and sort the Cohens out and then go home and have an early night.' She smiled. 'Dad's playing bridge at his club and your brother has Yusuf for the evening . . .'

Mehmet slipped an arm around her waist and pulled her in close to his body. The airport doors swished open to allow their departure and the couple just paused a moment to make sure that Jak and Estelle were still behind them before moving on towards the airport car park. It was dark outside, and confusing for an expatriate like Jak and a confused, ageing lady like Estelle. The Süleymans waited for their guests to catch them up.

'Çetin and Dr Sarkissian will be home tomorrow,' Mehmet said as they waited for the others. 'They're leaving Muratpaşa in the morning.'

'You'll be glad when they're back.'

He kissed her lightly on the mouth. 'I've missed them.'

Zelfa smiled. As ever it had been a mixed blessing having

Mehmet back in her life once again. She didn't always know where he was, even less what he was thinking. But he was, she knew, at least trying to be more thoughtful. And he was, she recognised, suffering from a lot of self-doubt with regard to this latest, still unsolved, investigation. He was also still having problems with what he had seen and done at the Neve Şalom Synagogue explosion. She knew both professionally and just as a human being that that would not go away for a long time. Berekiah had been badly hurt, the Cohens traumatised, innocent people had died. Mehmet was going to be angry and would suffer from nightmares for a long time to come.

But at least İkmen was soon to be home from his rather mysterious Cappadocian travels. Mehmet had spoken to him at length on the phone and in very excited terms, but Zelfa knew very little about it. She was just glad that her husband's friend was returning and that soon he would feel a little bit more secure once again. Mehmet relied upon İkmen in ways the older man would probably never have recognised. His sense of self worth was very tied in with İkmen's opinions. She looked at him again and thought how good it was for Yusuf to have his father back in his life. The child was even sleeping more easily now. For herself, she knew that she loved her husband, in spite of herself, and whatever he did. She might hate him, too. When he had gone off with another woman she loathed him. But she loved him – loved his smile, his intensity, his unfailing generosity. He was also, she thought as she almost laughed out loud, a very good fuck.

As the Cohens caught up with them, Mehmet put his free

arm round Estelle's shoulders and led Jak and 'his' women out towards his car.

A lot of people turned out to see the policeman from İstanbul and the two Armenians prepare to leave the village. Altay Salman was particularly sorry to see friends from 'civilisation' leave, as was Rachelle Jones who even shed a few tears on İkmen's behalf.

'It's going to be quiet around here without you guys,' she said as she took one of İkmen's hands warmly in her own.

İkmen smiled. She was probably right – at least for a little while longer. When the Senar case came to court it would probably bring a fair few media people into the area who would wish to sensationalise what had happened for a while.

'I've put some börek for you in a plastic tub with some pide,' Menşure said as she thrust an enormous blue bag into İkmen's hands. 'I imagine you'll stop off at different restaurants on the way but at least you won't have to eat any of their ghastly and unhygienic food.'

'No, Menşure.'

He moved forward as if to kiss her, but she just stepped back and, looking at her feet, said, 'Well, say goodbye to Kismet.'

Both İkmen and Arto Sarkissian looked downwards.

'Goodbye,' the policeman said to the cat. The doctor waved, a frozen expression of horror on his lips. Kismet sneered back expansively.

'Well, Inspector, this is it,' a cheery English voice interjected.

'Tom!' He felt his heart literally sink in his chest as he

contemplated this particular parting. Tom Chambers had become special in so many ways. He was, after all, a tangible part of Alison, a part that was still very much alive. İkmen threw his arms round the young man and then softly patted his back. 'Tom, what will you . . .'

Tom Chambers pulled himself gently away from İkmen and pointed towards the two women at his side. 'Em, Dolores and I are going to stay on a bit longer and then we're all going to go off down south.'

'Catch a few rays before the winter comes right in,' Emily Bronstein said as she shook first İkmen and then the two Armenians by their hands. 'Pity you can't come, Inspector.'

'I agree.' He smiled and turned to the other woman. 'And you, Miss Lavell, are you looking forward to catching some "rays"?'

'Yes.' She took one of his hands in hers. 'Thank you, Inspector.'

'Dolores is coming back afterwards, aren't you?' Tom said. 'Yes.'

'She's going to see what she can do for that poor Kemalettin,' Tom continued. 'Seems he has the same thing your dad suffered from, doesn't he, Dolores?'

'Yes,' she said, looking very deeply into İkmen's eyes.

'Coincidences! My God!' Tom said.

But Dolores Lavell and Çetin İkmen knew that this, unlike Tom's meeting with the policeman, was not a coincidence. İkmen had told the American about Kemalettin and his relationship to her. She, though initially shocked by this revelation, was hardly surprised. Her father had been quite the ladies' man in his time.

'I'll do what I can for Kemalettin. I may even take him to the States. Who knows what can be done for people like him now?' she said as she leaned forward in order to kiss İkmen on the cheek. 'Don't worry, he'll never know who I am,' she whispered gently in his ear.

İkmen, for many different reasons, but mainly for Kemalettin's sake, had decided not to let Nalan Senar's shame spread any further than Dolores Lavell's ears. Against all expectations Nazlı Kahraman had taken her father's old love rival into her home and he, simple soul, seemed to be enjoying the company of the old woman and her slow young husband. He would never be well and eventually his condition would kill him, but at least Kemalettin had people to be with as well as, possibly, the best care Dolores Lavell was able to arrange. She had promised İkmen and Kemalettin himself that much.

'Come on, Çetin,' Arto said as he slid into the driving seat of his black Mercedes. 'Atom!'

The younger Armenian, who was across the road from the pansiyon speaking German with Ferdinand Mueller, indicated that he was almost ready.

'Oh well . . .' İkmen shrugged as he surveyed the now-familiar faces around him.

'Thank you.'

The voice was old and cracked and it was one that İkmen had not heard anything from since the whole village had gathered to hear the İstanbul man's investigative wisdom. He turned. 'Haldun Bey!'

'Thank you for finding out who killed my daughter, Çetin Bey,' Haldun Alkaya said.

'I'm just so sorry you cannot bury her yet, Haldun Bey,'

İkmen said. 'But I promise you that as soon as the forensic people have done what they have to I will get them to return her to you.'

Although originally Aysu Alkaya's remains were to be driven back to İstanbul by Arto Sarkissian, their fragile state now made that impossible and so her corpse was to be flown out from Kayseri to İstanbul the following day.

'I knew that you and the DNA would find my daughter's killer,' Haldun Alkaya continued. 'It was indeed written, Çetin Bey.'

İkmen took one of the old man's hands in his and lifted it first to his lips and then to his forehead in a gesture of respect. 'Haldun Bey, it has been an honour.'

And so İkmen said his goodbyes and was waiting for Atom to finish his when he suddenly thought of something and went back over to Tom Chambers once again.

'Tom,' he said, a little nervously, the Englishman felt.

'Yes?'

'Tom, please, would you do something for me when you get back to England?'

'Name it,' the young man said. 'I mean, if you ever want to come over we've got each other's addresses now.'

'No, well, that would be very nice, but . . .' İkmen swallowed hard as he watched Atom Boghosian get into Arto's car. 'Would you go to Guildford in Surrey and put some flowers on to Alison's grave for me? I would do it myself, but . . .'

'Of course.' Tom put his arms around İkmen one last time and hugged him tightly. 'She loved flowers, she loved you.'

As quickly as he could, İkmen jumped into the back of the doctor's car and then wiped his 'leaking' eyes with the back of his jacket sleeve. Although most of the snow had now melted there was still a lot of slush on the roads as they sloshed their way out of the tiny troglodyte village of Muratpaşa. İkmen looked at the strange phallic shapes and biblically dressed people that characterised the village as they passed. Old slights to honour, imagined or real hurts, assumed enormous proportions in places like this. İkmen leaned back in his very comfortable rear seat and wondered whatever would happen to that wonderful fresco he and Tom had seen in the cave with the mummy. Without Erten's involvement, would the expert still come down from Ankara to preserve it? He hoped so. After all, whatever horrors had happened in that cave they had nothing to do with the fresco. That deserved to be seen by all, whatever the subject of the picture turned out to be.

As the car pulled up the hill and out of the village, Arto Sarkissian suddenly pointed out into the strange landscape to his left and said, 'Good God! What the . . .'

İkmen looked to where he was pointing, into the rising sun, to the lone figure of a woman dressed in a huge rainbow-coloured cloak bowing and stretching towards it.

'Oh, that's the Peruvian woman,' he said casually. 'She's praying to the sun god.'

'You know her?'

'Not exactly,' İkmen said. 'But I've heard some stories.' And then he took a cigarette out of his pocket, lit up and said, 'The country. Eccentric, gorgeously wild and potentially lethal. You can keep it. Come on, Arto, put your foot down!'

'Yes, well . . .'

'Got to get back to İstanbul. Got to help Mehmet Süleyman

with a very troubling business.' İkmen sighed with pleasure and, after he had finished his cigarette, slept and dreamed of the great crime-riddled city on the Bosphorus. His home, his İstanbul.

Afterword

The idea for this book came about, in part at least, as a result of a trip I made to Cappadocia in November 2003. A friend of mine, who lives in the area, wanted to do some travelling, and so I agreed to house and cat-sit for her for a month. It was a very interesting experience, not least because it was Ramazan, the Muslim month of fasting, for most of the time I was there. In addition, both staying in and getting around the district with local people and expatriates was great fun and very illuminating. Life in a Turkish village is very different from life in İstanbul. The pace of everything is much slower and (especially when I went which was outside the tourist season) it is very quiet. Fasting is, as I discovered when I tried not to eat, drink or smoke during the hours of daylight, a very intense experience. It certainly focuses the mind on higher things and amid the eerily weird landscape of Cappadocia, it can be disconcerting. Some of my lone walks out into the valleys whilst fasting were decidedly odd!

During the course of my stay in Cappadocia I was treated with unfailing kindness and understanding. Neighbours willingly helped this practical incompetent to change propane gas bottles and assisted me in the conservation of energy by always telling me when I had more than one electric light blazing. 'My' village was not the fictional Muratpaşa. Having said that however, some of the rather more remote hamlets that I visited have more than a passing resemblance to my fictional creation. Isolated communities across the globe were ever thus.

Whilst almost all of the characters in this novel are fictional, some of the events are very real. The bombings of the Neve Şalom and Beth Israel synagogues on 15th November 2003, as well as the attacks on the British Consulate and HSBC Bank (all in İstanbul) one week later, shocked the nation. It was quite by chance that some of my characters 'lived' opposite the Neve Şalom. But because of this and because of the magnitude of the explosion I was bound to deal at least with the Neve Şalom bombing on some level. Having said that, I have probably failed to do justice to the suffering that occurred on that terrible day, just as I cannot adequately describe the heroism of those who attended the injured and the dying – medics, police, fire service and military. Even in far away Cappadocia people unconnected with these events and with İstanbul were moved to tears by the images we all saw on our televisions over those two dreadful weekends.

Finally, if you are wondering who is *not* a fictional character in this book, it is the cat, Kismet. He is not, in reality, truly owned by anyone and quite terrified the cats I was looking after on occasion. But I do know him and whenever I have been in his presence, I have treated him with the utmost respect!

Barbara Nadel

Glossary

Anıt Kabir – Atatürk's mausoleum in Ankara

Belediye – local council

Bey – as in 'Çetin Bey', an Ottoman title denoting respect, still in use today following a man's first name

Börek – flaky pastry parcel

Cacık – yoghurt with grated cucumber and mint

Çay bahçe – tea garden

Djinn – evil spirits

Hamam – traditional Turkish steam bath

Hanım – lady, woman. Like the male 'bey', it is a title denoting respect for an older, usually married woman. It follows the woman's first name, as in 'Nazlı Hanım'

İftar – the meal eaten at sunset during Ramazan

İnşallah – 'God willing' or 'If God wills'

İskender Kebab – Döner kebab on flat (pide) bread with yoghurt, butter and tomato sauce

Jandarma – while the Turkish National Police are responsible for law and order in the urban districts, the Jandarma cover the rural areas. They are a paramilitary force under joint control of the military and the Interior Ministry

Kangal – Anatolian sheepdog

Kapıcı – Doorkeeper. Blocks of flats have kapıcılar, men who act as security, porters etc., for the apartment community

Kapalı Çarsı – the Grand Bazaar

Kismet – Fate

MİT – Turkish Secret Service

Mescit – small mosque

Meyhane – Tavern or bar

Müezzin – Cantor who sings the call to prayer

Pansiyon – Pension, guest house

Patlıcan salatası – Aubergine salad

Peris – Fairies

Rakı – Aniseed-flavoured alcoholic spirit

Ramazan – Ramadan. The ninth month of the Islamic calendar when Muslims, if healthy, are expected to fast during the hours of daylight

Şalvar trousers – Traditional baggy trousers worn by both men and women, mainly in rural areas

Şeytan – Satan

Şiş Kebab – Lamb or chicken cubes grilled on a skewer

TRT – Türkiye Radyo ve Televizyon, Turkish broadcasting corporation

Tavla – Backgammon

Yıldırım – thunderbolt

Turkish Alphabet

The Turkish Alphabet is very similar to its English counterpart with the following exceptions:

- The letters q, w and x do not appear.
- Some letters behave differently in Turkish compared with English:

C, c	Not the c in cat and tractor, but the j in jam and Taj or the g in gentle and courageous.
G, g	Always the hard g in great or slug, never the soft g of general and outrage.
J, j	As the French pronounce the j in bonjour and the g in gendarme.

- The following additional letters appear:

Ç ç	The ch in chunk or choke.
Ğ, ğ	'Yumuşak ge' is used to lengthen the vowel that it follows. It is not usually voiced (except as a vague y sound). For instance, it is used in the name Ayşe Farsakoğlu, which is pronounced *Farsak-erlu*, and in öğle (noon, midday),

	pronounced öy-*lay* (see below for how to pronounce ö).
Ş, ş	The sh in ship and shovel.
I, ı	Without a dot, the sound of the a in probable.
İ, i	With a dot, the i in thin or tinny.
Ö, ö	Like the ur sound in further.
Ü, ü	Like the u in the French tu.

Full pronunciation guide

A, a	Usually short, the a in hah! or the u in but, never the medium or long a in nasty and hateful.
B, b	As in English.
C, c	Not the c in cat and tractor, but the j in jam and Taj or the g in gentle and courageous.
Ç, ç	The ch in chunk or choke.
D, d	As in English.
E, e	Always short, the e in venerable, never the e in Bede (and never silent).
F, f	As in English.
G, g	Always the hard g in great or slug, never the soft g of general and outrage.
Ğ, ğ	'Yumuşak ge' is used to lengthen the vowel that it follows. It is not usually voiced (except as a vague y sound). For instance, it is used in the name Ayşe

	Farsakoğlu, which is pronounced *Far-sak-erlu*, and in öğle (noon, midday), pronounced *öy-lay* (see below for how to pronounce ö).
H, h	As in English (and never silent).
I, ı	Without a dot, the sound of the a in probable.
İ, i	With a dot, the i in thin or tinny.
J, j	As the French pronounce the j in bonjour and the g in gendarme.
K, k	As in English (and never silent).
L, l	As in English.
M, m	As in English.
N, n	As in English.
O, o	Always short, the o in hot and bothered.
Ö, ö	Like the ur sound in further.
P, p	As in English.
R, r	As in English.
S, s	As in English.
Ş, ş	The sh in ship and shovel.
T, t	As in English.
U, u	Always medium-length, the u in push and pull, never the u in but.
Ü, ü	Like the u in the French tu.
V, v	Usually as in English, but sometimes almost a w sound in words such as tavuk (hen).
Y, y	As in English. Follows vowels to make diphthongs: ay is the y sound in fly; ey is the ay sound in day; oy is the oy

sound in toy; uy is almost the same as the French oui.

Z, z   As in English.

Deadly Web

Barbara Nadel

A naked teenage girl is found dead near the beautiful Yoros Castle on the shores of the Bosphorus. She has stabbed herself through the heart but there is evidence of bizarre sexual practice. In another part of Istanbul, a young boy seems to have committed suicide in similar circumstances. What dark rituals could have compelled them to fatal self-abuse?

Inspectors Çetin İkmen and Mehmet Süleyman follow a trail that leads them to an underworld of Goth nightclubs and Satanic worship. But even these murky shadows hide more than they reveal and the answer to an ever-increasing number of suspicious deaths is more shocking and terrible than they could ever have imagined.

Praise for Barbara Nadel's novels

'Intelligent and captivating' *Sunday Times*

'The delight of the Nadel book is the sense of being taken beneath the surface of an ancient city which most visitors see for a few days at most. We look into the alleyways and curious dark quarters of Istanbul, full of complex characters and louche atmosphere' *Independent*

0 7553 2128 6

headline

Harem

Barbara Nadel

The body of a teenage girl is discovered in a cistern deep below the city of Istanbul. For the Turkish police force's most idiosyncratic and talented officer, Çetin İkmen, this is a difficult case. The girl was his daughter's friend and her attire, that of a nineteenth-century Ottoman, offers no easy explanation.

With his promise of justice to the dead girl's mother still fresh on his lips, İkmen is taken off the case. He's reassigned to the kidnapping of an ageing movie star's wife. The star is hiding something and so, İkmen fears, are his superiors. A powerful secret exists in the labyrinthine city, one which those on either side of the law will do anything to prevent escaping. But for İkmen, there's no choice, only the truth.

Praise for Barbara Nadel's İkmen series:

'Really refreshing to encounter something as idio-syncratic and evocative . . . as Barbara Nadel's Istanbul-set thriller' *The Times*

'Unusual and very well-written' *Sunday Telegraph*

'Intriguing, exotic . . . exciting, accomplished and original' *Literary Review*

'Full of complex characters and louche atmosphere' *Independent*

'My reader rates this author higher than Donna Leon' *Bookseller*

0 7472 6720 0

headline